Only You at Christmas

Christmas Town Book 3

by

Ginny Baird

ONLY YOU AT CHRISTMAS
Christmas Town Book 3

Published by
Winter Wedding Press

Copyright © 2017
Ginny Baird
Trade Paperback
ISBN 978-1-942058-23-6

Edited by Sally Knapp
Cover by Dar Albert

About the Author

From the time she could talk, romance author Ginny Baird was making up stories, much to the delight—and consternation—of her family and friends. By grade school, she'd turned that inclination into a talent, whereby her teacher allowed her to write and produce plays rather than write boring book reports. Ginny continued writing throughout college, where she contributed articles to her literary campus weekly, then later pursued a career managing international projects with the U.S. State Department.

Ginny has held an assortment of jobs, including schoolteacher, freelance fashion model, and greeting card writer, and has published more than twenty works of fiction and optioned ten screenplays. She has also published short stories, nonfiction, and poetry, and admits to being a true romantic at heart.

Ginny is a *New York Times* and *USA Today* bestselling author of several books, including novellas in her Holiday Brides Series. She's a member of Romance Writers of America (RWA) and Novelists, Inc. (NINC).

When she's not writing, Ginny enjoys cooking, biking, and spending time with her family in Tidewater, Virginia. She loves hearing from her readers and welcomes visitors to her website at http://www.ginnybairdromance.com.

Books by Ginny Baird

Christmas Town Series
The Christmas Cookie Shop
A Mommy for Christmas
Only You at Christmas
The Doctor Orders Christmas

Holiday Brides Series
The Christmas Catch
The Holiday Bride
Mistletoe in Maine
Beach Blanket Santa
Baby, Be Mine

Summer Grooms Series
Must-Have Husband
My Lucky Groom
The Wedding Wish
The Getaway Groom

Romantic Ghost Stories
The Ghost Next Door (A Love Story)
The Light at the End of the Road
The House at Homecoming Cove

Romantic Comedy
Real Romance
The Sometime Bride
Santa Fe Fortune
How to Marry a Matador
Counterfeit Cowboy
The Calendar Brides
My Best Friend's Bride
The Borrowed Boyfriend
Tara (Beach Brides Book 2)
Crazy for You

Bundles
Christmas Magic:
The Complete Holiday Brides Series (Books 1 – 5)
The Holiday Brides Collection (Books 1–4)
A Summer Grooms Selection (Books 1–3)
Romantic Ghost Stories (Books 1 – 3)
Real Romance and The Sometime Bride
(Gemini Editions 1)
Santa Fe Fortune and How to Marry a Matador
(Gemini Editions 2)
My Best Friend's Bride and
The Borrowed Boyfriend
(Gemini Editions 3)
Wedding Bells Bundle

Short Story
Special Delivery
(A Valentine's Short Story)

Ginny Baird's

ONLY YOU AT CHRISTMAS

Chapter One

Olivia Livingston bustled out the door of Jolly Bean Java wearing her parka, hat, and gloves. She held a coffee cup in one hand and a paper bag of cherry cheese Danishes in the other. She'd just returned from Sleigh Bell Stables and needed to get herself together for her three o'clock meeting with Nick. Nick Claus was the architect Christmas Town had brought in from Bangor, Maine to help restore the Grand Hotel. Olivia was the Town Council representative designated to work with him. She'd supposedly been pressed into service because of her background in interior decorating. Though Olivia suspected she was largely tapped for the project due to her proclivity for volunteering. It was a weakness she had, competing only with her addiction to those sinfully delicious dark-chocolate-cherry truffles sold at Nutcracker Sweets.

It had snowed another eight inches last night, and a blanket of white was everywhere, glistening brightly in the afternoon sun. Big billowy clouds hovered low, casting their shadows over the cleared sidewalks lining South Main Street. Given the heightened influx of tourists in the area, Olivia's little brother, Sheriff Carter

Livingston, saw to it that their contracted snow removal company stayed busy working overtime. Christmas Town certainly couldn't have its visitors skidding and falling. What sort of welcome would that be? And, they'd welcomed plenty of new faces yesterday. It had been the first Saturday after Thanksgiving and Olivia's friend and sister-in-law, Hannah Livingston, owner of the Christmas Cookie Shop, had unveiled the latest editions of her famed Virginia Cookies. They were based on a secret recipe that had belonged to Hannah's great-grandmother, and were rumored to—among other things—inspire true love.

This was the second year that Hannah had sold her special cookies, and they were apparently an enormous hit. People came from all around just to try them, which was a tremendous boon to businesses in this small town. Olivia's shop, in particular, had benefited greatly from the added number of holiday shoppers. Her store, All Things Christmas, which sat directly across the street from Jolly Bean Java, offered all sorts of seasonal items, including home décor, Christmas tree decorations, and festive holiday-themed barrettes.

Olivia self-consciously glanced at the auburn braid that draped forward over one shoulder. Of all things! There were tiny pieces of hay sticking out of it! Olivia had to hurry home and clean herself up. Particularly as she imagined Nick might arrive for their meeting in business attire. Olivia definitely needed to wash the grime off her skin and the stench out of her hair. She'd spent most of the morning cleaning out Blaze's stall, and was certain she smelled very horsey at this point. And not in a really positive way. Fortunately, her modest apartment was located directly above her store, so a hot shower wasn't far away. She scurried across the empty street, which stayed quiet on Sunday afternoons, spotting a couple of bundled-up figures pushing baby buggies and heading her way.

As they drew closer, Olivia was pleased to see they were friends of hers! She paused as wintery winds whipped around her, awaiting the arrival of what she'd secretly dubbed "the baby brigade." Hannah, who was married to Olivia's brother, Carter, pushed one carriage containing a chubby infant swaddled in a fuzzy pink snuggly blanket. Hannah's warm brown eyes lit up when she spied Olivia ahead of her. "Olivia, hi!" she called with a cheery grin. Chin-length brown hair peeked out from under her winter hat, and she wore a nicely cut peacoat and snow boots.

A pretty blonde with long wavy hair and bright blue eyes walked along beside her. She wore a puffy white parka, mittens, and sparkly earmuffs that looked like powder puffs with tinsel poking out of them. Sandy Winchester, formerly Claus, smiled happily, pushing her own pram loaded with a set of twins. Sandy was married to Hannah's brother, Ben, and their girls were called Holly and Rose. Each had bright pink cheeks and blue eyes. Hannah's baby was named Amanda. All three children had been born in September, with Sandy's twins arriving two weeks before Hannah's little girl, the only dark-eyed one in the group. Amanda also had very thick dark hair. Sandy's twins both had downy blond locks, but who knew how that might change in time?

"Out for some fresh air?" Olivia asked cheerfully.

Hannah halted her carriage when she reached Olivia on the sidewalk, and Sandy paused beside her.

"We thought we'd take advantage of the break in the weather."

Olivia peered into the strollers to find all three warmly swaddled babies snoozing peacefully. The twins had their tiny heads contentedly titled toward one another. "Looks like it's naptime for the little ones," she said with a chuckle.

"The motion helps," Sandy offered. "Holly was hollering when we left the house."

"That got Rose going," Hannah confided in a whisper.

"Yes," Sandy said, lowering her voice a notch. "I'm afraid they really startled Amanda."

From what Olivia had heard, Amanda was the ideal baby. She slept and ate on schedule and was generally good-natured. Sandy's twins were apparently another story. But, it was little Holly who was already proving herself to be the mischief-maker.

Hannah and Sandy had always been close; now that they had children practically the same age, they spent even more time together. Since Hannah and Carter lived in a cabin on River Road, Hannah often visited Sandy when she brought Amanda into town for her weekend strolls. Sandy and her husband, Ben, owned a craftsman-style house on Church Street not far from the Christmas Inn. Apart from the twins, they also had a precocious nine-year-old daughter from Ben's first marriage, Lily. Sandy and Ben had eloped last Christmas Eve, stunning and pleasing everyone in town, including Hannah and Carter, who'd been on their honeymoon in Bermuda at the time.

Olivia smiled sweetly at her friends. "Well, they seem to be sleeping like angels, now." Olivia hadn't really thought much about having children of her own, until this recent baby boom erupted in Christmas Town. Apart from Hannah and Sandy having newborns, their fourth Monday lunch-bunch pal, Jade Scott, had a darling six-month-old boy named Josiah. His big brother, Alexander, was seven and in the first grade. Olivia's "baby" was a six-year-old Tennessee Walking Horse, which reminded her of her need for a shower. She quickly checked her watch, seeing it was twenty till three. "Oops! Will you look at the time? Sorry, guys," she told them brightly. "I'd better scoot. I've got a…"

Sandy leaned forward to tuck the edge of a snowman receiving blanket around Holly, as the baby had apparently kicked it off in her dreams. Holly was dressed in dark green, while Rose wore deep red. Sandy claimed to always keep them in the same colors so that their daddy, Ben, could tell them apart. But Olivia guessed Sandy's choice of a fashion palette for her children had more to do with Sandy's love of everything Christmas. That passion was evident throughout Sandy's house, though her décor wasn't quite as over the top as it had been when she was single.

Before Sandy stood upright, Olivia caught a glimpse of a man positioned behind her on the sidewalk near the intersection with Santa Claus Lane. The tall rugged guy had a solid frame and a handsome face. His hands were shoved into his field coat's pockets and he appeared to be examining the outside of the Grand Hotel. Olivia sucked in a breath, hoping that he wasn't Nick! She couldn't meet him looking—and smelling—like this! Olivia blinked and nervously backed away as

Sandy glanced over her shoulder. "Oh hey, look!" Sandy chirped joyfully. "There's my brother—"

Olivia blanched, her eyes darting to the front door of All Things Christmas. She could be through it and up the back stairs in two minutes flat if she made haste. "Sorry, girls! Gotta dash!"

Olivia turned away in a panic, but Hannah caught her coat sleeve. "Olivia," she whispered kindly. "What's the rush? That's Nick Claus." She viewed Olivia tellingly. "I'm sure Sandy wants you to meet him."

"I…er…will!" Olivia swallowed hard. "Soon! Very soon! At three o'clock!" She tried to pull away, but Hannah had latched on tight.

"Don't let her go," Sandy instructed, enthusiastically waving at Nick. "He's already seen us!"

Olivia's eyes widened in horror as Nick turned their way. Next, he was ambling toward them at an easy gait, a smile spreading across his handsome face. Gosh, he was good-looking! With chiseled features, short dark hair, and dynamite blue eyes. As he approached, his grin broadened and a dimple settled in his left cheek.

Olivia's heart hammered and her knees felt weak.

"Nick!" Sandy called loudly. "Come and meet Olivia!"

He strode right up beside the baby buggies, nodding pleasantly at Hannah. "Hannah, good to see you again."

"Nick and Hannah met earlier at my house," Sandy explained. She turned toward Olivia, who felt frozen in place. "Olivia, this is my brother, Nick." She stared from Nick to Olivia. "Nick, meet Olivia Livingston, the wonderfully capable woman you'll be working with on the Grand Hotel."

He observed Olivia's stunned expression, his gaze landing on the section of her braid that seemed to be sprouting hay. "Hi," she offered lamely as heat torched her cheeks.

Nick's blue eyes twinkled. "Been at a barn today?"

"Yeah, sorry," Olivia gasped in shame. "I've got a horse there and—"

"Please don't apologize." His deep voice rumbled. "I'm fond of animals myself."

"Nick has a special way with them," Sandy offered uninvited. "When he talks to them, they listen!"

"A horse whisperer?" Hannah asked with pleased surprise.

Sandy twisted her lips. "Something like that, yeah."

Meanwhile, Nick's eyes hadn't left Olivia's. She didn't know why, but she had the weirdest notion that he knew about her cherry cheese Danish. Before she'd left Jolly Bean Java, she'd snuck a pastry out of her to-go bag to take a tiny nibble. Okay, maybe not such a tiny one. A huge whopping bite! It had smelled so good she hadn't been able to resist.

"Don't listen to my sister," Nick said good-naturedly. "She sometimes stretches the truth."

Sandy gaped at him, apparently affronted. "That is so not...*oh....oohhh...*"

Something totally strange was going on with Sandy's carriage. Little Holly had woken up and had begun kicking her legs. At the same time, her stroller's front wheels appeared to rise right off the ground! Sandy squeezed her mittens around the handlebar,

holding on tight. She gave a solid push and—*oomph*—
the carriage wheels smacked the sidewalk again,
bouncing hard. It was then that Olivia noticed Nick's
broad hand gripping the carriage's side and keeping it
steady.

Olivia wondered if her imagination had been
playing tricks on her. Hannah, who'd been busy finding
Amanda's pacifier in her stroller, hadn't seen a thing.
Amanda started to gurgle and coo as the twins began
fussing. Holly, especially, seemed to be experiencing a
sudden bout of ill temper.

"Looks like the natives are getting restless,"
Hannah said, addressing Sandy.

"Um, yeah. Right!" Sandy grinned extra tightly at
Olivia, then turned to her brother, Nick. "I think I'd
better get the twins home. Holly, especially," she
added, sending Nick a sidelong glance.

"Good idea," he confirmed with a nod.

Olivia sensed this was her opening. "I…I was just
going to wash up," she said, addressing Nick. "We're
still meeting at three, right?"

"Three is fine," he said warmly. "But there's really
no rush." His gaze snagged on the coffee shop sign
across the street. "Why don't you take your time
changing, while I grab a hot drink? Maybe you can
come and get me when you're ready?"

Olivia was still awash with embarrassment when
she raced up her apartment steps. Sandy might have
warned her that Nick was *hot*! She also might have
taken pity on Olivia and *not* forced an introduction
when she smelled of manure. But that was just Sandy's
way. She was so genuinely sweet that she only saw the

good in everybody. Hannah was actually like that, too. Olivia, on the other hand, wasn't afraid to call a spade a spade. Thank goodness she hadn't met Nick in an enclosed space. She'd just come indoors, and already her stench was filling the place!

When Olivia reached the bathroom in her apartment and stared in the mirror, mortification seeped through her. There were dark splotches on her cheeks and her hair made her look like she'd been rolling in hay. Her boots were muddy and her earth-encrusted jeans were worn through at the knees. The only part of her that actually looked decent was her light green parka. *No, wait! That has mud on it, too.* Olivia sighed heavily and turned on the shower, to let the water heat up. Then, she dashed into the bedroom and shrugged out of her parka, boots, and jeans. At least this was just a business meeting, and not a date. In that case, she'd have real worries. It was actually very hard to undo a first impression.

Nick sat at a table at Jolly Bean Java with his cocoa, thinking about how impressed with Olivia he'd been. She was nothing like he'd expected. The image of an interior designer conjured up someone extremely polished and poised: a lady wearing tailored slacks with high heels and a European-print fashion scarf. Not that he was opposed to that look; it was more that he'd found Olivia's presentation charming. She was clearly a very earthy woman. Nick also loved horses…and farm animals…domestic pets, and reindeer. Though he didn't suspect they had much of the latter around here. He took a thoughtful sip of his cocoa, wondering briefly if he shouldn't have ordered a peppermint mocha. While its ingestion did help tamp down some of his natural instincts, Nick didn't normally have the need for peppermint these days. Why then did he have the sudden inkling that Olivia had naughtily snuck a bite of cherry cheese Danish before hustling out of this shop?

Nick glanced around the cozy café with its tall metallic stools facing the high counter opposite the large picture window. He was seated near the front door, so had a clear view of the street… *When what to my wondering eyes should appear, but Lou and Buddy Christmas wearing Santa headgear!* Nick shot to his feet as the middle-aged couple entered the shop. Lou's light brown eyes shone merrily as she grinned at her husband. "Buddy! Look who's here!"

Lou rushed toward Nick and he hugged her warmly, the felt from her Santa hat tickling his nose. Her medium-brown shoulder-length hair was frosted at the tips. It was a more modern cut than the one Nick remembered Lou wearing when he was a kid. When he complimented her on the new style, she thanked him with a titter.

"You're looking awfully well, too." She eagerly elbowed the stout man, with a plump round belly and a snowy white beard and mustache, beside her. "Isn't he, Buddy?"

"*Ho-ho-ho!* Indeed, it's so!" He pulled Nick into a bear hug and soundly patted his back. "It's good to see you, son." He leaned back to study Nick. "How long has it been? At least ten years?"

Nick smiled fondly at the older couple. They and his parents had been very good friends, and when Sandy and Nick were younger their family had visited often. "Try twenty!"

"My! Has it been that long?" Lou blinked in shock, grinning up at Nick. "It hardly seems like five years have gone by."

"Yes, but look at him now, dear," Buddy said reasonably. "The teenage boy has grown into a man."

"And what a man, too," Lou said admiringly. A lightbulb seemed to go off inside her crafty head. "It's so nice that you're staying through New Year's." He'd told her this when he'd made arrangements at Sisters' Row, since Lou managed the rental. Nick had also asked to extend his lease for some additional months, as he'd be making repeated trips to Christmas Town to oversee his project. Lou had replied that a month-to-month contract was no problem, especially for somebody performing good works on behalf of the community.

"Surely, the Grand Hotel can't be restored in such short order?" Buddy queried.

"No, but I should have the blueprints done by Christmas," Nick answered. "Once the restoration gets under way, I plan to make periodic trips to Christmas Town to keep an eye on the progress."

Lou shot Buddy a sly smile. "Have you...?" Her brow rose with interest as she leaned toward Nick and whispered, "Met Olivia?"

"Only briefly."

"She's a *very* nice-looking young woman, wouldn't you say?"

Buddy awkwardly cleared his throat. "Sweetheart, let's go pick up our coffees."

"But I was just about to tell Nick—"

"We have to get to the church," Buddy explained politely. "Planning session for our annual Christmas bazaar."

Lou clapped her gloved hands together. "I hope you'll join us next Sunday at five? Olivia will be there." She winked confidentially. "She always is."

Buddy snagged her by the elbow. "Come along, darling."

"But, I—"

"Yes, yes. I know. Plenty of time for everything."

What did that mean? Nick wondered.

As Buddy tugged Lou away, she shot a gleeful smile over her shoulder. "Olivia's thirty-six, you know! Not getting any younger, just like you!"

The door chime tinkled and Nick spun around to find Olivia standing there with her cheeks burning bright pink. Long red hair fell past her shoulders as her eyes locked on Nick's. They were a spectacular shade of green, a cross between emerald and jade. While Nick had been entranced by her eyes before, he suddenly found them even more enchanting.

It had been a long while since Nick had taken note of a woman's eyes. Mostly, because he'd grown weary of the dating game... Developing a real relationship was always so complicated. Largely in thanks to his family history.

Lou saw Olivia standing there and cried without a hint of shame, "Olivia, dear! We were just talking about you!"

"I...er...gathered that." She stole a glance at Nick and grimaced. "Sorry," she shrugged, walking toward him, before confessing in low tones, "Lou's kind of that way."

"No problem." Nick took her in again, reflecting once more on how pretty she was. Lou had certainly gotten that part right. Olivia's beauty appeared totally organic. She didn't seem to be wearing a bit of makeup, but she really didn't need it. Her creamy complexion colored naturally at her cheeks and temples and her lips were a dusty rose. Thick dark eyelashes offset her stellar green eyes. "I've known the Christmases for a long while. I'm sure Lou only means well."

"Yes." Olivia's blush deepened. "So? Shall we walk down to the Grand Hotel, or would you like to sit a while and finish your coffee?"

Lou and Buddy retrieved their orders, then Lou angled back in their direction with a smile. "How nice! You're already getting along!" She cagily appraised her husband. "Maybe we can join them at their table? Just for a quick minute?"

"Let's walk," Nick said sotto voce to Olivia and she giggled.

"Getting the hang of the town, I see," she whispered back.

"It's been a while." He ditched his empty paper cup in a waste can and held open the door, so Olivia could walk through it. "But certain things are coming back to me, yeah."

Lou yelled out, startled. "Wait! You're leaving?"

"Sorry, Lou!" Olivia said. "Work to do!"

Nick waved a cordial goodbye to the couple. "Great seeing you both!"

Chapter Two

Olivia strolled nervously beside Nick, questioning what he must think of her. Lou had very clearly been talking about her, and more than likely trying to get the two of them together. That was Lou and her matchmaking ways! At least Nick didn't seem fazed by them.

"How was your drive?" she asked, attempting to focus on something casual.

"Long, but uneventful." He grinned and that devastating dimple settled again. "I'm pretty much used to driving in the snow."

"I'd guess so, living up in Bangor!"

Nick surveyed the plowed streets as they neared Santa Claus Lane. The Grand Hotel lorded over the T-intersection across from the Merry Market on the South Main Street corner and the Snow Globe Gallery on the corner with North Main. Nick's sister, Sandy, was the artist who ran the gallery. "It appears you get nearly as much snow here."

Olivia nodded in agreement. "We do get a lot, that's true. Sometimes I wonder if Santa placed a magical spell over this town to ensure it's nearly always white," she said, teasing. "I mean, in winter, anyhow. We do get our share of green in sum—"

"Santa?" Nick asked, apparently still stuck on the reference.

Olivia cupped a hand to her mouth, remembering his last name and feeling like she'd made a misstep. "Oh, gosh. I'm sorry, Nick. You've probably heard all the Santa jokes you can stand by now."

"Actually, I don't mind them."

"No?"

"I can probably recite almost every one. I was absolutely peppered with them in elementary school." His dimple deepened as he began his rehearsed litany. "What do you call a kid who doesn't believe in Santa?"

Olivia pursed her lips and waited.

"A rebel without a Claus."

"Oh!"

"Why does Santa go down the chimney on Christmas Eve?" They halted at the curb. "Because it *soots* him."

"Ha-ha!"

"What do you call a broke Santa?" Nick was apparently on a roll. "Saint-NICKEL-LESS."

Olivia's chuckles erupted in full-blown laughter. "Stop! You're killing me!"

"One more… Who says—" He surprised her by doing some sort of reverse moonwalk while swinging his arms. "*Oh-oh-oh?*"

Olivia stopped laughing to catch her breath, then guessed, "Santa walking backwards?"

"Very good." His blue eyes danced. "There may be a place for you in the Maritime Provinces."

"Maritime Provinces?" she asked, confused. "Don't you mean the North Pole?"

"Quite right," he said with a jolly wink. "*There*."

Apart from failing to mention his great looks, Sandy had never told Olivia her brother was so much fun. Olivia had known him less than an hour, and already he had her in stitches. "Let's cross here," Olivia said, still smiling. She'd worried that working with a stuffy restoration architect from Maine might prove difficult. Now, she saw she had nothing to fear in the way of pretense from Nick Claus.

She gestured to the Grand Hotel ahead of them. The boarded-up building was a Victorian-era structure with four full floors stacked above a partially in-ground basement that had the top half of its windows emerging out of window wells. Several steep steps led to a wide wraparound porch and an enormous front door. Olivia had the key in her pocket.

As they crossed the road, she asked him, "Where are you staying? At Sandy's?" The last Olivia had heard, Sandy was keen on Nick lodging with her.

"*No-ho-ho*," he said jovially. "My sister and her husband have a houseful with Ben's little girl and those new babies. I prefer the peace and quiet of Sisters' Row. Especially since I'll be working."

"You've taken the rental?" Olivia asked, referring to the place where Hannah had stayed when she'd first come to Christmas Town.

"The one and only around, according to Lou."

"Yes, that's right," she commented, as they climbed the stairs to the dilapidated building. "The other two units are owned."

"One of them used to be owned by my sister."

"I know!"

"I met the new person who lives there this morning."

"Liz?"

"That's right. Liz Martin."

"She's really sweet," Olivia said. "Salt of the earth kind of person. And a great temporary neighbor to have. Jade and Wendell are awesome, too. Have you met them?"

They reached the porch and Nick shook his head. "Not yet."

"Well, you're in very good company at Sisters' Row," Olivia assured him. "Liz just moved in this September when she started her new job. She used to work at *Santa's* Sandwich Shop." She shot Nick a wink and he chuckled. "That's a real place here, I swear," she continued lightly. "Anyway! Now Liz runs Jingle Bells Booties."

"Sounds…" Nick's eyebrows shot skyward. "Racy?"

"Racy?" Olivia asked, wondering if he'd misheard her.

"Forgive me for saying so, but Jingle Bells Booty brings all kinds of pictures to mind, and not exactly nice—"

Olivia hooted. "Not that kind of booty!" She hugged her middle in a fit of giggles. "*Booties*, as in baby shoes!"

The tips of Nick's ears reddened and Olivia wondered for a brief second if she'd embarrassed him. Or rather, if he'd embarrassed himself.

"It's the new daycare in Christmas Town," she filled in further. "Run out of the courthouse building."

"The large building down at the roundabout?" Nick surmised.

"There was extra space on the first floor," Olivia told him. "Two nice-size rooms with sunny windows and a little patio area out back. Once we experienced this recent baby boom, the Town Council came up with the idea. That's where Sandy's twins stay during the day. It's ideal because Ben's chambers are upstairs, so he can check on them. Carter finds it convenient for Amanda, too, since his office is in the building.

"In any case, nothing in Christmas Town is really that far away. Jade, who runs the Elf Shelf Bookshop, also keeps her baby, Josiah, there. And Liz's older brother, Stan, has his youngest child enrolled. His wife, Della, helps out part-time as does Carter's secretary, Tilly, who only works for the sheriff's office three days a…"

Olivia bit into her bottom lip, realizing she'd been prattling on, while Nick had been patiently waiting for her to unlock the door. "Oh, wow. I'm sorry Nick! I didn't mean to unload so much baby stuff on you."

"Just don't give me a test on all those names." He grinned pleasantly, and Olivia's pulse pounded. "Not just yet."

"Right, right!" Olivia said crisply, feeling fire in her cheeks. "No problem."

She pulled the key from her pocket and slid it into the keyhole on the antiquated door. As she did, Nick removed a small notepad and a pen from an inside jacket pocket. "I'm just going to jot a few things down."

"Of course!"

"I find it very helpful to make lists."

"Do you always *check them twice?*" Olivia couldn't help saying, then she gulped because she understood how that must have sounded. Like she was flirting.

Nick's ears reddened again, and this time color also swept his temples. His gaze poured over her and a slow smile graced his lips. "Generally, yes."

Olivia's heart hammered and she felt warm all over. He was looking at her like... Like, she didn't know what... Like, he thought she was interesting, or pretty, or something. Olivia hadn't experienced that sort of perusal from a guy in a long time. Maybe that's because she never went anywhere anymore, besides Sleigh Bell Stables. Olivia felt a sudden, inexplicable urge for a dark-chocolate-cherry truffle. Fortunately, she had a whole box of them back at her apartment and she could have one the moment she got home. "I...um...er..." She anxiously fumbled with the key, finally getting it to turn. "Let me just open this door!"

"Chocolate-cherry?" Nick mumbled.

"What?" Olivia stood ramrod straight and stared at him.

"Oh, uh... Sorry," he said, seeming to shake something off.

"You just said something about candy?"

"Did I?" Nick shared an innocent look.

"I could have sworn...?"

"I was just thinking about that shop," he confessed, glancing back across the street to where it stood to the left of the Snow Globe Gallery on Santa Claus Lane. "Nutcracker Sweets. Do you know it?"

But the look in his eyes said he guessed that she did. She scarcely knew Nick! The last thing Olivia wanted him to discover was her hidden addiction to chocolates. Could she help it that they lent her solace and lightened her spirits? Everybody had their weaknesses. "Only by name," she offered hurriedly.

Olivia pushed the huge door ajar with a shove, then gasped as the stagnant air hit her. The cavernous entryway hung heavy with musty air as dust motes spiraled toward the ceiling then twirled back toward the floor, riding on the wintery wind blowing through the open doorway. Two enormous high-ceilinged rooms stood on either side of the foyer, with ornate crown molding and cobweb-covered chandeliers.

Nick surveyed the scene in wonder. "No electricity, I suppose?"

Olivia pulled a flashlight from her pocket and shut the door. "That's why I brought this," she said, clicking it on.

Nick stared around the glorious old space, marveling at the possibilities. This entryway must truly have been *grand* back in the day, with that impressive curved staircase and its carefully crafted mahogany banister leading down from the upper level. Olivia led him through one of the large front rooms, her flashlight casting a broad beam of light ahead of them. "I think this was the original lobby."

The floors were solid oak, and elegant crown molding fashioned from plaster framed the ceiling with spiraling rose petals forming blooming flowerets. The impressively made chair railing complemented the decorative baseboards secured by matching toe molding. Faded pale pink wallpaper with worn vertical magenta stripes showcased hand-painted white rosebuds on tiny ivory-colored creeping vines climbing toward the ceiling. The wallpaper was torn in several places and peeling in the corners, but it was a gem that was worth keeping and restoring to its original form. An enormous wood-burning fireplace, with an intricately carved mantel, was centered on the left outside wall, but it had been sealed off.

"Impressive," Nick said, taking it all in. "I'll bet it was glorious once upon a time."

Olivia smiled wistfully. "It's a pity it's been closed for so long."

Nick noticed the former oil lamp sconces on the walls had been refitted to accommodate electricity. "When was it last in operation?"

"Lena Winchester closed it down when her husband, Emmet, died in 1966. The Grand Hotel was in Emmet's family since it was built in 1789. He took over running the hotel from his parents at about the time he and Lena married in 1920. Lena was Hannah's great-grandmother, you know." She smiled softly, shadows outlining her pretty face. "She's the one who started the Christmas Cookie Shop."

"Oh, yes. I've heard of it—from Sandy."

"It's a very special bakery." Olivia's green eyes glimmered. "Some say Hannah's cookies work magic."

"Magic, hmm." Nick thoughtfully surveyed her. "Those must be pretty special cookies."

"They are. Lena actually invented the recipe. It was lost for a number of years, but luckily Hannah found it."

Now Olivia had him intrigued. "What kind of magic do these cookies supposedly make?"

Olivia blushed deeply. "There are three varieties."

"Three?" Nick thoughtfully stroked his chin, thinking of the cookie tin he'd found in his freezer back at Sisters' Row. "What do these varieties look like exactly?"

"Hannah intends to vary them slightly each year, but there are three basic types of Virginia Cookies." Olivia appeared increasingly animated in the telling. "The first is the Charity—"

"I'm sorry," Nick asked, perplexed. "Did you say *Virginia* Cookies?"

"Virginia, as in Virginia O'Hanlon." Olivia smiled, reflecting on the tale. "The little girl who wrote to the New York *Sun* back in the late 1890s to ask about the veracity of Old Saint Nick. She was starting to doubt in the legend, and her dad said that everything printed in the newspaper had to be true. So, when she wrote to the editor and asked if there really was such a thing as Santa, he wrote back saying—"

"*Yes, Virginia, there is a Santa Claus?*"

"Yeah, that's the one!"

"Well, that editor certainly got his answer right in explaining the true meaning of Christmas." Nick knew the story well, as his and Sandy's parents had often referred to it when they were growing up.

"That's what Lena thought, too. That's why she decided to bake these special cookies that could help people—and help the town—rekindle its faith."

"In...?" he wondered.

"Christmas! Goodness and forgiveness." She paused unsurely before continuing. "And, oh...um...also..." Her eyes met his and Nick's heart skipped a beat. "*Love.*" The way she said it was super sassy, like she didn't believe in the legend for a minute.

"Something tells me you're not sold on their act."

"It's not that I see anything wrong with it. Hannah's Virginia Cookies are enormously popular and folks seem to have great fun pretending they have these powers."

"To inspire love?"

Olivia held up one finger. "True love."

"Ah."

"And goodness. That's the Charity kind. It features a little angel. The Christmas-tree-decorated Clemency Cookie fosters forgiveness, and the Commitment Cookie says—"

"*Forever Yours*," Nick filled in knowledgeably and Olivia gasped.

"But, how did you—?

"Someone left a little housewarming gift in my freezer." Nick winked and Olivia's whole face reddened.

"At Sisters' Row? But, who?" Nick could practically hear the wheels turning in her brain. "Maybe it was a mistake? Maybe they weren't meant for you? It's possible that Hannah left them behind when—"

"It wasn't Hannah, and they were meant for me. I'm sure of it."

"But...how?" Olivia asked, flummoxed.

"A yellow sticky note on the tin said, *For Nick, Enjoy some cookies with your milk!*"

Olivia gaped at him. "There was no signature or anything?"

"Nope." Nick shook his head. "When I saw Hannah with Sandy this morning, I tried to thank her for them, but she acted like she didn't know what I was talking about."

"Hmm." Olivia narrowed her eyes in thought. "Could have been Lou, I suppose? She does have a key to the rental."

"Good point. I'll be sure to ask her about them."

"But, Nick…" Olivia suddenly appeared alarmed. "I'd be careful, if I were you. I mean, careful with those cookies. Especially if it was Lou who left them there. The woman has legendary matchmaking tendencies."

Nick chortled in response. "Not seconds ago you said you thought the whole thing was bunk."

"Yeah, but…" Olivia worriedly bit into her bottom lip. "Nobody's really sure."

"I appreciate your concern, I do. But I've been having cookies and milk for *years* without any ill effects."

"Maybe you should talk to your sister—about those Commitment Cookies, in particular?"

"What would Sandy know about Hannah's Commitment Cookies?"

Olivia swallowed hard. "Maybe more than you think?"

She was obviously very worried about this, so Nick decided to humor her. "Okay, you have my solemn vow," he said, dropping his voice a notch. "I will not even take one tiny nibble of a Commitment Cookie until talking to Sandy."

Olivia heaved a breath of relief. "Thanks."

A little while later, they were traipsing down the ancient staircase. Olivia noticed that some of the spindles holding the banister were cracked, and that the wallpaper adorning this area was battered and peeling, too. After touring the kitchen, with its 1950s-era appliances, the dining room, parlor, and library, she and Nick inspected the former ballroom across the foyer from the lobby, before heading upstairs. The two middle floors each held six bedrooms but only one communal hall bath, both with white-and-black-checkered tile floors and claw-foot tubs housing shower conversions. Every room in the building, except for the bathrooms, had a non-working fireplace, and all had the freestanding radiators that had been installed later for warmth.

Nick found a separate door on the third floor hall leading to a walk-up attic, and a small apartment that was once apparently used by the hotel owners as their personal space. Olivia was delighted to find the fourth-floor apartment had a private hidden staircase leading all the way to the kitchen. She and Nick went down it, then climbed back upstairs again, descending a final time by the large staircase ending in the front hall.

On their journey, they were pleased to discover a dumbwaiter and a laundry chute on the guestroom floors. The dumbwaiter ran back and forth from the kitchen, while the laundry chute apparently landed in the basement. Nick cautioned against exploring that lower level until they returned with more light. Though the sky was clear outside, the fractured sunlight bouncing in through the beveled windows only partially illuminated the gargantuan rooms. Since the basement was mostly underground, it was bound to be even darker down there, and Nick wanted to take care in case it was in poor condition.

Nick said he had work lanterns he wanted to set up, so he could take measurements and photos, and make some preliminary notes and sketches. With the building being so old, he'd also need to bring in professionals to test for lead and radon hazards, as well as to check the quality of the plumbing and wiring, both which he guessed needed gutting and replacing. A heating and cooling contractor would need to be consulted, too. As would an inspector, to assess both the indoor and outside aspects of the structure... He added those items to the list he'd started on his small notepad, annotating the professionals he should call, and what he needed to bring with him tomorrow when he returned to officially begin his job. Nick wanted to get the lay of the land, before arriving at restoration ideas to present to the Town Council. He suggested Olivia might want to help him with the brainstorming, and she'd eagerly agreed to that.

"I suppose it might help if I had my own key?" he asked, when they were nearly to the bottom of the staircase. Nick was just a few paces ahead of her, as she trained her flashlight's beam before them.

"Of course! I brought a spare one." Olivia dug into her jeans pocket and the next thing she knew— *crunch*—her left boot crushed straight through a step and she tumbled forward, losing her grip on the flashlight. It banged hard against the bottom step, splitting open and spilling its batteries into the foyer. Nick spun quickly to catch Olivia as she fell, her left ankle wrenching in pain. "Oh!"

"Olivia! Are you okay?"

She stared up at him, bolstered in his strong arms, and winced. "I think...so."

Nick's brow creased in concern as he slowly lifted her off the stairs and gingerly set her down in the foyer, while still supporting her. "See if you can put any pressure on it?"

Olivia shifted her weight to her left foot and pain spiked up her shin, causing her knee to buckle. Her arms shot around Nick's neck as she held on tight.

Nick centered his gaze on her left boot. "You must have twisted your ankle." He worriedly scanned her eyes. "Does anything else hurt?"

"No, I…" Another wave of pain hit hard and the room spun around her.

Nick tightened his embrace and her heart hammered. He was so strong and steady, and so very close. Closer than she'd been to any man since Ted. "That old step must have rotted through," he said, glancing down at the splintered wooden plank. "I guess we're lucky it wasn't worse. You might have fallen and hit your head."

"Yes, I know."

"Do you mind if I take a look?"

She nodded weakly and Nick shifted her in his arms, gently lowering her toward the second step to the bottom. Olivia placed one hand behind her, steadying herself as he sat her down on the stairs.

Nick crouched low and tenderly touched the part of her left calf extending out of her boot. She had her jeans leg tucked into it, and still wore her coat and heavy sweater. As there was no heat in here, the interior of the Grand Hotel was chilly. "Does this part bother you?"

"No," she replied. "Lower. I think you're right. I must have twisted my ankle."

"We can't tell for sure without removing your boot."

"I think it might hurt too much to do that."

"Is there an urgent care center nearby?"

"Not in Christmas Town," she told him. "The closest thing we have is the Christmas Town Clinic, but that's closed on Sundays."

"Kurt Christmas runs that, doesn't he?" He surveyed her kindly. "I'll bet he makes house calls."

"I'd hate to bother Kurt." Olivia pushed herself forward and tried to stand, but the second she did she went tumbling backwards again and Nick had to catch her.

"If I didn't know better," he said teasingly. "I'd say you were doing this on purpose. Falling into my arms." He shot her a wry smile and Olivia's skin burned hot.

"I...er...no! It's just that—"

"Not that I'm complaining." His blue eyes twinkled. "But I *am* calling Kurt. Do you have his number, or should I phone Lou and ask her to—?"

"No, no!" Olivia said hurriedly. "Don't call Lou! She'll wind up coming too, and maybe even bringing Buddy!" She quickly extracted her cell from her coat pocket. "I'll call Kurt. I've got his number right here."

Chapter Three

Kurt Christmas arrived at the Grand Hotel with his medical bag ten minutes later. With that buff athletic build, light hair, and dark eyes, Nick could see why Kurt was a magnet for the ladies. Though Sandy told Nick that Kurt dated plenty, she'd also confided she secretly believed Kurt still carried a torch for his former high school crush, Savannah. Nick recalled Kurt showing him a photo of the pretty redhead when they were both teens, but—in Nick's opinion—Savannah's big sister, Olivia, was the real looker in the family. He'd only vaguely heard about her and the Livingston girls' brother, Carter, prior to getting contacted by the Christmas Town Council about the hotel project here. Olivia and Carter were still relatively new to Christmas Town, while the members of the Christmas family were all long-time residents of the historic area.

"Kurt Christmas!" Nick said, extending his hand. "Great to see you again."

"And you!" Kurt pulled him into a bear hug then stepped back to view him fully. "Just look at yourself. All grown up!" Kurt was three years younger than

Nick. The last time they'd seen each other, Kurt had only been fourteen.

"Looks like you did as much growing up as I did," Nick returned jovially. He motioned to Kurt's black bag. "Med school and everything."

"Yes," Kurt answered, peering past Nick at Olivia on the stairway. "How's the patient?"

Olivia waved wanly. "My left ankle's had better days."

Kurt approached her, eyeing the broken tread a few steps above from where she sat. "I see that." He knelt in front of her, placing his bag on the floor. "You two need to be careful in here," he said, addressing them both. "This building hasn't been inhabited in a long while."

"We're hoping to fix that," Nick said confidently before querying with concern, "How's it looking?"

Kurt had slowly removed Olivia's boot and was gently palpitating her ankle. He carefully supported her heel in his hand and tried gingerly manipulating her foot in different directions.

Olivia squirmed, pinching her lips together. "Ooh."

"Sorry." Kurt shot her a compassionate smile, then turned to Nick. "It doesn't appear that anything's broken, and I have good news." He gradually released Olivia's foot, setting it down. "I don't think it's a sprain, either. More likely a strain or a tendon pull from the way you landed." He opened his medical bag, removing an elastic bandage and a small pair of scissors. "Keep it iced and elevated for a few days, and things should be as good as new."

"A few days?" Olivia asked worriedly. "I can't possibly... I've got my store to think of, and my horse.

And, Tuesday afternoons I have the kids out to the stables."

"Not this Tuesday you won't," Kurt said with a wink.

He carefully pried off her sock than began wrapping her foot while Olivia stuck her leg out to help him, attempting to keep it steady. At the same time, she was still protesting. "I can't let down the kids."

"You'll be letting them down more if you turn a simple injury into something worse by not taking care of yourself."

She looked pleadingly at Nick, but he took Kurt's side. "You probably should listen to the doctor."

"Ice, elevation, ibuprofen," Kurt instructed. "Should be noticeably better by Wednesday." He finished up, clipping the end of the bandage with his scissors and securing it in place. "If it's not—or if the pain gets worse in the meantime—call me."

Nick could tell Olivia wasn't happy about Kurt's orders, but she also appeared resigned to comply with them. "All right," she said, thanking him. Kurt replied that it was no problem. He was glad that she'd called.

"Will you be okay getting home?" Kurt asked. "I can drive you?"

"It's only half a block," she contested before Nick glanced her way. She was right. It was a short distance, and he was more than happy to walk her back. In part, because he was worried about her, but also because the idea of being around Olivia just a little while longer held appeal.

"Do you think you could make it with my help?"

Olivia grabbed onto the banister railing and cautiously tested her foot. "It's a little better than before," she said, looking up at Nick. "I should be able to manage."

"Not on your own," Kurt said in a scolding tone. "You'll let Nick take you."

"Yes, Kurt." She sighed, sounding exasperated, and arched an eyebrow. "I'm not that stubborn, you know."

"She can be sometimes," Kurt whispered to Nick, but he said it right in front of her like she was meant to hear.

"Ha-ha!" Olivia said fake cheerily.

Nick loudly clapped his hands together. "Great! We've got that settled." Next, he extended his grip to Kurt, who'd already stood and grabbed his bag. "Thanks again for coming, man."

"Any time."

As he departed, Kurt shook his finger at Olivia. "Ice, elevation—"

"Yeah, yeah. I know."

"And leave that boot off," he cautioned. "Or else it might get stuck due to the swelling."

"Aye-aye, sir!" She gave an exaggerated eye roll, then said to Nick, "Kurt's everybody's big brother in this town."

Nick watched Kurt slip out the door, thinking the life of a small-town doctor must be nice.

"Doesn't sound like such a bad thing to me."

Nick was just ushering Olivia toward the door, when an odd scratch-scratching sound came from outside it. "What's that?" she asked, leaning into him. Nick had his left arm around her waist, while Olivia looped her right arm over his broad shoulder. She moved in small hopping steps as Nick stabilized her. In her left hand, she held her boot.

"I don't know." He laid his hand on the doorknob, tugging the door open. "Let's see."

Olivia stared down at the fluffy gray cat with a white star on its chest. "Tulip!" she cried with surprise.

The cat meowed and blinked up at Nick.

"That's—" Olivia started to explain, but Nick preempted her.

"Lily's cat, I know. Lily introduced me to her when I was at Sandy's earlier."

"I don't know what she's doing outdoors," Olivia remarked, stunned. "She's an inside cat. She must have slipped out somehow."

Tulip mewed again and Nick viewed her thoughtfully. "Yes."

The gray feline planted herself by his feet and looked up expectantly.

"Can you hang on just a sec?" Nick asked Olivia. She nodded and latched onto the doorjamb so he could bend toward the cat.

"Come here, you," he said, picking her up. Tulip started purring immediately. "What kind of mischief are you up to?" Nick raised the loudly humming animal up to his ear then laughed.

"What is it?"

Nick grinned at Olivia. "Tulip says she's not the troublemaker; that's her son, Jingles."

While this was true, Olivia couldn't fathom how Nick knew this. Then she surmised that either Lily or Sandy had filled him in. Tulip's two offspring, Jingles and Belle, now lived with Hannah and Carter. Jingles did keep things lively with his penchant for stealing shiny objects. He was always sneakily taking something and hiding it under the bed.

Nick surveyed Olivia suddenly. "Is that right?"

"Oh, yes! Absolutely! Jingles is quite the little scamp. Fortunately, his sister cat, Belle, is very mellow. Or else they'd be double-trouble."

"Something like Sandy's twins," Nick joked.

Despite the throbbing pain in her ankle, Olivia couldn't help but laugh. "Yeah." She fretfully eyed the cat in Nick's arms. "What are we going to do with Tulip?"

Nick considered the cat and then Olivia. "Maybe she can wait here until I see you home? Then, I'll take her back to Sandy's."

"Aren't you scared that she'll run—?"

The minute she said it, a loud barking echoed toward them.

"Cocoa! No!" It was Tilly Anderson, racing down the sidewalk in hot pursuit of her brown toy poodle, who'd apparently gotten loose. Cocoa scampered ahead of her, yapping sharply and dragging his sequined leash behind him. Tilly teetered along in bright pink leggings, hiking boots, and a thigh-length glittery purple sweater under a red-and-green plaid ski vest. Her short red curls bounced as she ran. Olivia spied a decorative Christmas barrette in her hair, but couldn't discern its type from this far a distance. Although, as Tilly bounded closer, she thought it looked an awful lot like one of the penguin ones.

Tulip spotted Cocoa fiercely tearing her way and she panicked, wiggling free from Nick's hold. The cat leapt from his arms and sprang onto the porch before skittering down the steps as Cocoa quickly covered ground, closing the distance between them.

"*Cocoa! Ohhh...*" Tilly's cry was frantic. The stout middle-aged woman was scurrying along so fast she nearly tripped.

Nick glanced her way then observed the dog, gaining on poor Tulip, who was headed toward Santa Claus Lane. If the cat ran down that street toward the North Pole Nursery, she might get lost in the woods flanking the mountain ridge towering over the town.

"Cocoa," Nick commanded, in a calm even tone. "Sit!"

The little dog stopped on a dime and sat obediently, curiously gazing up the steps to the Grand Hotel and locking its small dark eyes on Nick's. Olivia was amazed that the little creature had minded him. Cocoa didn't even know Nick! Neither did Tilly.

Tilly approached her tiny pet, huffing and puffing and holding her sides. "Thank you!" she called, staring in awe at Nick. "I don't know how on earth you did that."

Olivia had no clue, either, and Cocoa was still sitting there, not even moving a muscle.

"Come on, you little love muffin." Tilly bent toward her dog to pick him up, and he tilted his head at Nick.

"You go on home with your mama," Nick told him. "And mind your manners for the rest of the day."

Cocoa whimpered and stood, tucking his tail between his hind legs. Then he turned disconsolately toward Tilly and blinked up at her.

"I'm sure he's sorry," Nick offered from afar.

"No doubt you're right!" Tilly scooped Cocoa up and nuzzled him against her chin. "You scared me half to death, you mongrel. Don't go running away like that again."

"He won't," Nick assured her with a confidence that stymied Olivia.

"Well, thank you…?" Tilly stared at Olivia then back at Nick.

"It's Nick!" he told her. "Nick Claus!"

"Well, thank you, Mr. Claus!" Tilly grinned gratefully. "And, welcome to town!"

"How did you do that?" Olivia asked Nick, as he locked the door to the Grand Hotel.

"I thought Sandy told you?" Nick said lightly.

"You're Dr. Doolittle." Olivia lowered her voice a decibel. "*Right*."

Nick chuckled deeply. "I wouldn't exactly go *that* far."

"Well, you obviously have a way with animals…" Olivia fretfully surveyed the street. "What are we going to do about Tulip?"

"No worries. I'll find her." He smiled reassuringly. "But first, let me help you home."

Olivia limped along beside Nick during the short journey down South Main Street to her shop. He steadied her as they went, his strong arm around her waist and his masculine scent washing over her. It wasn't exactly cologne, more like the clean smell of soap. Something that gave off a spicy aroma that was earthy and appealing. Just like Nick. Olivia hadn't expected to find herself instantly drawn to him, or feel under the sway of his spell. But when he gazed at her with his deep blue eyes, Olivia's heart gave a little flutter.

Her heart hadn't fluttered in a long while. The last time she'd opened it up to someone the results had been devastating. Her breakup with Ted had been so bad, Olivia had nearly convinced herself she was done with men altogether. And, until now, she'd done just fine without them. She had a job she loved, as well as plenty of extracurricular activities to keep her busy. But, busy didn't fill her long, lonely nights. Books and an unhealthy supply from Nutcracker Sweets took care of that.

She shot a cursory glance at his handsome profile as they neared her door. He had the rugged look of an outdoorsman, yet he was clearly a polished professional. Olivia had been impressed by his remarks on the condition of the Grand Hotel when they'd gone through it, and was interested to discuss ideas with him about its renovation. Only now she had this silly injury to deal with. Olivia sighed heavily, wishing her boot had never gone through that step.

"Doing all right?" Nick asked with concern, eyeing her. "We're almost there."

"Yeah, thanks." She smiled up at him, and Nick's heart pitter-pattered. He swallowed hard, wondering what was going on. While animals minding him was not unusual, he seemed to have an uncanny knack for communicating with them today. He'd also had the distinct impression that Olivia had been thinking about dark-chocolate-cherry truffles earlier. Were those a weakness of hers, he wondered? Something she privately craved? It would be interesting to learn Olivia

had a secret hankering for chocolate when she was
otherwise so outwardly healthy. She certainly stayed fit
enough to eat anything she wanted and get away with it.

Nick found himself inexplicably yearning to know
more about her. She was a very beautiful woman, and
accomplished in her own right. Nick was further
intrigued by her efforts at Sleigh Bell Stables. When
she'd discussed the place with Kurt, it sounded as if she
ran a charity program for children involving horses.
That was something else that engaged Nick about
Olivia; she was clearly good-hearted. A woman who
thought about others, and didn't just focus on herself.
Nick found that characteristic extremely appealing.
After the stuffy confines of the dating scene in Bangor,
being around Olivia seemed like a breath of fresh air.

Olivia's womanly scent wafted toward him and he
guessed she wasn't wearing perfume. Yet her skin gave
off hints of lavender and other natural extracts like
olive, hemp, and jojoba oils. This left him questioning
whether Olivia purchased her bathing products at the
interesting store in town his sister Sandy had
mentioned: Mystic Magi, which stood to the left of the
Christmas Cookie Shop.

Olivia let herself into her darkened storefront. Nick
could spy the festive retail space behind her adorned
with Christmas decorations like indoor wall wreaths,
homespun Christmas stockings, and freestanding
ornamental reindeer. Shelves stocked with holiday
knickknacks lined the sides of the room, and an array of
fake trees dripping with ornaments occupied the area in
back. The large front window showcased a pretty
Christmas village display, complete with miniature
Victorian-era houses, streetlamps, and undulating swirls

of pretend snow. A checkout counter holding a register sat in the center of the room, and there were was a door located directly behind it and between the stands of artificial Christmas trees. He guessed the stairway to her upstairs apartment was through there, and found himself wishing he could see it.

"Thanks for walking me home," she said. "It was really nice of you to do that."

"I couldn't very well have let you hobble home by yourself."

Olivia laughed in agreement. Then she cringed, shifting her raised foot.

"You'd probably better get that elevated."

"Yeah."

"Do you need me to get some ice for you, or something?"

Olivia shook her head. "I probably have enough in my freezer, and if I run out..." She studied the ground beside him. "I guess I can always use snow."

Nick chuckled heartily. "Ah, but that would mean another trip downstairs."

"True."

"And, I have the feeling the good doctor meant for you to stay put."

"I'm going to be bored out of my mind," Olivia admitted. Then she added shyly, "The truth is I don't sit still very well."

Nick could understand that sentiment. He was much the same way. "Do you have enough groceries?" he asked, thoughtfully. "Supplies?"

"Yes, thanks. Fortunately, I went to the store just yesterday morning."

He was running out of excuses to stick around. "Well, if you need anything," he said, thumping the doorframe. "I'm not really far away." Since Sisters' Row was kitty-corner from the Grand Hotel on North Main, it was just down the street.

"Thanks, Nick." Her pretty green eyes sparkled and the back of Nick's neck felt hot. "It was really great meeting you today."

"Yeah, you too."

"I can't wait to hear your ideas for the Grand Hotel."

"How about I call you on Tuesday, once I've had a chance to examine everything more closely tomorrow?"

"That sounds super, thanks."

"Take care of that ankle in the meantime."

"I will." She sighed sweetly, obviously resigned to her predicament. "Thanks."

Nick's pulse pounded all the way back to the Grand Hotel. It picked up even more steam when he hit Santa Claus Lane. Nick stopped and found himself staring into the storefront for the Christmas Cookie Shop. That made him think of those legendary Virginia Cookies, as well as the mysterious tin in his freezer. He was betting that Olivia was right. Lou Christmas probably put them there, and from what Nick had witnessed this morning, Lou definitely was the matchmaking kind.

But the goal Nick needed to focus on now was finding Tulip. His niece would be crushed if anything happened to her cat, and Nick was determined to prevent that. Nick ambled down the empty street toward the North Pole Nursery, which stood in the old train depot building. It was closed up tight, late afternoon shadows falling around it, as snowcapped mountains towered in the background. "Tulip!" he called. "Here, kitty, kitty!" He looked left and right, scouring every inch of the sidewalk. *Where in the world is that cat?*

Over here!

Nick turned with a start, nearly jumping out of his skin. He'd heard something; he was sure he had! Nick surveyed the area across the street where he believed the sound had come from. There, huddled up on the stoop of the Elf Shelf Bookshop, crouched Tulip, shivering and looking afraid.

"You poor thing." Nick hurriedly crossed the street, striding toward her. She waited patiently until he approached and picked her up. "You've really had quite a day, haven't you?" he asked the shaking feline, holding her close. The minute he snuggled Tulip against his chest, she began to purr. "There, there," he said, stroking her head. "Everything's okay now. You're going home to Lily." Tulip purred louder then, understanding she was safe.

Nick stared up the street at the broad outline of the Grand Hotel, thinking what an interesting town this was. There was something special about it, too. Special and unique... Just like that interesting legend about Hannah's Virginia Cookies, Nick thought, his gaze snagging on the front of her shop. He was going to have to remember to ask Sandy about those.

Chapter Four

Lily rushed into the foyer the moment Nick
appeared with her cat in his arms. The nine-year-old
girl had big dark eyes and pigtails. She wore a powder
blue and white snowflake-design sweatshirt and jeans.
Nick noted she had a decorative reindeer barrette
clipped in her hair to the left of her center part. It had a
bright red nose, just like Rudolph.

"Tulip!" she cried happily, rushing past Sandy,
who held back the door. She gazed gratefully up at
Nick. "Uncle Nick! You found her!"

Nick carefully transferred the hefty feline into
Lily's arms. She held Tulip up to her face, rubbing her
cheek against the cat's fuzzy head. "Where did you go,
you silly kitty?"

"I think she might have followed me to the Grand
Hotel," Nick answered, deciding not to mention the
episode with Tilly Anderson's dog lest that worry Lily.

"Followed *you*?" Sandy beckoned him inside,
shutting the door behind him. "But, why? Tulip's never
gone outdoors!"

"She's cold," Lily reported. "Her fur's all wet,
too."

"Why don't you take her into the kitchen and dry her off?" Sandy suggested gently. "Then, you can give her something to eat."

Lily nodded and walked away, holding Tulip close. When she'd gone, Sandy latched onto Nick's coat sleeve, tugging him toward her and away from her front hall sentinel, Frosty. The three-foot-tall snowman wore a black top hat, and had a corncob pipe and two eyes made out of fake coal. He was wound from top to bottom in blinking Christmas lights.

Sandy glanced through the dining area as Lily disappeared into the kitchen, then asked quietly, "What's going on, Nick?"

"I don't know," he said, a bit confounded himself. "Something, though. I met one of your townspeople, Tilly Anderson—and her dog."

"Cocoa?" Sandy's forehead rose. "What happened?"

"I'm not exactly sure," Nick returned, stroking his chin. "He obeyed me, but that's not unusual."

"You've always been good with animals," Sandy agreed. "Especially with Grandpa's."

"I know, but I've never heard…"

"Heard what?"

He shook his head, deciding his ears must have been playing tricks on him. "It was probably nothing."

Nick glanced into the cozy living area, which included a candy-cane-striped sofa and two end tables shaped like kettledrums. A brightly decorated Christmas tree stood at the far end of the room and three Christmas stockings hung from the mantel of a wood-burning fireplace. Comfy red armchairs nestled by the hearth facing the coffee table between them and

the sofa, which was actually a child-size sleigh that had
been outfitted with a Formica top. Nick recognized the
green and gold sleigh as having belonged to Sandy
when she was little. His grandpa had made him a
similar one, painted gold and red, when he was a boy.

"Where are the little ones, and Ben?" he asked, not
seeing any of them around.

"Ben's over at the Christmas Inn helping Walt with
a project." Sandy cocked her head toward the staircase
behind her. "Holly and Rose are napping upstairs."
Nick bemusedly recalled Holly's aborted flying act
with her carriage.

"That was quite a trick Holly played on the side—"

"Shhh," Sandy said in hushed tones. "Lily will hear
you."

"Does Ben know?"

Sandy grimaced slightly. "I think he's kind of
guessed."

"There are worse abilities to have, I suppose." Nick
cast his gaze at the ceiling. "Have you noticed anything
about Rose?"

"Not yet, but they're still so tiny."

"Yeah."

"Would you like to stay for coffee?" Sandy
offered. "Ben will be back in a bit."

"Can't today," Nick replied. "I need to finish
settling in at my rental. Plus, I've got a few notes to
work up on the Grand Hotel."

"Still making those lists, huh?" Sandy said
teasingly.

Nick shot her a friendly wink. "You know it."

"How'd everything go with Olivia?" she asked,
when he turned to go.

"Just fine. Only…" Nick's lips creased in a frown. "She had a small mishap on the stairs."

"Oh, no!" Sandy's blue eyes rounded. "She didn't get hurt?"

"Twisted her ankle, but Kurt says it should heal quickly."

"If you brought in a doctor, it must have looked bad."

"We decided better safe than sorry."

"Good call."

"I'm just glad that Olivia's going to be all right, and that it wasn't worse." Nick smiled thoughtfully. "It was great seeing Kurt again. I only wish it had been under better circumstances."

"I'll give Olivia a call later to check on her," Sandy said. "Thanks for letting me know."

When Nick laid his hand on the doorknob, Sandy added, "Olivia's *very* pretty, wouldn't you say?"

Nick chuckled deeply. "Now, you're sounding like Lou Christmas."

"You didn't answer my question."

"I'm not sure I noticed." Nick stared back over his shoulder. "Olivia and I were talking business."

Sandy smirked. "Nicholas Claus, don't play cute with me."

His eyebrows arched innocently. "Cute?"

"You know exactly what I mean," Sandy answered. "And, for the record, I think you like her."

"What makes you say that?"

Sandy crossed her arms in front of her and spoke with a knowing air. "You're already starting to detect whether she's been naughty or nice."

Nick trudged back toward Sisters' Row, with his hands shoved into his jacket pockets. Today, he'd neglected to wear his gloves. He wouldn't make the same mistake tomorrow. Snow clouds loomed overhead, crowding out the fading afternoon sun. This brief break in the storm wouldn't last long. Christmas Town was predicted to get several more inches of snow this week. Sharp winds blew and Nick hunched his shoulders forward, wondering when his baby sister had become such a know-it-all. While Nick wasn't one hundred percent certain he'd read Olivia correctly, one thing was sure. Sandy had used one of her special skills by creeping into Nick's mind. She must have sensed him thinking about Olivia eating that Danish.

At least, Sandy hadn't been around later when that other weird stuff was going on. Being descended from the Clauses, who were distant relations of the Christmas family, both Sandy and Nick had inherited certain unusual abilities. Their parents had warned these special talents would strengthen once each of them met their potential mates. But Nick hadn't come to Christmas Town to settle down and get married! He'd been summoned by the Town Council to work on the Grand Hotel. Though it was true that Olivia was an extremely attractive woman, that didn't mean Nick couldn't work with her without becoming romantically involved.

And anyway, just look where his past romantic involvements had gotten him. Let down and left alone, every time. There was more to his unusual family's history than most ordinary women could handle. Sandy had been extra lucky to find Ben. When she'd told him the truth about her history, he'd accepted her with his whole heart. All right, maybe there'd been a few speed bumps in the road along the way. But, ultimately, his sister and Ben had arrived at their happy ending. And, just look at them now. They had a beautiful family with Lily and the twins, a lovely renovated historic home, and both Sandy and Ben had their dream jobs. Sandy actively worked as an artist while running the Snow Globe Gallery and Ben served as the Christmas Town Justice of the Peace. Thinking of their fairytale courtship reminded Ben about those Virginia Cookies at Sisters' Row.

He paused at the corner by the old stone church and slapped his forehead. He'd meant to ask Sandy if she knew anything about the mysterious gift in his freezer. What's more, at Olivia's prodding, he'd intended to ask Sandy about her personal experiences with the rumored romantic powers of the enticing Christmas treats. There surely couldn't be anything to the Virginia Cookie legend. But Olivia's insistence that he speak with his sister regarding the Commitment Cookies in particular had stimulated his curiosity.

Nick crossed North Main Street and headed south, strolling the few short blocks to Sisters' Row. The collection of three Victorian-era town houses huddled together behind a wrought iron gate. All shared a broad covered front porch, and were painted dusty rose with green gingerbread trim. On the far side of the building, Sandy's gallery occupied the spot on the corner of North Main Street and Santa Claus Lane. He'd nearly reached the stoop, when Nick's stomach clenched. It knotted like a balled-up fist, then pinched even tighter. *Whoa!* Nick fiercely clutched his belly while curiously smacking his lips together. There was an odd sensation on his tongue, and a very distinct taste, too. Dark-chocolate-cherry. *Omphhh*. A lot of it.

Olivia hurriedly ditched the other half of her last remaining truffle back in the empty box, and reached for her phone. She couldn't believe she'd demolished a whole box of the sweets—again! Particularly as she'd only intended to eat two or three. Not *twelve*. For goodness' sakes! Now she felt sick to her stomach.

"Olivia?" a familiar voice said. "Hi! It's Sandy!"

"Sandy, hi!"

"I'm calling to see if you're all right? Nick said you had a fall?"

"At the Grand Hotel, that's right." Olivia sighed and extended the leg she'd propped on a pillow on top of the coffee table. "I stepped through a rotted tread on the stairs and twisted my ankle."

"I'm so sorry to hear it."

"Kurt took a look. He says I'll be all right. After keeping it elevated and iced for two days," Olivia continued with a groan.

"Oh, no," Sandy said sympathetically. "I know that's going to be rough on you."

"At least it's just a few days and not weeks."

"That's true," Sandy replied sunnily. "Things could be worse." She paused a moment before continuing. "I was thinking about tomorrow and our girls' lunch," she said, referencing the regular Monday date she, Olivia, Hannah, and Jade had at Santa's Sandwich Shop.

"Yeah, I know," Olivia answered sadly. "I'm afraid I'll have to miss it."

"Not if we bring the lunch to you!"

Warmth pooled in Olivia's eyes. She'd never known such great friends before coming to Christmas Town. "I'd hate to put you ladies out."

"Don't be silly. It will be a refreshing change. I've already run it by the others, and they thought it was a fine idea."

Olivia was so touched she wanted to cry. "Thanks, Sandy. That's very kind."

"Now, all you have to do," Sandy continued brightly, "is look at the menu online and text me your order."

Chapter Five

Nick had just carried his luggage upstairs at his rental at Sisters' Row when he heard a knock at the front door. There were two bedrooms in the townhome, one facing the back patio and the other facing the street. He opted for the one in front since it was slightly larger. A full bath was in between them in the hall, with a half-bath beneath it downstairs right off the living area. Apart from the dining table in the nook facing the patio, and the seating arrangement opposite the walled-up fireplace, there wasn't a whole lot more to the first floor. The kitchen was modest but functional, and Nick had noticed one of Sandy's paintings, an outdoor winter scene, mounted over the mantel in the living room.

Someone rapped crisply again as Nick skipped down the stairs. "Coming!" he called, wondering who his visitor might be. It was nearly dinnertime and he certainly wasn't expecting anybody. Nick opened the front door to find Lou Christmas standing on the stoop smiling broadly. She wore her animal print coat and gloves. A tall, slender woman in her thirties with delicate features and honey-brown skin was with her.

"Welcome to Christmas Town!" the younger woman said congenially. She handed Nick a cloth-covered wicker basket, and the aroma of homemade soup drifted toward him. "I'm Jade Smith."

"And you know exactly who *I* am," Lou said, sounding chipper.

"The Christmas Town mayor?"

"Too true, but guess again!"

"Lou's on the Christmas Town Welcoming Committee," Jade happily explained. "I'm her substitute assistant."

"Sandy generally helps," Lou said with a wave of her glove. "But, you know. Busy with babies!" She smiled effervescently, peering over Nick's shoulder.

"Oh, right. Right. Sorry, Lou. Won't you ladies come in?"

Jade replied with a shake of her head. "I probably shouldn't. I've got a baby of my own to get back to."

"Little Josiah?"

"That's right." Jade's entire face brightened. "How did you know?"

"Olivia mentioned that he went to daycare with Sandy's twins."

"And a very fine daycare it is, too," Lou reported. She grinned proudly at Nick. "I helped name it, you know."

Nick chuckled to himself, wondering why he should be surprised.

"Jingle Bells Booties," Jade filled in. "Isn't that cute?"

"As a button!" Nick agreed heartily.

Jade's eyes darted toward her door. "In any case, Josiah will be waking any minute from his afternoon nap, so I'll want to get home."

"Wendell can only handle one boy at a time," Lou whispered confidentially to Nick.

"That's not...exactly true," Jade said a tad self-consciously. "It's just that—ever since the new baby came along—Alexander's become a tad rambunctious."

"Even more so that he was before," Lou proclaimed glowingly. "Just ask Frank and Victoria Cho about his influence on little Bobby."

Jade nervously cleared her throat. "It's quite the other way around, Lou." The natural dark hue on her cheeks deepened. "Quite the other way!"

A sharp wind blew, calling Lou up short. "My, it's getting chilly…"

Nick motioned them inside and both assented, saying they could only stay a quick minute.

"The basket contains a homemade Brunswick stew and a couple of sub sandwiches," Jade told Nick, once he'd shut the door behind them. "There's fruit and cheese in it, too. As well as a tin of salted nuts."

"Thanks so much. That sounds delicious," Nick answered gratefully. "I hadn't yet decided what I was going to do for dinner."

"Not many choices around here on a Sunday," Lou told him.

"We included a bottle of local wine, too." Jade smiled pleasantly. "I hope you enjoy!"

"And, don't forget the cookies for dessert," Lou added.

"I meant to thank you for those," Nick said, setting the basket on the entryway table with a painted mirror hanging over it. "That was really nice of you to leave some in the freezer."

"Freezer?" Lou's eyebrows rose. She stared questioningly at Jade, who turned to Nick.

"She meant the ones in there," Jade said, pointing to the basket. "Peanut butter chocolate chip. They're very good. Lou's granddaughters made them when they were home for Thanksgiving break."

"I….uh…" Nick looked from one woman to the other. "So you didn't…?" he said, addressing Lou. "Supply a little welcome gift?"

Her face fell appreciably. "Oh, dear. Isn't this enough?" She worriedly glanced at Jade. "I told you we should have brought a bigger basket for a man. His appetite's bound to be much—"

"No, no!" Nick said, cutting her off. "This basket's more than perfect. A very special welcome treat. I can't thank you enough." He scratched the side of his head. "I just wondered who gave me that very nice tin of Virginia Cookies, that's all."

Both women alerted at this.

"Virginia Cookies?" Jade asked, surprised.

Lou angled closer. "Really? What kind?"

"Why, all three, from the looks of it." Nick stared at Lou expectantly as she drummed her gloved fingers against her chin.

"No, nope. Wasn't me."

"Maybe it was Hannah?" Jade offered.

Nick shook his head. "Hannah said she didn't know anything about them."

"No?" Lou's eyes shone brightly. "Well, this *is* a mystery."

"Wasn't there any kind of note?" Jade inquired.

"Only one with my name on it, saying the cookies were for me."

Jade spoke surely. "Then it sounds like you were meant to have them!"

"Yeah, but who…?"

Lou shrugged then said with a leading edge, "Maybe you've got a *Secret Santa*?"

Nick bid the ladies adieu, thanking them again for their generous gift. Their thoughtful gesture was going to make his first night here so much easier. He wouldn't even have to cook! Nick carried the basket to the kitchen and set it on the counter, unpacking its treasures. When he got to the package of cookies wrapped in a clear plastic baggie tied shut with green and red ribbon, his gaze trailed toward the freezer. It was mighty odd that his two primary suspects hadn't owned up to gifting him with those Virginia Cookies. And neither Hannah nor Lou had appeared to know anything about them.

He opened the freezer door and pulled out the cookie tin, studying its decorative lid portraying Santa in his workshop with some elves. The yellow sticky note he'd seen earlier was still in place. He tugged it off the top of the tin to examine it more closely.

For Nick, Enjoy some cookies with your milk!

Well, what do you know? In the bright kitchen light, Nick saw something shining through from the back side of the page. It looked like more squiggly writing. He flipped the small yellow paper over in his hand, then chortled in stunned laughter.

P.S.
Don't forget to share with Olivia!

Interesting, very interesting indeed. Nick shook his
head with a broad grin, thinking there was more than
one intrepid matchmaker in town. He was definitely
calling Sandy to learn about these legendary Virginia
Cookies. But he'd wait until after he'd had dinner, and
Sandy and Ben had put the kids to bed.

"I can't believe my big sister gets hurt, and doesn't
tell me. I have to hear it through the grapevine!"
    Olivia pressed her phone to her ear with a pleased
smile. "Savannah? Is that really you?" She hadn't heard
from her baby sister in eons. But somehow their
periodic breaks in communication hardly seemed to
matter. Each time they reconnected, it was like no time
had passed at all.
    "Yeah, sugar, it is. And, seriously," she added, but
she said it sweetly. "Why didn't you call?"
    "Honey, it's only happened today!"
    "But Carter said you had to go the doctor's and
everything?"
    Olivia might have suspected that Carter had been
the snitch. Hannah must have told him, after Sandy
called Hannah about modifying their girls' lunch by
making it a carry-out affair. "Honestly, Savannah. It
isn't that bad. I just twisted my ankle a bit. And I didn't
go to the…" She hesitated in mentioning Kurt, given
the rough history between Savannah and him. "What I
mean is, a local medic took a look at it and said—"

"Wait a minute. What local medic? You mean, you called 9-1-1?"

"Heavens, no! I told you—"

"You can't expect me to believe you just grabbed some dude with a stethoscope off the street!" Why oh why was Savannah always so insistent?

Then Savannah gasped in understanding before whispering into the phone, "It was Kurt, wasn't it? Kurt's the Christmas Town doctor."

"Yeah, so?" Olivia began to fiddle nervously with a strand of her loosely coiled hair. She normally wore it in a braid, not all long and sexy like someone out of a shampoo ad. Olivia hadn't wanted to admit it, but secretly she'd wanted to look nice for Nick. Particularly since she'd appeared so unkempt when they first met.

"So, that means Kurt checked out your ankle, but you didn't want me to know."

Olivia could practically see Savannah's pretty mouth puckered in a pout. She had green eyes like Olivia's but her build was more slender, and her skin even more pale. While Savannah lived and worked in Miami, you'd never know it from her complexion. She burned extremely easily and took care to stay out of the sun.

"What do you think I am, Olivia? Fifteen? I'm way over Kurt by now." She tried to sound convincing, but Olivia still found herself wondering if that was true.

"I know you are," she answered kindly. "But I also know sometimes it's hard. First loves, and all that."

"I never hear you mention Henry Meeks?"

Olivia laughed heartily. "Oh…my…gosh! I haven't thought of him in years!"

"I'll never forget how scared you were to kiss him when you got braces."

"Stop!" Olivia cried, but she was chuckling.

"He had them too, and Carter teased you by telling you not to get any big ideas, because your braces might get locked together."

"He was *such* a pesky little brother."

"Yeah, and a protective big one, too." Savannah sighed heavily. "I guess he meant well."

"You know he did," Olivia insisted. "He still does, pretty much all of the time."

"I'm sick that I missed his wedding," Savannah said. She'd had an accident of her own at the time, requiring surgery, and hadn't been able to make the event last year.

"Everybody missed you," Olivia told her. "I really wish you could have been here."

"I'll make the next one," Savannah assured her.

"The next what?"

"The next wedding in Christmas Town, silly." Then, she added a bit impishly, "Maybe it will be yours?"

"Ha-ha. Seeing as how I don't have a boyfriend—"

"You're still not dating, Olivia?" Savannah was trying to be supportive but her disappointment shone through. "Honey, you've got to get back out there."

"Yeah, well, I suppose you haven't noticed because you haven't been here, but Christmas Town's not exactly teeming with eligible bachelors."

"Not even one?" Savannah seemed astounded. "What about that new guy? That architect from Maine you said you were going to be working with?"

"Nick? Well, he's…" Olivia's face flamed when she remembered being steadied in his strong embrace, then leaning against his muscular frame as he escorted her home. "What I mean is, I've barely met him."

"Is he single?"

"Yeah."

"Young?"

"Well…uh…not *too* young. He's my friend Sandy's older brother."

"*Hot?*"

"I…er…didn't exactly notice."

"What's wrong with him, then?"

Olivia recalled his deep blue eyes on hers and her skin burned hotter. "Nothing! It's just that he's here to *work with me* on a project. Not, you know…" She shrugged lamely. "Date me."

"Nothing wrong with killing two birds with one stone!"

Spoken just like Savannah. She was such a multitasker.

"How about you?" Olivia asked, turning the conversation around. But already her mind was racing, wondering what that would really be like. Going out on a date with Nick. Would their conversation flow just as easily as it had when they were talking this afternoon? Would Olivia find herself once again falling into Nick's strong arms? It wasn't hard for her to imagine wanting him to hold her. Because the fact of the matter was that Nick *was* hot, and smart and funny. Not to mention, very, very sexy in his own unique and charming way.

"How about me?" Savannah asked, sounding a bit caught off guard.

"What's the current story with James?" Olivia asked, inquiring about Savannah's on- and off-again boyfriend, a respected pediatric heart surgeon who traveled often.

"Oh, you know…" When her words trailed off, Olivia suspected she did. Though Savannah had stuck with James for years, something told Olivia that their relationship wasn't exactly the most fulfilling one for Savannah. James, on the other hand, appeared to like things the way they were just fine. "He's gone again," Savannah finished wistfully. "He's always gone lately, it seems."

Olivia frowned in sympathy. Savannah was basically in a long-distance relationship with a guy who lived in the very same town. "That must be hard—on you, and the relationship."

"I think it's good we can each have our space," Savannah said unconvincingly. "I stay busy with school," she said, referring to her job as a high school guidance counselor. "Did I tell you?" Savannah's voice became animated. "We're putting on a new play!" Olivia knew that Savannah and the drama instructor were close, and that Savannah often helped with productions.

"Excellent. Which one?"

"It's a musical: *Oklahoma*."

"'There's bright, golden haze on the meadow'?"

"Yeah, I've always loved that song."

Savannah sang it exceptionally well, too. She had a beautiful voice and had done a lot of theater in high school. Carter used to rib her by saying it was the perfect fit since Savannah was such a drama queen. He never teased anyone like that anymore. After Carter had gone to college, and especially once he'd gone into the army, he'd become much more serious. He'd become so stoic in fact that Olivia had actually started to worry about him. Then Hannah Winchester came to town, and she'd changed everything. Olivia guessed that love and happiness could do that to a man, because Carter sure appeared to be in great spirits most of the time now. Married life obviously suited him, and he really doted on his daughter.

"You'll have to send me a video of the show," Olivia said, aware that the drama department at Savannah's school always taped them.

"Will do. I promise!" She altered her tone to sound serious. "Now here's something that I want you to promise me… One, that you'll get better soon, and two, that you'll give Nick a shot."

"What?"

"Come on, Olivia. It's not that hard. Nick's from out of town, right? So, it's not exactly like you're pushing for a long-term commitment. Just dinner or something? A cup of coffee? But, whatever you do, make it a real date. I mean, don't wear your hair in that braid of yours. And don't wear muddy jeans. Oh! And, if you've been at the barn—"

"Savannah!" Olivia said abruptly. "Stop being so bossy!"

Savannah issued her sassy retort. "If I don't boss you, who will?"

"Nobody! That's the point."

"No. The point is you haven't been out with a guy since Ted. And Ted was three years ago. That's a long time, Olivia. Too long to give Ted that sort of power over you."

"Who says Ted has any power?" she asked, inwardly questioning whether her sister was right. Savannah was, after all, an expert at relationships. Even if she couldn't manage her own.

"I'm hoping he doesn't… Any longer." Then Savannah added a challenge. "There's one sure way to find out."

"By going out with Nick?" Olivia asked incredulously.

"Put yourself in the line of fire and see what happens," Savannah suggested. "If you go out with Nick and all you can think about is Ted, then you've got a problem. But, it's not a problem we can't fix," Savannah amended hurriedly. "I can recommend some great books, and maybe even help you find someone in your local area to talk to."

Olivia didn't need therapy! She had her own ways of dealing with her pain, she thought, guiltily eyeing the empty truffle box from Nutcracker Sweets. "And, what happens if I don't…think of Ted?"

"In that case, I'd say you might be in for a very merry Christmas!"

"*Ho-ho-ho!*" Nick chimed merrily when Sandy took his call. "You never told me Christmas Town was such a friendly, welcoming place."

"Yes, I did, and you know it," she said before asking excitedly, "What's happened? Something with Olivia?"

"Olivia. *Olivia…*" he chanted. "I'm starting to suspect a ringing in my ears. First there's Lou, then there's—"

"When did you see Lou?" She stopped herself, evidently remembering. "That's right! She must have brought the welcome basket by. With Jade! How did you like her?"

"Jade's a lovely woman. So is Louise. A little more eccentric than I remember."

"Some folks would say that about the Clauses," Sandy cautioned. "That we're eccentric."

"I guess the Christmases and the Clauses have that in common."

"Probably why our families have remained close," Sandy agreed.

"I can't believe it's been twenty years since I've set foot in Christmas Town."

"A lot has changed around here," she said. "You haven't met Ray Christmas's wife, Meredith, or their boy, Kyle. And Walt's girls, Noelle and Joy, are already in college."

Nick remembered meeting Walt's late wife, Rose, during his last trip here as a teen. Walt and Rose had married right out of college, and she was expecting their twins. The eldest Christmas brother, Ray, was still a bachelor at the time. "Kurt's probably changed the most," he said. "At least the other two were grown-ups then."

"You'll probably be hearing from Walt soon," she told him. "Ben said he mentioned having you stop by for a drink at the Christmas Inn."

"That would be awesome. I'd love to see the place—and Walt, of course."

"You can expect a call from Hannah, too."

"Hannah?"

"She and Carter are having a dinner party at the end of the week and they want to include you."

"I think I'll appoint you as my new social secretary," he said, joking.

"You might need one," he sister returned quickly. "Fasten your seatbelt. This is Christmas Town!"

"Not a sleepy little place?"

"That depends on how you look at it. For some of us, it's hopping."

"I know it is for you. Between work and family you must stay plenty busy."

"Ben helps."

"I'm sure that he does..." Nick pensively stroked his chin. "Which reminds me of a question I wanted to ask you."

"Question?"

"It's about Hannah's Virginia Cookies?"

"Oh?" Oddly, there was a note of trepidation in her voice. "What about them?"

"Olivia said I should ask you about your experience with those Commitment Cookies?"

"She did, did she?" Sandy asked, sounding slightly annoyed. Then she dropped her voice in a whisper. "Why?"

"Why, indeed? Maybe you can tell me?"

Sandy took a moment to process this. "I hardly see how I'm the expert on Commitment Cookies. If you want some real answers, you should probably ask Hannah."

"Perhaps I will... But, in the meantime, what am I supposed to do with the stash in my freezer?"

"Stash? What stash?"

"My Secret Santa left me a little welcoming gift," Nick said, testing the waters. If Sandy had snuck those Virginia Cookies into Sisters' Row, now was her chance to fess up.

"Well, it wasn't me!" Sandy huffed. "Is that what you're thinking?"

Nick was running out of reasonable prospects. "If not you, then who?"

"I have no idea." She sounded just as stymied as Nick felt.

"There was note attached," he offered further. "Encouraging me to share them with Olivia."

"Somebody is definitely up to something," Sandy commented in thoughtful tones. "And, that something is matchmaking… Have you talked to Lou?"

"Lou said it wasn't her."

"I'm not sure who else has a key?"

"That's the odd part, isn't it?" Nick asked.

"Yeah."

"In any case," he continued. "From what Olivia said the cookies' powers are all pretend, anyway. Totally make-believe."

"Huh. She said that? Then, why did she tell you to talk to me?"

"Maybe she thought you held a different opinion?"

"Well, I…" Sandy hesitated an awkward beat. "…er…don't!"

"O-*kay*."

"It's not like Ben and I wouldn't have fallen for each other regardless," she rushed in. "We were head over heels from the start! Love at first sight! And that was *way* before either of us had taken even one little bite!"

Nick pondered her explanation. "I see." He also knew that when Sandy got nervous she tended to blabber a lot.

"And, when Ben ate his," she barreled ahead. "It was all a big mix-up! I didn't mean to give him my heart and he didn't expect to feel *grateful*, but he did. Oh my goodness!" Sandy sucked in a breath. "Oops, I've said too much."

Nick chuckled warmly. "It's okay. Your secrets are safe with me. All of them. And, for the record, I believe you. You and Ben are a great match. I have complete faith that you would have made it, with or without those cookies."

"Thanks," she said, still sounding breathless.

"So, I suppose I'd better take care in eating mine?"

"Right! Especially the 'Forever Yours' kind. Be extra careful who you're around when you eat that one. Be sure to choose wisely!"

"But you just said you agreed with Olivia's assessment?"

"I did? I…um…" Next, she jumped in quickly. "Oh, yes. I did! Do! And, I meant that. One hundred percent. It's just that, Nick?"

"Yeah?"

"It never hurts to be cautious. You know what I'm saying? Particularly at Christmas."

Chapter Six

Nick woke up the next morning surprisingly alert. He also felt that jolly glow about him like someone had done an awfully good deed. The warmth started in his belly then settled in his chest, lending him a happy, contented heart. And the face that came to mind was...*Olivia's*. Nick sat bolt upright under the covers, thinking this through. When he was a kid, telling who'd been naughty and nice was child's play. He didn't even have to work at it, really. The impressions just slammed him whenever he looked at someone just the right way. As he grew older, all that internal chatter became distracting, so he'd investigated ways to forestall it. Luckily, he'd learned that ingesting peppermint seemed to tone the problem down.

He had a pack of peppermint gum in the glove box of his SUV, and a jar of starlight mints by his drafting table at the office. He also kept a steady supply of peppermint teabags in his desk. Nick wasn't keen on being in on everybody's business all the time, especially when he was working. His parents had called this skill one of his talents, but to this day he was unsure of who it benefited. There were certain things a guy just didn't want to know. Like the fact that his coworker had cheated on his diet, or that the new office assistant bought a skimpy lingerie set for her boyfriend at Valentine's. Nick supposed the sexy getup had been both naughty and nice. No doubt the boyfriend appreciated it. It wouldn't even have qualified as naughty, if the secretary hadn't blushed when she bought it.

This naughty and nice business didn't just impact Nick's emotions. It affected the hearts of others around him. It was how they *felt* about their actions that mattered the most. Fortunately, that meant that true sociopaths were off Nick's radar, since they had no empathy or remorse whatsoever. He was glad he didn't have to deal with those folks, on top of everyone else.

The situation with Olivia was special. Something odd was happening there. Something Nick couldn't quite explain. He was receiving impressions of the woman without even being within range of her! Not unless you counted a few city blocks as "within range," and Nick had never read anybody at a distance before. Curiosity tugged at him as to why this was happening now.

Just last Christmas, Sandy had experienced a similar phenomenon with Ben. She'd inherited family abilities too, and the minute Ben arrived on the scene they appeared to strengthen. In fact, they'd gathered so much steam that the situations Sandy found herself in had scared her nearly half to death. Until she'd decided to embrace who she was and let Ben in on her secrets. Things had apparently resolved themselves then... *With Sandy and Ben getting married.*

Nick swallowed hard and drew the covers to his bare chest. He'd slept in his Christmas boxers, the ones with teams of reindeer prancing across them. All of Nick's underwear sported a holiday theme, though— obviously—not many others were aware of it. A few of his ex-girlfriends had found this weird. But seriously, where was their Christmas spirit? Nick was a huge fan of the holiday but he didn't advertise it quite as loudly as Sandy.

She had Christmas *everywhere*. In her work, in her gallery, in her home… She even dressed her kids that way. Nick, on the other hand, was much more understated in his approach. Although, it was true that he loved to decorate, and had a very big weakness for cookies and milk. It was a good thing Lou had supplied him with an alternate cookie source, or he very well might have gotten into those Virginia Cookies in his freezer. If only he could guess who'd placed them there to begin with?

For the moment, Nick had something more pressing to focus on. He had to know why he'd woken up with visions of Olivia dancing in his head. Perhaps he'd stop by to check on her before heading to the Grand Hotel. He could bring her a surprise from the coffee shop across the way, and he didn't think he'd wake her. Nick had a keen sense that Olivia was an early riser.

Olivia ended her call with Sleigh Bell Stables feeling satisfied. Her group of little girls wouldn't have to miss their regular Tuesday afternoon meeting with the horses, after all. Olivia's friend at the barn, Maggie, had offered to run the program for her. Olivia had called to ask Maggie to look after her horse, Blaze, for a few days while she recovered from her minor injury, and Maggie had volunteered one step further. She'd said she'd love to fill in for Olivia with the children, and Olivia was grateful for her help.

The horse program was valuable in two ways. It was great for the kids to become comfortable with the animals, and the rescue horses benefited from the low-key exposure to the gentle little ones. Some of the rescue horses had come such a long way, Olivia had been able to train them for riding. After getting to know the horses, several of the girls became desperate for riding lessons. With the children's parents' approval, Olivia had been able to arrange the classes with another friend at the stables who was a certified instructor.

Olivia decided to do something nice for Maggie to thank her. She limped toward the kitchen area which opened up on the living room with an island standing between them. The island had three tall chairs facing a dining counter on the living room side. Olivia was proud of the pretty green-and-white checked seat cushions she'd sewn specifically to fit them. They added a homey touch to the place and matched the curtains framing the large window at the front of the living area, which looked out on the street.

The room housed a futon with a forest green slipcover, which doubled as her guest bed, and a couple of cranberry-colored director's chairs. An old steamer trunk served as her coffee table, while holding the linens for the futon and extra blankets. She had a small television set that she rarely turned on, and bookshelves teeming with books. She had favorites that she'd read several times, but Olivia never tired of the stories. One book in particular was special to her.

It was an older edition of *The Night Before Christmas* by Clement C. Moore. Her dad had bought it for her when she was little and Olivia had become enthralled with the magical tale of Old Saint Nick's fanciful late-night ride. Even to this day, it still gave her goose bumps, wondering what it would be like to *really* see Santa Claus. Olivia knew it was silly to imagine that as an adult, but there was just something so wonderful about Christmas that it made you want to believe. Not that she'd ever tell her friends this. They all thought of her as the reasonable one. And, rightly so, since she generally was.

Olivia reached the cupboard to the left of the kitchen sink, spying her treasure trove through the paneled glass. The community garden she oversaw had yielded an abundant crop last summer, and Olivia had taken advantage of the fresh vegetables by putting up lots of homemade salsa, spaghetti sauce, sweet pickles, and chutneys. She'd make a special gift package for Maggie using one of the handbaskets she had around. She had plenty of extra green-and-white checkered cloth with which to line it, too. Olivia was just putting her basket together when the downstairs doorbell buzzed. She hoped it wasn't a shopper arriving early. Olivia checked her watch. All Things Christmas didn't open till ten, and it wasn't even eight o'clock.

The doorbell sounded again and Olivia called out as she limped down the stairs, "Coming!" *Honestly, who expects a Christmas shop to be open this early on a Monday morning?* When she reached the door, she saw it wasn't a prospective customer at all. It was Nick!

His bright blue eyes twinkled as snow lightly drifted around him. "I hope I didn't wake you?" he queried as a courtesy, Olivia was sure. She was clearly already dressed for the day in her red sweater and jeans.

"No, I've been up for a bit." She hobbled backwards, allowing him passage into her darkened shop and out of the wind. As she shut the door, Olivia noted he held a coffee cup and a white paper bag stamped with the logo from Jolly Bean Java.

"I wanted to check on you, and be sure you're okay?"

Olivia was truly touched. "That's really nice of you, Nick." She leaned into the doorframe, stabilizing herself with one hand, and he briefly viewed her raised foot.

"Is the ankle any better this morning?"

"It seems a lot less swollen today," she reported, gratefully. "The rest helped."

"Were you able to sleep all right?"

"Yes! Fine. I had sort of weird dreams, though," she admitted with a chuckle.

"Yeah?" Nick appeared intrigued.

"Santa was flying with his reindeer, and I was in his sleigh!"

"Wow."

"I know! Pretty crazy, right?"

"Um…well…"

Olivia was suddenly embarrassed she'd told him. What a goofy thing to admit. "That's what I get for reading that book before bed again," she said, trying to shrug it off.

"Which book?"

"*The Night Before Christmas*."

"I know that poem; it's very good!"

"Yes."

He seemed to suddenly remember his mission. "Oh, right! Here," he said, lifting the bag in his hand. "This is for you."

"Me?"

"I stopped by Jolly Bean Java to grab some coffee and thought you might like a morning treat."

Olivia's cheeks flushed hot. "How sweet."

"They're cherry cheese Danishes." He studied her appraisingly before adding, "I had a hunch you might like them."

Olivia was stunned, but also pleased. "They're my absolute favorites! But, how did you—?"

"I asked the fellow at the counter. I believe he said his name is Devon?"

"Devon Slade, yes," Olivia said, relieved. For a moment, she was starting to worry Nick could detect her cravings. She'd woken up this morning with a dire hankering for Danishes, but hadn't wanted to risk scuttling across the icy street with her bum ankle. "Devon attends community college nearby, but he still works there part-time."

"Still?"

"He's had the job since high school. His parents run South Pole Pottery right down the street."

"I like the sound of that place. I'll have to stop by. When I'm taking a break from the Grand Hotel, that is. Business first!"

"Business first!" Olivia echoed perkily. But all she could think about was Savannah's suggestion that she ask Nick out—on a real date. *Give me a break. I can't do that! Talk about awkward with a capital A!*

A dimple settled in his left cheek as he passed her the bag. "Well, here you are. Enjoy!"

She accepted his offering, her pulse pounding. Olivia was in the habit of doing things for other people. It was a tad humbling to have someone doing something for her. Particularly when that someone was *male*, and *single*, and *devastatingly handsome*, standing there in his open field coat, work boots, and jeans. He wore a navy blue sweatshirt beneath his coat and there was a hint of a white T-shirt underneath.

"Thanks! I'm sure I will."

"I'll call you tomorrow when I have more news about the Grand Hotel." His neck colored slightly above his open collar. "Maybe we can get together on Wednesday or Thursday, if you're feeling better?"

"That would be great." Olivia was eager to bounce around ideas about the renovation. She was also secretly desirous of spending more time with the handsome architect, though she had a hard time admitting this to herself. Perhaps Savannah was right. Olivia had been out of circulation for too long. She couldn't even recall feeling attracted to a man the way she was to Nick. Then again, there weren't a whole lot of guys like Nick in Christmas Town, apart from the Christmas brothers. Ray, of course, was married, and Kurt—being her sister's old flame—was strictly off-limits. Walt was a wonderfully good man and incredibly handsome, too. Yet Olivia had never felt any sort of interest in Walt, or Kurt for that matter, beyond friendship.

Nick shifted on his feet before asking thoughtfully, "Did you work everything out at the stables?"

He must have recalled her fretting over not being able to conduct her Tuesday program during her conversation with Kurt. "Oh, yes! I spoke with Maggie just this morning. She's a friend of mine at the barn, and she offered to fill in."

"It's great to have good friends," he commented. But the way he was looking at her made Olivia guess he was contemplating something else. "I hope we'll be friends, Olivia. I mean, beyond working together on the hotel project. I'll be here for a few months, and don't know too many people in town."

"Ah, but you know some important ones!"

He chuckled deeply. "The Christmas family and my sister, yes." He cocked his chin to the side, apparently waiting on her answer.

Olivia swallowed past the lump in her throat, her face flaming. "Of course we'll be friends! Ha-ha. One can never have too many."

His eyes danced and Olivia's heart hammered. She felt hot all over, like she was breaking out in a sweat.

"So, I guess I'll see you later?"

"Later! Sounds good," she chirped, clutching her pastry bag until it crinkled. "And, uh… Thanks for the pastries!"

He locked on her gaze. "Any time."

The room twirled around her and Olivia tightened her hold on the doorframe. If Nick didn't leave soon, she was going to fall again—and he was going to have to catch her. That thought made her heart race faster.

Nick reached for the doorknob, his coat sleeve brushing her arm. "May I?" he queried politely and Olivia realized she'd been unwittingly blocking his exit.

Or maybe she'd subconsciously done it on purpose!
Gosh.

She hurriedly hopped to one side. "Oh…er…ah, yeah! Of course!"

"Have a nice day, Olivia." The way he said her name was as smooth as silk, caressing. Olivia's pulse pounded and her right leg shook.

"You too, Nick! Thanks for stopping by!"

Then, he was gone, leaving Olivia catching her breath.

Chapter Seven

Hannah was the first in the door at one o'clock. "And just what are you doing up, little missus?" she asked Olivia, carrying in a couple of bags from Santa's Sandwich Shop. "We all thought your store would be closed?"

Jade came in behind her, carting a cardboard tray holding four drinks, and Sandy brought up the rear, waving her loaded mittens. "I've got the straws and napkins," she said with a winsome wave.

Olivia turned toward them and forced a play smirk. "Kurt said to take it easy, not stay in quarantine!" She sat behind her register with her foot diligently propped on a footstool. A bag of ice rested on her ankle, which was actually feeling much better. The swelling was appearing to go down as the day went on. The girls scuttled over to her and peeked over the counter, taking a look.

"Poor you!" Sandy said with a frown.

"Have you noticed any improvement?" Jade asked.

"Yes, I'm much better today. Just not quite back to normal."

Hannah's expression brightened as she held up her bags. "Eating will help."

"Hannah thinks that eating is the answer to everything," Sandy teased.

"A little nutrition never hurt anyone," Hannah retorted sassily.

"Be careful," Jade warned in a whisper. "You never know when she's talking about those Virginia Cookies…"

Hannah's eyes widened defensively but then she laughed. "Am not!"

"Who needs Virginia Cookies when there are other sweets around…?" Sandy set her straws and napkins on the counter and stealthily reached for the bag sitting beside the register. "Jolly Bean Java?"

"Olivia, you didn't?" Hannah asked, aghast.

"She's right," Jade concurred. "Crossing the street in your condition might not have been—"

Olivia rushed in with her protest. "But, I didn't!" When the others stared at her she continued, "What I mean is, I…er… The pastries were a gift."

The others exchanged puzzled glances. "A gift?" Hannah asked. "From who?"

"Nick brought them by." Olivia felt warmth seep into her cheeks. "This morning."

Sandy blinked in delighted surprise. "Nick?"

Olivia hesitated in telling Sandy too much. She'd mentioned her brother's status as an eligible bachelor more than once. In fact, for the past several months, it had become a recurring theme. *It's so great that Nick's coming to town! And, that he's working with you on the Grand Hotel project. By the way, did I mention that he's single?*

"Uh, yeah," Olivia said. "He just wanted to check up on me, I think."

"Well, *that* was sweet of him," Jade quipped with a knowing air.

"Yes, very," Hannah agreed, grinning.

"Isn't it great that Nick's in town?" Sandy asked, gleefully addressing Olivia. "And, that he's working with you on the Grand Hotel project!"

"Did she mention that he's *single*?" Hannah and Jade parroted together, obviously well versed in Sandy's pronouncements, too.

"Guys!" Olivia rolled her eyes. "Yeah, yeah. More than once, okay? I get it." She studied her friends, who watched her with curious faces. "But Nick isn't here to be on some kind of reality television dating show. He's in Christmas Town to do a job."

Hannah enthusiastically leaned forward. "You two will be working very closely, I hear."

"On the hotel project, sure," Olivia defended, but her face was steaming.

Jade cupped her hand to her mouth. "Ooooh," she reported to Sandy and Hannah, "I think Olivia *likes* him."

"Naturally, I like him. Nick's a really nice guy!" Olivia had the sense this was going to be a very long lunch. She loved her friends dearly. Honestly, she did. But sometimes they could really be buttinskies.

Hannah eyed her carefully. "We can't wait to hear how yesterday went."

"I bet that place is *so* romantic on the inside," Jade said, referring to the Grand Hotel. "It's such a fantastic old building."

Sandy sighed breathlessly. "I know. I hear it has a ballroom, but I've never seen it."

"It's got more than a ballroom," Olivia told them, recalling her and Nick's exploration of the grand old mansion. "You wouldn't believe all the details!"

"Please share," Hannah said, smiling warmly. "Only, let's talk over lunch. Our food is getting cold."

By the time Olivia's girlfriends left, they'd wheedled several confessions out of her, including the fact that she found Nick wickedly hot. They'd all squealed at that, and Sandy had stood up and danced around the room. But, seriously? What did the others imagine? Appreciating how a man *looked* and acknowledging that you found him *interesting*...didn't necessarily mean you were on course to have a relationship with him!

Olivia was a grown woman and she could be professional when she needed to be. The fact that Nick had hinted at being friends didn't change things in the least. On the contrary, that made everything better. Nick had clearly set the boundaries between them regarding their future interactions. Friendship was good. Olivia hadn't been romantically involved with anyone in so long, it wouldn't make sense to rush in headlong now. She needed to approach getting back on track in her dealings with men, not suddenly—in leaps and bounds—but slowly, by taking baby steps.

The instant she'd thought that, Olivia regretted the analogy. Baby steps only made her think of infants, reminding her that all three of her closest friends now had tiny bundles of joy to hold. Olivia guessed that she'd make a decent mother. Her own mom had served as a fine example, and Olivia did have a nurturing side. Just look at all the care she took with her animals! Blaze was wonderful and she loved her horse dearly. But Olivia couldn't tuck Blaze into bed at night, or sing her lullabies…

Olivia raised a hand to her cheek and discovered that she'd been crying. Up until now, Olivia had believed her life complete. She had a great job, wonderful friends, a nice place to live, and several excellent hobbies. But, right here at this moment, Olivia found herself questioning if those things were really enough? For, way down deep in her very tender heart, Olivia secretly yearned for something more. Marriage. Family. A baby of her own to cuddle…

Savannah was right. Olivia would never get from here to there without taking some intermediary measures. Perhaps this new friendship with Nick would be a good thing. It could pull her out of her funk and prime her for full-fledged dating down the road. Olivia sighed heavily, hoping that wouldn't mean the involvement of Lou Christmas. As soon as Lou learned Olivia was open to going out again, she was sure to jump in quickly with her suggestions. Lou knew all the *best bachelors* in the surrounding towns. Yet, the only bachelor that interested Olivia at the moment was one who had short dark hair and bright blue eyes. She couldn't wait to talk to Nick again on Tuesday. Until then, she'd secretly be counting the hours.

Nick set his fancy camera back in its bag and zipped it, tucking the camera case inside the backpack he planned to take home this evening. He'd also stuffed the backpack with his tape measure, electronic distance meter, clipboard, and the pages of extensive notes he'd compiled. On his way to Jolly Bean Java this morning, Nick had dropped the backpack off at the Grand Hotel, along with a folding stepladder and several work lanterns. He'd been especially grateful for the extra light sources, given the gloomy day outside and the looming shadows cast by the high ceilings indoors. Dusk was settling in, with the remnants of any natural daylight fading, so Nick decided it was time to pack it in for the evening.

He slung the backpack over his shoulder, once again observing the magnificent staircase, which was the focal point in the elegant foyer. Nick had restored several commercial spaces, like old theaters, and historic homes, including plantations, but no project had gotten his blood pumping like this one. He felt so energized being in Christmas Town. While Nick hadn't traveled here in many years, the moment he'd reached the town sign at the roundabout, he'd experienced an uncanny sense of coming home. The town was quaint and picturesque, and its people were warm and friendly.

He'd enjoyed seeing Buddy and Lou, and Kurt again, and looked forward to renewing his connections with Ray and Walt. Sandy had mentioned many others here that Nick was sure he'd like to get to know. But the resident who intrigued him the most had long red hair and incredible green eyes. Olivia Livingston sure was pretty. There was an inherent goodness about her, too. Nick could tell she was a generous-hearted person, and his in-person impression only reinforced what Sandy had previously told Nick about Olivia.

Nick knew Sandy had been not-so-secretly trying to get him and Olivia together, and Olivia seemed like a wonderful woman. Under normal circumstances, Nick would have fallen easily under her spell. But Nick had to take care to guard his emotions. Not just for his own benefit, but primarily for Olivia's sake. He wouldn't want to put her through the situation his former girlfriends had endured. It wouldn't be fair to Olivia, and Nick was far too scared to risk it. She was his sister's good friend, and was close to many folks in Christmas Town, and Nick was—first and foremost— here to restore a building. Not think of romance.

It would probably take him all of tomorrow morning to finish up his basic building assessments. Then, he could head back to Sisters' Row to make phone calls and run some searches on the Internet, before touching base with Olivia. Nick also needed to establish a makeshift office by setting up the portable drafting table he'd packed in his SUV. If he moved the furniture around a bit, he thought he could make space in the second bedroom and take care of that sometime tonight.

Nick shook his head, remembering the weird feeling he'd had upon waking this morning. He'd sensed in his gut that Olivia had done something nice for someone, and later he'd learned that she had. She'd made sure that the kids in her Tuesday program were taken care of so that they wouldn't be disappointed. She also might have worried that the horses could have felt let down. Nick was well aware that animals had feelings. They were also very primed to routines, so any change at the barn might have proven unsettling. Nick was sure Olivia had considered all of them: the kids and the rescues. She was good-hearted that way.

But Olivia's heart was something he had no business thinking about, Nick admonished himself sternly. Perhaps this morning's *impression* had been a fluke. Maybe his powers weren't gaining strength, after all. Nick held onto that thought until he pulled open the hotel's front door, and was greeted by a mob scene on the porch! *Yikes!*

A huge horde of animals crowded together. Lots and lots of cats and dogs! A possum and a raccoon, too! Winter birds and squirrels perched on the railing, and a family of deer stood on the steps as rabbits nestled beneath their legs. Nick glanced nervously up and down Main Street, relieved to spy no other folks out in the snow. The animals watched him raptly with curious rounded eyes. They seemed fine in each other's company, none intent on fighting with the others. They appeared to be waiting on Nick to say something, but he hadn't a clue *what*.

"Run along home, guys," he croaked in a whisper. "Scat!"

But instead of moving, they all just tilted their heads as a blue jay squawked.

Perspiration beaded Nick's hairline. This was crazy. Beyond nuts! Animals had always liked him, but he'd never drawn a crowd before. He began to hear odd snippets of conversation. Nick tried cleaning out his ears, but the background noise continued.

He's real! He's really real!
Red fox at ten o'clock.

I told you there's a Santa Claus.
Nick whipped his head around. Big buck!

Santa Claus is coming to town...
Santa Claus is coming to town...
A pair of hyper singing chipmunks?

It's not Santa, I tell you; it's Sandy. Sandy *Claus!*
Insistent skunk, excitedly jumping up and down.

It's Sandy Winchester now.
Astute brown owl on the railing.

And that's Sandy's brother, Nick.
Fluffy gray feline! At his feet!

"Tulip?"
Okay, now Nick knew he'd lost his mind. Nick
dropped his backpack and reached for Lily's cat,
picking her up and holding her close.
"Go on, fellas!" he rasped hoarsely at the others.
"*Please.*"
They stared at Nick with disappointed faces, then
one by one began turning and scampering off, or taking
flight. The last white flick of a deer tail had just
disappeared down the lane, when a pair of headlights
sliced through a curtain of fast-falling snow. Soon, a
red Ford truck appeared with a shimmering blue light
planted above its cab. The fellow behind the wheel
stopped at the curb and lowered his passenger side
window. As he did, Nick saw he was wearing a
uniform.
"Need a lift somewhere?" the sheriff asked,
angling toward him.

Nick studied the cat in his arms, thinking of getting Tulip home safely to Lily.

"That would be great, Officer! Thanks!"

Chapter Eight

On their way to Sandy's house, Carter Livingston introduced himself. Nick was happy to meet Olivia's younger brother, who had a solid build and dark green eyes. Unlike his sisters, he was dark-haired, though. He'd removed his sheriff's hat and it rested on the console between them. Given the worsening weather, Nick was grateful for the ride. He told Carter so as icy snow slapped against the windshield.

"It's no problem," Carter told him. "It's nice to finally meet you. Sandy's been talking to Hannah about you nonstop. Your sister's awfully excited to have you in town."

"I'm really glad to be here."

Carter stole a glance at Lily's cat, apparently recognizing her. "What's Tulip doing out? That's not like her?"

Nick hedged, before answering, "She tracked me down at the Grand Hotel."

"It's lucky a friendly face was there to greet her," Carter said.

"Aren't most faces friendly in Christmas Town?"

Carter chuckled warmly. "Yeah, they are. That's true. We've got a lot of nice folks here..." He pulled to a stop at the corner of North Main and Church Street before making his turn at the old stone church with a high steeple. "And one of the nicest among them is my big sister, Olivia." Before he started driving again Carter turned to Nick in the cab. "I'm going to level with you." There was a seriousness in his eyes Nick hadn't expected. "I know that Sandy is bent on getting the two of you together." Carter pursed his lips, and Nick sensed his inherent disapproval. "But Olivia's a big girl, you hear? She makes up her own mind."

"Of course! I wasn't planning on—"

"I may be her brother, but I have eyes. I know she's an attractive woman, in more ways than one. I'm also well aware that Olivia has a heart of gold. And, if that heart gets broken..." He leveled Nick a look that spoke volumes. Nick swallowed hard.

"I...understand. Really, I do. I feel the same way about Sandy. I mean, *felt*, before she and Ben—"

"I just want to get one thing clear," Carter interrupted. "There are to be no Virginia Cookies involved."

"Virginia Cookies?" Nick asked unsurely. He glanced down at the purring cat in his lap then back over at Carter. "What makes you say that?"

"Because I know my wife, and I know your sister," Carter said solemnly. "I also know that everlasting love can be a wonderful thing."

Love? "Hang on! Slow down!"

"But anyone who wins over my sister," Carter continued as if he hadn't heard him, "is going to have to do it the good old-fashioned way, or not do it at all."

Carter put his truck in park and Nick realized they'd arrived at their destination. "Get what I'm saying?"

"Sure!" Nick stared at Carter wide-eyed. "I do understand. Understand perfectly what you're saying, but I assure you you'll have no worries from me."

"Good." Carter placed his hat on his head and tamped it down, then stared hard at Nick. Nick suddenly realized that Carter was waiting on him to exit the truck.

He nabbed his backpack and reached for the door-handle, cradling Tulip close in the opposite arm. "Well, um… Thanks again for the ride! Great meeting you, Carter!"

"Yeah, you too!"

As Nick climbed from the cab, Carter tipped his hat Nick's way.

"Enjoyed our little chat."

A few hours later, Nick found himself at the Merry Market. While Lou and Jade's generous welcome basket had gotten him started with supplies, he needed to pick up something for tonight's dinner as well as a few extras. Nick was also determined to stock up on peppermint. He'd received the sheriff's message loud and clear: *Stay away from my sister*. He'd also been more than slightly freaked by the animal scene on the front porch of the Grand Hotel, and wasn't sure what might happen next. Just to be on the safe side, he'd need to quell his crazy family abilities before they got any more out of control.

He rounded the corner of the candy and coffee aisle, nearly running right into his sister.

"Nick!" Sandy exclaimed in surprise. She was pushing a small shopping cart and had it loaded with pasta, fresh fruits, and veggies. A pretty bouquet of fresh-cut flowers was laid sideways on top of her produce.

"Sandy! Hello." Nick glanced to the right, spying a large box of prepackaged cookies on the shelf beside him. He nabbed it deftly, dropping it into the hand-held basket that draped from one arm. Sandy stared down at the cookies then back in his eyes.

"You can probably get better ones at Hannah's shop."

"Yeah, right. Been meaning to check that out."

Sandy eyed him curiously. "That's all you're eating for dinner?" She reached down and lifted the edge of the cookie box. Beneath it, Nick had hidden four new twelve-packs of candy canes. "Well...well..." she said suspiciously. "What have we here?"

Nick blanched and grabbed for a box of white peppermint bark biscotti, tossing it onto the heap in his basket. "Just snack foods. *Ho-ho-ho.*"

"Snacking?" Sandy's blue eyes rounded in incredulity. Then she said in scolding, mother-hen-like tones, "I thought you knew better than that, Nick. You need to watch the sweets. Big bellies run in our family."

"Yeah, well. Thanks! And, anyway, I wasn't planning on eating *everything*." Nick thought quickly. "I'm preparing to decorate my tree!"

Sandy's whole face glowed. "You're putting up a Christmas tree at the rental? How great! Need help?"

"No, no. I can handle it."

"I have plenty of extra decorations," Sandy insisted. "Lou probably has a few she can spare, too. I can stop by later if—"

"The fact is I'm still settling in, sis. Haven't exactly *bought* my tree. But, I will. Very soon!"

"Ray Christmas sells them at—"

"The North Pole Nursery, yes. I've been meaning to stop by and see him."

Sandy viewed him appraisingly. "You're acting awfully edgy."

"Just a busy first day!"

"First day... Hmm." Sandy briefly studied the ceiling, apparently putting things together. "This has something to do with Olivia, doesn't it?" she asked with a happy gasp.

"Well, no. Not entirely. I mean—"

Sandy narrowed her eyes at him.

"Okay! All right, yes!" He dropped his voice into a hushed whisper. "If you must know the truth, it's happening."

"It?" Sandy practically shouted and he quickly shushed her. "Oh, yeah. Sorry," she whispered back after a couple of other shopping patrons had passed them by. "What do you mean?" she asked sotto voce. "Your powers are strengthening?"

"I'm certainly getting that *impression*. Yeah."

"Nick, that's awesome!" Sandy couldn't have looked more pleased. "I told you that you and Olivi—"

"But I can't!"

"Can't?"

Nick furtively glanced around before adding, "I was ambushed by the sheriff."

"Carter Livingston?" Sandy asked, surprised. "What did he say?"

"Basically, not to mess with Olivia."

"Oh! Well!" She appeared mildly befuddled. "Don't worry, I'll have Hannah straighten Carter out about that."

"But there's nothing going on," Nick told her.

"Not yet, maybe..." She shared an impish smile. "But, maybe soon... You've got to admit she's cute."

"Yeah, yeah. Just darling. But I can't let this happen. Not now."

"What's wrong with now, Nick? You're practically thirty-eight. An old man."

"Hey!"

"Next thing you know, you'll have a snowy white beard and whiskers like Grandpa. You might even grow the tummy." She giggled at his supply of candy canes. "Especially if you keep eating like that."

"Thanks for your support."

"You shouldn't try to fight it," Sandy continued. "It's just like you told me with Ben. If you go with the flow, things will get better."

"No, this is different."

"I can't see how?"

Nick envisioned hordes of bison stampeding down South Main Street. If his powers kept increasing at the speed things were going, his reach might extend to Wyoming! "I'm worried, that's all." He grimaced with his confession. "Worried that things are spiraling out of control."

"People always feel that way when they're falling..." she whispered to him. "Even regular people, Nick."

"I am *not* falling, Sandy," Nick contested hotly. But he was whispering back.

"Fine! Have it your way," she retorted. "You can deny it if you want. But, in the end, you only have two choices, you know."

Nick's forehead rose.

"A: give in." She said the first option giddily then lowered her voice even further. "Or B…" She enunciated carefully. "*Peppermint.*"

Nick certainly wasn't giving in. This wasn't just about his attraction to Olivia; it was about his whole wacky life going haywire. If this was really the beginning of true love, then *love* was for the birds…and squirrels…and rabbits. *And, what was with those hyper singing chipmunks?*

"Nick," Sandy hissed. "Nick? Did you hear me?"

"No, sorry." He focused back on her gaze. "I was temporarily lost in thought."

"Well maybe you need to start paying a little more attention."

"To?"

"All that stuff you're putting in your basket?"

Nick looked down in horror to see his basket brimming over with just about every sort of sweet treat on the aisle. "Don't worry!" he said quickly. "I'm putting most of these back."

"Everything except the candy canes. Hmm."

"Yes," Nick said decisively. "For now."

Before she turned to go, Sandy added, "If you're concerned about Olivia, I wouldn't be."

"Why not?"

"She's a pretty tough woman." Sandy winked. "I'd say tough enough to handle any sudden surge in your animal instincts."

That was just like Sandy. Nick hadn't told her a thing about the critter crowd at the Grand Hotel. She must have sneakily read some of his thoughts again. When Nick had brought Tulip back to Sandy's house, he'd handed the cat off to Ben, who'd been working at home and was leaving to meet Lily's school bus. In Christmas Town, schools apparently stayed open in spite of snow, unless blizzard conditions were expected. Nick's gaze flitted to the door of the Merry Market as Sandy departed, her arms loaded down with bags.

This certainly was a different situation. Normally, Nick was the calm, collected one, handing out rational advice. Now, it seemed it was Sandy's turn to play the grown-up. Nick grumbled to himself as he finished up his shopping. He wasn't comfortable with the role reversal, and he especially wasn't fond of his little sister telling him what to do.

Nick strode to the register and paid for his order, anxious to get back to his rental. Snow was coming down hard and quickly coating the sidewalk and streets. The Jolly Bean Java stood just to the right of the Merry Market as Nick faced the road. Olivia's store and her apartment were directly across the way from it. It was after six, so All Things Christmas was already closed. The apartment above it had bright lights glowing in its window. Nick dug into his paper shopping bag extracting a carton of candy canes, determined to put a stop to this nonsense right then and there. After quickly shedding the sweet's wrapper, he popped the straight end of the peppermint stick in his mouth. *There*, he said to himself. *Much better!*

At that precise moment, Olivia appeared in the window and seemed to be scanning the street. Nick jumped and wedged the candy cane box deep in his bag. Then, he stepped off the stoop and hustled down the sidewalk. Was it possible Olivia was developing *impressions* of him? *That's unheard of! Absurd.* He glanced over his shoulder, spying her still standing in the window, and Nick's heart thudded. She seemed to angle his way, cupping her hands to the glass in front of her eyes. Nick's temples throbbed and his face burned hot as he beat it toward Sisters' Row. Nick was definitely doing some family research when he got home.

Chapter Nine

Olivia stepped away from the window, flummoxed. Wasn't that Nick Claus she'd seen scuttling down the sidewalk? Why was he in such a hurry? And, what was he clutching in that brown paper bag? It appeared he'd just been shopping. It had also looked like he'd had a candy cane clamped between his teeth! She'd caught a glimpse of the red-and-white treat as he'd popped it in his mouth—right there on the stoop of the Merry Market. Of all people, Olivia understood the need for a sugar fix. But even *she'd* been able to make it out of Nutcracker Sweets without opening her box of truffles. Olivia's face flushed hot when she recalled her dip into her pastry bag at Jolly Bean Java only yesterday morning. All right. So maybe she wasn't perfect.

She stared at the empty chocolate box on her coffee table, knowing she'd need to be strong. There'd be no dashing out for more dark-chocolate-cherry bonbons until she'd given her ankle one more day of rest per doctor's orders. Olivia hobbled back to the futon, lowering herself onto it. Then, she picked up the children's picture book she'd been perusing last night. Olivia didn't know why, but she had the strangest compulsion to read the story over and over again. It was almost like she was an investigator, searching for clues. Perhaps if she read it one more time, Olivia would cure her hunger for this whimsical tale.

Nick finished unpacking his groceries, setting his stash of candy cane boxes on the kitchen counter. Tomorrow evening, after work, he'd pick up one of Ray Christmas's evergreens. That would give Nick a rational excuse for having so many candy canes in the house. If he didn't eat them all first in the meantime. Nick was relieved that he hadn't spied any animals on the streets. He was also glad Olivia hadn't spotted him making his mad-dash getaway. Nick had to admit it was odd that she'd come to the window at the exact moment he'd been across the street. If he didn't know better, he'd suspect she'd had the sense that Nick was near.

His stomach rumbled, but Nick decided he could wait a while to eat. First, he needed to research more about his abilities going out of whack and study up on how to control them. While peppermint had served him well in the past, it was merely a cure for mildly annoying impressions. He'd never had half the forest appear on his doorstep before!

When Nick turned eighteen, his paternal grandfather had given him a small present. *As you get older*, he'd said, *you'll find the answer to all of your questions in here*. Nick hadn't had much occasion to use the tiny gift, but he typically kept it with him just in case. The handy resource was rife with ready answers, hinging on North Pole secrets.

Nick crossed through the living area and climbed the stairs, turning into the back bedroom off the hall.

He'd left some work supplies and his drafting table in it earlier, but had yet to assemble the latter. Nick lifted his laptop case off the bed then sat in a corner chair, resting his open computer on his knees. Next, he dug into a computer case zippered pocket where he kept his special item stashed. Nick withdrew the compact flash drive that had been given to him by his grandfather. Its logo featured a miniature smiling elf in a green hat holding up his hands to support the title, which arched above his head like a glittery rainbow: *Santa's Little Helper*.

If ever Nick needed help, it was now, he decided, sliding the flash drive into the slot on his computer. Mechanical sounds hummed and whirred as the database began to load. Then suddenly, a hearty *Ho-ho-ho* boomed through his speakers. "Welcome to *Santa's Little Helper*!"

A cartoon elf appeared against an animated background showing Santa's workshop, where other elves were busily at work, packaging toys and setting them on conveyor belts. The youthful male elf in a green outfit with jingle bell accents walked forward and smiled through the screen.

"Hello, Nick! How can I help you today?"

Nick found it uncanny how his granddad had programmed this. Everything was so life-like!

"You can select one of the categories from the drop-down menu," the elf said, gesturing with one hand. "Or, enter your search term there!" He pointed to a blinking cell in the upper right corner.

"If you require technical support, please click *here*," the elf continued, indicating the relevant link. "Please be aware that, due to seasonal demands, you may experience unusually long wait-times between Thanksgiving and Christmas."

Yeah, Nick was well aware of those, which was why he was determined to find his own answers. He clicked on the drop-down menu and selected "Table of Contents."

Right there in the As, Nick spotted a number of sections relating to animals.

ANIMAL:

Aeronautics…
No, no.

Bathing and Care…
Not quite.

Communication…
Warmer.

Control…
Aha!

Nick clicked to that section, quickly scanning through it.

ANIMAL CONTROL
A male Claus's ability to influence and control animal behavior develops simultaneously with his animal communication skills. He should take care to always approach the animals gently and with genuinely kind intent. Never speak in negatives. Instead, positively communicate instructions and the specific outcome you

expect. This is particularly important concerning night-sky navigation.

Nick gawked at his computer screen, nearly afraid to keep reading whatever might come next. This was not what Nick wanted! He didn't ask for these abilities, nor did he pine for them to get stronger. He fumbled in his computer bag for a piece of peppermint gum, unwrapped it and popped it in his mouth, nervously starting to chew. While he was the youngest male heir on the Claus side, Nick had always been quite clear in his ambitions. He wanted a *normal* life—as an architect in Bangor. And, his parents had been fully supportive. Just as they'd supported Sandy's goals of working as an artist and opening a gallery.

He returned to the Table of Contents, searching the Ns until he located:

NAUGHTY & NICE
The ability to discern whether someone has done a benevolent deed or been mischievous develops in male Clauses in late childhood. Expect this skill to strengthen throughout adolescence and peak at the point of long-term romantic pairing. See MARRIAGE *for a list of potential signs that a Claus has met his or her ideal mate.*

Nick held his breath and clicked the link.

MARRIAGE
First and foremost in their talents, Clauses have the ability to detect their ideal DNA match in the individual best suited to helping them perpetuate the

family line. Expect any inherent talents to increase exponentially when the love interest is around. Normal remedies (such as peppermint) won't work in the face of true love.

Nick gulped hard, accidentally swallowing his gum. This was what his parents had told him and Sandy about when they were teenagers. Though neither one had mentioned peppermint one way or another, his folks had shared that his and Sandy's powers would increase once they met their special matches. Neither he nor his sister had believed their folks at the time. It was only when Sandy started experiencing strange phenomena around Ben that she and Nick began to suspect there was some truth to their parents' prediction. And now here it was in writing! Smack-dab in the middle of the guidebook relating to all things Claus...

Nick's gaze locked on the screen.

When a Claus meets his or her ideal partner, one or more of the following signs may appear in order to encourage that perfect union. These signs may become evident while in that person's company, or when merely thinking about them. Please note these are additional markers above and beyond regular romantic attraction, which typically exists concurrently.

Warning: *A Claus's failure to heed such signs could lead to the unfavorable consequence of this remarkable gene pool becoming extinct over time, thereby severely diminishing holiday joy and forever compromising the magic of Christmas.*

Gee, nothing like pressure, Nick thought, starting to sweat.

MATING INSTINCT SIGNS
Strengthening of natural abilities.
Emergence of new abilities. *
Heart palpitations on contact.
Lightheadedness.
Urge to fly.

Now, wait a minute! Nick flipped shut his computer, but then he opened it back up due to the footnote that had caught his eye.

* *In extremely rare circumstances, love interests can develop abilities of their own.*
See MRS. CLAUS.

MRS. CLAUS
Mrs. Claus should be caring, generous, and kind, and be good with animals and children. In rare circumstances, Mrs. Claus may receive a transfer of certain abilities from her husband, with levitation being the most common.
She further may develop impressions telling her when Mr. Claus is coming home. The male Claus subconsciously communicates his proximity as he draws near, hoping that the missus will happily anticipate his arrival. Optimally, with a tray of cookies and milk...

Nick shut his laptop again, and dragged the back of his shirtsleeve across his sopping brow. This was crazy stuff. Ridiculous family lore. Nick didn't know why he'd taken the time to go through it. It hadn't cleared up anything at all; only left him more confused. *Forget about dinner!* Nick suddenly had a really strong craving for something sweet.

He laid his laptop on the bed and descended the stairs, entering the kitchen. The basket Lou dropped by yesterday was still on the counter beside the refrigerator, but it was mostly empty. He peered inside it, dismayed to see he'd eaten the rest of the homemade cookies. If Sandy hadn't guilted him into putting the others back, he'd at least have some of the store-bought kind to dig into. As it was, all he had left was…

Nick's gaze rolled toward the freezer compartment of the refrigerator. While he'd promised to exercise caution with the Commitment Cookie, he really couldn't see the harm in sampling the other two kinds. The Charity Cookie would only inspire good works, and the Clemency Cookie—forgiveness. How much trouble could come from that?

Not much at all, Nick decided, taking the holiday tin from the freezer. Now, all he needed was a cold glass of milk and a plate for his cookies. He carried them to the dining room table, where he intended to further ponder his situation with Olivia. Nick had to know if she was the one causing him these unnerving problems, and there was only one way to find out. He had to see her again in person, and soon.

Nick sat at the table admiring his two lovely Virginia Cookies. Both were heart-shaped and smelled deliciously of gingerbread, with hints of orange and cloves…and something else mysterious Nick couldn't quite detect. The first had a pretty angel painted on it with white icing. She had blond curls, blue eyes, and a small golden halo above her head. This was the Charity Cookie, he surmised. The other, with the green Christmas tree design, had to be the Clemency Cookie. At Sandy's strict orders, Nick had left the one with the frothy pink-and-red border and the message saying *Forever Yours* in the freezer.

Nick chuckled and took a big bite out of the Christmas tree cookie, thinking it was funny that Olivia was superstitious about these cookies too, when she appeared so levelheaded otherwise. Then again, if she had her doubts about the true effects of Hannah's Virginia Cookies, perhaps that indicated her mind would be open to other sorts of magic? Nick rolled the cookie bit around in his mouth, thinking it was actually very tasty. He'd have to compliment Hannah on her cooking when he saw her, for sure. Nick took a swallow of milk, pondering the question of who'd left these cookies in his freezer in the first place.

While he'd quickly suspected Lou as the culprit, she'd been vehement in her denials that she'd put them there. Nick set down his milk glass, a sly thought occurring. As the landlady, Lou was the only one with a key, so if she hadn't snuck the cookies into Sisters' Row herself, perhaps she had craftily loaned her key to someone else, so she could distance herself from the deed? *But, who? Hmm.* The next time Nick saw Lou, he was going to attempt to finagle an answer.

Chapter Ten

Olivia woke up the next morning feeling phenomenal. Oddly, she'd had that Christmas Eve flying dream again. Only, rather than being an old fat guy in a red suit, the Santa guiding her sleigh had looked really sexy… Sort of like… Olivia opened her eyes and blinked at the ceiling. *Nick.* She tossed back the covers and sat up in bed, placing her feet on the floor. Pain pinged in Olivia's left ankle and she realized it hadn't healed completely. When she stood and gently placed pressure on it, though, she confirmed that it was getting better. Olivia limped toward her closet and pulled out her robe, sliding into its fuzzy warmth.

She was surprised to see by her clock that she'd overslept by an hour! Olivia rarely slept in, and now would have to hurry in order to get her shop open in time. She scuttled into the kitchen and started her coffee, noting the snow was still coming down outdoors. She'd only been confined in this building for a few days, but already Olivia was feeling cage crazy. At least she'd be hearing from Nick this afternoon. If she was lucky, maybe she could convince him to come over. Olivia couldn't wait to hear his thoughts on the

Grand Hotel. She was also mildly curious about why he'd been rushing down the sidewalk last night. If he didn't readily volunteer something about it, she might ask him.

Olivia was headed to the bathroom to take her shower, when, *Oh! Oh, dear!* Some kind of weird *impression* hit her, nearly sending her stumbling backwards. It was the same thing that had happened last night just before she'd spotted Nick on the street. There wasn't a concrete thought in her head, merely a vague notion of someone…approaching? *No… Returning.* Returning was more like it. But returning from what?

Olivia cautiously hobbled toward her front window that looked down on South Main. A man's form emerged from Jolly Bean Java and Olivia gasped out loud. It was Nick! Gripping a paper cup of coffee, and…*now that's pretty weird*…sucking on another peppermint stick? Olivia held her breath in fright, hoping he wasn't coming here! She glanced down at her robe in a panic and back down at the street. Fortunately, Nick had pivoted toward the north and was making his way toward Santa Claus Lane, apparently headed for the Grand Hotel. Relief surged through her, as heat flooded her face. What on earth was happening? How could she have sensed Nick being so close by? Not one time…but two?

Olivia's gaze returned to the window where she observed the quiet street. She was probably making too much of nothing. Seeing Nick outside her window had just been a coincidence. Both times. Uh-huh! Sure! Olivia shook her head, deciding to put that storybook away for a while. No matter how tempted she felt to read it, contemplating the magic of a mythical figure was starting to make her imagination run wild. She snagged *The Night Before Christmas* off her coffee table and carried it back into the bedroom, setting it high on a closet shelf. Then, she selected a new outfit for herself and began to get her day in order.

At a little past four, Olivia sat behind her register with her foot diligently propped and iced. Though she wasn't sure her ankle still needed nursing, she'd decided to listen to Kurt and baby it for one more day. By this time tomorrow, Olivia would be up and running again. Okay. Not running maybe. But she should be walking with very minor difficulty at least. Olivia couldn't wait to get back to the stables and into her routine. She missed Blaze and she was going to miss seeing the kids this afternoon. Olivia was trying to focus on her work in going through receipts, but that nagging sensation was gnawing at her again. She sensed that something was going to happen, and that feeling put her slightly on edge. Surely, this didn't mean that Nick—

The door chime tinkled and Olivia blanched. Nick Claus had just walked into All Things Christmas!

"Good afternoon," he said cheerily. "How's the injury doing today?"

"Oh, so much better!" She blinked at him like he'd suddenly appeared out of thin air. "I'll be back to normal by tomorrow, I'm sure."

He grinned and walked toward her carrying something in his hands. Olivia's heart pounded as he approached. "I brought you a little something to cheer you up," he said.

Olivia started to protest, but when she saw the box was from Nutcracker Sweets, she cracked a bright grin. "Truffles? You shouldn't have!"

"I wanted to," he said, smiling back, and Olivia's face warmed all over. "I was thinking about you at lunch today, so I went over and picked these up. As a…" He hesitated a beat. "Friendly gesture."

"That was really sweet of you, Nick. Thank you."

"I also checked out Hannah's shop."

"How did you like it?"

"I bought one too many cookie," he whispered confidentially as his blue eyes twinkled. Olivia burst into laughter.

"No worries, I understand," she confessed, mock solemnly. "I've got a sugar problem, too."

"It's only a problem if you think it is," he said sincerely.

"Oh?"

"Dark-chocolate-cherry bonbons aren't such a naughty treat, Olivia." His eyes danced and Olivia felt her color deepen. "You could do far worse."

"How did you know what kind I like?"

"I saw the empty box in here yesterday morning."

"What? Where?"

He motioned to the wastebasket by her register. Olivia thought hard on this, trying to recall where he'd stood when he'd come into her store to bring the Danishes by. She didn't recall disposing of her truffle box down here. Olivia had been quite certain she'd put it in the trash upstairs…? Either way, the type of truffle hadn't been written on the—

"In any case, here you go!" He passed her the box and his hand grazed hers as she took it. Nick froze in place staring down at their hands. The tips of their fingers were barely touching, but Nick appeared entranced. "*Boom-boom…boom-boom…boom-boom…*" he uttered, totally transfixed. Though Olivia didn't believe he'd meant to say that out loud.

"Boom what?"

Nick blinked hard and quickly released the box. He let go so fast Olivia nearly dropped it. "Nick?" she queried cautiously. "Are you all right?"

"Yeah, I…" He blinked again then cleared his throat. "Just fine." Nick pulled a package of peppermint gum from an inside coat pocket, offering her a stick.

"No, thanks," she said, still puzzling over their earlier exchange. She didn't know what had gotten into him, but Nick had appeared really out of it. "I'll wait for my truffles later."

He popped a piece of gum in his mouth, seeming to mull something over in his head. "The project's coming along," he said finally. "Got my basic evaluation wrapped up this morning."

"That's great!" Nick had promised to call Olivia about it. Seeing him in person was so much better. Even if he was acting a little strange.

"I lined up some contractors to come by, too. We'll get the place tested for any environmental hazards next week. Once all that's cleared, we can work on a formal proposal for the Town Council. Meanwhile, I plan to use the rest of the week drafting ideas to share with you."

"I'm really excited about this project," she told him eagerly.

"Yeah, me too." He met her eyes, studying her. "Olivia?"

"Huh?"

"Are you…? Did you…?" He shook his head, seeming to think better of it. "Oh, never mind."

"Why don't you go ahead and ask me?"

"All right." Nick shifted on his feet. "It's about last night—"

Just then, Lou Christmas burst in the door, sending the chime tinkling wildly. "Hello! Hello!" She glanced from one to the other, then back again. "I'm not *interrupting*, am I?" she asked, smiling gleefully.

"Lou, what a pleasant surprise," Olivia said. "Of course not. Come in!"

Lou scurried over to where she sat and peered over the counter. "Oh dear, it's true. Kurt said you had a serious injury."

"It's not so serious, really!" She looked at Nick for reinforcement. "I'll be as good as new tomorrow, won't I Nick?"

"That's what the doctor said," Nick agreed.

"Well, thank goodness it wasn't worse." Lou straightened her spine and stared around the shop. Eventually, her gaze fell on the counter where Olivia had set her new package.

"My gracious, Olivia," she said as if she knew differently. "Tell me you didn't hobble all the way over to Nutcracker Sweets with that bad ankle?"

"I brought the chocolates," Nick volunteered. "I thought Olivia might need a little cheering up. Being store-bound and everything."

Lou gave Olivia a slow perusal and Olivia's cheeks steamed. Then she wheeled on Nick with a smile. "How considerate of you, Nick!"

"I almost couldn't help it," he appeared to confess. "I woke up this morning wanting to do a good deed."

Olivia stifled a gasp.

"The next thing I knew," Nick continued undaunted, "I was ready to forgive someone, too."

Uh-oh.

"Forgive who?" Lou asked perplexed.

"Why you, you clever woman," he said in light tones. "For trying to fix me and Olivia up!"

Olivia sure wished she knew where Nick was going with this because she was certain her face couldn't possibly get any redder. It had to have gone from pink to crimson by now.

"Admit it, Lou," Nick said with a wink. "You might not have put those Virginia Cookies in my freezer *yourself*...but you know who did..." he continued in a rollicking way. "You might even have had something to do with it, you sprightly rascal." He eyed her knowingly and Lou took a giant step backwards.

"Cookies?" she asked, obviously thrown. "I told you before, it wasn't me... And I...I have no idea who put them there." She seemed to ponder this a moment. "Though, I must say, that was a very good idea... Kudos to whoever thought of it! I wish I could take credit. But, no." Lou sadly shook her head and Nick appeared deflated. He apparently had believed himself onto something in solving his cookie mystery.

"Nick...?" Olivia asked haltingly. "You didn't actually *eat* any, did you?"

He shrugged looking sheepish. "I had a weak moment."

Olivia gasped.

"I was clean out of cookies," Nick explained rapidly, as Lou watched him with a pleased grin. "It was an emergency. Couldn't really be helped. And anyway," he added, heaving a breath. "I only ate the white one and the green one." He shot a pointed stare at Olivia. "I had it on good authority to steer clear of the Commitment kind."

"Phooey!" Lou said, as Olivia sighed audibly. "You shouldn't just *eat* that final cookie, you should *share it* with Olivia."

"Precisely what the note said…" Nick reported, eyeing Lou suspiciously. He evidently couldn't shake the thought that Lou had something to do with it, and Olivia could understand why. Lou did have quite the reputation in this town.

"Nick Claus," Lou replied a tad indignantly. "I'm surprised at you. Questioning my integrity! I've never had to use cookies in getting people together before, and I certainly don't intend to start now." She turned and addressed Olivia. "I didn't do it, I tell you." Then she snickered softly. "Not that I *wouldn't have*…if somebody hadn't outfoxed me and thought of it first!"

"Can I help you with something, Lou?" Olivia asked her, trying to redirect the conversation.

Lou appeared to remember her mission. "Oh, yes! I'm here to buy some of those pretty Christmas barrettes: the new ones that came out this year that look like Hannah's Virginia Cookies."

"They're right in back," Olivia told her. "On the small tree beside the Christmas ornament display."

Lou thanked her and excused herself to go shopping. "I wanted to pick a few of those up for Noelle and Joy while they're still off at college," she said, striding toward the back of the store. "Early Christmas presents for them both, as sort of a welcome home."

"What a nice idea," Olivia called after her as she traipsed away. "Let me know if you have any questions!" When Lou was out of earshot, Olivia eyed Nick with a giggle.

"You did a very naughty thing, Nick Claus."

"Naughty? Me?"

"You dug into those Virginia Cookies when I warned you against them."

"Wrong. I did a *nice* thing, by not eating the one that says *Forever Yours*." He stepped closer and her heart hammered. "That *was* your request, wasn't it, Olivia?"

Olivia swallowed past the lump in her throat. "My request was that you talk to Sandy," she replied in a hushed whisper.

"I did," Nick whispered back.

"And?" Olivia asked with interest.

"And..." His gaze washed over her. "The results were inconclusive."

"What's that mean?" she asked, angling closer.

"That means..." Nick rested his elbows on the counter and leaned toward her until his face was just inches from hers. Olivia's lips trembled and her breath hitched. "Nobody knows for sure about those Virginia Cookies."

"Somebody must know. Somewhere," she said weakly.

Nick sexily cocked an eyebrow. "We can ask Hannah?"

"Hannah? When?"

"She's asked us both to dinner this Friday, I understand."

"I…uh…" Olivia self-consciously licked her lips. "Yeah."

"You're going, I hope?"

"I'd planned on it."

"Sandy wants me to drive you."

"Sandy? Oh!" She thought on this then asked haughtily, "And what do you want, Nick?"

His blue eyes danced. "I'd like to drive you, too."

"Found them!" Lou proclaimed from the back of the room.

Nick and Olivia quickly backed apart.

"It only makes sense," he continued to Olivia. "With me staying right down the street."

"It's rational, of course," she said calmly, but inside, her pulse was racing.

"You never know how your ankle will be feeling."

"I'm sure, by then, just fine."

"Are you declining my offer?"

"Declining? No, no… It's just that I'd hate to…er…be a bother!"

"Not a bother at all. In fact, I imagine you'll be a help."

She raised her eyebrows, waiting on Nick to finish.

"I've never been to Carter's cabin, and I hear the road it's on is unmarked. It apparently won't come up on a GPS."

"I thought you Clauses were pretty good at getting around," she teased lightly. "In your sleighs and all."

"Oh, we are. I assure you. We just need to have the right equipment along." He winked and Olivia's skin tingled. "Or, the right navigator."

Chapter Eleven

A few nights later, Nick sat by the fireside with Walt Christmas at the Christmas Inn. After catching up on chitchat, they'd meandered into conversations about Nick's life in Bangor and how Walt was faring back here, with Noelle and Joy away. Joy was at a state school studying art, and Noelle had won a scholarship to a private university where she was majoring in English.

Walt appeared proud, yet melancholy, while discussing his daughters. His fondness for them showed in his dark blue eyes. Of the three Christmas brothers, Walt was the bearded one who also wore a mustache. He had darker hair than the other two and was an inch or so taller, even though he was the second son in line. Ray was the eldest, with Kurt bringing up the rear. Walt was the middle child and three years older than Nick, meaning he'd just turned forty. Nick teased him about that, asking how he was holding up in middle age.

"Forty's the new fifty," Walt bantered, raising his glass. "Haven't you heard?"

"That's good to know," Nick countered with a chuckle. "Especially since it's looming closer for me."

He glanced around the cozy study with its stocked bookshelves and the decorated tree beside a rolltop desk. "Got your tree up early, I see." This reminded Nick that he needed to get busy with his. He'd told Sandy he was buying one on Tuesday, but he'd been so overcome by events, he'd totally forgotten.

"The girls helped me decorate when they were home last weekend," Walt explained. "We like to keep it festive for the guests."

"Do you get many this time of year?"

"In Christmas Town? Sure! Last weekend we were booked solid. Mostly on account of Hannah's special promotion at the Christmas Cookie Shop. You probably missed all the hubbub by coming in Sunday."

"Sounds like it was quite an event," Nick commented.

"Promises to be so each year." Walt thoughtfully sipped from his drink. "That was a very good thing Hannah did by coming back here. The whole town seemed to turn around after that."

"How so?"

Walt shrugged. "People pulled together to help her get her operation going again. Once galvanized by that, other things started taking shape. The Grand Hotel project is a case in point."

"I'm glad to see Christmas Town returning to its glory days," Nick said, before adding humbly, "And, very honored to be a part of its restoration."

"We're glad you're here," Walt said, toasting Nick in the air with his glass.

Nick raised his glass in return then took a sip of Kentucky bourbon. He liked it on the rocks. Icy cold. "Thanks for the welcome."

"We like to keep things friendly," Walt said with a jovial grin.

"Speaking of friends..." Nick began treading lightly. "Now that your girls are away, any chance that a lady—?"

Walt slowly shook his head. "Nope, not a one. How about you?"

"Well, I... The truth is I stay pretty busy in Bangor."

"Say it ain't so!" Walt ribbed enthusiastically. "There's not even *one* interesting female in town?" That depended entirely on which town Walt was talking about, Nick thought but didn't say. There was a particular female in Christmas Town that was starting to interest Nick plenty. How had she *done* that? Made his heart go *boom-boom, boom-boom, boom-boom*? It was like Nick had been listening to his own pulse through a stethoscope. One with the volume turned way up high!

"There have been women," Nick confessed. "I won't lie. But nothing's ever worked out."

"That just shows how shortsighted those gals are in Maine," Walt returned heartily. "Maybe you should consider moving to Tennessee?"

"Moving?"

"There's nothing wrong with our little town," Walt assured him. "You actually might come to like it if you stay a while."

Nick's liking Christmas Town wasn't the problem. It was his feelings for one of its residents that had him thrown for a loop. Ever since seeing her on Tuesday, Nick hadn't been able to stop thinking about Olivia. He'd tried to forget about her by pouring himself into his work, but had wound up sketching pictures of her on his drafting paper instead! Totally by mistake of course.

"I don't know what my plans are long-term to tell you the truth." And, wasn't that a fact? Nick had no clue what all this Claus stuff meant. With his impressions growing stronger, and his mating instinct appearing to develop a mind of its own, he was afraid to think too far ahead. Particularly if that meant, eventually hanging his hat in the Maritime Provinces. *No-ho-ho-ho!*

"Excuse me?" Walt stared at him. "Did you say something?"

"Uh…sorry! Frog in my throat."

"Maybe you're putting too much pressure on yourself?" Walt said kindly. "Why not just enjoy things as they are now, and see how it goes?"

"You mean, enjoy being in Christmas Town."

"Sure!" Then Walt added with a hint of mischief, "I hear you've got a very pretty guide to show you around."

"You're talking about Olivia."

"Uh-huh, and she's single."

Nick was about to ask Walt whether *he'd* put the Virginia Cookies in his freezer. Then another idea occurred. Perhaps it had been Kurt? It was hard to say which traits those boys had inherited from their mother, Lou. "Have you been over to Sisters' Row?"

"Sisters' Row?" Walt asked, surprised. "Not lately. Why?"

"Nothing. It's nothing," Nick answered, deciding not to mention the Virginia Cookies, after all. Walt was already teasing him about Olivia. Why add fuel to his fire?

"We had a beautiful wedding reception last year here at the Christmas Inn." Walt grinned warmly. "I wouldn't mind hosting another one."

"Perhaps you should think of finding a wife for yourself," Nick told him, chuckling.

"Let me get my girls through college first."

"You'll have one foot in the grave by then!"

"Ha-ha, yes. Perhaps. But you know what they say…" Walt finished his drink with one long swallow. "It's never too late for love."

"So what did Walt talk to you about last night?" Sandy asked Nick. They sat in the café area of the Elf Shelf Bookshop having an afternoon coffee. Nick had asked his sister to meet him on her break, because he had something to ask her. Mainly, he wanted another person he trusted to verify he wasn't going insane.

"We did a lot of catching up," Nick said. "Old times."

"Great!"

"He also hinted at current events."

"Current events? What do you mean?"

Nick scooted his chair closer and whispered, "About me and Olivia?"

"It's going well, huh?" Sandy asked with a rosy glow. "I just knew that it—"

"Sandy," he hoarsely spewed back. "It's not going at all. I mean, nothing's happened! No, that's not right." He perplexedly scratched his head. "A lot *has* happened. It's just stuff that doesn't make any sense. Things I can't explain."

"Are you attracted to her?" Sandy asked quietly.

Nick's heart started to *boom-boom* just at the thought.

"Apparently, yeah."

"What do you mean, *apparently*?" Sandy asked, sounding annoyed. "It's a yes or no question, Nick."

"Okay, then… Yes." Nick swallowed hard. "Naturally, I find Olivia very attractive. She's sweet, and smart and kind… And…" The back of Nick's neck grew hot and his heart felt like it was about to burst. He brought a hand his chest to quell the relentless pounding.

"Nick?" Sandy's brow creased with worry. "What's wrong?"

"I don't know how much longer I can take this."

"I know. Love is a terrible thing."

"Love?"

"Terrible—but wonderful, too!" she added hastily. "It's the height of joy, I promise! You've just got to sludge through all that other stuff to get there."

"What other stuff?"

"The Claus stuff." Sandy grimaced. "Sorry. It's kind of like a family curse."

"Spoken like one who's lived through it."

"And, lived to tell the tale!" Her smile sparkled. "I've got to tell you, it was worth it! Every horrible moment!"

"Gee, thanks."

"What's your worry, Nick? This is a good thing. Olivia could be your future! The woman of your dreams!"

"The scary part is she's already dreaming about me, and doesn't know it." Nick latched onto Sandy's arm. "And, when Olivia does discover the truth, she's going to toss me back. Just like an unwanted catch and release!"

"That is so not true." Sandy viewed him sympathetically. "You're just not thinking clearly because your emotions are out of whack. I understand, because that happened to me—with Ben."

"I'm not so sure this little dinner party tonight is a good idea."

"Of course it is," Sandy contested. "It was very sweet of Hannah and Carter to invite us, and we're all going to go and have a great time."

"You, Ben, me, and...Olivia."

"I'm so glad you're picking her up."

Nick sat back in his chair. "Why am I suddenly feeling outnumbered?"

"That's because you are! This is Christmas Town, remember?"

Nick heaved a sigh.

"You know what I think?" Sandy said sincerely. "I think you should try to relax and just have fun. Don't worry about the future, our family issues...or anything you read in *Santa's Little Helper*."

"Hey, I didn't say—"

"Nick," she said, stopping him. "I mean it. Just for tonight. One night. Relax. Let go!" Her blue eyes twinkled. "You might be surprised by what happens."

Chapter Twelve

Olivia was as nervous as a filly in a rainstorm. All she had to do was get ready for a casual dinner party at Hannah's, for heaven's sakes. It wasn't like she had a formal date! Nick had texted to say he'd stop by at six forty-five. Since Carter and Hannah's cabin wasn't that far out of town, that would give them plenty of time to get there. Olivia stared in the mirror, thinking her hairstyle made her look like she'd been working too hard. She had the top sections pulled back on each side and braided. Then those smaller braids connected in back, leaving the rest of her hair falling loose past her shoulders. What was she doing? Auditioning for a fantasy series princess position?

Olivia normally wore a lot of flannel. But a red-and-black-checked shirt and the fairy princess hair definitely didn't match! She quickly undid her plaits, glancing at the clock on the bathroom shelf. Nick would be here at any minute, and now she had creases in her hair. Little crimp lines caused by braiding those top sections while her hair was still wet. *Great.* She looked like she'd stuck her finger in an electrical socket! Plus, this top was awful. It simply had to go!

She dashed to the closet and ripped out a pretty turtleneck sweater. It had shimmering threads inlaid so it sparkled like new-fallen snow. Yes! This would do— as long as Hannah didn't serve spaghetti, in which case Olivia would likely spill the sauce all over herself. *Boy!* She was a wreck. Olivia's pulse raced and she had the feeling Nick was getting near. She rapidly shucked her shirt and yanked the sweater over her head, hopping into her brown leather boots. The left ankle was a little tender, but doing well enough that she'd been able to return to regular footwear. Next, she finger-combed her hair into a high ponytail. It wasn't her customary style, but it felt light and breezy. Casual, yet comely… Maybe even slightly sexy, with wispy strands framing her face.

Olivia's heart hammered at the thought. *Do I really want to look sexy for Nick?* She dashed to the bathroom mirror, and aligned the hem of her long sweater over her stretch jeans. Then she tightened her casual ponytail and soundly pinched her cheeks. Though she truthfully didn't know why she'd bothered. Olivia seemed to blush bright red every time Nick was around. In her mind's eye, Olivia saw Nick exit Sisters' Row. Then, he climbed into his SUV and was headed her way. In a flash, she'd nabbed her coat from the closet and had hustled down the stairs. She'd just locked the door behind her, when Nick pulled up to the curb.

"Good timing!" he said, as she climbed into the passenger seat.

Olivia shut her door against the blustery snow and dusted off the top of her basket, which had become coated with flakes. When Nick asked her what was in it, she said she'd brought a small hostess gift along:

homemade garden salsa and some organic blue corn tortilla chips. Nick motioned toward a bag on the back seat.

"I brought a microbrew beer. They should go well together."

When she buckled in, he added, "You look nice with your hair that way."

"Oh, um…thanks." Olivia fiddled with the cloth covering her basket. "So do you!"

He shared an amused grin. "I always wear it like this. It's short."

"Ha-ha! Yes!" She laughed stupidly then bit into her bottom lip. "What I meant was…it suits you! You somehow don't look like a long-haired guy."

"That just proves you didn't know me in my reckless youth." He sent her a wink and set his SUV in drive.

"You had a reckless youth?" she asked, surprised. "Somehow that's hard to imagine. I thought all you Clauses were as good as gold."

"Oh, I wasn't bad, necessarily," Nick told her as they headed toward the roundabout. The snow was coming down steadily, so he was driving with extra caution. "I just had an independent streak." He shot her a wicked grin. "And I did have long hair."

"Did not!"

"Did so. Right down to…" He tapped one of his shoulders. "Here. I'm sure I've got a photo around somewhere to prove it."

"This I've got to see," she said, laughing. After a beat, she queried playfully, "Tattoos?"

"Now you're getting personal."

"Nick Claus!" she shouted above her giggles. "You are one big tease!"

"Don't tell me you never did anything to displease your parents?"

"Me?" Olivia thoughtfully shook her head. "That was Savannah. She was the rebel in the family."

"I didn't realize there was a quota?" he said, raising his brow.

"Did you do anything else?" she asked, genuinely curious. "To annoy your parents?"

"They always thought I drove too fast."

Olivia's glove gripped her armrest. "Oh!"

"Not on city streets," he tried to reassure her. "In Canada."

"Canada?"

"Up at my grandpa's farm," Nick explained. "He taught me to drive when I was very young. Never said a thing about speed limits."

"Wow!" She shifted in her seat to view him more fully. "I guess you were lucky you were out in the country then."

"Yeah, there was nothing like it. Feeling the wind and the snow on my—"

"Wind and snow?" she asked, perplexed. "You weren't in a convertible in winter?"

"Convertible?" he asked, like he'd never heard the word. "No, it wasn't that." Nick glanced through the windshield ahead of him as they entered the roundabout. "Which way here?"

"First right," Olivia directed. "That one's River Road."

Nick took the turn, surveying the darkened courthouse building, and the old library and the post office that stood nearby. A sign beside the flagpole in the central island read:

Welcome to...
CHRISTMAS TOWN, TENNESSEE
Where everyday dreams come true!

"Catchy motto," he said, peering in his rearview mirror, as the roundabout became swallowed in a swirl of snow behind them.

"Yeah, and it's fitting," Olivia told him. "People stay pretty happy here. In Christmas Town."

Nick acknowledged her statement with a nod. "Sandy's dreams sure came true."

"Hannah's too." Olivia sighed wistfully and stared out her window. The small-town lights were fading and their beaming headlights framed the darkened road.

"What about your dreams?"

"Mine?" She turned to him, surprised. "Well, I don't exactly... What I mean is, I'm not much of a dreamer to tell the truth."

"No?" he challenged, cocking an eyebrow. "Just this week, you told me you'd dreamed about Santa Claus?"

Olivia laughed lightly. "Okay, that's true. But that's different."

"How so?" His query seemed sincere.

"Because night dreams are different from daydreams. Everybody knows that."

Nick tightened his grasp on the wheel. "I've heard that night dreams can mirror daydreams. Sometimes they even reveal things about our secret hopes and fears."

"Okay! You've got me," she said jauntily. "I've secretly always wanted to fly."

"Really?" He seemed earnestly intrigued.

"Gosh, Nick! No!" Although the idea was kind of cool when she thought about it.

"You're not afraid of heights?"

"Why would that matter?"

"A rooftop's pretty high up there…"

"Stop!" she said, chuckling loudly. They came to a fork in the road by the Reindeer Pub, and Olivia indicated they should keep left.

"You know what I think?" Nick asked, briefly eyeing her. "I think you're dodging the question."

"Which question?"

"About what you really want, Olivia? Have you found it? Found everything you're looking for in Christmas Town?"

She stared at him a while, contemplating his question. "I've got a great job," she told him. "Wonderful friends."

"A good horse," he filled in.

"An excellent horse. Only…" Olivia's words fell off and her lips creased in a frown.

"Olivia?" Nick asked worriedly. "What's wrong? Is it something with Blaze?"

"Actually, yeah. It is," she confided. "I'm not sure what's the matter, but ever since I returned to the barn on Wednesday, she's seemed different."

"Different how?"

"I'm not sure. Just off somehow. Not herself."

"Do you think she's sick?"

Olivia worriedly shook her head. "I had the vet take a look. He couldn't find anything physically wrong with her."

"Maybe it's emotional?" Nick suggested. "Do you think she became upset when you were away?"

Olivia shrugged disconsolately. "I don't know. Maybe. It was only for a few days."

Nick considered this a beat before offering kindly, "Would you like me to take a look at her?"

Olivia knew Nick was great was animals, but she wasn't convinced that he could help. Then again, perhaps anything was worth a shot. "I'd hate to put you out. I know you're busy drafting your plans."

"I can make some time tomorrow." His generosity of spirit warmed Olivia's heart.

"That would be really nice of you, Nick. Thank you."

Olivia spied Carter and Hannah's cabin up ahead of them. A snowy white field sat between the log-frame house with a tin roof and the river. Dark mountain peaks towered beyond the river's banks. "This is it, right here."

Nick observed the homey house with a covered front porch and whistled appreciatively. Cheery light shone through its windows and smoke coiled from its chimney through the slanting snow. Another SUV was in the gravel drive, parked behind a red Ford truck and a compact sedan. "Nice digs!"

"Yeah, Carter and Hannah's cabin is really cute."

"Ready to go inside?"

Olivia found herself momentarily wishing she could stay right here with Nick. She'd enjoyed the intimacy of their conversation, and had been truly touched by his offer to try to help Blaze. But they'd have more time for talking later, Olivia reminded herself. Nick was driving her home. Olivia felt herself blush deeply when she realized this actually was starting to feel like a real date. Already, she was wondering what it would be like for Nick to kiss her goodnight. She forestalled that thought by answering casually, "Sure!" But, deep inside, Olivia was already giddily anticipating the ride home.

Nick stared at Olivia, reluctant to exit his SUV. She looked so pretty sitting there in the soft light reflected from the cabin's windows. Her hair was swept up high exposing a hint of her alabaster throat above a sparkly turtleneck collar. Little wisps of hair framed her face and her cheeks were bright pink. And those incredible green eyes…were gorgeous enough to make a million mountains crumble. They were certainly making putty out of him. And Nick was normally a rock-solid guy.

His gaze landed on the pack of peppermint gum on the console between them. He thought of picking it up and offering Olivia a stick, so he could have one himself. Then he recalled Sandy's advice about enjoying the evening. Why on earth not? The peppermint didn't seem to be working very well, anyway. At least, not in regard to Olivia. Nick wasn't as sure about its impact on his connection to animals. Then again, he should have no worries about that tonight. It was only when they were halfway to the door that Nick remembered Hannah had Tulip's two offspring as pets, and that their names were Jingles and Belle.

Chapter Thirteen

Hannah opened the door and grinned, greeting Nick and Olivia with warm hugs.

"Hello, hello! Welcome!"

The living area was cozy and warm with a glowing woodstove positioned across from a couch facing the front porch. There were a couple of armchairs accompanying the sofa and one appeared to have been pushed forward to accommodate a cheerfully lit up Christmas tree partially blocking some bookshelves in the corner. The two extra chairs that completed the seating group had been borrowed from a table in a nook abutting the kitchen. Tasteful Christmas decorations adorned the room, with a pretty rustic wreath hanging on one wall.

Carter was right behind Hannah. He hugged Olivia as well and offered his hand to Nick.

"Good seeing you again." Nick smiled cordially, recalling their previous conversation in Carter's truck. Given that he'd arrived here with Olivia, it was hard not to.

"I brought a six-pack of holiday cheer," Nick said, handing Carter the beer. Carter studied the label's cartoon design and chuckled.

"Santa's Sleigh Malt. Nice," he said, eyeing the jolly old fellow in a red suit and his reindeer team on the package. "Where did you pick this up?"

"The Merry Market," Nick explained. "You'd be surprised by their Christmas offerings."

"Oh no, he wouldn't," Sandy declared, emerging from the kitchen. She wore a holiday apron and apparently had been helping prepare the food.

"Everything in Christmas Town is all about Christmas!" Ben said, completing Sandy's thought as he followed her into the living room. Ben was dark-haired and dark-eyed like his sister, Hannah.

"That's why you love it so much here," Sandy sassily told her husband.

Ben leaned forward and kissed her cheek. "Certain things have grown on me, yeah."

Hannah rolled her eyes at Olivia. "They're still newlyweds. Technically."

"Hey!" Sandy retorted. "Technically, so are you. Your anniversary's not until next weekend."

Nick thought to himself that the two couples had gotten to work quickly in producing their babies. From the children's birthdates, they had to have been conceived on those honeymoons, if not soon after. Not that Nick begrudged anyone wanting to get started on a family. His eyes inadvertently traveled to Olivia and she blushed under his perusal.

"Uh, here!" she said suddenly, shoving her basket at Hannah. "This is for you! A little hostess gift."

"Why, thanks, Olivia!" Hannah graciously accepted the basket, examining its contents. "Is this some of your legendary homemade salsa?"

Olivia beamed proudly. "It is."

"Then, we'll have to open and try it!"

"Most definitely," Carter agreed. "Should go great with Nick's beer."

"Can I take your coats?" Ben offered helpfully, as Carter carried the beer to the kitchen and Hannah followed him.

"Maybe you can set those on the bed upstairs?" Sandy suggested. She made her apologies to Nick and Olivia as they slipped out of their coats. "Just got to check on my cornbread." Before she left, she pointed to the ceiling and winked. "Don't get into too much mischief while I'm gone."

Nick glanced skyward, seeing he and Olivia were positioned beneath a sprig of mistletoe just inside the front door. For an insane second, he had the impulse to kiss her. Just imagining Olivia in his arms sent Nick's heart *boom-boom*ing again. He met her eyes and she stared back, appearing utterly mortified. Not exactly the expression Nick hoped for.

"Sandy's so bad!" she whispered.

In spite of himself, Nick stepped closer. "Yeah."

"Totally ridiculous with this matchmaking thing."

"Totally."

She peered up at him and Nick's heart hammered. Olivia was gorgeous standing there in that pretty white sweater and jeans that outlined her athletic figure. Olivia wasn't any shrinking violet. She looked strong and able. For a fleeting instant, Nick wondered if Sandy was right. While none of Nick's previous girlfriends could deal with his family, was it possible that Olivia was the one woman who could?

Nick ducked his chin, his mouth involuntarily moving closer to hers.

"Nick, I…"

Color warmed her cheeks and Olivia licked her lips. Lips that left him aching to taste them. Didn't have to be here. Didn't need to be now. But most definitely was going to be someday. Somewhere deep inside, Nick had just crossed that line and there was no turning back.

On the threshold to the kitchen, someone loudly cleared his throat. Nick turned to see Carter holding two beers. "Olivia," he asked, shooting Nick a questioning look. "Would you like one of these? Or, would you prefer wine?"

Olivia self-consciously adjusted her ponytail. "The beer's great! Thanks!"

Carter handed one to her and another to Nick and both thanked him.

"Can I uh…help in the kitchen?" Olivia asked awkwardly.

Carter thumbed in that direction. "Why don't you go ask Hannah?"

Olivia glanced shyly at Nick before heading that way. When she'd gone, Carter cocked his chin.

Nick flagged a palm in Carter's direction.

"No cookies. I swear."

"Sure looked like some kind of magic to me."

"Blame it on the mistletoe."

"Ah." Carter squared his shoulders.

Just then, two cats scampered down the stairs, followed by Ben who was chasing them. "Sorry, man!"

he told Carter, hoofing it down the steps. "They got out ahead of me."

Nick didn't have to ask why the pair had been sequestered in the bedroom. The orange-striped tabby was very naughty. While the fluffy gray cat with little white boots and a white stripe on her nose was apparently the nice one. Both reached the living area, parading right up to Nick. They sat obediently at his feet and stared up at him in tandem.

"Well, will you look at that," Carter said, amazed. "I guess they came to give you a welcome."

Nick bent low to pet each cat. As soon as he touched Jingles, a peculiar image came to mind. Belle shook her head as if to say that when the pair was locked away, it had already been too late. Nick stood, his impression strengthening. In his mind's eye, he saw a set of car keys. He could even detect the make of the automobile by its manufacturing emblem. "Anyone missing a set of car keys?" he asked the other men.

Carter replied that he always kept his out of reach, as Ben patted down his pants pockets. "Hang on. I thought I'd put mine…" Ben's brow wrinkled as he looked around. "On the coffee table, right…there," he said, pointing to an empty spot beside a stack of magazines. He shot Nick a quizzical look, as if wondering how Nick had known about the missing keys.

"Hannah?" Carter called into the kitchen. "Jingles has been at it again!"

"Jingles? Oh, no!" She appeared in the doorway with Amanda in her arms. Nick spotted a baby swing behind them, and assumed that's where Amanda had been when Hannah answered the door. The infant appeared alert and happy, her dark eyes shining brightly as she cooed. "How did he get out?" Hannah asked, referring to the tomcat.

"It was my fault, sorry," Ben said before Carter added that the mischief had evidently occurred before Hannah had put the cats away.

She sighed, passing Amanda to Carter. He reached for his daughter, joy filling his face. "Come to Papa, you."

Amanda gurgled contentedly as Carter lifted her high in his arms, then snuggled her against his chest. "This fatherhood stuff is rough business," he said lightly.

"Yeah, we can tell it's killing you," Ben ribbed, and the guys all chuckled.

Hannah, meanwhile, had snagged Jingles and was carrying him upstairs. "What's missing this time?" she asked the others.

"Ben's car keys," Carter said, shifting from foot to foot to gently body-rock his daughter. Nick couldn't help but feel moved by their connection. He'd never really felt ready for children himself. But, once Sandy had gotten married, he'd begun to think about it. She was six years younger than him, and already she had three! Not that it was a contest or anything. But watching Carter and Amanda together made Nick wonder if he was getting left behind...and missing out on something wonderful.

"I have a pretty good idea where to find them," Hannah said. "I'll be back for Belle in a flash."

But poor Belle hadn't done anything. Nick hated to see her punished for her brother's transgressions. Then she rubbed up against Nick's leg and he got an inkling of her intention. She had very big plans to beg during dinner. So, perhaps she was a bit of an imp herself. Nick stifled a chortle, thinking his ability with animals wasn't such a bad thing. In fact, he might be able to use it to help Olivia's horse, Blaze. He sure hoped so, because he hated seeing Olivia worried. Nick also disliked the fact that something was bothering her horse. He'd do his best in addressing that tomorrow.

Meanwhile, he'd have to mind his p's and q's under the watchful eagle eye of her brother. Nick hadn't done anything untoward, yet he felt like Carter had him under a microscope, just daring him to make a wrong move. At the same time, Sandy was intent on pushing him and Olivia together. This was going to be an interesting evening all around. But Nick was a big fellow, and old enough to fend for himself.

As Hannah returned to retrieve Belle and cart her upstairs, Ben made casual conversation. "How are things going at the Grand Hotel?" he asked Nick.

"Very well!"

"Don't start that conversation yet," Hannah cautioned, as she hurried up the steps. "I want in on it, too!" She returned a few moments later, producing Ben's key ring and handing it to him. "I'd love for you to fill us all in during dinner," she said sweetly to Nick. "It's almost ready." Hannah smiled brightly at her husband. "You mind taking Amanda upstairs and tucking her in?" Then she explained to Nick, "We planned to start dinner after putting her down."

"And, unlike in my house," Ben said in jovial tones, "things *here* go according to plan."

"You have a few more kids to deal with," Hannah told him with a laugh.

"I'll bet Lily is a big help with the twins," Carter commented.

"Oh, she is," Ben agreed. "She's just not quite old enough to babysit. We'll give her another couple of years." He turned toward Nick. "Liz Martin is helping us out tonight."

"Liz?" Nick said, remembering meeting his plucky neighbor. "That's great."

"She works at the daycare, too," Hannah added.

"That's what I heard."

"Five minutes!" Sandy called from the kitchen.

"Oops!" Hannah said. "That's my cue!" She shot a pointed glance at Carter.

"And, mine," he said, winking at the others. "I'll be back in a little while."

"Take your time," Hannah told him. "We're doing appetizers first, so dinner won't be for a while."

"Have I mentioned my wife is an excellent hostess?" Carter asked, heading for the stairs.

"No need to," Ben said kindly. "It's evident."

"Yes," Nick agreed and he and Ben clinked beers.

When Hannah entered the kitchen Sandy giggled. "I think it's working," she whispered while Olivia pulled the hot crab dip from the oven. "Nick nearly kissed her under the mistletoe."

"They are made for each other," Hannah whispered stealthily. "You were so right!"

Olivia wheeled on them both and asked craftily, "Right about what?" She'd set the steaming casserole dish on a burner behind her and was slowly removing her oven mitts.

"I…well…er!" Hannah bit into her bottom lip.

"We were talking about your salsa!" Sandy lied.

"My salsa." Olivia arched an eyebrow. "Right."

"It's perfect for tonight!" Hannah rushed in. "The perfect precursor to chili!"

"And I am perfectly not that *stupid*." Olivia set her hand on her hip. "I know you were talking about me, guys."

Hannah gasped.

"I heard every word."

"You did?" Sandy asked, abashed. "Whoa. I thought we were being really qui—"

Hannah elbowed her before she could finish, and Olivia chuckled. "It's okay, girls. I'm not mad. Really."

"No?" Hannah's face brightened.

"We're only trying to help," Sandy offered meekly.

"Maybe I don't need your help," Olivia said saucily.

"What?" Sandy looked incredibly pleased.

Hannah beamed. "You go, girl!"

"You mean...?" Sandy leaned toward her. "You and Nick...?"

"Nuh-uh."

Hannah's face fell in utter disappointment. Olivia was actually a little touched. She hadn't realized this was so important to Hannah, too. Of course, Hannah did run the shop reputed to inspire romance...

"Not yet," Olivia continued mysteriously, shocking them both.

"What's that mean?" Sandy demanded in a whisper.

"Yeah, what?" Hannah echoed in low tones.

Olivia giggled as she envisioned herself gathering up her nerve. "I'm going to ask Nick out."

"What? You?" Hannah looked like she wanted to sing and dance.

Sandy was already springing up and down on her heels, and clapping her hands. "When? Where? I won't ask why, because I'm sure I know! I think you *like* him!"

Olivia rolled her eyes at her wacky friends, but she loved them both dearly. She kind of wished that Jade was here to share in their fun and secrets. Unfortunately, Alexander was down with the flu, so she and Wendell had to stay home.

"That's a lot of questions for just five minutes," Olivia replied reasonably.

"Yeah, so? Then just answer the first two." Sandy cracked a grin as Hannah waited expectantly next to her.

"I'm going to suggest we go riding."

"Riding? Oh?" Olivia didn't know why, but Sandy looked mildly disappointed.

"Nick's going with me to the stables tomorrow to meet Blaze," Olivia continued undaunted. "So I'll have the perfect opening to suggest we go riding some other time."

"That's not exactly a date, Olivia," Hannah told her, apparently siding with Sandy.

"Why not?"

"It's just not very…romantic?" Sandy replied gently.

"We were thinking candles…" Hannah said dreamily. "Moonlight…"

"Dinner at the Peppermint Bark!" Sandy filled in.

"Everybody does dinner at the Peppermint Bark," Olivia said, slightly exasperated.

"Well then, think of something different," Sandy challenged.

"I don't see what's wrong with a ride through the snowy countryside?"

"On separate horses?" Hannah asked, sounding dismayed.

Olivia harrumphed, feeling like they'd turned against her.

"It's all right," Sandy jumped in quickly, obviously worried she'd hurt Olivia's feelings. Which she had, actually. They both had. Quite a lot. "Horseback riding can be fun! Nick loves horses!"

"That's why I thought of it to begin with," Olivia contested gloomily.

Hannah gently touched her arm. "You just do whatever works for you. I'm sure that Nick will love just about any suggestion."

"Yeah," Sandy agreed. "As long as you're together—and alone—you can give things time to work!"

"Things?" Olivia asked curiously. "Which things?"

"Oh…I…er…" Sandy nervously dusted her hands on her apron. "Those natural things. You know, that bring men and woman together."

"I don't want you to get your hopes up," Olivia told her friends. "Just because I'm thinking of going out, that doesn't mean I'm ready to get serious. I haven't been serious about anybody in a long time."

"We know," Hannah said sympathetically. "That's why Nick seems ideal!"

"Ideal for a friendly outing, sure," Olivia answered.

"You said a date." Sandy smirked good-naturedly. "Don't backpedal on us now."

Olivia had no intention of backpedaling. She also wasn't prepared to move forward at the breakneck speed her friends were apparently envisioning. She'd decided to take Savannah's advice, that's all. To test the waters and see how things went. It wouldn't be fair to make Nick think their relationship could lead to something more. He likely wasn't looking to get seriously involved any more than Olivia was.

"I thought you gals would be serving chili by now." Carter surprised them by appearing in the doorway.

"We were just about to bring out the hors d'oeuvres," Sandy said.

"Is Amanda sleeping already?" Hannah asked him.

Carter smiled fondly. "Out like a light."

Sandy slid on the oven mitts to carry the hot dip into the living area, while Olivia finished arranging chips around a special platter into which she'd already poured her salsa.

"Want to grab a couple of things and help us?" Hannah asked her husband.

Carter agreed congenially, grabbing the bowl of mixed nuts and a tray of fruit and cheeses. "I'm not sure anyone will be able to eat chili after snacking on all of this."

"Oh, they'll be able," Sandy insisted. "And, they'd better serve a big helping of my cornbread, too," she added, inspiring lighthearted laughter.

"Don't forget my cookies for dessert!" Hannah said, and the others turned to stare at her. "Not Virginia Cookies, guys. For heaven's sakes. Just a regular old variety pack of holiday selections from my shop."

"We'll have to tell everybody to save room," Olivia said.

"Trust me on this." Sandy playfully rolled her eyes. "Nick always has room for cookies!"

A few hours later, the happy group was finishing up their dinner in the living area. They'd eaten buffet style in order to appreciate the warmth of the woodstove. It was still snowing hard outside. Nick had enjoyed his conversation with the others, and even Carter had seemed to loosen up after a beer or two. Nick was sure that Carter was a great guy. He had a feeling Carter would genuinely come to like him, too, once he learned Nick only had honorable intentions. Although he'd been sorely tempted by Olivia's magnificent lips under the mistletoe, he'd reined himself in. And, just because he was still thinking about kissing her, that didn't make Nick a bad guy. On the contrary, he was actually a decently caring and considerate person. Nick had never hurt anyone on purpose, and didn't have plans to start doing anything like that now.

He did want to get to know Olivia though, on more than a casual basis. Nick couldn't help but feel drawn to her. She was interesting and attractive, and oh-so-easy on the eyes. Olivia also held that inexplicable power over him. The one that sent his pulse racing. Nick further suspected that Olivia was starting to develop an ability of her own: knowing when he was around. Whether or not Nick believed what he'd read in *Santa's Little Helper*, he had to find some way to make sense of what was happening between them. Maybe, as he spent more time with Olivia, his course would seem clearer?

"Anyone for dessert?" Hannah asked, standing and starting to clear their dishes. Carter got up to help her, and their guests followed his cue.

"I don't think I could eat another bite," Olivia said contentedly. "Everything was so delicious!"

"Yes, Olivia, especially your salsa," Ben said. "It was great to finally try it."

"It was superb," Nick agreed, nabbing a fistful of empty bottles from the coffee table.

"I loved Sandy's cornbread," Carter commented.

"Your five-alarm chili was pretty great, too," she returned with a grin.

"I can't believe nobody's going to have my cookies," Hannah said disappointedly, setting her dishes in the sink.

Nick alerted at this. "Cookies? Which cookies?"

"I brought some sugar cookies home from my shop," Hannah explained. "Mexican wedding cookies, too. And gingerbread men and snickerdoodles."

"Well, I won't be shy," Nick said and everyone laughed. "I'll take one of each!"

"I have a couple, too," Ben chimed in.

Hannah smiled at the two men, pleased, then glanced at the others.

"Oh, all right," Olivia said, grinning. "I'll cave. But, just one. I'll take a gingerbread man."

"Smart," Sandy said, teasing. "Might as well choose the big kind if you're only having one!"

"None are as large as Hannah's special Virginia Cookies." Carter shot a look at Nick. "It's a shame she sold out again this year."

"I always keep a few extra around," Hannah said lightly. She turned to Carter who was behind her and saucily kissed his lips. "For emergencies."

Ben chuckled. "Yes, well. Sandy and I have had our share of those."

Sandy widened her eyes at him, like she didn't want Ben to go there.

"You should have seen what happened when—"

"Sweetheart!" Sandy said, cutting him off. "Don't you think we should phone Liz to see how it's going?"

Ben suddenly checked his watch, before addressing the group. "Sandy's right. The twins can get a little ornery at this time of night, especially Holly."

"She doesn't settle down very well?" Olivia asked him.

"Oh, she settles all right. It's just what happens when she wakes up. Even though she's so little, I'd swear she's already having dreams."

"Really?" Carter asked, intrigued. "About what?"

Ben stared at Sandy who pointedly twisted her lips. His temples reddened. "Uh…yeah. Right! Let me just go and make that call," he said, excusing himself as he stepped into the other room.

The rest of them helped Hannah and Carter load the dishwasher and clean up the kitchen, before settling back in the living room with mugs of coffee and cookies. When they joined Ben there he was just ending his call.

"Everything all right at home?" Sandy asked him.

"Actually, it sounds like Liz kind of has her hands full." He grimaced apologetically at Hannah and Carter, then glanced at Sandy. "It might be good if we headed home."

"Oh dear, poor Liz!" Sandy frowned sympathetically. "I thought Lily might be able to help her."

"She did! She tended to Rose while Liz was busy cleaning up the nursery."

"The nursery?" Sandy asked with alarm. "What happened to it?"

"Liz wasn't sure," Ben said. "She heard the sound of glass breaking then found Rose's Christmas snow globe shattered on the floor. Little Rose woke and starting wailing, then—"

"How did that happen?" Hannah asked, amazed.

"I…uh…"

"Maybe Holly kicked the crib?" Nick suggested smoothly. "Wasn't the shelf holding the snow globe nearby?" Nick hoped to help his sister out by offering a rational explanation. Though, secretly, he understood there was much more to the situation than Sandy and Ben would be willing to let on.

"Yeah," Sandy said enthusiastically. "Yes, that's it!" She shot a look at Ben, and he nodded vehemently.

"Must have been the vibrations. Sure!"

Olivia frowned worriedly. "I'm glad no one was hurt."

"Nope! No one at all," Ben told her. "But, we'd better get going."

"Right," Sandy agreed, heading for the stairs. "So sorry, Hannah and Carter. It's been a great time."

"Excellent," Ben agreed, as they went to grab their coats.

Soon after Ben and Sandy departed, Olivia sent Nick a meaningful look. He could tell she was ready to leave, too. It had been a great evening, but neither of them wanted to overstay their welcome.

"Thanks again for everything," Nick said, as he and Olivia bundled up and prepared to go. "I especially loved those cookies, Hannah. You have a real gift for making them."

"Especially the Virginia kind," Olivia teased. She looked up at Nick. "Did you ever learn who left them in your freezer?"

"Freezer?" Carter asked, surprised.

"Yeah, it was odd. I mean, a very nice gesture, but a little strange, too. Somebody left me a housewarming gift, but they didn't sign their name."

"That is strange," Carter said, stroking his chin. His gaze roved over Hannah and she play-swatted at him in the air.

"Go on! It wasn't me! I already told Nick that." She turned to Nick for confirmation. "Right?"

When Nick assented, Carter inquired, "What kind of Virginia Cookie did this mystery person leave you?"

"All three, and I've got to tell you the first two were very good. Excellent in fact."

Hannah blushed at the compliment. "Which kind did you eat?"

"A Charity Cookie and the Clemency Cookie. Olivia warned me against trying the other type," he said lightly, and it was Olivia's turn to redden.

"I merely said to exercise caution," she corrected.

"Excellent advice," Carter agreed.

"Did the cookies…have any effect on you?" Hannah asked tentatively.

"Well, since I had a big glass of milk with them, they did make me sleepy."

Carter seemed to laugh in relief. "That sounds like the intended consequence."

"Is *not!*" Hannah contested. "My cookies have special powers."

"Yes, dear. I believe you," Carter told her warmly. "But it appears their powers may not work on everyone."

"That's because I'm immune," Nick told them with a wink.

Olivia's eyebrows rose. "Immune? How?"

"Magic doesn't work on magic," Nick explained sunnily. "That's double-dipping."

Olivia viewed him wryly. "You're saying you're already special enough?"

Nick's blue eyes sparkled. "You tell me?"

Hannah laughed out loud. "Now, you're sounding just like Sandy," she said to Nick. "Teasing must run in the family!"

"Lots of things do," he assured her, zipping up his coat. He dipped his chin their way. "Carter, Hannah, thanks for a great evening."

"Yes, thank you!" Olivia said. She cast a sideways glance at Nick, like she was still mulling over his previous response. "We'll see you both again soon."

After Olivia buckled her seatbelt in Nick's SUV, she turned to him and gaped. "'Magic doesn't work on magic'? Hmm. Care to explain any further what that means?"

"You said yourself I'm pretty special."

Olivia laughed and shook her head. "Maybe I should have added that you have an enormous ego, too?"

"It's not as big as you think."

"No?"

"What would you say if I really was?"

"Really was what?"

He stared at her expectantly and she waggled a finger. "Oh, no you don't, Nick Claus! You're not roping me in with your joking again."

"Again?"

"Like you just tried to do in there." She rolled her eyes toward Hannah's cabin, and he chuckled in understanding.

"I see. You think I was trying to dupe you."

She scrutinized him a moment, thinking that some of the most convincing lies landed close to the truth. Nick was hiding something about who he was; Olivia just wasn't sure what.

"But, you told me initially that you didn't believe in the legend of the Virginia Cookie," Nick said.

"I...don't."

"And still you told me to be careful."

He had her there. Olivia heaved a breath. "Listen, I realize that sounded contradictory, but that's just because I wasn't sure. I mean, not one hundred percent. Most people believe Hannah's cookies work like self-fulfilling prophecies. That those who believe in their magic, will experience it."

"A lot of magic works that way, don't you think?"

"I wouldn't know."

"Because you don't believe…" Nick's forehead rose and Olivia's pulse pounded. "You don't believe in much, do you?"

"Of course I believe! I believe in goodness, and faith and friendship and family! I believe in home and hearth and—"

"Love?"

Olivia nearly swallowed her tongue. "I'm…not so sure about that."

"Rough seas?"

"If my last relationship had been a ship, it would have been named *Titanic*."

"I'm sorry, Olivia."

"It's all right, really," she said, but inside she didn't totally believe it. She'd been engaged to marry Ted when she'd discovered him in the cask room with his hospitality manager, Elizabeth. Ted owned a vineyard, but he'd apparently been tending to more than the vines.

"How long have you been afloat?" Nick viewed her kindly. "On that life raft of yours?"

Olivia swallowed hard. "Three years."

"That's a long time."

"I know." She couldn't help wondering about him. He was such an attractive man, and so accomplished. "How about you? Smooth sailing?"

Nick resolutely shook his head. "I guess I've never had the right…boat." He appeared pensive a moment, shadows outlining his handsome face. After a while, he turned to her. "Are you ready to go home?"

"Not yet," she answered honestly.

"Is there some place we can talk?"

Olivia thought a moment. "There a park a little ways past here. The Lena Winchester Memorial Park. It's right alongside the river."

"Sounds nice," he said, cranking his engine. "Why don't you show me the way?"

They pulled up to the park, Nick's headlights illuminating the playground equipment that had been built by Buddy and his sons and Carter. A large wooden climbing structure was fashioned like an old-timey train, the sort that used to traverse the looming mountains ahead of them back in the day when Christmas Town was a railroad whistle-stop. A thicket of pines stood to their left housing the opening to some sort of trail. Snowy hills rose behind them tumbling toward the snowy riverbank.

"Looks like a great place for sledding," Nick said.

"It is," Olivia agreed when he put his vehicle in park. "I've never been, but I hear it's great." She peered through the windshield and pointed to the trailhead he'd seen. "I prefer cross-country skiing myself."

"Really?" Nick was very pleased. He enjoyed the sport immensely himself and he told her so.

"Maybe we could go sometime?" she asked hopefully. Then her cheeks reddened. "What I mean is…if you want to…and have…?" Olivia covered her face with her hands, and mumbled to herself. "Lame, so lame. About as bad as horseback riding!"

Nick leaned toward her and asked softly, "What's so wrong with horseback riding?"

She peeked at him between her splayed fingers. "It's not very…romantic." Her cheeks burned hotly. "For a first date."

He lightly touched her arm. "Is that what you're doing? Asking me on a date?"

"I…um…" Olivia lowered her hands and hung her head. "I'm terrible at this, aren't I?" she asked when she faced him again.

"Actually, I think you're doing pretty well. You named two things that I love to do anyway. I'm sure I'd have twice as much fun doing them with you."

Olivia's face brightened. "Really?"

"*Ho-ho-ho*! Of course!"

She giggled and covered her mouth. "You do that a lot, you know that?"

"What?"

"Never mind." Her grin broadened. "I think it's cute."

Nick's voice caught in his throat. "Cute?"

"Yeah." Olivia's green eyes danced. "I can tell you don't even know that you're doing it."

"*No-ho-ho*—" Nick halted abruptly, looking chagrined. "It's pretty bad, isn't?"

"Does it happen a lot, or only with me?"

"It seems to be happening more lately. A lot of things do."

"Like?"

There was no way that Nick could tell her. She'd totally think him nuts! "Like, I've been having a hard time getting you out of my head," he said, settling on a truth.

"I know what you mean."

She looked up at him and Nick's heart hammered. *Boom-boom, boom-boom, boom-boom!*

"I've been thinking a lot about you, too." She studied him a moment and Nick's pulse raced faster.

"You know, it's funny. The other night? I was thinking about you, and then you were out there."

"Out where?" Nick inquired, although he already knew.

"On the sidewalk, outside of the Merry Market. And then the next morning, something similar happened again. Only, that time, you were getting coffee. And tonight…"

Her words trailed off. Probably because Nick's eyes kept growing wider and wider.

"Are you all right?"

"Yeah. I just…think that's incredible—that you can sense me that way."

She shrugged uncertainly. "You don't think it's a little weird?"

Nick uncomfortably cleared his throat. "I've heard of people having premonitions."

"Yeah, but this isn't exactly like that." She thoughtfully set her chin. "It's different."

Her gaze swept over him and Nick's temperature spiked. "Something about *you* is different, isn't it?"

"Most guys like to think of themselves as unique!"

"That's not it." She narrowed her eyes in a challenge. "What are you hiding from me, Nick Claus?"

Nick's heart stilled and his palms felt clammy. "Nothing. Nothing much."

"You don't have a dark past, or something?"

"Dark? No, not dark! Snowy white. I promise!"

"If we go out on a date, will you tell me?"

"Just one date?"

Olivia chuckled in disbelief. "Two?"

"How about three?" Nick swallowed hard. "Three should work!"

"You drive a hard bargain," she said, laughing.

"Perhaps," he recovered quickly. "But, I'm an awfully good at what I do."

"Yeah?"

"Absolutely! I got some great sketches drawn this week."

"I'm so excited to see them."

"Maybe we can meet up on Monday to kick around ideas? I've got contractors coming by in the morning, but I'm free in the afternoon."

"My shop's open until six."

"We can do dinner in that case?"

Olivia smiled in agreement. "In the meantime, can you still see Blaze?"

"Of course I'll still see Blaze. I promised to take a look at her tomorrow."

"Then, there's the church bazaar…"

Nick slapped his forehead with a laugh. "That's right! I nearly forgot. That's this Sunday, isn't it?"

"Yes, and you'd better go," she told him sternly. "Or else, Lou Christmas will never forgive you."

Nick chuckled, his tensions easing. "Thanks for the heads up. I'll make sure to be there." He turned and stared out the windshield at the driving snow. "It's really pretty out here."

"And peaceful," Olivia said. "Christmas Town is a nice place."

"It keeps getting nicer," he said, his voice husky.

"Yeah," Olivia said happily. "It does."

When Nick drove her home a little while later, Olivia felt as if her heart had sprouted wings. While tonight hadn't been a planned date, in the end it had seemed like one. And, Olivia couldn't have had a more marvelous time. She'd had fun with her friends at Hannah's, and her conversation with Nick at the park had been warm and intimate. She liked so much about him, even his mysterious parts. Olivia figured that Nick was just a cautiously guarded person, and that he'd reveal more about himself eventually. He'd pretty much said as much.

She was excited he'd gotten started on ideas for the Grand Hotel, and was especially thankful he was willing to try to help her with her horse. More than anything, Olivia was really happy she'd have several more occasions to see Nick again—in the very near future.

"Well, thanks for the ride," she said, climbing from his SUV.

"I had a great time with you, Olivia." He smiled warmly and she grinned back.

"Yeah, me too."

"So, see you in the morning around eight o'clock?"

"Eight will be fine!" she agreed happily. Since her shop was open on Saturdays, they'd need to get to the stables and back before then.

As she shut the door, Nick shot her a wink and Olivia's skin burned hot.

"Pleasant dreams."

Oh, she was going to have pleasant dreams, all right. Lots and lots of them… And, if she was lucky, they'd involve the ultra handsome Nick Claus and her riding in Santa's sleigh.

Chapter Fourteen

The moment Nick and Olivia stepped from her truck, a herd of horses came galloping toward them from the pasture. Nick had walked to Olivia's store and she'd offered to drive, since she knew the way and joked that she didn't mind her truck getting dirty. The gravel road leading here was covered with a frozen combination of ice, mud, and muck, but Olivia's vehicle was accustomed to taking the bruising. And it was worth the drive every time.

Snow blanketed the ground and covered the barn rooftop nearby. The horses that had been put out for the morning all wore blankets, and their breath clouded the air as they hoofed in Olivia's direction.

"Come on!" She motioned to Nick and he followed her, as she went through the swinging gate then securely shut it.

Olivia was taken with the beauty of the morning. A slight mist rose off the surrounding mountains, as gray skies closed in from above. More snow was expected soon, but they were experiencing a temporary break in the weather. She loved Sleigh Bell Stables and never could get enough of the place. Olivia was especially proud of the program she'd started for the kids.

"Looks like the gang's all here," she said, smiling as the horses approached them. She laughed and turned toward Nick. "They must have heard my truck."

While Olivia was accustomed to the horses greeting her, she was stunned to see them angling toward Nick. He stepped into the field and soon he was surrounded by seven curious faces nosing in at him. The horses snorted and whinnied, stomping their hooves on the ground while prancing around Nick in a curious circle. "Looks like they're interested to meet the stranger," Olivia said in awe.

"Yeah." Nick smiled her way then he addressed the horses, patting each one on its withers or stroking its nose. "How are you? Yes, yes, I know," he said to Violet. He spoke to Jim Boy as he nuzzled closer, crowding out the others. "Nice to meet you! You don't say?" Olivia was amazed by the ease Nick displayed with the animals he'd never met before. They all seemed to take right to him! Only Blaze held back from the group, shyly hanging her head while watching Nick with big dark eyes. Olivia walked over to her and took her by the bridle, leading her in Nick's direction.

"Nick," she said proudly. "This is Blaze." Then she told her horse, "And, this is my friend, Nick."

Blaze eyed Nick cautiously as he slowly raised his hand to pet her right behind her ear. "Hey there, Blaze. How are you?"

Blaze stared at him and cocked her head.

"Hmm, right." He glanced at Olivia. "Do you think we could have a moment?"

"Well, I…" Olivia stared at him, flummoxed. "Sure! I guess."

Nick shot her a wink, indicating he had things under control. Then he strode toward the fence and Blaze trotted after him. The other horses started to follow, but Nick calmly raised his hand. "We'll be back," he said, and the horses stopped in their tracks, hanging their heads in disappointment.

Olivia's mouth gaped open. She'd never seen anything like this in her life. And, she'd been around plenty of horses—and horse people. Nick leaned into the fence, resting his elbows on the top rail, as Blaze aligned herself next to him facing the barn. Every once in a while, Nick shook his head, reassuringly patting the horse, but as far as Olivia could tell, Blaze was just standing there staring straight ahead. After a bit, both Nick and Blaze turned toward the riding ring, looking that way. Nick nodded again and said something to Blaze. She pranced on her front hooves, pounding the snowy ground, then she pivoted and galloped away. As she did, the other horses perked up and followed after her, racing toward the woods near the pasture's edge.

Nick strode back to Olivia as she watched him wide-eyed. "Want to tell me what just happened?"

Her pretty green eyes locked on his and her cheeks were pink with the morning cold. She wore a warm hat, a parka, a scarf, and gloves. He had his field coat and work boots on, and Olivia wore riding boots and jeans.

"It's about your Tuesday program," he told her.

"What about it?" she asked, concerned.

"You mentioned some of the rescues have been outfitted for riding?"

"Both Jim Boy and Violet were ready."

"Well, now Blaze thinks she's ready, too."

She appeared confounded by the suggestion. "But Blaze has always been so timid! She's been the least approachable with the children. I mean, she's good with them, but sometimes I think they overwhelm her."

"Not the 'little one,'" Nick corrected.

Olivia raised her brow. "The 'little one'?"

"The one who brings her carrots," Nick explained.

Olivia gasped in understand. "Lily?"

"Is it Lily?" Nick asked with pleased surprised.

"It must be," Olivia said with sudden understanding. "Lily's a petite child, a little smaller than the other children. She's also taken a particular shine to Blaze. In fact, she's one of the few children Blaze is comfortable with approaching her." Olivia worriedly viewed Nick. "I'm not sure about riding, though. I don't know what Ben and Sandy would say."

"How about Lily?"

Olivia cracked a grin. "She'd be over the moon."

"Then, let me talk to Ben and Sandy. Blaze is a gentle horse, and she's bonded with Lily. Don't you think it would be good for someone to ride her?"

"Besides me?" Olivia asked. "Of course. It will help with her socialization, and in building her trust with people." She paused to study him. "Just one question…?"

"Huh?"

"How did you know that? Know what was troubling Blaze?"

"I just had an instinct about it."

"Yes, but—"

"Or, more like a strong impression."

Her pretty face glowed. "Hannah was right! You are a horse whisperer!"

Actually, it was more like they whispered to him. He just listened. But Nick decided not to correct her. "I've always liked animals," Nick explained. "And been good with them. My grandpa is, too. He taught me some of his tricks on the farm."

"His farm in Canada?"

"That's right."

"Does your granddad keep other animals besides horses?"

"Oh, yes! All kinds, even reindeer."

"Reindeer?" She chuckled in disbelief. "Go on!"

"You don't have to believe me, if you don't want to."

She smiled brightly. "I'd like to see that farm of your grandpa's. It sounds amazing."

"It really is." He studied her a long while before saying, "Maybe someday I'll take you."

An hour later, Olivia and Nick sat at Jolly Bean Java drinking hot coffee. After introducing Nick to Blaze, she'd shown him around the barn and the office area where the business aspects of the horse rescue were coordinated, which was located in a trailer. She'd also given him a tour of Blaze's stall and checked on the horses' feed before leaving. The hefty barn cats, Chester and George, had scampered after Nick as he'd returned to Olivia's truck, almost like they'd wanted to go with him.

Nick certainly had an uncanny ability with animals. She was still at a loss to understand how he'd communicated so clearly with Blaze, but Olivia was

very glad that he had. Blaze's spirits had seemed
brighter immediately after Nick had talked to her, and
hopefully the horse's outlook would continue to
improve. Particularly, if Nick helped work out the idea
of Lily taking riding lessons with Sandy and Ben. And
Nick had promised he would.

"Thanks again for coming to the stables," she told
him. "I can't tell you how much I appreciate your
making an effort with Blaze."

"She seems like a wonderful horse."

"She is."

"So which one will I get to ride?" He peered at her
over the rim of his cup. "When we have our date?"

Olivia laughed in pleased surprise, so glad he was
still considering it. There was nothing she'd enjoy more
than combining her love of horses with her interest in
this exciting new man. "I was thinking about Jim Boy.
He's a sturdy stallion."

"I like Jim Boy." Nick smiled warmly. "And the
rest of them. Thanks for showing me around Sleigh Bell
Stables."

"Now that you know where it is…"

"I'll be back for sure." He studied her a thoughtful
moment. "How about next Sunday?"

"Sunday?"

"For our ride? I'll be done with more work by then,
and it will be good to take a break."

"I'd love that, Nick," she said, meaning it
absolutely. "And Sunday's perfect. That's a slow
afternoon out here."

"Great! Then it's a date." He clinked his coffee cup
to hers and she smiled shyly.

"I thought we already had one on Monday."

"That's right," he said, remembering. "To discuss business."

She perused his handsome face, her pulse racing.

"I won't mind having a working dinner with you."

"You know what, Olivia?" He reached out and took her hand, and Olivia's heart fluttered. "I won't, either." His voice was husky when he said, "I like being around you; you've got to know that... I'll make any excuse." Heat warmed her cheeks, and Nick held her hand tighter.

"I like being around you, too."

"That's really nice to know."

They parted with plans to see each other tomorrow evening at the church bazaar. There was a Christmas pageant there each year, complete with a children's reenactment of the Christmas story and a family dinner and craft-making session afterwards. Nick was looking forward to going and meeting more folks from the town. Most of all, though, he was looking forward to seeing Olivia again. He felt so comfortable around her, and each time he was with her he only wanted to see her more. Perhaps he shouldn't have held her hand this morning, but he hadn't been able to stop himself. And Olivia certainly hadn't protested. To the contrary, she'd seemed to welcome his affection and respond to it.

Nick had loved Sleigh Bell Stables and had truly enjoyed meeting the horses. His impressions around them today had been particularly keen. Nick wondered if that was in part due to Olivia being near. Her presence appeared to bring out the best in him, in some of the most unusual ways. Nick was just approaching

Sisters' Row on foot when he spied Lou Christmas standing on the stoop holding a big cardboard box.

"There you are," she said, turning toward him with a friendly smile. "I knocked, but thought you were sleeping!"

"Not this late in the morning," Nick said, with a *ho-ho-ho*. "Got somewhat of an early start today."

She viewed his muddy work boots and her eyebrows rose curiously. "Oh?"

Nick climbed up on the porch and pulled his keys from his coat pocket. "Went out to Sleigh Bell Stables," he said, unlocking the door.

Lou traipsed inside and handed him the hefty box with a pleased grin. "Sleigh Bell Stables means Olivia, doesn't it?"

"It might," he said noncommittally before glancing down at the box. "What have we here?"

"Christmas decorations!" Lou proclaimed with delight. "Sandy said you were in need…" She glanced around the simply furnished living area, spotting the bare Christmas tree by the rear bay window. "Ray said you picked out a tree yesterday morning, so I figured you were ready!"

Nick chortled in understanding. The eldest Christmas brother, Ray, ran the North Pole Nursery. Ray was tall and nice-looking like the other boys, yet his face was more weathered given that he spent most of his time outdoors. Apart from running the nursery, he and his wife Meredith owned a Christmas tree farm out on River Road. They also had a twelve-year-old boy, Kyle, who helped his dad with Christmas tree sales when school was out.

Nick guessed that Ray must have told his mom, Lou, that Nick had stopped by to purchase a six-foot Frasier fir. Everybody appeared to know everything about everyone else in Christmas Town, but that didn't bother Nick. Coming from a line of Clauses, he was used to folks being in on other people's business. Sometimes more often than they wanted. He thanked Lou for her thoughtfulness and set the box down on the coffee table, opening its folded-together flaps.

Nick jerked back his hand with a start. The first item staring back at him was positively frightening.

Lou reached for the stuffed object and lifted it out of the box. "Meet Mr. Noodles!"

Nick supposed it was supposed to be a…snowman? The poor creature had a big round body with stubby arms and legs poking out of it. The snowy white head wore a little black hat and had buttons for its mouth and eyes. The mouth button was so large, Mr. Noodles appeared to be screaming. Or maybe choking…? Perhaps due to the sparkly winter scarf wound extra tightly around his neck? "Wow," Nick replied. "I don't know what to say!"

"I know." Lou tittered proudly. "Amazing, isn't he? I made him myself from all natural materials."

"Uh-huh. Great!"

Lou worriedly glanced around. "You don't have any cats in the place?"

"Cats? No, why?"

"Because *last year*…" She lowered her voice confidentially. "Mr. Noodles and that naughty feline, Jingles, had a bit of a run-in."

"A run-in, I see," Nick said, sure he could imagine it.

"In any case," Lou continued in an upbeat manner. "There's plenty more in there!"

"Wow, I don't know what to—"

"No need to thank me," she went on. "Seeing your place all dolled up for the holidays will be thanks enough." Then she added with a wink, "Don't think I won't be back to check, now!"

"You're welcome back here anytime. Lou. Of course!"

"Lovely!" Lou clapped her gloves together. "But, at the moment, I must dash! Lots to do for the bazaar tomorrow." She paused and scanned his face. "You *are* planning to join us?"

"I am."

"Excellent. We'll see you there at five o'clock. And, don't be late! You won't want to miss the pageant."

Chapter Fifteen

When Nick pulled into the parking lot of the Corner Church, it was already packed to the gills. He'd meant to arrive early, but had gotten caught up reviewing some blueprints and had lost track of time. He was very excited about the ideas he had for renovating the first floor of the Grand Hotel and was interested to hear Olivia's concepts for the upper floors. He entered through the side door by the parking lot, which led to a large Fellowship Hall area. Several round tables had been set for dining, and a hot buffet line, containing crockpots and covered casserole dishes, occupied two long tables. At the far side of the room near the entrance to the kitchen, more tables were established as craft stations. A separate section of tables held interesting-looking items on display, like children's books, elegant pottery, and even some of those Christmas barrettes he'd seen for sale at Olivia's shop. Pieces of paper were taped to the table in front of these objects and pens sat near by. This was evidently the makings of a silent auction of some sort, likely as a fund-raiser for the church.

Nick heard voices swell in an opening Christmas hymn and hurried through the empty hall and into the narthex, where Kurt Christmas stood holding a collection of programs. "Olivia's in there," Kurt whispered, handing Nick a program. "If you want to sit with her." Kurt pointed to the fourth row from the back and Nick spotted Olivia standing near the center aisle, holding a hymnal. Nick nodded his thanks and quietly made his way down the aisle, scooting in beside her.

"I was worried you might not make it," she whispered with a pretty blush. Nick saw Jade and Wendell standing on the other side of her. Their baby, Josiah, was snoozing, slumped against Wendell's shoulder.

"Sorry I'm late," Nick told her.

"Alexander's in the pageant. He's one of the wise men," Olivia explained quietly.

"Glad he's feeling better," Nick returned in hushed tones.

"His friend, Bobby, is too." She craned her head toward the dark-haired couple standing on the far side of Jade and Wendell. "Those are Bobby's parents, Frank and Victoria Cho. Victoria is—" she started to tell him, when the hymn came to an end. Olivia cupped her hand to her mouth and giggled. "Later," she said, silently mouthing the word as they were seated.

Nick smiled, thinking about what a warm and wonderful woman Olivia was. No wonder she had so many close friends here. A gray-haired minister with a kindly face ascended to the lectern, addressing the congregation. Though he'd naturally grown older, Nick recognized him as Pastor Wilson from meeting the clergyman several years before. "Merry Christmas, one and all. May the joy of the season be with you!" He stepped aside, introducing a pale blonde in her thirties with light eyes and freckles. Her name was Della Martin and she was apparently coordinating the children's pageant. She motioned a young boy forward with light hair and dark eyes. "That's Kyle Christmas," Olivia whispered, as the preteen opened his Bible and began to read. Nick glanced around, spying Kyle's dad, Ray, seated in the front row beside a stately brunette Nick took to be Ray's wife, Meredith. Lou and Buddy Christmas were with them, as was Walt.

Walt had mentioned to Nick during their visit at the Christmas Inn that his girls were going through final exams and wouldn't be home until next weekend. Nick was sure that Walt missed them, but found it nice that Walt had come to support his nephew's participation in the event tonight. It was good of Kurt to be here, too.

Nick looked around at the packed church seeing other faces he recognized. His neighbor, Liz Martin, was sitting by a tall slim man with a similar profile who looked to be five or six years older than her. Nick guessed that was Liz's brother, Stan. Olivia had mentioned that Stan and Della had four children, and Nick figured the toddler boy sitting on Stan's lap to be the youngest. As three little angels appeared proclaiming the good news to the Virgin Mary, Olivia whispered that they were the three Martin girls. Nick was pleased to recognize Lily as the child playing Mary, and she was doing a fine job, cradling a baby doll wrapped in swaddling clothes, as a young boy about her age paraded down the aisle beside her, heading toward the makeshift manger by the altar.

Someone tapped Nick on the shoulder, and he saw it was Sandy, wanting to join him in the pew after the kids had cleared the aisle. He gently nudged Olivia and everyone slightly slid over, making room. "Sorry," Sandy whispered to Olivia and Nick. "Had a hard time with the twins and the sitter…"

"What happened?" Olivia asked softly, leaning forward.

"She bailed!" Sandy replied, cringing. "Poor Ben had to stay home."

"Who was the sitter?" Olivia questioned quietly.

"Miss Thurston," Sandy confided. "The young art teacher from the high school." She pulled her cell phone from her purse and turned on the video feature. "I told Ben I'd film it," she said in low tones.

Nick almost felt sorry for Sandy. Almost, but not quite. Though she definitely had her hands full with her twins, overall her life was pretty wonderful. So any minor difficulties she endured were bound to be worth it.

"You're totally right about that," she said, beaming up at him, and Nick knew she'd read his thoughts again. He focused back on the play, determined to fix his attention on that rather than on the gorgeous redhead beside him. There were only so many things Nick intended to share with his sister. And his amorous leanings were none of Sandy's business.

"Amorous?" she asked, pleased. "Really?" And Nick pinched her.

"Ow!" she cried quietly, rubbing her arm.

Olivia curiously viewed their exchange. "Guys, shhh…" she said, hushing them. "Here comes the best part."

Kyle finished reading and the children at the altar sang a Christmas song ending in a gleeful shout of *Hallelujah!* Nick chuckled, thinking to himself what cute little rascals they were. And each of them had been good this year. He had no doubt that Santa would fill their stockings.

The pageant ended and the congregation rose, singing another hymn.

"Great service," Jade commented softly when it had ended.

"Everyone did a super job," Wendell agreed, as Josiah kept sleeping.

Frank Cho leaned forward, reaching past the others to take Nick's hand. "Welcome to Christmas Town."

The pretty brunette in a tight chignon beside him smiled. "Nice to see you, Nick!"

"Thanks," he said to the Chos, before addressing them and the Scotts. "Your boys were both great wise men." Nick turned to Sandy. "Lily was perfect as Mary, too."

"Will you sit with us at our table?" Olivia asked him. "Hannah will be there with Amanda." For the first time, Nick noticed Hannah had been seated a few rows behind them. She toted an alert-looking Amanda in a baby carrier and was accompanied by a middle-aged man with salt-and-pepper hair, which was graying even more heavily at the temples. "That's Hannah and Ben's dad," Sandy explained quietly. "Carter's on duty tonight."

"That sounds great," Nick replied, smiling down at Olivia. He looked around at the friendly group. "I'd love to join you. Thanks!"

As they exited the sanctuary, Pastor Wilson took Nick's hand. "Nick Claus, aren't you a sight for sore eyes! What a pleasure having you back in Christmas Town."

"It's great to be here this season," Nick returned. "And so nice to see you again, Reverend."

"How long will you stay?"

"Through New Year's at first. But I'll be in and out."

"He's working with Olivia on the Grand Hotel project," Sandy offered from beside them.

"Yes…" Pastor Wilson's warm brown eyes glinted. "I'd heard about that. Marvelous, just marvelous to think of how Christmas Town is coming back."

"I'm happy to be a part of things," Nick said.

Pastor Wilson warmly patted the back of his hand. "And we're delighted to have you here."

Nick was amazed by how quickly the evening flew by. While he'd expected that entire families would sit together, it appeared that the children were happier scampering off to sit in groups with their peers. This left just him, Olivia, Jade, Wendell, Frank, Victoria, Sandy, and Hannah and Amanda and her dad to all get better acquainted. The table was outfitted for eight, but they'd squeezed in a few extra chairs, including one to accommodate Amanda's baby carrier.

Frank Cho was a boisterous man with closely cropped hair and a broad smile. He kept them all in stitches with anecdotes about his encounters with Christmas Town residents while working as the local electrician. His story about first seeing Hannah and Carter together at the Christmas Cookie Shop made

Hannah blush, though she'd laughed at the tale along with the others. Hannah's dad was a nice man, but on the quiet side. He appeared contented just being around his daughter and grandchild, and feeling included in the happenings around him.

Olivia perhaps seemed the happiest of all. She loved being here in Christmas Town, Nick could tell. She was also incredibly fond of her friends, and had found a welcoming place here. Nick was sorry she'd had a bad time in the romance department, but he couldn't believe that someone as great as Olivia wouldn't get a second chance at love someday. Nick swallowed hard when he realized he'd been secretly wondering if that "second chance" might be with him.

He scooted his chair farther away from Sandy's lest she pick up on his internal vibes. His little sister was already nosy enough. Even after she'd gone to man her Christmas tree ball painting station, she kept shooting Nick telling looks as he stayed at the table to visit with Olivia, Wendell, and Hannah and her father. Jade was assisting with the silent auction, while Frank and Victoria oversaw the making of advent wreaths.

At the end of the evening, after Nick and Olivia helped everyone clean up, Nick walked Olivia to the door. "It was really great seeing you tonight," he told her when no one else was around to hear them. "I enjoyed getting to know your friends better, too."

"I'm really glad you came," she said sweetly.

"Do you need a ride home?" he asked, staring out the darkened window at the driving snow.

"Thanks! But Sandy's taking me."

"All right then. I guess I'll see you tomorrow?"

"We're having dinner? Isn't that right?" Her green eyes danced and Nick's heart stuttered.

"I was thinking you might come to Sisters' Row so we can go over my blueprints and sketches? I'd planned to order pizza."

"From the Reindeer Pub?"

"Yes, that's the place."

"Their pizza's the best! I'm definitely in." She shyly ducked her chin. "I'm also excited about seeing your plans."

"I can't wait to have your feedback." Nick also couldn't wait to be alone with her, just the two of them. As they'd been out in the pasture at Sleigh Bell Stables, and also in his SUV at River Run. While he loved being around her in any kind of circumstances, Nick relished her company in private the most.

"What time should I be there?"

"Want to say seven?"

"Seven sounds great," Olivia answered. "That will give me time to get off work at six and take a little breather before coming over."

"Super," Nick said. "See you then!"

As he stepped out the door and into the snow, Nick was surprised to be greeted by Buddy Christmas.

"Buddy!" he said fondly. "How are you?"

"Fine! Fine!"

"Where's Lou?"

Buddy glanced sneakily back at the door. "She's still inside putting things away in the kitchen."

Nick eyed him curiously, wondering what Buddy was up to. Clearly, it was something.

"I just wanted to ask…" Buddy continued brusquely.

The Chos barreled out the door, laughing loudly at something Bobby was chattering about, and Buddy stopped talking. Once they'd walked past and waved goodbye, Buddy stepped closer.

"I wanted to ask if you found the cookies."

"Cookies?" Nick blinked hard. "You mean, the—"

"Virginia Cookies, yes," Buddy whispered hoarsely. "I left them for you and Olivia."

Nick couldn't have been more stunned. "*You* did? But why?"

Buddy dipped his heavy chin then said confidentially, "Because they worked on me and Louise when nothing else would."

"Wait a minute—"

"That was years ago, of course," Buddy barreled ahead. "Lou and I were spring chickens then. And they were Lena's cookies, naturally, not Hannah's. Yet, they did push me over the edge!" He winked knowingly at Nick. "They got me to propose."

Nick swallowed hard. The last person on earth he'd expected to be in on the matchmaking was Buddy Christmas!

"You've got to promise you won't say a word to Louise," Buddy said with a pleading look. "I'm always scolding her for her romantic interference, so I can't have her learning that—now—I've gone and done it, too. I'd never hear the end of it…of that much, I'm sure." His face reddened as he further confessed, "Lou always keeps the rental key on the same hook by our laundry room door. I never would have gone there if I didn't believe this to be some kind of true emergency."

"Emergency?"

Buddy gripped Nick's shoulder through his coat until it pinched. "There's a lot riding on this, Nick. Much more than you know." Buddy squeezed harder. "You're a Claus, son, and you can't forget it."

"Of course, I can't… Won't." Nick carefully surveyed Buddy's ruddy features. He very much resembled Nick's father, even though they were only distant cousins. "Have you been talking to my dad?" Nick asked suspiciously.

Buddy angled toward him and spoke in a rough whisper.

"He phoned before Thanksgiving to talk about your visit here…"

"And?" Nick pressed, needing to know. It wasn't like his father to meddle in his personal business.

"He's worried about you, boy. And, not just about you. About the entire future! About Christmas!"

"I think you can count on Christmas to take care of itself," Nick said a tad more defensively than he intended.

"*No-ho-ho*, you can't," Buddy warned him sternly. "Each of us has to do our part, Nick. Don't go figuring yourself for the exception."

At that exact moment, Lou bustled out the door. "Why, there you are," she said, addressing Buddy. "I've been looking for you everywhere!"

"I'm sorry, dear," Buddy said deferentially. "I just wanted to tell Nick goodbye and thank him for coming."

Lou narrowed her eyes at her husband then gave Nick a slow once over. "Just what has Buddy been saying to you? You look positively petrified!"

"Nothing, dear!" Buddy jumped in merrily. "Just sharing some Christmas cheer."

Lou turned skeptically toward Nick then asked with compassion, "Is that true?"

"*Ho-ho-ho,*" Nick replied, smiling tightly at Buddy. "Absolutely! Merry Christmas, Lou." Then, he hugged her warmly and strode off through the snow. Do his part? What did that mean? Nick felt like the weight of the world had been placed on his shoulders. Plus, his left shoulder still smarted from Buddy's death-grip.

"Don't forget!" Buddy called after him.

As Nick raised his glove in a wave, he heard Lou starting to bicker with her husband. "Buddy Christmas," she admonished solemnly, "what have you done?"

Chapter Sixteen

Olivia was happy to meet her friends the next afternoon for lunch at Santa's Sandwich Shop. They all stayed so busy with their growing families, it was becoming harder and harder to get together for "girl time" these days. While all of them stayed true to their regular ritual of a Monday lunch, they'd unfortunately had to limit their early Saturday morning brunches to much more sporadic gatherings, as their schedules allowed. Now, more often than not, those weekend get-togethers occurred in the evenings and also included the husbands: Wendell, Carter, and Ben, which left Olivia feeling awkwardly like a third wheel. Though the rest of them worked hard to make her feel included, by attempting to limit the couples' and baby talk.

"How's the ankle doing?" Jade asked, as Olivia slid into the booth beside her. Sandy joined them next, waving cheerfully as she sat beside Hannah. "Things were so busy at the bazaar, I totally forgot to ask you!"

"Great! Just great," Olivia replied. "I hardly notice it at all. It's just mildly sore when I come down on it a certain way...like when I'm climbing out of bed. Otherwise, it's fine."

"You and Nick seemed to be getting along pretty well during dinner," Hannah commented happily.

Sandy enthusiastically leaned forward. "And also during dessert..."

"Too bad there weren't any of those Virginia Cookies on hand," Jade said, teasing.

"Nick already has some," Olivia informed her.

Sandy chirped, "He's already eaten two!"

Jade's eyes widened. "Yeah?"

"The Charity and the Clemency kind," Hannah said, glumly. "Apparently he didn't feel a thing."

Olivia fanned herself with her menu. "Nick claims it's because he's magic," she said, chuckling.

"Oh!" Sandy sat up with a start. "He said that, did he?" Hannah and Jade turned to stare at her and she slunk down in her seat. "I mean...er...that's silly, right? Totally absurd."

"Well, I guess if you believe in the magic of a Commitment Cookie," Jade said slyly. "You could believe in the magic of a man..."

The others giggled.

"Yeah, right," Hannah said. "I'd venture to guess that human magic is more powerful, anyway."

"If you're talking chemistry," Sandy quipped. "Then there certainly seems to be some between you and Carter!"

"Between you and Ben, too," Hannah said, grinning.

"Don't leave me out," Jade said play haughtily. "Wendell and I have our wild side."

The others gasped and then giggled. "We just don't flaunt it, that's all."

Suddenly, all eyes were on Olivia. "What? What are you all looking at?"

"There's something going on, isn't there?" Sandy asked sneakily. "Between you and Nick? I could have sworn I sensed it last night. I got a very strong vibe."

"You don't mess with Sandy's vibes," Jade put in. "They're very serious."

"And, accurate," Hannah added. For some reason, she was blushing hard. "So, did you?" she pressed, addressing Olivia. "Did you actually ask Nick out on a date?"

Jade appeared keenly interested, as she was the only one who hadn't been in on this.

"Well, kind of..." Olivia shyly lifted one shoulder. "I did mention horseback riding, and—"

Sandy appeared dismayed. "You didn't?"

"And...uh...cross-country skiing, too!"

Hannah groaned. "Cross-country skiing? Really?"

Olivia blushed hotly. "Nick said he loves them both!"

"Oh!" Sandy blinked like this was a new angle she hadn't considered. "Then, that's good, isn't it?" She nodded encouragingly at the others. "Great!"

"We're also having dinner...tonight," Olivia added with an impish smile.

"Now that's more like it," Jade said, beaming.

"Where?" Hannah asked.

"At Sisters' Row."

"Dining in?" Sandy questioned. "I like that! Is Nick cooking?"

"We're getting pizza and discussing our plans..." Her friends gaped at her. "For the Grand Hotel," she finished, puzzled. "What's wrong with that?"

"Nothing! Nothing at all," Hannah said sweetly. "The important part is that you're going to be together."

"They probably won't get a lick of work done anyway," Jade said, joking.

"Well, I hope you have a wonderful time," Hannah said lightly. "Nick's a really great guy."

"And great guys are hard to find," Sandy followed up quickly.

Jade grinned devilishly and added. "Has she mentioned that he's single?"

Nick flipped over a page on his legal pad, going through his list for the umpteenth time. He'd made his notes and checked them more than twice. What was wrong with him? It wasn't like he was giving a presentation to a large gathering of corporate executives, or something. He was merely sharing his thoughts on the project with Olivia. *Olivia.* That made Nick recall that she was due here within the hour. It was already after six o'clock and soon he'd need to call in the pizza. Nick had learned the Reindeer Pub delivered, and was grateful for the added convenience, especially given all the extra cleaning up he had to do!

Nick scuttled around his rental removing sticky notes. There were several all over the place in his temporary office, but Olivia probably wouldn't come in here since he planned to review ideas with her at the dining room table. He should nab the one off the doorframe, though.

Church bazaar at 5!

If he'd put that up on the bedroom side of the door, he might not have run late.

There were more sticky notes lining the wall in the hall, all relating to people Nick had to call and errands he needed to run. He pulled them off one at a time, stacking them neatly then dashing back to deposit them in a pile on his drafting table.

Nick darted into the bathroom next, yanking another note off the mirror.

Shower, Shave, Beer—

That one had been from Friday night. Nick gave a cursory glance in the front bedroom, spying a pair of his Christmas boxers lying on the floor. He quickly scooped them up and dumped then in a drawer. Not that Olivia was coming upstairs anyway. Still, it never hurt to be careful. Nick rapidly tugged up the covers on his unmade bed and fluffed the pillows, checking his watch. It was almost time to phone the Reindeer Pub. *Hang on!* What if Olivia didn't like the kind of pizza he ordered? Better to check with her first. Then, they could put in their order together. Nick spotted a sticky note glued to the lampshade on the nightstand beside his bed and panicked.

Research Mrs. Claus?

He yanked it off, crumpling the note and shoving it in his jeans pocket, before spotting another note on the closed plantation blinds.

186 Only You at Christmas

8 a.m.

Then, there was the really embarrassing one under his alarm clock.

Olivia, Olivia, Olivia…
Olivia Claus?
Olivia L. Claus?
Nicholas and Olivia Claus?
Mr. and Mrs.—

Nick's face fired red. He couldn't believe he'd woken up in the middle of the night to write that down! What was he? In middle school? Nick shoved that note in his pants pocket with the others, and tore down the stairs, hoping he wouldn't find worse in the kitchen. Nick didn't even recall creating so many notes. His list-making wasn't even conscious a lot of the time. He just did it.

There were only a few stickies in the dining area, and another by the phone in the kitchen. The latter said:

HVAC guy…

Oh yeah, that one was important. Nick needed to confirm with him in the morning, so he'd leave that where it was. There was a grocery shopping list on the fridge. Nick decided that was inoffensive enough, and another sticky on the stove.

Electrician—

Exactly. He needed to call Frank Cho to have him look at the wiring.

The doorbell rang and Nick jumped. A sticky note on the coffeemaker read:

Buy coffee!

He guessed he wouldn't be offering that.

Nick paused to stare at his reflection in the mirror by the front door, deciding he looked panic-stricken. That wasn't exactly the air he wanted to project at the moment. He heaved a deep breath and let it out slowly, then smoothed down his hair which was standing up at crazy angles. He wore a nice sweater over a polo shirt and jeans, and otherwise appeared decently put together. He didn't appear to be sweating visibly, but inside he was broiling. When he opened the door, his skin burned even hotter.

Olivia looked gorgeous standing there in her green parka and holding a bouquet of fresh-cut flowers. Nick had never had a woman bring him flowers before. Ever. "Olivia, hi!" he said, nearly stumbling backwards. Nick wasn't sure why he was nervous. They were just getting together for dinner, and to discuss the Grand Hotel. Never mind that he'd stayed up half the night thinking about her. And when he hadn't been awake and thinking, Nick had been asleep and dreaming.

He kept seeing the two of them together in a wintery sleigh. Olivia wore a gorgeous red velvet cape with a stunning white fur collar, and on her head she wore a tiara while a long red braid was slung forward over one shoulder. In his vision, Nick was extraordinarily pleased and proud to be with her. But, for some reason, all he could utter was *Ho-ho-ho!* When the diamond on her finger glinted in the moonlight, he'd awakened with a jolt and had begun writing weird things down.

"These are for you," she said, handing him the flowers. "I thought they might brighten up the place… Oh, look!" she said, smiling happily at his tree. "You've already decorated!" She walked into the living area, noting the scary snowman on the back of the couch. "Mr. Noodles?" she queried, arching an eyebrow.

Nick set the vase of flowers on the entryway table and crossed to the sofa, pulling the sticky note off the odd fellow's tummy. "I forgot that note was there!" He laughed lamely. "Lou brought him by. She made him, you know."

Olivia chuckled at this and removed her coat. "That was sweet of Lou."

"She also brought more innocuous things, too," Nick said. "Like the Christmas balls and lights for the tree."

"It looks very nice," she said, also observing the candy canes hanging from several boughs. "If you decide you want anything else, I've got plenty of cute things at my shop."

Yeah, but the cutest of all stands right here in this room, Nick couldn't help but think to himself. "Here," he said, remembering his manners. "Let me take your coat."

She passed it to him and he carried it to a hook by the door. When he reached up to hang it, a couple of balled-up pieces of paper spilled out of his jeans pocket. "Oops!"

"Here," Olivia said, rushing forward. "Let me help!" Before Nick could stop her, she'd already swooped down like a bird of prey and had nabbed two crumpled stickies off the floor.

"I'll take those!" Nick jutted out his hand, desperately grabbing for them.

"What are these?" she teased lightly. "State secrets?"

Nick's pulse pounded and the back of his neck felt hot. "Of course not! Just…work notes. Reminders!"

To his horror, she opened one and started to read. Her whole face colored. "What does this mean?" she asked, looking up. "Research Mrs. Claus?"

"It's…uh…" Nick racked his brain. "For the design!"

"Design?"

"A fresco at the Grand Hotel!"

"A fresco? I see."

"In the ballroom," he told her. "I thought it might be whimsical… Fun! To have a fanciful scene on the wall…of Mr. and Mrs. Claus hosting a party at Christmastime?" He paused to catch his breath, then inquired uncertainly, "What do you think?"

"Why, Nick!" Her eyes sparkled merrily. "I think that's a great idea. Sandy could help us with the final design."

"That's just what I was thinking."

"What other excellent ideas have you had?" She started to pry open another balled-up sticky note in her hand, but Nick plucked it out of her grasp.

"Nuh-uh," he said sternly. "No peeking! I can't let you in on all my ideas just yet." He shot Olivia a conspiratorial wink. "Then, what would we have to discuss over dinner?"

She chuckled good-naturedly in return. "I suppose you're right. We wouldn't want to rush things." Olivia smiled, then indicated the flowers she'd brought with a nod of her head. "Do you mind if I add some more water to them in the kitchen?"

"*No-ho-ho*," Nick responded. "Go right ahead." The minute her back was turned, Nick quickly opened up the sticky note he'd just taken from Olivia.

Olivia, Olivia, Olivia…
Olivia Claus?
Olivia L. Claus?
Nicholas and Olivia Claus?
Mr. and Mrs.—

Olivia peered out of the kitchen and Nick crushed the sticky note in his hand. Sweat beaded his hairline.

"Can I get you a glass of water or something?" she offered. "You look a little hot?"

Nick deftly shoved the note in his pocket, way down deep past the side of his cell phone. "Ice water sounds fine! Would you like some, too?"

"Sure," she returned happily. "Then, afterwards, maybe we can open the wine?"

"Of course! I've got some in the cupboard."

"I brought some, too." She smiled at the large handbag she'd deposited on one of the living room chairs. "Maybe you should grab it out of my purse, and we can open it and let it breathe?"

"All right."

Nick turned that way and Olivia popped open the freezer, reaching for an ice tray. Everything was so antiquated here, there wasn't even an icemaker. Just the good old-fashioned plastic trays holding a divided section of cubes. Her fingers were almost to it, when she spotted the colorful Christmas tin shoved to the back of the frigid space. It had a cute drawing on its lid of Santa in his workshop with some elves. There was another one of those curious sticky notes on top. Olivia wondered if Nick had put it there, or if this was the note that he had mentioned as being attached to the Virginia Cookies. She stood up on her tiptoes to read it:

For Nick,
Enjoy some cookies with your milk!

Oddly, there was a little arrow drawn across the bottom of the page, apparently pointing to something on back. Olivia carefully lifted it up with the tip of her finger. Even when reading upside-down, she could pick out her name.

"Find the...ice?"

Olivia sprang back from the fridge, gripping the ice cube tray in her hand. "Yup," she said without giving anything else away. "Found it!"

Nick scrutinized her a beat. "Well, good," he finally offered. "Then let's have a drink!"

"Water?" she asked tentatively.

"Perhaps we should pour some wine, too?"

"I think that's a really fine idea," Olivia said, hiding her blush. She reached into a cabinet for some wine glasses.

"It looks like you know your way around the place," Nick commented from behind her.

"I was over here a lot," she said, her back still turned. "When Hannah lived here."

Olivia spun around to find herself practically in Nick's arms. "I was just, uh…" His temples reddened. "Reaching for the corkscrew by the dish rack, there."

She caught a glimpse of it, handing it to him. Their fingers touched and Nick met her gaze.

"You're an incredibly beautiful woman."

Olivia's breath hitched. "You're not a bad-looking guy."

One half of his mouth turned up in a grin. "Is that a backhanded compliment?"

She blushed heatedly. "No, no. I meant it as a straight-up one."

"Then, I'll take it as you intended."

Olivia's heart hammered and her knees felt weak. She held two wine glasses in her hand. "Shall I…take these into the living room?"

"Yes, we can serve the wine in there."

His blue eyes sparkled and Olivia felt caught up in his swell. Like he was this gigantic wave that had just swept her away. Her words were a breathy whisper. "Thanks for having me over."

"Thanks for saying yes." His voice grew thick. "You must have guessed how much I like you."

When she nodded in response, he continued, "I'm sure hoping you like me, too."

"I do," she said, as her lips trembled. "I do like you, too."

A smile warmed his face. "Then let's go pour some wine and begin our evening." He gently lifted one of the glasses out of her grasp, then took her free hand in his. Olivia's spirit soared and her heart felt light.

"Sounds like a plan," she said, as he led her into the dining area. Nick pulled a chair back from the table and offered her a seat. After she took it, he uncorked the bottle of wine he'd already placed there. Olivia noted a pile of sketches at the far end of the table along with a few sets of blueprints.

"We can order the pizza whenever you'd like," he said, filling her glass. "I can either call it in now, or after we discuss ideas."

Olivia shyly took a sip of wine, watching him above the rim of her glass. He was so cool and sexy. She was sure he was talented, too. Just look at the idea he'd had about the mural! It had been spectacular, and so avant-garde! "Let's tend to business first," she decided. "Then, we can relax."

"Business first," he said, toasting her glass. "That works!"

Chapter Seventeen

Olivia was very impressed with Nick's proposal. He'd sketched out some different ideas for the downstairs and had run some models on a computer program as well, which he showed her on his laptop. He explained the Santa and Mrs. Claus mural for the ballroom had been a last-minute brainstorm, which he'd yet to incorporate in his design.

"I love your ideas for the ballroom," she said, referring to his suggestion that it be left as an open area for hosting town functions. The other large room downstairs could be easily converted to a restaurant, since there were kitchen facilities behind it. Naturally everything would have to be updated. "The restaurant, too!" The wheels in Olivia's mind were turning. "If we added glass French doors leading into the foyer on either side like you propose, those could be opened during larger functions to allow for flow between the dining area and the ballroom space for dancing."

"It would be ideal for a wedding," Nick said, and Olivia blushed.

"Yeah, and other things, too. Perhaps we could hold exhibits in the ballroom from local artisans."

"Great thought!" His eyes twinkled. "That leads me to my ideas for the upstairs." He flipped to another screen on his laptop showing a 3-D image of the upstairs hall. "Each of the old hotel rooms could function as individual galleries. What do you think?"

Olivia pondered this a moment. "Galleries or working studios?"

"Why, either one, I'd think."

"I visited a place like that in Charlottesville, Virginia once," Olivia said. "Several artists in residence had working studios they left open to the public a certain number of days a week."

Nick leaned toward her with interest. "Were the artists juried in?"

"They were grant recipients."

"Hmm, we'd have to investigate how to make that work."

"Maybe the visual arts are too limiting for a town this size," Olivia said. "What if some studios were for painters...others for ceramics..."

"Wood workers?" Nick asked.

"Yes!" Olivia cheered, growing excited.

"How about having a toymaker in one of the studios?"

Olivia laughed with delight. "That would be perfect for Christmas Town."

"Buddy Christmas might have some suggestions in that regard."

Olivia thought of Ben's connection to the nearby university, with which he was collaborating to establish a pro-bono law clinic. "I wonder if the college would be interested in getting involved? I'd be happy to go and talk to someone in their music department, for example.

How cool would it be if we could secure an artisan who handcrafted instruments?"

"Very," Nick answered enthusiastically as she went on.

"Like…I don't know…violins?"

"How about instruments with a bit of local flavor, like fiddles or mandolins?"

"That would be truly amazing!" Olivia replied, feeling energized.

"So, then," Nick surmised, making some notes on a legal pad. "The downstairs would be public and community space, with the two middle floors being filled by working studios of all different kinds."

"The Slades of South Pole Pottery might have some thoughts on this."

"Good point. We should go and talk to them," Nick said, writing this down. He also made a note about toymakers and Buddy Christmas and contacting the university's music department.

"I'd love to see a photographer included, wouldn't you?"

"Dynamite idea, Olivia. Especially if their work covers this part of East Tennessee."

"Maybe we should make that a requirement of the artisans?" Olivia suggested. "That they work with locally sourced materials and keep their products authentic to the region?"

"Yes! Excellent! I like it." A smile lit up his handsome face. "You're pretty good at this."

"Just wait until we get started on interior design," she told him. "That's my forte."

"And also a bit down the road. But when we get there," he said, his dimple deepening, "I know you'll do a superb job.

"I can take everything we've talked about and work up a formal proposal to submit to the Town Council," he told her. "What about the basement?"

"Couldn't that be used for storage? We'd probably need to keep a selection of extra tables and chairs on hand to use for certain events in the ballroom."

"And the attic apartment?" Nick asked. "Any ideas there?"

Olivia thought hard a moment. "We've been talking about the arts, but one element we've neglected is theater," she said, thinking specifically of Savannah and her love for the stage.

"Do you believe Christmas Town is large enough to support a community theater?" Nick asked, sounding surprised.

Olivia shook her head. "I don't honestly know. Perhaps that is too ambitious."

"What about a children's theater? The town seems to be experiencing a baby boom, and there are already trailers at the elementary school. Walt told me that when he was talking about how much Christmas Town had grown in just the past two years."

"A children's theater?" Olivia repeated, thinking this over. "That's really innovative, Nick. And something that very well might fly in Christmas Town."

"You'd need a coordinator to run it, of course," Nick continued. "But if local children were in the productions, then perhaps the parents could get involved to help with things like sets and costumes?"

"The theater wouldn't be very big."

"The upstairs apartment consumes the entire fourth floor," Nick answered. "We wouldn't have to install permanent seating, so the space would be more flexible. Maybe other groups could use the area for small performances, like music recitals?"

Olivia's thoughts were still focused on the kids. "Or puppet shows? Wouldn't that be fun?"

"There could be lots of uses for that space," Nick agreed. "Managing it might be a full-time job. A pretty fun one for someone into theater and the arts."

"Yes," Olivia agreed, thinking once again about Savannah. "My sister double-majored in theater in college. She might be able to give us some ideas."

"Does she live in Christmas Town?"

"No, Miami. But, Carter and I have been wanting her to come visit."

"There's no rush on the fourth floor," Nick assured her. "We'll have enough to do with the downstairs and middle floors. A project this large will need to be done in stages."

"When do you suppose it could all be completed?"

"It depends on how soon the Town Council gets behind it and how much more money they raise." Nick rubbed his chin. "But I'm thinking, optimistically, by this time next year."

Olivia beamed with joy. "We could have a grand opening at Christmas!"

"Now, that would be fitting."

"With a Christmas Town Ball and everything! People could dress up, and drink champagne, and dance!" Olivia sighed dreamily, gazing at Nick. "Wouldn't that be *grand*?"

He grinned warmly. "That sounds like a party I wouldn't want to miss."

Nick was stunned to see on the mantel clock that it was already past nine. He and Olivia had been having so much fun with their planning, the time had escaped them. They'd also nearly finished their bottle of wine. "Oh, wow," he said, pulling his phone from his jeans pocket. "We'd better call in that pizza."

"Nine-fifteen!" Olivia proclaimed, astounded. "Where did the last few hours go?"

Nick motioned to the table cluttered with their notes and some additional rough sketches he'd drawn as they'd been talking. "Not to waste, that's for sure," he said with a chuckle. Then he quickly covered the mouthpiece on his cell and whispered, "What would you like on your pizza?"

"I like it all," Olivia said with a grin.

Nick nodded and ordered them a large everything pizza, thinking Olivia must be starved. "They said it will be about forty minutes," he said when he ended his call. "Would you like some cheese and crackers in the meantime?"

"I'm all right," she said lightly. "I can wait." She glanced down at the floor beneath his chair. "Looks like something fell out of your pocket when you pulled out your phone."

Nick stared down at the crumpled yellow sticky note and his heart raced. "Oops!" He grabbed for it, but Olivia reached it first. She scooped it up quickly, shooting him a saucy look.

"What other great ideas have you been hiding?"

"Olivia, don't—!"

But before he could stop her, she'd smoothed the top part of it out on the table.

"Olivia?" She laughed. "That's me!" Then she finished opening the note and her cheeks burned bright red. "Claus?" she asked weakly. "Olivia L. Claus? Mr. and Mrs. Nicholas—?"

Nick slapped his palm down on the table, covering his horrifically embarrassing exercise. "Olivia, I…" he stammered, breaking out in a sweat.

Her eyebrows arched quizzically.

"What I mean is… You see… The truth is…"

"Yes?"

"I…sometimes make lists."

She peered down at his splayed fingers. "And, check them twice?"

"Oh, yes! At least. Generally, two times. Uh-huh. At a minimum." Nick face-palmed with his free hand. The other one was still glued to the table.

"Nick," she said, gently. "It's all right."

He dropped his hand and stared at her. "You probably think I'm nuts. Immature. Hopeless."

She studied him a long moment and there was tenderness in her eyes. "Actually, I don't find you any of those things. I think you're smart, and talented, and funny… And, well, all right, a little absent-minded in the sticky note department. I'm sure you didn't even remember that note was in your pocket when you pulled out your phone."

Nick laughed with relief. "You've got me there."

Her smile gleamed in return. "So you have a crush on me, huh?"

Nick's ears burned hot. "I suppose, if it wasn't obvious before, the cat's out of the bag now."

"Well, it's nothing to be embarrassed about," she told him casually. Then she added in a sultry whisper, "Sometimes crushes work both ways."

Nick's heart skipped a beat.

"There," she said resolutely. "Now you know my secret, too."

She stared at him a long while and he became lost in her lovely green gaze. After a beat, her eyebrow arched. "Well, Mr. Claus?" she asked sassily, pushing back her chair. "Aren't you going to do anything about it?"

"I...uh...sure!" Nick pulled himself together and got to his feet. Then he took Olivia by her hands and tugged her up to meet him. In an instant she was in his arms, all soft, womanly, and warm, and wrapping her arms around his neck.

She looked up at him with daring in her eyes. "Can you really make magic?"

When he nodded, she closed her eyes and said, "Show me."

Olivia's lips were luscious and inviting, her beautiful red hair spilling past her shoulders, as her chin tilted up toward his.

Nick lowered his mouth to hers and sleigh bells rang, jangling loudly. "Wait!" he said, pulling back. "Did you hear that?"

"Um-hmm," Olivia said, hanging on tighter. She stood up on her tiptoes and gently kissed his lips. Fire raged through him while icy prickles danced down his spine. Nick's fingertips were tingling and so were his toes, as well as everything else in between. "I hear music," she said, kissing him again, and this time he kissed her back fully.

A thousand fireworks exploded in Nick's veins…their staccato crackling and popping only overshadowed by the *boom-boom, boom-boom, boom-boom*ing of his heart. Nick felt like he was falling and spinning… Next, a torrent of wind lifted him up, and he was rocketing through space, carrying Olivia along with him beneath a broad canopy of stars.

"Oh!" she whimpered in his embrace. "Oh, Nick."

"It's okay," he said, holding her closer. "I've got ya."

Then he ran his fingers through her hair and showed her how a real Claus could kiss.

The doorbell rang and Nick pulled back, warmly stroking Olivia's cheek. "That must be our pizza," he said, and she nearly fainted. Her head was light and her legs felt like limp pasta. She didn't know where Nick had taken her, but she wanted to go there again. Olivia had never had a man kiss her like that. In her life! She'd felt hypnotized, glorified…exhilarated…free…and so, so *hot* and sexy…and wow! Nick tried to step away but she grabbed for his arm, not trusting her own legs to hold her. She tried to speak but there were no words. Olivia was pretty sure she was panting, though. Very heavily.

Nick worriedly surveyed her face, as the doorbell chimed again. "Here," he said kindly. "Let me help you to the sofa." As he led her that way, Olivia had the phantom sensation that she was floating, or that she'd been *flying* or something. The whole room was spinning around her. *Whoa.*

As Nick eased her down on a sofa cushion, Olivia found her voice. "I...feel like I just got off of a rollercoaster."

"I'm sorry about that." Nick viewed her apologetically. "I didn't mean to come on so strong."

"No, no," she said, still catching her breath. Her hands gripped the sofa cushion. "You came on just right." *Boy, did he ever! Boy-oh-boy-oh-boy! Ted? Who's Ted? Ted was a lame excuse for a guy, but that Nick Claus... Now he's a real man. Weeee!*

As Nick answered the door, Olivia eyed the seat of his jeans, thinking he filled them out perfectly. His shoulders were broad and buff, and his back extremely muscled beneath that sweater. When he'd held her against him, the front of him had been pretty darn firm and sexy, too. Olivia had the weird sensation that she was levitating off of the sofa and clenched the sofa cushion harder in her hands.

Nick paid the pizza delivery person and turned back to her. "You look like you need a glass of water," he said. "I'll get it!" He left the pizza box by the door and brought Olivia her water glass from the table. She drained it all in one long swallow.

Nick's brow crinkled in concern. "Better?"

Olivia nodded unsurely, noticing that the hand holding her water glass was trembling. Nick carefully took it away from her and set it on the coffee table. Then, he sat down beside her. Olivia's heart was still beating fast, but it was finally starting to reestablish its regular rhythm.

"Yeah," she said, still gasping for air. "Think so."

Nick tenderly took her hand. "For the record, you took my breath away, too."

She studied his gorgeous profile and rugged frame. "Was that...*normal* for you?"

"Normal?"

"What I mean is, does that happen with all women?"

"Nope." His fingers tightened around hers. "It's only happened with you."

They both stared straight ahead for a long while.

Finally, Nick said, "There's nothing wrong with a new normal, though." He grinned and that dimple settled in his cheek. "If we work at it, we could probably get used to it."

"Sure, sure!" Olivia agreed, her cheeks steaming. "As long as we take it slow."

"My thinking, exactly."

He released her hand and brought his arm around her, snuggling her up against him on the sofa. "You're a pretty excellent first date," he said, kissing the top of her head.

She smiled up at him, about ninety-five percent recovered. "Yeah, you too."

He lightly squeezed her shoulder. "Ready for that pizza yet?"

"I'm still not sure I can stand," she said with an amazed laugh.

"Then how about I bring some to you?"

A little while later, Nick and Olivia said goodnight by his front door. He'd tried to insist on walking her home, but she'd refused, saying she lived so close by she could make it on her own. At last, they'd compromised on Nick watching her from the front porch of Sisters' Row until she'd safely reached her shop.

"Thanks for a great night." Her cheeks held a rosy glow. "Your plans look great, and the pizza was delicious.

"I had a great time, too." He took her in his arms but she gently pressed back on his shoulders.

"Nick," she said shyly. "I don't think we'd better. I need to be able to make it home."

"I know." He leaned forward and gave her a firm peck on the lips. "There! How was that?"

Olivia's eyes glimmered in understanding. "Pretty perfect."

"I'll work on revising my plans this week. Then we should probably go over things again, before talking to the Town Council."

"Yes, I agree."

"How about Friday?"

"Another working dinner?" she teased.

"Somehow I don't imagine working with you is going to be a chore." He dipped his chin toward hers again, and Olivia brought a finger to his lips.

"Let's wait until next time." The way she said it made Nick's pulse pound and his heart soar.

"Next time, it is," he said, his voice husky.

"Do you want to come to my place?"

"Why don't you let me arrange something?"

"There's only one other restaurant in town open on Friday evening."

"Is that a fact?" he asked with a mysterious grin.

Chapter Eighteen

Olivia was dying to talk to Savannah, but with all of her sister's play rehearsals, they hadn't been able to catch up until Thursday. *Oklahoma*'s opening night was tomorrow, so the cast and crew had been given tonight off. They were in for a busy weekend ahead, including two performances on Saturday and a Sunday matinee.

"I hate to admit it when my little sister is right," Olivia told Savannah when she answered. "But you were right."

Savannah gasped with glee. "You went out on a date?"

"Sort of," Olivia replied dreamily. "Yeah."

"What's a 'sort of' date?"

"Nick and I have been out twice," Olivia reported breezily. "Three times if you count the visit to the stables. No! *Four*, if you include the church bazaar, but we kind of only saw each other there."

Savannah squealed with delight. "I want to hear every sordid detail."

"None of the details are sordid, Savannah. Nick's a very nice guy."

"Oh." She almost sounded disappointed. "In any case," Savannah continued, her tone brightening. "Nice is good! Better than naughty, I suppose. Although, naughty can be fun too, Olivia," she teased with a giggle. "Maybe sometime you should try it!"

"Who says that I haven't?" Olivia returned saucily. Savannah spoke in low tones. "*Do* tell."

"I don't kiss and tell, thank you very much."

"You *kissed* him? Woot! Olivia," she continued, evidently pleased. "I'm so proud of you."

"Yeah, well. I'm proud of me, too. I'm also glad that he kissed me back. Otherwise, that might have been... You know..." Olivia shrugged. "*Awkward*."

"And...?" Savannah pressed nosily. "How was it?"

Olivia sighed, reflecting on that gloriously long moment. "Magical."

"Cool!" She hedged before prying gently, "No thoughts of—?"

"Ted? Not a one! Other than the fact that he doesn't hold a candle to Nick. I mean it. Ted is like this teeny weeny flickering match, and Nick is like...this great big flaming torch!"

"Whoa."

"Hot! Sexy! Sooooo good-looking. And that dimple! Oh my goodness, don't even get me started!"

"Wow."

"I know, right? It's so crazy that he already wants to marry me!"

"*What?*" Savannah's shrill cry echoed down the line. "Slow down, sis. I think we've got a bad connection."

"It's not bad, it's the truth! I caught him red-handed, that sneaky man. Did I mention Nick likes to write lists? Lots and lots of lists! He's nothing if not organized!"

"No, um…you didn't."

"And that he likes cookies?"

"Cookies?"

"Oops! There's my kitchen timer! Hang on a sec." Olivia set her phone on the kitchen island and slid on her oven mitts, removing one piping hot tray from the oven rack and dropping another one in its place. Cooling racks lined the countertops and they were all brimming over. She'd made *dozens and dozens* since Tuesday! She'd gone back to the Merry Market twice because she kept running out of supplies. When she returned to the phone Savannah asked her what kind she was baking. Olivia glanced appraisingly around her kitchen.

"Oatmeal scotchies, chocolate chip, peanut butter, jam thumbprints, shortbread, gingersnaps, and sugar cookies with icing!"

"Don't tell me you made all those today?"

"No. I got started a few days ago. There might be other kinds in my freezer that I've forgotten… I can go and check."

"Olivia!" Savannah shouted, stopping her. "What in heaven's name are you doing?"

"Baking cookies," Olivia stated like it was the most natural thing in the world, because at present it seemed like it was.

"But, why so many?"

"Because I felt like it."

"You're not going to a…cookie exchange, or something?" Savannah asked hopefully.

"Nope! No exchange!" Olivia laughed giddily. "Then I might not have enough for Nick."

"Seriously?"

"He totally loves them. I can't wait to show him all the kinds I've made!"

"Uh…maybe you shouldn't?"

"Shouldn't? Why not?"

Savannah was clearly trying to put this gently. "Aren't you worried he'll think it's a little strange? That you've made such a variety and…er…*abundance* in such a short time?"

The notion hadn't even occurred to her. On the contrary, she had the feeling that Nick would be extraordinarily pleased. "Nope."

"So, when was the last time you saw him?"

That was a tricky question. Olivia had *seen* Nick every morning this week. The only thing was, she hadn't actually talked to him. Nick apparently had this really fun little routine where he went to pick up coffee at Jolly Bean Java before starting his work day. He was generally there around eight. Sometimes a little after. Often, before. And every single time, Olivia had been able to sense him, she thought with a giggle. He'd sensed her, too. Without fail, he'd looked up at her window with a bright smile and waved. Even from across the street she could see that dimple!

And then, there were the animals that appeared to follow Nick down the street. Dogs tugged at their owners' leases and cats meandered after him. Birds alighted from lampposts and squirrels scurried down trees… It was the wildest thing Olivia had ever seen, and it happened day after day! Just this morning she would have sworn she'd seen Nick conversing with a robin that had perched on his shoulder.

"Olivia?" Savannah's voice rose with alarm. "Olivia, are you still there?"

"Oh! Um. Yep! Here I am!"

"I was worried that you'd fainted or something."

"Almost did—when Nick kissed me." She giggled with delight. "My head was so light! Lighter than air! Almost dizzy!"

"You guys weren't doing anything weird? Nothing illegal?"

"Drugs?" Olivia asked, terribly affronted. "Savannah! Get ahold of yourself! You know me better than that."

"Thought so. Only…"

"Only, what?"

"I've just never known you to be like this. So…"

"Happy? Yes, I am!" Olivia felt a grin warm her face. "Isn't it awesome? Who knew baking cookies could be so much fun?" She paused to reflect. "Oh yeah, wait a minute… Maybe Hannah."

Savannah gasped. "It was those Virginia Cookies, wasn't it? You got into them somehow!"

"Did *not*."

"Then, maybe it was Nick? You said he has a sweet tooth."

"Yes, that's true, but I'm afraid you've got it wrong. Magic doesn't work on magic. That's double-dipping!"

"Who told you that?"

"Nick!"

"I'm getting a little worried about this guy," Savannah started in a cautionary tone. "Maybe I shouldn't have pushed you to—"

"You didn't. I would have done it, anyway!"

"Oh yeah?"

"Of course! The moment he brought me those chocolates, I knew he was the guy for me."

"Which chocolates?"

"Dark-chocolate-cherry truffles from Nutcracker Sweets."

"Those sound delicious."

"They are." Olivia lowered her voice confidentially. "Do you want to know a secret?"

Savannah hedged uncharacteristically. "I...uh...I'm not sure."

Olivia shared her confession anyway. "I think Nick can tell when I've been naughty and nice," she said in a whisper.

"Oh...my...word.

"That's not all! He can talk to animals!"

"You know what," Savannah said calmly. "I think you've been putting too much pressure on yourself."

"Pressure?"

"Taking too much on. You've got your shop, the program at the stables, the community gardens, and now this Grand Hotel thing. All of that on top of your horrible break-up with Ted. Anyone can see that would be too much, even for the strongest person."

Olivia gaped at her cell. "Just what are you suggesting?"

"Remember when we discussed you seeing someone?"

"First off, *we* didn't discuss that, Savannah," Olivia said curtly. "*You* did. Secondly, I said I wasn't interested in going to counseling. I didn't require it then, and I'm in even less need of it now."

"How do you figure that?"

"Everything's so much better. I feel so happy! And hopeful and alive!"

"I see."

Olivia wrinkled up her nose, thinking she detected a charred odor. "Uh-oh! I also think I'm burning my cookies! I forgot to reset the timer! *Yikes!*" Her gaze darted toward the oven and the black smoke pouring from it, as the smoke alarm blared. "Sorry, Savannah! Gotta go!"

"Wait!" Savannah yelped.

Olivia dropped her phone on the counter, nabbed an oven mitt, and yanked the scorched tray of cookies out of the oven, slamming it down on the stovetop.

She picked her phone back up, breathing hard. "What? What is it?" Olivia asked, waving a dishtowel in the air below the blaring smoke alarm.

"Carter!" Savannah shouted. "Does he know?"

"Know what?"

"All that stuff—about Nick!"

"No… No, I haven't said anything to him."

"Good." Olivia huffed and shook her head as Savannah finished. "Take a sisterly word of advice: *don't.*"

Olivia testily ended her call then cracked open a window to let in some fresh air. Seriously, she would have expected Savannah to be happy for her! Not all up in her face about seeing a counselor. *Really.* Her sister had gotten her so annoyed, Olivia had totally forgotten to mention the children's theater idea for the Grand Hotel. Well, maybe that was a good thing. Who needed Savannah's opinion, if all she intended to do was rain on Olivia's parade! Olivia was having a great time in Christmas Town, and for the first time in her life she was enjoying the attentions of an unbelievably hot, smart, and sexy man. That was something to celebrate, and not have to become defensive about. *Gosh.*

Olivia stared around her kitchen at the mountains of cookies that were stacked everywhere. She was going to need to buy more cookie tins in order to put all these away, and Olivia knew just where to find them, too. In the kitchen section of Sugar Plum Feed Supply.

Sugar Plum Feed Supply was essentially an enormous hardware store situated in an old warehouse building. They didn't have much in the way of kitchen supplies. Only some basics like cast-iron skillets and ceramic Dutch ovens. They did sell oven mitts, though, and a cute selection of aprons. Those were in the barbecue section, which also contained assorted outdoor grills, fire pits, and Tiki torches. The torches made Olivia think of her comment to Savannah about Nick, and her face flamed hot.

Now, where were those silly Christmas tins? Aha! Olivia spied a special holiday display bordering on the pet area. A nice arrangement of Christmas cookie tins was shelved there. She approached the area then began to hand-select a pretty array of designs. No two of them should be the same if she could help it. Variety was the spice of life! She sure hoped that Nick would think so, too, and that he'd enjoy the many kinds of cookies she'd baked him.

Olivia held a stack of five tins in an arm, with the top one tucked under her chin, and was just about to examine another when a familiar voice sounded over her shoulder.

"Fancy meeting you here."

"Carter!"

Olivia spun in alarm, dropping all five cookie tins at once. They collided with the cement floor in a cacophony of sound, their loud dings and clanks echoing up to the rafters. Olivia gasped and began to chase the one that was rolling away!

Carter eyed her curiously and bent down to help her, popping a few of the lids that had bounced off back onto their tins. He passed her three tins as she held the others numbly in her hands. "Baking…?" His eyebrows rose. "Cookies?"

He was out of uniform so this was clearly his night off.

"Um…yes! That's right!" Olivia said, straightening. "Baking! Cookies!"

"Quite a lot of them?"

"Quite a lot of them, uh-huh!"

"Christmas cookies?"

"Christmas cookies, yep!"

He scrutinized her. "Olivia."

"Huh?"

"Why are you repeating everything that I'm saying?"

"Everything that you're saying!"

Carter narrowed his eyes and Olivia gulped. "What are you doing out and about?" she asked hoarsely, deflecting his question.

He thumbed over his shoulder. "Hannah sent me on a little errand. I'm picking up some Santa treats for Jingles and Belle."

"They still get stockings? How sweet!"

Carter beamed proudly. "This year, we'll have one for Amanda, too."

"Of course!"

He curiously viewed her stack of tins. "What kinds of cookies are you making?"

"All! All kinds!"

"Wow."

"Yeah, I know. That's why I ran out...of tins."

"I'll have to tell Hannah you're into it. Is this a new hobby?"

"Kind of!"

"Well, that's cool, I guess."

Olivia smiled tightly.

"How's Nick?"

"Nick?" she said like it was a new word.

"We enjoyed having you guys over to the house the other evening."

"Oh yeah! That was great. Thanks again!"

"No doubt you've seen him since?"

"*Seen* him?"

"Hannah said that he was at the bazaar?"

"Oh right! There!"

"She also might have mentioned that you were getting together for work purposes." He leaned toward her. "After hours."

"Well, ha-ha! That's only natural. Since I have a full-time job, and—"

"Olivia," he said in a brotherly way. "Careful there."

"Carter Livingston," she said, disbelievingly. "I'm two years older than you. I don't think I need your protection."

"Maybe not, but I still don't want to see my big sister getting hurt."

"Nick's not a hurting kind of guy," she said a tad too defensively.

He viewed her worriedly. "It's gone that far already?"

Olivia blinked. "But I...I didn't say a thing!"

"You didn't have to," he told her. "It's written all over your face."

The cookie tins slipped in her grasp and she clutched them harder.

"This didn't by any chance involve those Virginia—?"

"No!"

"Because I told Nick—"

"*What* did you tell Nick?" Olivia stared at him agape. "Carter Livingston...?" she warned in scolding tones.

The look she gave him must have been formidable, because after a while, he said, "Nothing."

"If you went inserting yourself in my business again, I'll...I'll..." Olivia stomped her foot, nearly dropping the tins for a second time. "Scream!"

"Please, don't do that." He stared at her pleadingly, then glanced around. "Not here."

"You're just like Savannah," she said heatedly. "Thinking you can run my life."

"Savannah? What did she say?"

"I hardly think it matters."

"In that case, it must matter a lot."

Olivia huffed. "Don't you have some catnip to buy?"

"Sure, sure." Carter held up both hands. "No problem."

Before he turned to go, Carter said, "Olivia?"

"What?" she snapped.

He shot her a lopsided grin. "You know that I love you."

"Yeah, yeah." Olivia let out a breath, thinking that families were complicated. "I love you, too. Just don't go telling me who to date, all right?"

"Got it," he said with a wink. As he walked away, he said jauntily, "I can't wait to tell Hannah that you and Nick are official."

"*Official?* No, we're not!"

That's all Olivia needed, for a rumor like that to start flying around.

"Getting there?" Carter asked craftily.

"Arghh!" Olivia cried, groaning at the ceiling.

Then she hauled her purchases to the checkout counter and went home to more happy pursuits. Like putting her cookies away and dreaming of Nick.

Chapter Nineteen

Nick was pleased with how the week had gone. Despite its age, the Grand Hotel had passed muster and the various building inspectors had declared it fit for restoration. Most of the heavy lifting would need to be done on the main floor, where the former lobby and ballroom were located. The middle two floors would require minimal upgrades to allow the former hotel rooms to function as studios, and the bathrooms on each of those floors would need to be modernized. The building would further have to be made handicap-accessible by the installation of a ramp, perhaps by the side door leading into the planned restaurant area. The redesign of the old apartment on the fourth floor would take additional work. And, a small elevator would need to be installed somewhere to allow access to the upper floors. Nick thought the space currently housing the dumbwaiter could be enlarged and converted in that regard, but he'd need an expert to look at it.

Depending on how the Town Council decided to use the apartment area, this could tack a few extra months onto the completion date of the project. But Nick was confident he could get the bulk of the restoration completed by this time next year, and he loved Olivia's idea about having a Christmas Town Ball to celebrate the building's formal reopening. Most of the exterior work was cosmetic, but the building would need a new roof, leaf-protected gutters, and downspouts. Nick also wanted to recommend that a landscape architect be brought in to oversee the outdoor touches, like new plantings that might appropriately frame this grand old lady in restoring her to her original elegance. Since Olivia was good with gardening, perhaps she could help with some oversight in that area, too.

Nick stood on the sidewalk across the street, admiring the Grand Hotel's structure from his vantage point by the Snow Globe Gallery. The building had good bones; it just required some important upgrades. Nick was excited about presenting the ideas he and Olivia had discussed to the Town Council, and hoped to do this soon, so he could move things along. There was no sense in going into detailed designs until he had the Town Council's approval. Though Olivia had assured him its members were bound to be as excited about his and Olivia's prospective plans for the space as they were.

Olivia was the perfect business partner in this regard. Nick had never enjoyed working with anyone more. And, when Olivia grew excited, her green eyes sparkled in a way that made his pulse race and his heart feel light. Nick loved seeing Olivia happy, which was one reason he'd worked so hard on the surprise he'd planned for her tonight.

"I thought that might have been you!" Nick turned to find Sandy peering out her gallery's door.

"Hey, sis," he said buoyantly. "Happy Friday afternoon!"

"Want to come in for some cider?"

A sharp wind blew, nipping at his chin and nose, and Nick decided that sounded like a fine idea. Snowflakes gently fell around him as he ambled toward the gallery door. Sandy held it open for him then shut it with a shiver.

"Brrr! Getting colder out there!"

"You're blood's getting thinner," he teased her. "You used to be able to handle all sorts of cold back in Maine."

"That's what I get for moving south, I suppose."

Nick chortled. "It hasn't felt like the south here much."

"Not since you've been here, no. But things do warm up in summer." Sandy lifted a carafe from a counter near her register that held an artsy selection of Christmas mugs. Nick noticed that one of the mugs was filled with candy canes. She caught him eyeing them and offered, "Would you like one with your cider?"

"No, thanks. I'm cutting back on peppermint these days."

Sandy filled two mugs with steaming hot liquid that smelled of apples, cloves, and cinnamon, and handed one to him. "Oh, really?" she asked with a grin. "This couldn't have to do with Olivia, could it?"

"It might," Nick replied, unable to repress a smile.

"I haven't seen you around much this week."

"I've been busy." Nick glanced around the nicely arranged gallery, observing Sandy's stunning paintings on the wall. All were Christmas scenes, including one of a couple in a horse-drawn sleigh, embracing under a blanket and sharing a heart-shaped cookie. "Apparently, so have you! You've done all these since moving to Christmas Town?" he asked, impressed.

"I've actually painted more. I've sold several already and can barely keep up with the demand. But that one you're looking at is special. I'll never let it go to strangers."

Nick stepped closer to examine its title on a small brass plate: *Winter Wedding*.

"It features Lena Winchester's Virginia Cookies," Sandy explained. "The original ones from back in the day. Hannah was quite taken with it when she first saw it. I figure if I ever give it to anyone someday, it will be to her."

"You two are very close, aren't you?"

"Like sisters."

"It's good you have each other then, right here in town."

"I wouldn't mind having my brother—right here in town—either," she said leadingly.

"Well now, Sandy…"

"Come on, Nick! Don't tell me that you haven't thought about it? Imagine what fun it would be to live in Christmas Town."

"I haven't had time to think that far ahead."

"Says the man who can't stop making lists."

"What's that supposed to mean?"

"You always plan things out, Nick," Sandy told him stubbornly. "Sometimes way in advance."

"Yes, well." Nick awkwardly cleared his throat, thinking of the Mrs. Claus note Olivia had found. "Maybe this time I'm more focused on the present."

Nick strode to the gallery window facing North Main Street. It held Sandy's whimsical snow globe showcasing a small red barn and a farmhouse surrounded by a tiny stand of pines and a herd of miniature reindeer. Smoke curled from the farmhouse chimney and a slender red-and-white-striped pole turned slowly in the snow-covered yard, casting out glimmering bits of light that collided with the falling snowflakes making them each glisten like twinkling stars.

"Glad you found a good place for that."

"It's the gallery's best feature."

"Wrong," he said sweetly. "The gallery's best feature is its artist in residence."

"You're such a great big brother," Sandy said appreciatively, before adding wistfully, "I just wish you didn't live so far away."

"Yeah, I know." He beheld her sweet face, thinking that Sandy appeared happier than he'd ever seen her. Almost glowing. "You really like it here, don't you?"

"In Christmas Town? I *love* it, Nick. 'Like' is too mild a word."

He chuckled at this. "I can see why. It's a very nice place."

"With lots of nice people, too."

"I can sense that."

Even though they were the only ones in the place, Sandy lowered her voice in a mischievous whisper. "Not too many naughty ones around, eh?"

"Not too many, no," he agreed, smiling. "And, none of the transgressions are terrible ones… Which reminds me," he said suddenly. "About Holly?"

Sandy's brow crinkled in concern. "What about her?"

"She didn't break that snow globe on purpose."

"What?"

"Last Friday when we were at Hannah and Carter's for dinner—?"

"Now Nick, it's kind of you to care, but Holly is a little imp. She sometimes—"

"Not that time," he told her surely. "She wasn't destroying Rose's snow globe out of envy, if that's what you're thinking. Holly was actually trying to help."

"Help?" Sandy asked, perplexed. "How?"

"Little Rose wanted to see the snowflakes in hers, so Holly was trying to bring it closer. The trouble is, Holly's telekinetic skills are just developing, so unfortunately she dropped it. Quite by accident, I assure you. Holly cried over the episode as much as Rose did."

Sandy gasped in surprise. "You mean, Holly was trying to do a good deed?" A tear glistened in the corner of her eye. "That little stinker! And there Ben and I thought this was the start of some kind of sibling rivalry thing. That she'd smashed Rose's snow globe on purpose."

"Clauses can only use their abilities for the good," Nick reminded her. "And Holly has half your genes."

Sandy cupped her hand to her mouth. "Of course, you're right. I don't know why Ben and I got so worried."

"New parents worry about all sorts of things."

"Ben's not so new at it. Lily's nine now."

"Yes, but the twins present a brand new set of challenges, I'm sure."

Sandy thoughtfully twisted her lips. "That's true." She impulsively set down her mug to give Nick a hug. "Thank you for that. You made me feel better."

Nick affectionately patted her back. "You're a wonderful mom. Don't ever doubt that."

"I won't..." She grinned before adding, "Ever again!" She viewed his zipped up field coat. "You must be warm in that. Do you want me to hang it up?"

"No, thanks," he said, finishing his cider. "I really can't stay. I have some errands to run this afternoon."

"Work errands?" she asked, looking concerned. "But it's nearly six o'clock?"

"I never said they were work errands," Nick answered slyly.

"Ooohhh..." Sandy said in knowing tones. "Olivia errands."

Nick grinned mysteriously. "They might have something to do with her."

"I never heard how your evening was on Monday? Olivia said you had a working dinner?" Her eyebrows arched expectantly. "Did you get a lot done?"

"Yep."

Sandy folded her arms with a laugh. "I'll bet."

"I'll see you later, sis," he said, giving the top of her head a kiss. "Thanks for the cider!"

"Glad it's going well!" she called as he went out the door.

Chapter Twenty

Olivia skipped down the stairs as Nick approached All Things Christmas. She was super excited about their date and couldn't wait to give him his cookies! Made with all natural ingredients and everything! Since they'd had pizza on Monday, Olivia assumed they were going to the Peppermint Bark since it was the only other game in town. Santa's Sandwich Shop was just a lunch place and Jolly Bean Java closed at six, like most stores here.

She'd dressed in a calf-length tan suede skirt, brown leather boots, and a pretty cocoa-colored V-neck sweater over a cream silk blouse. She'd worn her hair long and had a section pulled back on one side with one of those new Virginia Cookie barrettes Liz had designed. The fake-gingerbread heart matched her outfit's muted color scheme. The cookie's frothy pink border and the dainty red lettering saying *Forever Yours* added pops of color!

Olivia had started to wear a Charity Cookie barrette—which actually matched better—but she'd run down to her shop at the last minute and switched them out. The new Commitment Cookie barrette made Olivia feel emboldened! Sexy! *Oops!* She nearly tripped over her feet, scurrying down the steps. Olivia raced through her darkened shop feeling like she was sprouting wings. Just the knowledge that Nick was nearby made her want to fly. *Yippee!* She raced to the door and threw it open wide, only to be greeted by a blast of snow.

When the frigid haze cleared, she saw Nick standing there looking as handsome as ever in his field coat and dark chinos. He held an umbrella in one hand and a white envelope in the other. "Good evening," he said, his blue eyes sparkling.

"Hi," Olivia said giddily, fully taking him in. He was even more handsome than she remembered. *Yay!* During one fit of cookie-baking Olivia had experienced the tiniest burst of doubt. *No one* was *that cute*, and *that sexy* and *that tall* and *that built*… Oh, yeah they were! And his name was Nick Claus! *Weee!*

"Uh…" Nick shifted on his feet and Olivia noticed he was wearing very nice loafers, not his usual work boots. "Mind if I come in?" She'd almost forgotten that rugged face and that insanely gorgeous dimple.

"Yeah, sure!" Olivia stepped aside and he collapsed his umbrella, handing her the envelope. Olivia shut the door, then met his eyes. *Zing!* Wow, that felt terrific!

A warm grin graced his face. "You look dynamite, Olivia. Very pretty."

"Oh, thanks!" She was still tingling a little bit from that *zing* thing. Olivia wasn't quite sure what had happened. But she'd liked it. Liked it a lot. It was like they had electricity or something. She glanced down at the envelope he'd given her, wildly curious. Maybe it was a gift certificate of some kind? Or a letter? No, a list! Another one of Nick's crazy lists. Olivia blushed hotly recalling his "Olivia Claus" yellow sticky.

"Go on, open it," Nick urged gently.

She did and saw it was on letterhead from Sleigh Bell Stables. *Wait a minute.* Olivia recognized this form. It was a standard consent form for riding lessons along with registration paperwork. Lily Winchester's name was on it! And, Ben and Sandy had added their signatures to the bottom. Olivia's eyes felt hot as she blinked back her tears. "Lily's riding Blaze?" she asked, her voice shaky.

"If that's still what you want?" Nick questioned gently. "The Winchesters are all for it."

Olivia sprang at Nick and hugged his neck, clutching the paperwork in one hand. "Thank you!" She kissed his cheek. "Thank you, thank you!" And then the other! Next, she planted a really hot one on his lips.

"Wow!" He chuckled, holding her. "Who else can I get to sign up?"

"Come on," she said, eagerly taking his hand. "I have something for you!"

Nick bellowed a laugh as Olivia practically pulled him up the stairs. "*Ho-ho-ho*! Just where are you taking me?"

"To my apartment, of course!"

He was actually looking forward to seeing it. When they reached the upstairs, he found Olivia's place just as homespun and lovely as her. There were lots of feminine touches around like scented candles and artistic picture frames. There were photos of Olivia with her friends and also several of her family. Nick spotted a group shot that had apparently been taken at

Hannah and Carter's wedding, where Olivia had been one of the bridal attendants. Nick pointed to an older couple standing at Carter's side. The woman was a petite redhead and the gentleman had graying hair. "Are those your folks?"

"Spencer and Janet, yes," she said, beaming proudly. Nick hunted for Olivia's sister but didn't see her with the others.

"Savannah couldn't make it," she explained. "Everybody missed her."

"Have you had a chance to ask her about the Grand Hotel?"

"Oh! Ah...not yet! But I will." Olivia dragged him away from the photo display on the bookshelf and toward the kitchen, motioning grandly to a cookie tin display on a counter that had bar stools in front of it. "Surprise!"

Nick blinked hard, counting fifteen cookie tins stacked in groups of three. "Wow! What have you been baking?"

"Cookies!" The delight in her eyes was evident, and Nick couldn't help but smile. "Lots of lots of cookies! All kinds!"

"All?"

"Name your heart's desire. Which is your absolute favorite?"

"Um... Chocolate chip macaroons?"

Olivia held up one finger then stated with authority, "In the freezer!" She released his hand and strode briskly toward the freezer door, yanking it open. It was so packed with cookie tins the two measly ice cube trays were stuck in sideways. Nick goggled at the sight. "You must have been baking for weeks."

"Nope," she reported staunchly. "Just since Tuesday!"

She slammed shut the freezer door. "Would you like to try one?"

"Sure! I just don't want to ruin my dinner."

Olivia staged a frown and Nick's heart melted. "You're right. One little cookie could hardly make a difference."

"Do you want a macaroon?" she asked hopefully. "Or one of the others?"

Nick was so floored he didn't know what to say. Nobody had ever given him a gift this extravagant. It touched him all the more that the gesture had come from Olivia's heart. No wonder he'd had that feeling day after day that she'd been doing something really nice for him.

"Go on, lay it on me," Olivia challenged. "Name any kind of cookie you want. What are you hankering for?"

All of a sudden Nick had an insatiable urge. He hated to put Olivia on the spot, but wouldn't he love to have one if she'd made it? He crinkled his brow and asked tentatively, "A walnut chocolate bourbon ball?"

Olivia set her hand on her hip. "Nick Claus, that's not technically a cookie, and you know it!"

"It's not?" he asked, flummoxed.

Olivia giggled with joy. "Third tower over," she said, nodding toward the stacks on the counter. "Second tin down."

Nick couldn't believe how wonderful this was. He felt like a kid on Christmas morning. And all of his confectionery wishes were coming true. He carefully approached the center island, selecting the tin that

Olivia had indicated. When he removed the lid, a delectable scent rose up in a puff. Kentucky bourbon, chocolate, and walnuts. *Yum!* Nick gingerly picked up the little round treat covered in confectioners' sugar, and took a big bite.

"Oh…my…goodness," he said, moaning. "Olivia! These are delicious!"

Her smile lit up the room. "I'm so happy that you think so. I've made plenty more!"

"Yes. Yes, I see that." He finished the bourbon ball, licking his fingers. Nick tried thinking back to see if he'd ever tasted anything this good. Categorically, the answer was, no. Olivia was his dream chef. Where had she been hiding these talents?

"Would you like a glass of wine or anything?" she offered. "To go with your sweets?"

"I really shouldn't have any more." But already Nick was tempted to know what was in those other tins.

Olivia indulgently shook her head. "You can probably have another and it won't kill you."

"Kill me, no. But you haven't seen my grandpa. Or maybe you have…"

"You look plenty fit to me!"

"Now, sure." He glanced around the room, trying to keep himself from salivating. All sorts of wonderful aromas were filling the air. Cinnamon sugar. Gingerbread. Sugar cookies with a hint of orange somewhere… "Give me another ten years of eating like this…"

"You won't be eating like this, if I have anything to say about it," Olivia told him resolutely. "You'll have to eat your dinner first, and stay mindful of getting plenty of exercise."

Nick twinkled at her. "Yes, ma'am."

"That can include horseback riding," she reminded him. "We're still going Sunday?"

Nothing made Nick happier than the thought of trotting through a snowy forest with Olivia at his side. "Of course!"

He selected another bourbon ball then she took away the tin, snapping on the lid. "The great thing about cookies is…they freeze!"

"But your freezer is full?"

"I guess I'll have to buy another! I can keep it in the back room downstairs."

Nick roared with delighted laughter. "You, Olivia Livingston, are one special woman."

"And you are one special man!" She set the cookie tin back on the counter before asking, "Now, do we have time for a glass of wine, or do we need to make our reservation?"

Nick checked his watch. "We can spare a moment or two."

"Great," she said, offering to take his coat. "You sit. I'll pour."

Nick had never known Olivia to have a bossy side, but he kind of liked it. He somehow had the inkling he wouldn't mind being bossed around by her. Nick handed her his coat then sat on the futon, noticing the swags of Christmas holly framing the window that looked out on South Main Street. For the past several days he'd spotted her there in the mornings, just waiting on him to appear. Knowing she was there brought a warm comfort to his soul, like a gentle swaddling blanket. While there were other Christmas decorations around, Nick didn't spot a Christmas tree.

"I would have thought the owner of All of Things Christmas, of all people, would have a Christmas tree in her place?"

"I've got three of them downstairs in the shop," she said wryly, handing him a glass of merlot. Nick took a sip thinking it was the perfect complement to those bourbon balls. "They're fake trees, but nonetheless, I plan to put up a real one someday."

Nick stared around the crowded room. It was cozy and warm, but there wasn't an inch to spare. "I suppose you are a little tight on space."

"What's your place like?" she asked, sitting beside him. "Up in Bangor?"

"I've got a sleek new condo. All chrome and glass."

"You?" she asked, apparently astounded. "I would have pegged you for something without so many hard edges."

Nick shrugged mildly. "My home style fits with my architect image."

"Yes, but you're a *restoration* architect," she observed. "Supposedly into old stuff?"

"That's true." Nick found it both incredible and delightful that she could read him so easily. "That's why I've always pined for eventually owning a bungalow."

"A bungalow?" she asked him. "You mean like those little craftsman houses down on Church Street?"

"Exactly like those."

"Sandy and Ben bought one, and restored it."

"Yeah, and their place looks great."

She studied him a moment and her cheeks colored sweetly. "Thanks for taking me out tonight. For a moment, I almost forgot that we're supposed to talk business."

"We don't have to talk about it too much."

"No?"

Nick shot her a satisfied grin. "How about we talk about it just enough?"

"Okay," she agreed easily. "Where do we set the limit?"

"How about…" He viewed her thoughtfully. "No work talk after dinner?"

Olivia's blush deepened. "All right."

Nick fell into her eyes, so badly wanting to hold her. Yet, he knew if he did, they'd probably never leave. "I have a very special night planned for us, Olivia. I hope you'll be pleasantly surprised."

"If you thought it up, I'm sure I'll love it," she said.

Olivia took a slow sip of wine and he watched her every movement. The light flutter of her eyelashes, the pretty glimmer of her hair as it fanned across her shoulders, the subtle movement of her lips…the warm heat in her eyes, as she set her gaze back on his. Nick had never been so captivated by a woman, nor ached so desperately to please her.

"Promise me something," he said, his voice husky.

She set her wine on the coffee table and waited.

"Don't go making cookies for any other guy."

Olivia gave a stunned laugh, but it was a kind one. "I promise you, I won't! Not any time soon."

He brought his hand to her cheek, and spoke from the depth of his soul.

"I meant… Not ever."

Olivia swallowed hard and licked her lips. "Nick…"

"It would break my heart."

"Oh, babe," she said softly. "I would never do that."

Olivia gazed at him lovingly and all of Nick's fears melted away. He leaned forward and gently kissed her. Her lips were warm and tender, trembling just slightly. And, her sigh was like a song, filling his soul with music. That sweet, sweet melody unique to only her.

Chapter Twenty-One

Nick wrapped his arm around Olivia as he shielded them from the pounding snow with his big umbrella. Her heart was still beating wildly from that kiss, as they strolled up South Main. Olivia had never known a man to take her breath away like Nick could. She was falling and sinking fast. Or maybe, she was completely sunk already. It was hard to imagine feeling this strong of an attraction with anybody else, just as it was impossible to believe her emotions were fleeting.

Perhaps when she'd spoken to Savannah, she'd sounded nuts. But what was more overwhelmingly crazy than the beginnings of true love? The situation was different for everybody. Just because it hadn't happened to Savannah that didn't mean it couldn't happen to her. Olivia sure hoped Savannah would experience this kind of joy someday. Because it was a pretty special feeling that made every day shine a little bit brighter, and the nights glow with tender warmth.

Nick snuggled her closer, as cold winds blew, threatening to upend their umbrella.

"Doing okay?" he asked.

When she nodded, he smiled tenderly.

"We're almost there."

As they approached the intersection with Santa Claus Lane, Olivia was surprised to see flickering light emanating through the Grand Hotel's first floor windows. "Nick!" she gasped with worry. "I think somebody's in there."

He reassuringly squeezed her shoulder. "Maybe we should go and see?"

She hesitated a beat. "Maybe we should call Carter? Do you think it's an intruder?"

"I have a notion that everything will be just fine," he said, ushering her up the front stairs. "Careful now, the steps are a little slippery."

Olivia held onto his waist as they climbed toward the porch together. As they did, the lights from inside appeared brighter. Nick was acting awfully calm about this, almost like he knew what was going on. When he slid his key into the lock on the front door, Olivia asked, "Should we call the restaurant?"

"No need." He grinned slyly and pushed open the door. "The restaurant's right here!"

Olivia stepped into the foyer and gasped with delight. An elegantly adorned table stood in the center of the ballroom, flanked by two chairs. LED candles flickered on either side of the floral centerpiece and were placed strategically around the room on empty shelves and windowsills. The old gold-framed mirror above the closed hearth caught the candles' glow, bouncing light back across the room in shimmering gold ribbons.

The table was set with bone-white china with an inlaid gold edge, silver flatware, and red-and-green crystal wine goblets. Ivory cloth napkins perfectly matched the accompanying tablecloth, which draped in swags to the floor. A champagne bucket on spindly silver legs held ice and a chilling bottle. Olivia was completely blown away.

"It's so beautiful."

Nick closed his umbrella, leaving it on the porch behind him as he shut the door. "Here, let me turn these on," he said, striding toward the first of four small battery-operated space heaters he'd positioned in the four corners of the ballroom. "They should take the chill out of the air."

But Olivia couldn't imagine feeling cold in this glorious place. Already her skin was warm and her cheeks were steaming. She slipped out of her coat, still marveling in awe. "When did you do all this?"

"Late this afternoon."

"You must have planned it before?"

Nick nodded and also removed his coat. "I started things in motion on Tuesday. The place settings are on loan, courtesy of the Christmas Inn."

"Bless Walt," Olivia said with a happy laugh. "He's terrific!"

"Yes." Nick took her coat and laid it over the banister with his. Then he followed Olivia into the ballroom, where she was still gazing around. "It looks phenomenal in here with all the candles going."

Nick lifted the bottle out of the ice, tilting it toward her. "Champagne?"

"I'd *love* some," Olivia said with unmasked joy.

He grabbed the towel draped over the back of his chair and expertly popped open the bottle. He filled two wine goblets and handed one to her. Olivia inhaled the sweet fizzy aroma, the bubbles tickling her nose. "This is…so lovely."

Nick grinned graciously. "I'm glad you approve." He raised his glass to hers. "Since we're working on restoring the Grand Hotel to its original glory, I thought we should give things a trial run."

Olivia replied lightly, "A Christmas Town Ball for two?"

"I should have worn my tux and tails."

She examined the azure sweater that brought out the hue of his eyes, noting that he wore a dress shirt and tie beneath it. "You look terrific just how you are."

He clinked her glass. "Here's to a new beginning for the Grand Hotel!"

"Here's to new beginnings!" Olivia took a sip of champagne and the bubbles tingled on her tongue. "What other surprises do you have in store?" she asked eagerly.

"Ah!" His brow rose as if he was just remembering. "Dinner."

She smiled at him. "Something tells me we're not going to the Peppermint Bark."

"No, the Peppermint Bark came here."

When she stared at him questioningly, he pulled out her chair. "Please, have a seat. I'll be right back with our food."

Olivia took her seat and looked up, meeting his spectacular blue eyes. "Can I help you?"

"I've got it. Just relax here."

As he departed through the foyer, Olivia saw him reach into his coat pocket on the banister and extract a small flashlight. He flicked it on, spreading broad beams of light across the wood floor in the lobby as he disappeared toward the kitchen. Olivia guessed he'd stowed the carryout containers of food there. He returned a few minutes later carrying a tray holding a couple of pretty salads, a basket of rolls and butter packets, and two steaming cups of scrumptious smelling soup. "I hope you don't mind my serving the salad and the soup together? The soup is potato leek and the salad is already lightly dressed in a vinaigrette."

"Nick," Olivia proclaimed, still stunned. "This is fantastic! How did you keep the soup warm?"

"The people at the Peppermint Bark were very accommodating. They let me borrow some of the transport containers they use while catering."

Olivia couldn't have felt more special. Nick had arranged all this just for her. "Wow, just wow, Nick. You've totally outdone yourself."

He ginned appreciatively. "I wanted to make it a special evening."

"Then you can consider it a success!"

"You don't even know what we're having for dinner!"

She could hardly see how it mattered. Olivia had never had a more wonderful date than this. Still, she decided to ask him anyway. "Do you want to give me a hint?"

"I couldn't decide between steak and one of their fish dishes, so I thought it might nice to do both."

"Surf and turf?" Olivia asked with hopeful glee.

"How does a petite filet mignon with a crabmeat béarnaise sauce sound? Accompanied by a fresh lobster tail with drawn butter?"

"Sounds like I've died and gone to heaven," Olivia admitted with a giggle. She took a spoonful of soup, finding it superb. "Oh, Nick. You're spoiling me."

"Don't forget this is a working dinner," he teased with a wink.

"Are you going to take it off on your taxes?" she joked in reply.

"Nice idea, but *no-ho-ho*. I don't think I'd better."

Olivia grinned warmly, totally enjoying herself. "How did everything go this week with the building examiners?"

"Excellent," he replied. "Better than expected for a structure this old. It was very well built and with quality materials, so all that helps."

"Will you be able to reopen the fireplaces?" she asked, glancing at the hearth.

"Most definitely. But, for safety's sake and energy efficiency, I'd recommend we make them gas burning."

Olivia's face fell slightly before she could catch herself.

"You're not much for gas fireplaces, I take it?"

"Oh, no. It's not that. I can totally see your point about that working better here, particularly as there are so many fireplaces in the building to contend with."

"But you'd like the other kind someday in your home," he surmised with accuracy.

Olivia sighed dreamily. "Yeah, that would be nice. Cozy, you know?"

He held her gaze a long while. "I know what you mean, exactly."

They talked a little more about Nick's work week and what he'd gotten accomplished, then he asked her how things had gone at All Things Christmas.

"Superbly," she told him. "Ever since last year, when Hannah reopened her shop, business has been booming. Commerce is so much better here now than it used to be. Christmas Town experienced a real slump when that new bypass went in diverting traffic to the highway."

"I suspect things will improve even further with the reopening of this place." Nick appraisingly glanced around. "It's really going to be something."

"Yes. I can't wait to present our plans to the Town Council. When do you think you'll have your proposal ready?"

"Probably by the middle of next week," Nick said, finishing his soup.

Olivia finished hers as well and they both started on their salads.

"There's a bottle of still water in the kitchen," he said. "I meant to bring it out earlier. I can grab it when I get our entrees?"

"Water sounds good," she answered. "But you seriously need to let me help."

"You can help afterwards."

She started to agree, thinking he meant she could assist with cleaning up the dishes, but then he continued, "I might need help breaking in the ballroom."

She viewed him quizzically.

"You will dance with me?"

Heat warmed her cheeks. "But there's no music?"

Nick's eyes sparkled. "Why don't you leave that to me?"

After an incredible meal, Nick surprised Olivia with a dark-chocolate-cherry mousse for dessert. "I've never seen this on the menu at the Peppermint Bark!" she exclaimed happily.

"That's because it's not." Nick winked, pleased that he'd gotten this part just right. "I had them make it special order. Since you love that kind of truffle, I thought this might be a nice touch."

He refilled their champagne glasses, delighted by the pretty glow on Olivia's cheeks and the merry twinkle in her eyes. She was obviously having a great time, and Nick was thrilled that his preparations had paid off. It was easy to treat Olivia like a princess because she had the confident demeanor of royalty. There was also a subtle grace about her, and a very natural beauty. Nick stared at her in the wavering candlelight, imagining her growing even more beautiful over the years.

Olivia savored her dessert and champagne. "I think this mousse is the best thing I've ever tasted!" She stared inquisitively at his portion, which he'd barely touched. "You're not eating yours?"

"It's delicious, but I'm honestly much more of a cookie man."

She laughed in understanding. "Don't get rid of it," she instructed merrily. "If you don't want it, I'll take it home."

"If I can swap out for some cookies, it's a deal."

"You can swap out for more than *some*," Olivia said with a chuckle. "Pretty please, take as many tins home as you want!"

Nick grinned in reply. "Maybe I should try to pace myself?"

"Are you worried you won't exercise restraint without somebody there to watch you?" she ribbed lightly.

"Actually…" His laughter rumbled with a deep *ho-ho-ho*, tickling Olivia's soul. "Yes."

"You've been pretty good at resisting the Virginia Cookie in your freezer."

"I know." He glanced at the pretty barrette in her hair. "It looks exactly like the one you're wearing."

She blushed deeply at this. "Do you like it?"

"It looks beautiful on you. And, I think it's perfect…for tonight."

"Do you plan to ever eat that Commitment Cookie of yours?"

"There's not really much need, now that you've made me a month's supply!"

She gaped at him. "You could really eat all those cookies in a *month*?"

"Well, I…might take a little longer, of course. Depending."

She giggled into her hand. "You're right. I'd better not send them with you all at once. You might go overboard, and then blame me for your tummyache."

His eyes danced with mischief. "Or my big belly!"

"I can hardly see you getting one anytime soon," she said, admiring his fit physique. She happily polished off her last bite of mousse then offered to help Nick clear the dishes.

There was actually very little to do regarding cleanup, and he told her so. The restaurant had simply asked that he discard any leftover food before returning the containers and the champagne bucket. Walt had sent the tableware over in a picnic basket, after wrapping it carefully in the cloth napkins and tablecloth. He'd also loaned Nick the folding table and chairs. The LED candles were products of Sugar Plum Feed Supply, where Nick had also been able to rent the four space heaters. Nick planned to carry the dishes home to Sisters' Row to wash them, and the restaurant said he could bring back the borrowed items in the morning, when he also planned to return the things to the Christmas Inn that Walt had loaned him.

"At least let me help you pack things away," she insisted.

"Don't forget you promised me a dance, afterwards."

She gazed at him sunnily. "You're very decided on that."

"I am decided. On that." Nick had also decided on a lot of other things, like the fact that he was burning to get Olivia back in his arms. "I'll bet nobody has danced in this ballroom in years." He met and held her gaze. "I want us to be the first."

Olivia's lips turned up in a sweet smile. "All right."

After they'd cleared the table and carefully packed the dishes away, Nick led Olivia back into the ballroom where the rest of their champagne was waiting. Olivia felt like a fairy princess in some distant realm. None of this seemed real, yet all of it was beautiful in the most spectacular way. Nick pulled her to him and took her in his arms, shadows lining his handsome face.

"I'm glad you enjoyed your dinner."

"Everything was amazing." She stared up at him and his gaze washed over her like a tumbling tidal wave. Olivia's knees felt weak and her lips trembled as he held her closer. She surrendered to his strong embrace as he threaded his fingers through hers on the hands they held high. Nick's other hand was centered on her waist. When it slid around to Olivia's lower back, her breath hitched. She gripped his shoulder as he slowly…and deliberately began to move her around the floor. First they were gliding by the mirror. Next, twirling by the doorway to the foyer. Circling back around again, making slow lovely turns around the table in the center of the room.

Suddenly, there was music! The soft sweet sighing of violin strings. Then another violin joined in, and a cello…a viola… It was a complete string quartet.

Nick sexily cocked an eyebrow and grinned down at her. "Can you hear it?"

It was faint, but yes. Yes! She heard it! "But, how…?"

"The two of us make magic together," he said huskily. "You and I."

Olivia was entranced, caught up in his spell. "I've never felt this way before. About anyone."

His eyes danced. "Neither have I."

"Will it always be this way?"

"Between us?" He spun her around again. "I hope so, yes."

His hand ran up her back as he held her closer. Olivia's pulse raced.

"There's something you don't know about us Clauses." Nick pressed his cheek to hers and whispered in her ear. "When we find our perfect match, special things happen."

He nibbled her earlobe and goose bumps skittered across her flesh.

"Nick…" The word was a sigh, a prayer… She caught her breath as her heart beat faster.

He gently kissed her cheek and then her neck, still moving them to the sultry rhythm of a faraway beat. Olivia didn't know what was happening or why. She just didn't want it to stop.

His kisses trailed to her chin and then to her lips. He claimed them commandingly, his hands sliding into her hair. Olivia couldn't tell if they were still dancing…or flying. The whole room kept turning around them in bright sunbursts of light. In her mind's eye, she saw the wide open sky and a whole host of stars twinkling in the night. There was wind but no chill, and snow without cold… Only the heat of being in Nick's arms. She was safe with him, so she surrendered, letting him take her father and farther away.

"My darling," he said, stroking her cheek, as he kissed her again. "My darling, darling one." His voice was raspy, growing thicker. "You must have been made just for me."

She whispered into his kiss, her pulse pounding wildly. "Yes."

He pulled back to gaze in her eyes. "And I for you."

She stroked his rich dark hair, then tenderly traced his dimple. "Absolutely."

Olivia knew what this was, and it wasn't any sort of crush. It was deeper, richer, and so much more profound.

"Will you stay with me tonight?" he asked, his voice husky.

When she nodded her assent, Nick grinned. "You're not afraid?"

"Of you?" Impossible. Olivia could never fear Nick Claus.

"Of us." His eyebrows rose. "And the magic we might make together."

"I could never be afraid of that," she said surely.

Nick shared a sultry smile then swept Olivia off her feet and into his arms.

"Nick Claus!" she cried with surprise. "What are you doing?"

"Practicing!"

"Practicing what?"

"Sweeping you off your feet."

She chortled with laughter. "You've already done that, you big goof!"

"*Ho-ho-ho*," he said, carrying her into the foyer. "You haven't seen anything yet!"

She glanced back into the ballroom in a panic. The space heaters were still going and the LED candles were turned on. Plus, they still had stuff left in the kitchen. Surely, he wasn't going to cart her out in the snow without either of them wearing their coats?

The next thing she knew, Nick stunned her by taking an unexpected turn. Rather than heading for the front door he was carrying her upstairs. She noticed someone had already replaced the tread she'd stepped through.

"Nick!" she said, kicking her feet while squealing with laughter. "Where are we going?"

He shot her a sultry look when he reached the top of the stairway. "I asked you to stay the night. I didn't say where."

They were on the second floor and gentle glowing light flickered from the back guestroom. The one at the end of the hall and closest to the hall bath. "*Here?*" she asked, giddily excited. This was reckless and daring and wild...and so, so unlike her.

"No, darling," he said, nodding toward the back room. "Not here, *there*." He cracked a devastating grin. "I forgot to mention some other things I picked up at Sugar Plum Feed Supply. A big air mattress and lots and lots of camping blankets."

Olivia dropped her jaw and she swatted his shoulder. "What if I'd said no?"

His eyes twinkled tellingly, as if he was awfully glad that she hadn't. Olivia was actually glad that she hadn't, too. "Then I would have walked you home, of course." As he carried her down the hall, he continued. "Did I mention that the plumber came by?"

"The plumber?" she asked, confounded. "No, why?"

"We now have working water. It's cold, but at least the toilets flush."

"Ah, gotcha," she said, laughing.

"I couldn't have you being uncomfortable staying here with me."

Olivia imagined she was about to get very, very comfortable. She tightened her arms around Nick's neck as he carried her over the threshold. The bedroom was beautiful and it obviously had been cleaned. Freshly polished floors gleamed in the candlelight below the enormous queen-size air mattress. It was piled high with plush blankets and an assortment of pillows. A lovely vase of lilies stood on the windowsill flanked by rows of glowing candles.

"How did you know that lilies are my favorite?" she asked, touched.

He smiled and gently laid her down on the bed. "I know a lot of things."

"Like whether I've been naughty or nice?" she asked in sultry tones.

"Yes," he said, easing himself down on the bed beside her. "And, lately…" He playfully thumbed her nose as they lay face to face. "You've been very, very good. I don't believe you've had a truffle all week."

Olivia gasped and her face steamed. "I can't believe that you know that!"

He brought his arms around her. "Why not?"

"Because that's not fair," she said, play pounding his chest. "Not fair for you to know my secrets when I don't know yours."

"All right," he said, snuggling her closer. "I'll let you in on one of them."

She gazed up at him expectantly and his eyes gleamed in the candlelight. "I'm wearing candy cane boxers."

Olivia burst out laughing. "Are not!"

Nick flipped onto his back then pulled her up and on top of him, with a hearty *ho-ho-ho*. "Want to find out?"

She cupped his face in her hands, stroking his cheeks with her thumbs.

"I want to know *all* of your secrets, Nick Claus."

He grinned sexily and Olivia's whole world sparkled like the crystals in a snow globe. "That could take some time."

Olivia fell into his kiss. "We've got all night."

Chapter Twenty-Two

Olivia and Nick sat bolt upright as bright sunlight beamed through the window. "I thought I heard something," she said with a start.

Nick stared at her in alarm.

Before they knew it, there were heavy footsteps on the stairs. Doors were popping open and slamming shut down the hall. Olivia clutched the blankets to her chest. She was wearing Nick's dress shirt and her panties, but nothing else.

"Nick," she hissed in a whisper. "What are we going to do?"

"I'll go check it out."

He frantically lunged for his boxers just as the door swung open.

"Carter!" Olivia yelped at the top of her lungs. "What are you doing here?"

Her brother shook his head, then cut a steely look Nick's way. "Maybe that's a question for you?" Carter was in uniform, so he'd clearly been making his rounds. Olivia had no idea what time it was. Her eyes darted to the watch on the mound of clothes she'd shucked beside the air mattress. Was it really after nine? How in the world had that happened?

"Hello? Anybody home?" A cheerful man's voice echoed from the stairs.

"Who's that?" Nick asked suddenly.

Olivia gulped. "Sounds like—"

Frank Cho appeared in the doorway.

Nick blinked hard, staring at the electrician. "We had an appointment, didn't we?"

Carter averted his gaze from Olivia, addressing Frank. "When I got to the office, Tilly said Mac from the Merry Market called first thing. He'd seen lights in here last night, then when he got to work this morning they were still glowing." Carter tugged at the brim of his hat. "Guess he was scared someone was burning the house down."

Frank clucked his tongue, not looking the least bit abashed. "Where there's smoke there's generally fire," he said, crossing his arms in front of him. *What? Was he planning to stand there all day?*

"Will you look at all these candles? Heavens!"

Noooo. Lou Christmas was downstairs!

"Who do you think did this, Buddy?"

Buddy's here, too? Oh, boy. Olivia face-palmed.

"Squatters?"

"Squatters don't generally drink champagne, dear," Buddy replied in a big booming voice.

"*Puh-leeze*," Olivia begged Carter in hushed tones. "Don't let them come upstairs."

"Lou! Buddy! What's going on? I saw the commotion from my gallery— Oh! Hi, Jade! Nice to see you!"

Sandy, too? And, Jade?

"Look," Jade said, apparently pointing out a window. "Here come the Slades from South Pole Pottery!"

"I don't think it's squatters," an intelligent male voice said.

Wendell?

"This looks like an inside job." Wendell paused and then asked the group, "Has anyone seen *Nick* or *Olivia* this morning?"

"Oh my goodness!" Sandy cried. "Look! There are their coats!"

Olivia gaped in shock, rasping hoarsely at Carter, "How did everyone get in here?"

"*Somebody* forgot to lock the front door," Carter answered pointedly.

Nick tightly pursed his lips and Carter turned to Frank.

"How about we leave these guys alone to get dressed?"

Frank just stood there with a dopey look on his face, goggling at the lovers.

Carter nudged him soundly.

"Oh, sure! Sure!" he said, coming out of a daze. As he followed Carter out the door, Frank whispered to Nick and Olivia, "Don't worry, guys. I won't say a word about this to anyone. I promise, not one word."

Olivia blushed hotly, thinking that Frank wouldn't need to.

There'd be several others in town eager to help get the word out first.

Olivia ducked out the back door of the Grand Hotel, her cheeks burning. There was still something approaching a party in the ballroom and front hall. Even more folks had shown up than before! All down Santa Claus Lane, store owners had temporarily shuttered their shops and scurried up the street to see what was occurring at the Grand Hotel. A robbery? A fire? An early-morning reception to which most of the town hadn't been invited? Olivia heard the speculations fly as fresh voices sounded in the hall. All were apparently relieved by Carter's presence, but for some reason he seemed to be having difficulty in getting the crowd to disperse.

Thank goodness Nick and Olivia had recalled the back staircase. The one that ran from the fourth floor apartment all the way down to the kitchen. They'd dressed quickly and clambered up to the top floor of the building by the main staircase before taking the secret one back down to the first floor. Nick leaned out the door to kiss her and Olivia shivered. Though it was sunny out, the temperature still had to be below freezing. "Your coat?" he whispered with worry.

"I'm not going to face all those people!" Olivia said in hushed tones. "I'd rather die."

"You very well may get sick if you go out like that." He worriedly surveyed her then seemed to make an instant decision. In a flash, he'd ripped off his sweater and had begun tugging it over Olivia's head. She raised her arms to help him as the warm snuggly garment fell around her. Nick's azure blue sweater was roomy and comfortable, and it smelled deliciously of him.

"Better?" he asked with concern. When she nodded, Nick hurriedly kissed her lips. "Love you!" he said, like it was the most natural thing in the world.

Olivia stared up at him, her heart pounding. "Wha…what…did you…?"

"I said, I love you, Olivia Livingston," he proclaimed convincingly. "And those are not just words said in the heat of the moment."

Olivia's heart melted, right down into a lovely rich pool of dark-chocolate-cherry. She beamed as she gave him a kiss. "I love you, too."

"You'd better dash," he said. "We'll catch up later."

"Later!" she said, nearly tripping on the stairs. *He loves me! Loves me! Weeee!* She turned to look at him thinking he was the most handsome man she'd ever seen at this time in the morning, even with his hair all a mess. His dimple settled deeply as he gave her a wave. "Careful walking home now," he cautioned quietly.

Olivia nodded and scooted toward the back hedge. There was an alley behind South Pole Pottery that led directly to the rear of her shop. Olivia could hustle to All Things Christmas without any of the nosy townspeople being the wiser.

She was bustling along, taking care to watch her step on the slick stone, when a pair of man's shoes appeared on the ground before her. Olivia halted abruptly, looking up.

"Pastor Wilson!" He was out walking his Pekingese and appeared just as startled to see her, as she was to see him.

"You're out without a coat on, my dear," he commented, like she might not have noticed.

"Oh, yes! I know! I was just…er…running a quick errand."

"Do you know what's happening at the Grand Hotel?" His brow crinkled with concern. "Mary said a mob was gathered there not twenty minutes ago," he said, referencing his housekeeper. Pastor Wilson's wife, Margie, had passed several years ago and he'd expressed no interest in remarrying. Even though there were several ladies in the sewing circle quite interested in him. "She worried that something was amiss, but didn't want to be nosy." That would make Mary unique in this town, Olivia thought sagely.

"Umm...somebody thought it was on fire," Olivia said hurriedly. "But—luckily—false alarm! Ha-ha!"

Pastor Wilson viewed her oddly. "It that a man's necktie hanging out of your purse?"

Olivia blanched. Nick's tie draped from one side of her purse like a kite tail. She must have shoved it in there when they were rapidly picking up! She cupped her hand to her mouth, hoping she didn't have his candy cane boxers in her bag, too.

"Seems to have a holiday theme?" Pastor Wilson said, examining the tie more closely. "Those look like little Christmas trees?"

"Christmas trees, right!"

"Very festive." Pastor Wilson nodded with approval. "I simply can't keep up with ladies' fashions these days." His face broadened in a grin. "Wearing men's ties as fashion accessories for your bags! What will you gals think of next?"

Olivia smiled with a plastered-on grin, unsure of what to say. Anything she could think of would only incriminate her.

He glanced down at his dog who stood obediently by his side. "Well, Pooks and I best be on our way.

Nice seeing you, Olivia." He bowed his head. "But next time, for heaven's sakes child, dress more warmly."

Olivia rapidly scuttled off, glancing over her shoulder as the minister meandered down the alleyway with his dog, pausing periodically to let Pooks sniff the curb. Once she'd put enough distance between them, Olivia frantically peered into her purse, half expecting a plethora of tiny candy canes to peek back her. Olivia gasped with relief seeing they weren't there. Then she had a quick memory flash of Nick yanking his chinos up over them and his taut, toned derriere. That image nearly made her lose her footing. *Eeek. I'm a mess!*

Olivia pulled her phone from her purse and rapidly sent Nick a text.

I think I took your tie.

Within seconds he texted back.

You naughty girl!

Olivia flushed and typed again.

What do you want me to do?

Keep it.

Keep it?

For now.

Olivia giggled at their escapades, then a gust of wind kicked up, hurrying her along.

Sorry!

His reply was lightning fast.

No-ho-ho you're not.

Olivia laughed happily, thinking it was true! In spite of their horribly embarrassing morning, she didn't regret spending the night with Nick. And, she'd never, ever change it. He'd been so charming, and wonderful and patient and kind... *Plus, he's a tiger in the sack. Roar!* Olivia paused in thought, questioning whether tigers roar? She smiled giddily, thinking that it didn't matter. She'd adored being with Nick and couldn't wait to see him again. Fortunately, they already had a riding date planned for tomorrow, and had agreed to meet at the stables.

We still on for 3?

Yup! See you there!

Olivia dropped her phone in her purse and wrapped her arms around herself, hugging Nick's fuzzy sweater, as she hurried along. The sky was bright and clear, and Olivia couldn't have hoped for a more glorious morning. *He said he loves me! Yay!* And she was utterly crazy about him. Olivia felt a sudden urge to preheat her oven, and picked up her pace, scurrying faster. The moment she got home, she'd need to check her supplies. Odds were she'd be dashing out to Sugar Plum Feed Supply for more cookie tins.

Chapter Twenty-Three

The next afternoon, Nick drove his SUV to Sleigh Bell Stables. Olivia had gone there early to tend to some paperwork concerning the next session of riding lessons that would begin in January. Nick's niece, Lily, was among those being enrolled in the beginners' class. Sandy implicitly trusted Olivia and her judgment. She'd easily convinced Ben of the merits of Lily learning how to ride in this part of the country. Ben had insisted that Lily take responsibility for the endeavor by volunteering her help at the barn a few hours a week after her lessons.

Lily had been over the moon, hugging Nick's neck tightly and telling him what a great uncle he was for helping arrange her lessons with Blaze. Lily was a precious little girl and very tenderhearted. It was simple to see how Sandy had immediately taken to her, and Nick was impressed by the bond the two of them had already established. If a stranger didn't know better, they'd assume Sandy to be Lily's biological mother, and not her stepmom.

Nick patted his coat pocket thinking of the special treat he'd brought along to share with Olivia. He'd been waiting for the perfect moment, and now the timing seemed right. Now, all Nick had to do was locate the ideal place... He entered the office trailer, finding Olivia sitting by herself at a desk bent over some paperwork.

She glanced up with a bright grin, then checked the clock.

"Is it that time already?" She was dressed in riding clothes today, including a closely fitted jacket, riding boots, and jodhpurs. Her hair was braided on one side and slung forward over her shoulder. There were no Christmas barrettes in her hair today. Nick suspected that was because they might interfere with the comfort of her riding helmet.

Olivia shuffled some papers on her desk, sliding them into a manila folder which she dropped into a filing cabinet. "Your timing was perfect." Her pretty smile gleamed. "I was just finishing up." She stood and walked toward him, and he pulled her into his arms.

"It's awfully quiet in here today."

"Sunday afternoons generally are."

"I'm excited about riding Jim Boy," Nick said, thinking that he hadn't been on a horse in years. Not since he was little at his grandpa's farm. He'd always loved it then, and had taken to it easily. Nick hoped his rusty skills wouldn't fail him.

"Great! I told him you were coming." She carefully scanned his eyes. "I don't suppose you brought any riding gear?"

"I'm afraid I don't own any."

"No matter," she said with a cheery twinkle. "There's plenty for you to borrow here."

A little while later, they were suited up and mounted on their respective horses. Nick rode Jim Boy and Olivia rode Blaze. He marveled at how natural she looked on a horse. It was like she'd been born to the saddle. As they exited the barn, Olivia giggled and held out her hand, catching a cluster of small white flakes.

"Oh, look! It's snowing!"

"It's coming down lightly, though." Nick studied the sky and the billowing gray clouds overhead. "Are you worried it could get worse?"

"I'm not worried." Olivia grinned. "Are you?"

"I've never minded the snow," Nick said contentedly. He glanced around at the snowy white field, the empty riding ring, and a few odd horses covered in blankets in the pasture. Most of the others were in the barn. Nick started to ask about the horses that had been turned out, then he became suddenly aware of them enjoying the feel of the wind on their faces and the tiny prickle of snowflakes on their noses.

"Don't worry about Georgia and Sam," Olivia said, as if reading his thoughts. "A hand will be along to bring them in shortly."

Nick nodded, following after her as Blaze broke into a trot. They were headed toward a rustic trail that led into the forest. "If the weather starts to get worse, we can always turn back," Olivia said in a reassuring way.

They still had a couple of hours of daylight left. Even though the day was gloomy, the slight mist formed by the horses' rising breath gave the forest a magical quality. Tree limbs curtsied in the wind and evergreen boughs hung heavy with snow, as more flakes dotted the air. Nick watched a herd of deer, prancing jauntily down a ravine flanking a frozen creek. Then they were joyously bounding up the other side of the hill, and disappearing into the underbrush with fast flicks of their white tails.

Jim Boy fell into step beside Blaze and the rhythmic clip-clopping of their hooves mirrored the pounding in Nick's veins. He felt so alive here. In his element. Nick loved being with Olivia, and being with her in nature—where she seemed to fit particularly well—was extra special. "This is a really beautiful place."

Olivia blushed. "I'm so happy that you like it."

"I like everything about Christmas Town," he told her surely. "And, each day, I'm liking it more."

Her smile took his breath away. "I'm liking it more, too," she said sweetly. "It's such a great town, I never could have imagined it getting better." She shot him a telling look. "And then you came along."

"I'm awfully glad that I did."

"I'll have to remember to thank Lou Christmas for asking me to spearhead this project!"

Nick chuckled warmly. "And I'll have to thank my sister for tapping me as the architect for the job."

Olivia sighed reflectively as they rode along. "You never know about fate. It's mysterious sometimes."

"Yes," he said, admiring her lovely profile.

As they continued into the dense wood, Nick noticed a thick shrub hedging the path. It had dark green oval-shaped leaves and waxy white berries. "Olivia, look!"

She pulled back on her reins, slowing her horse. When she saw he'd halted Jim Boy, she brought Blaze to a complete stop, too, swinging her around so she faced Nick. "How pretty!" Olivia's green eyes shone. "Mistletoe!"

"We seem to have wandered into an enormous patch of it," Nick said, eyeing either side of the trail.

"Funny! I've never noticed it here before." She was a vision, sitting there on her horse with her helmet and shoulders lightly dusted with snow. It coated the length of her braid and clung to the horn of her saddle, but Olivia scarcely seemed to notice. She stared in wonder, viewing their gorgeous surroundings. "It's so quiet out here," she said, her cheeks glowing. "I love it, don't you?"

Nick sensed this as his opening. "Yeah, I sure do." He paused, listening to the soft pitter-patter of snow falling around them. "But it's not only this, and not just here. It's more than Christmas Town, Olivia." He gazed at her tellingly and withdrew a small brown package from his coat pocket. "I meant what I said yesterday morning. I've fallen in love with you."

He side-stepped Jim Boy closer and set the package in her hand. "What's this?"

"A Commitment Cookie." Nick cracked a devilish grin. "Will you share it with me?"

Olivia's laughter rang through the forest. "Oh, Nick! You've saved it all this time?"

"It's been in the freezer. I'm sure it's still fresh."

"That's not it... What I mean is... Gosh, you took a while to share it." To his amazement, she almost sounded exasperated.

He chuckled at her response. "What? You wanted me to give it to you sooner?"

Olivia cocked an eyebrow. "Weren't those your instructions?"

"Instructions? Wait a minute…" Nick's laughter roared. "You peeked at that note, didn't you?"

She sassily shrugged her shoulders. "Might have."

"When?"

"When I was over."

Nick grinned and shook his head. "Aren't you going to open it?"

Olivia smiled and uncreased the bag's fold, extracting the prettily made heart-shaped cookie. "Did you ever find out who wrote it?"

"I did!" Nick said, evidently surprising her.

"Who?"

"Buddy Christmas." Nick decided not to mention Buddy's stated reasons behind it.

Olivia's mouth hung open. "You're kidding!" Then she giggled. "Who knew Buddy was the matchmaking kind? I had that down to Lou…and Kurt."

"Yeah, well." Nick grinned. "I suppose you never really know in Christmas Town."

She held the cookie toward him but he gallantly shook his head. "Ladies first."

"All right." She gave a shy smile and took a dainty nibble. "Oh…my…goodness! Good!" She stared at him curiously. "Should I expect something to happen?"

"I don't know," Nick said. "Maybe I should try some, too?"

Olivia handed him the cookie and he took a taste, deciding it was even better than the first two kinds of Virginia Cookie he had tried. "Really delightful."

"And?" Olivia blinked, waiting. "I don't feel any different, do you?"

Nick leaned toward her on his horse and whispered huskily, "Maybe that's because you've already experienced real magic."

"Ah," she said astutely, before snatching the cookie away and taking another bite. "I see." Blaze peered back at her with interest and Jim Boy began to stomp his hooves. Olivia held the remainder of the cookie out for Nick, and he devoured it with a gobble.

"So, what does this mean?" she asked, her green eyes sparkling. "That we're going steady?"

"I sure hope so."

Olivia held his gaze. "I hope so, too."

Nick leaned even closer. "Shall we seal it with a kiss?"

Olivia grinned and obliged, meeting his lips for a lingering moment.

"That felt pretty good," she said, straightening in her saddle.

"Better than the best."

Olivia peeked at the thickening clouds through the overhanging branches. "We should probably start heading back."

Nick nodded and swung his horse around.

"Lead the way!" he said, allowing her and Blaze to start out first.

"Nick?" Olivia asked, as they trotted along.
"Huh?"

"I hate to say I'm disappointed…"

Nick's heart sank. "Disappointed?"

"I mean, it's only a silly legend, and I never *really* believed…" She turned to look at him. "It's just that

Sandy and Hannah both seemed so sure about their powers."

"You're talking about the Virginia Cookies? I guess magic is in the eye of the beholder."

"Yeah," she answered doubtfully. "But, Nick?"

"Yes?"

"Sandy's your sister! How could they affect her, and not you?"

"Sandy and I are different."

"I know that, of course. Sandy's very sweet, but you're…" Olivia carefully scanned his eyes. "Special somehow, aren't you?"

Nick wasn't sure how far he wanted this conversation to go. He wasn't ready for it yet, and he doubted that Olivia was either. "I'd like to think I'm special to you," he answered warmly.

"You are, without a doubt. More special than anyone I've known." She startled in her saddle, sitting up ramrod straight. "Whoa! That's weird? For a moment, it felt like Blaze's hooves weren't even touching the ground!" Olivia squared her shoulders, seeming to shake it off. "I must have been imagining things. Ha-ha! Too much fresh air!"

Nick arched both eyebrows and studied Blaze's hooves, seeing them levitating slightly. Next, Jim Boy began to rise off the ground, too. Nick frowned and focused hard, trying to get the horses to land.

Olivia gazed ahead, smiling dreamily. "The snow's really piling up. I can barely hear our horses anymore!"

Nick furrowed his brow and increased his concentration. *Hooves on the ground, hooves on the ground, hooves on the…*

266 Only You at Christmas

"Are you okay?" Olivia asked suddenly. She stared down at the windswept trail then back in Nick's eyes. "What in the world were you looking at?"

"Nothing! Just admiring the...uh...snow."

Olivia shook her head with a smile and kept the lead. As she pulled ahead, Nick glanced over his shoulder at the trail behind them. For a stretch of about fourteen feet, there were no hoof prints in the snow.

Nick knew it now, things were getting serious. Olivia was becoming more like him, starting to absorb some of his energy. Maybe he'd given her too much of it last night. But, Nick hadn't been able to stop himself. With her incredible mind, her good-as-gold heart, and that unbelievable smile, Olivia had practically driven him crazy. And that was before he'd seen her fabulous body. What was a Claus to do? Nick was only human. But he was a special one, yeah. Olivia had nailed that part.

And yet, he was especially made for her. Nick would bet his life on it. He'd never felt this way about any other woman. He and Olivia fit together like a hand in a glove. Theirs was the perfect union. Glorious. Heaven-sent. And when she'd taken Nick in her arms and let him into her bed, Nick had known with a certainty that he could never bear to leave her.

This was no fleeting thing.

He wanted Olivia with him always.

After they'd put the horses away for the night, Nick and Olivia headed for the gravel parking area. "Thanks for taking me out riding today," he said. "I had a really great time."

"Thanks for coming along!" She beamed up at him. "I loved every moment, especially the Virginia Cookie surprise."

"You're not disappointed anymore?"

"I'm sorry that I ever said that," she said, looking ashamed. "I didn't mean it, Nick. You haven't done one thing to disappoint me yet."

That's what he was worried about. The "yet" part. Wasn't it inevitable that things between them would unravel in time? They had with every other woman Nick had grown close to. Then again, he'd never been as close to anyone else as he was to Olivia. Things were different with her. Electric and exciting. But that just made Nick's heart pound with trepidation all the more. For the more invested the two of them became, the more they had to lose.

"I've detected a real change in Blaze," she told him. "Did you notice?"

Nick had noticed that Olivia's horse was more lively-stepped and bright-eyed, and he told her so.

"Thanks to you," she replied gratefully. "And your instinct about what was bothering her. The moment I started training her to the smaller riding saddle, it was like she knew. I think Lily might have talked to her, too. Blaze has seemed happier ever since."

"I'm glad I was of help," Nick said sincerely.

Olivia viewed him with earnest green eyes. "You've been helping a lot of people around here. Once the Town Council approves your proposal, you'll be helping even more. The restoration of the Grand Hotel will be a tremendous boon to Christmas Town."

He hedged before asking, "Are you worried about facing them?"

She laughed in incredulity. "No, why?"

"Word's bound to have gotten around by then," Nick said, treading tenderly. "Rumors are surely getting started about you and me."

"So let them talk!" she said boldly. "Our relationship hasn't affected the quality of your work, or mine." She smiled shyly. "In some ways, it's improved it. Wouldn't you say?"

"I only hope the townsfolk will agree."

"Oh, they will. Trust me."

He eyed her doubtfully. "How can you be so sure?"

"Everyone might be into everyone else's business here, but at base the people of Christmas Town are all genuinely good souls." She lowered her voice in a whisper. "They're also all die-hard romantics."

Nick's eyebrows arched. "Oh, really?"

"Really," she said lightly. "That's one reason people lobbied so hard to get Hannah's shop back in operation. Even if they didn't work for us, people in general are taken with the legend of Lena's famous Virginia Cookies. Several couples even attribute their marriages to them." Nick recalled Buddy's confession about proposing to Louise, and was astounded to find himself believing this was true.

"Marriages, huh?" In the far-off distance, Nick thought he heard a melodious ringing in the mountains. He sharply turned his head that way. If the idea hadn't occurred to him consciously before, it must have been bubbling up under the surface…because now, his head was filled with fascinating visions of Olivia dressed in a sparkly, long white gown.

She wore a red velvet cape, though. With a fluffy fur collar.

Nick swallowed hard, thinking he'd need to consult *Santa's Little Helper* again. Though he doubted a mere flash drive could unlock the deepest secrets of his heart. It appeared only Olivia could do that, he thought, gazing at her longingly.

"So, what do you say?" Olivia continued questioningly, and Nick realized she'd been asking him something. "Will you come over for dinner?" She lowered her voice in a tempting tone. "I've got lots of cookies and milk for dessert."

Nick shared a broad grin, wondering how he could have gotten so lucky.

"A man would have to be crazy to refuse an offer like that."

Chapter Twenty-Four

The next morning, Olivia lay lazily in bed reliving her happy memories of yesterday spent with Nick, including all last night. He'd just run out to grab some coffee for the two of them from Jolly Bean Java. They both had full work days ahead, and Olivia had offered to set up the Town Council meeting through Lou Christmas as soon as possible. Nick imagined he'd have things ready on his end by late Wednesday. He was preparing a PowerPoint presentation with 3-D mock-ups, charts, and slides outlining the phases of the project and how and when they ideally should be undertaken. There was so much to consider, but Nick had covered every angle. He was such a brilliant man...not to mention a dynamite lover, Olivia thought with a contented giggle.

Someone rang the bell downstairs, which Olivia found curious as she'd given Nick her key. Perhaps he had his hands full with their coffees, or the key had somehow become jammed in the lock? It sometimes stuck that way and Olivia had been meaning to oil it. She slid out of bed with a happy sigh and stretched her arms long toward the ceiling. Nick's comfy azure sweater hit her mid-thigh. She'd slept in it, liking the feel of his clothing on her skin as he'd wrapped his arms around her. He'd teased her about the getup, but he'd also said it suited her. The outfit certainly complemented the new boxers he had on, which showcased lots of little white snowmen against a powder blue background. Olivia loved the way Nick was such a regular guy on the outside, but secretly so Christmassy underneath. In fact, she loved everything about him.

Olivia skipped merrily down the stairs, not bothering to grab her robe. It would only take an instant to let Nick in, then the two of them would be warmly snuggled back in bed. Since All Things Christmas didn't open until ten and it was only a little after eight, that gave them nearly two full hours to linger under the covers... Olivia's skin tingled at the very idea.

When she reached the front door, she halted in shock. She didn't spy Nick through the glass-paneled panes of her door—but, Sandy! Olivia cracked the door open with a tentative smile.

"Sandy! Hi!"

Her eyes looked a little panicked and her cheeks burned bright pink. "I've been trying to reach you." She bustled her way inside, nearly knocking Olivia over in the process, and yanked off her earmuffs. "Why haven't you been answering your phone?"

"My phone?" Olivia thought hard, trying to remember where she'd put it. "I...er..." That's right! It was still in her purse from Saturday morning. She'd set it to vibrate on Friday night, then after her run-in with Pastor Wilson in the alley and subsequent communication with Nick, she hadn't retrieved it.

Olivia had been so busy dreaming of Nick and baking cookies, she'd forgotten all about her phone. "I guess I left it silenced in my purse?"

"For two *days*?" Sandy asked, sounding astounded.

Olivia was a little surprised, too. Then again, since she and Nick had previously set the time for meeting up at the stables, she hadn't really missed it. It wasn't like she was expecting to hear from anyone, and that cookie baking had taken tons of time. Far more than she'd bargained for, actually. Probably because Olivia had quickly gotten bored with the run-of-the-mill kinds, and had started branching out into more exotic varieties. That double-batch of "Italian Meringue Hazelnut Macarons with Chocolate Hazelnut Spread" took *forever* to make. Then again, Nick's utter appreciation of them yesterday evening had made the entire endeavor worth it!

Sandy viewed her worriedly, her forehead wrinkling. "Olivia?" she inquired gently. "Are you all right?"

"Yup! Uh-huh! Just fine!" Olivia carefully eyed her friend, suddenly wondering why she was here. Sandy never visited her this early on weekday mornings. "How about…you?"

"*Me*?" Sandy appeared taken aback. "Honey, it's *you* the whole town is concerned about."

"Concerned?"

"It's like you disappeared off the face of the earth?" Sandy's eyebrows knitted together. "You and Nick, both! And, after the incredible hubbub at the Grand Hotel—"

"Oh?" Olivia asked casually, as if she had no idea. "Did something happen?"

"Yes." Sandy pointedly arched an eyebrow. "A very elegant dinner, apparently."

"How nice!" Olivia said, purposely obtuse. "For whom?"

Sandy crossed her arms in front of her. "Give it up, Olivia! We found your and Nick's coats hanging over the banister! I mean, really..." Her features softened and then she giggled. "Were you guys really so hot and bothered that you had to run home without wearing your coats?"

"Er...run home? No, we didn't—"

"Don't try to pretend with me, now." Sandy dismissively waved her hand. "And don't worry that I object, either. I've been *all for* you and Nick getting together. From the beginning! Remember?" Her gaze seemed to snag on Nick's sweater, before she continued. "I just wish you guys hadn't absconded like that—leaving the town in a titter before the big meeting, that's all."

"Is there...going to be a problem?"

"I don't think so. I just wanted to warn you, in case you didn't know. Any secrets you thought that you and Nick were keeping? They're out!" Sandy paused then continued briskly, "In any case, we'll expect you to tell us all about it today during our girls' lunch." Sandy viewed her worriedly. "You *are* still coming? We're your best friends on earth!"

"Er...yes! Of course!"

Sandy glanced again at Olivia's clothing.

"Say...doesn't that sweater you're wearing belong to—?"

"Hello, sis!" Nick said, by way of greeting, stepping in the door.

Sandy blinked while Olivia smiled tightly.

"Well," Sandy said, "I see that things are moving right along!" She shot a look at her brother. "I've been trying to reach you, too," she told him in scolding tones.

"Really?" Nick asked innocently. Olivia noticed that, apart from two steaming cups, he held a paper sack in his hand. Had he really brought her cherry cheese Danishes? The instant she'd wondered about it, Nick winked her way, indicating that *yes, he had*. Olivia felt her cheeks color, as Sandy studied them both.

"Yeah, really!" she said, answering Nick. Sandy sighed and threw up her hands. "I'll let your girlfriend fill you in."

Olivia's blush deepened at Sandy slapping that label on her. Though she and Nick had agreed to be exclusive, they hadn't told anyone else about it yet.

"I'll make sure she does that," Nick said with a cheerful grin.

Sandy shook her head at Nick, slightly annoyed. "I'll be seeing *you*, later."

When Nick's eyebrows rose, Sandy explained further. "We've got some family business to discuss."

Was it Olivia's imagination, or did Nick's sunny expression temporarily cloud over? It was just for a flash, though. Like a lightning strike over the desert. "Family, sure," he replied in jovial tones. "I'll give you a call this afternoon."

"Better make it this morning," Sandy said in a cautionary fashion.

Nick worriedly twisted his lips, before replying. "This morning, yeah. No problem!"

"Gee," Olivia said shortly afterwards, as she and Nick settled back in under the covers. "I hope everything's okay?"

"Are you talking about with the Town Council?" She'd briefly filled him in as to why Sandy had stopped by on their way upstairs.

"No, I meant with your family?" Concern was written in her dark green eyes and Nick could have kissed her for her genuine compassion. But he decided to hold off on the kissing until later—after they'd finished their coffees. He passed her a cup, trying to ease her worries.

"I'm sure everything is fine. Some things just come up occasionally with our grandfather's business, and Sandy and I are asked to help out."

Olivia took a sip of her coffee, saying it was delicious and thanking him for getting it. "What kind of business is your granddad in? You never did say?"

"It's a...rather broad enterprise."

"Enterprise? You mean, like a corporation?"

"Something like that."

"You said he lives in Canada, right?"

"Yes, uh-huh. My parents have retired there, too."

"But...your granddad is *not* retired."

"Nope. Not yet."

"Gosh! How old is he?"

"Plenty. Plenty old, actually."

"Don't your folks help him out?"

"They would if they could. But, I'm afraid...they...just don't have the skills!"

"Skills?" Olivia tilted her head to the side, and a wave of dark red hair fell over her shoulder. "What kind of—?"

"Would you like a Danish?" Nick asked abruptly, lifting the bag off the nightstand. "I brought your favorite!" He tried to shoot her a devastating grin, but she didn't take the bait. Evidently, her mind was focused on something else.

"Thanks! In a bit." Her expression softened in a smile. "I guess I'm just a little confused about what your grandpa does—specifically?"

Nick meant to say, *Oh, that!* Instead, it came out as, "*Ho-ho-ho!* That!"

Olivia screwed up her face and stared at him, and Nick swallowed hard.

"He's into manufacturing and distribution."

"Of?"

"Just about everything. You name it!" In spite of himself, Nick's voice squeaked. Heat flashed at his temples and the back of his neck felt really, really hot. This was not the time or place for this discussion. Nick needed to get certain things in order first.

"Wow. Impressive. Sounds like your grandfather is like a jack-of-all-trades, then? Some kind of huge business mogul?" Her brow rose with the question and Nick answered quickly.

"Yes, but no! What I mean is, he's not in it for the money. His business is more like a…non-profit. A charity. Yeah, that! A charity for the children. And, uh…those who are young at heart!"

"That sounds wonderful, Nick. Your grandpa must be an exceptional man."

"He is. Uh-huh! And a very talented guy!" Sweat was building at his hairline and Nick found himself wishing he'd ordered his coffee iced.

"You said before I'd get to meet him," Olivia said saucily before taking another sip of coffee. "I suppose that's what you meant when you said you'd like to show me the Maritime Provinces?"

"It is! Only…"

"Only what?" she asked sweetly.

"Only, we'd better eat these cherry cheese Danishes first," he said with an encouraging grin. "While they're still nice and warm."

"You got fresh ones?" she asked with obvious delight. "Yum!"

Nick passed her the bag. "Dig in!"

"Will you join me?"

Nick nabbed some napkins and dabbed his brow with relief.

"*Ho-ho-ho*, of course!"

Chapter Twenty-Five

Nick kissed Olivia goodbye, still inwardly fretting over Sandy's visit. Each time their parents called them back to Canada, Nick worried that things might be getting worse. While there had been a few minor slip-ups here and there as of late, nothing had been so serious that anyone had discussed their granddad abandoning his post. Grandpa Claus was top-notch at his job, and it was impossible to think of anyone replacing him. Nick had a few older cousins in line, *thank goodness*. Otherwise, that could mean that Nick might be tapped for the position. Not that Nick was opposed to spreading Christmas cheer throughout the world on an annual basis... He'd just always hoped he could accomplish that another way. Like by being a really good, kind, and thoughtful *normal* person!

If Nick didn't get the present situation cleared up with Sandy soon, the uncertainty would eat away at him all day. That's why he decided to stop by her gallery on his way back to Sisters' Row, before showering and changing for work.

"Well, don't you look like something the cat dragged in?" Sandy proclaimed gleefully as he walked in the door. Nick glanced at his image partly reflected in the window, thinking he didn't look *that* bad. Just because he hadn't yet shaved or combed his hair...

"I wanted to catch you before you opened your shop," he said in urgent tones. "Why don't you tell me what's going on?"

Sandy's lips creased in a frown and she strode briskly to the door. "Hang on," she said, locking it and drawing the blinds. Next, she traipsed into the back room and returned with a small tarp.

"What are you doing with that?" Nick asked, surprised.

Sandy carefully draped it over the shimmery snow globe in the front window. "Taking precautions," she whispered back.

Nick didn't like the sound of this. One bit.

"Has something happened?" he asked, his heart sinking. "Something to Grandpa?"

Sandy stepped toward him and confessed quietly. "It's his driving," she said, with a furrowed brow. "He's had two collisions on practice runs just this week!"

"Oh, no."

"Dad says this can't go on..."

"And, Mom?" Nick asked.

Sandy surreptitiously glanced toward the street to ensure nobody was approaching. "She thinks Grandpa can hang on a little longer..." Sandy lowered her voice even further. "With assisted care."

"Assisted care? What's that?"

"He'll need at least one little helper," Sandy explained. "Maybe two...with him at all times."

"But Grandpa is so independent."

"I *know*, Nick. But just think of the potential consequences."

Nick didn't really want to, because all of them were messy.

"It started about this time last year," Sandy told him. "With little things…like Grandpa forgetting to lock the gate. The reindeer were getting out, and all sorts of things."

"What about Grandma Claus?"

"She's extremely troubled by Grandpa's decline, and she's determined to help out. It's just that…" Sandy worriedly bit into her bottom lip. "Mom says that Grandma's way of helping involves baking *more* cookies! And Grandpa's getting chunkier as he ages," Sandy continued to confide. "Which makes it *even more* difficult for him to maintain control of his sleigh."

Nick raked a hand through his hair, not liking the sound of any of this. "Have SJ and Kris been contacted?" he asked, referring to his two older cousins on his dad's side.

"Of course. They'll be there, too."

"Be where?"

"At the NPCC meeting next weekend."

"Next weekend? But that's right before Christmas."

"Exactly, big brother," Sandy told him seriously. "Now, you're getting the point. Something has to be decided about how to handle this situation. Something before Christmas Eve."

"Are you thinking Grandpa might not be able to work this Christmas?"

"I'm hoping he can, and at least a few more."

"It would kill him to step down."

"I agree that he's not ready."

"So fine," Nick said decidedly. "We'll put a support system in place. The best we can find, so Grandpa can continue in his post for as long as possible."

"That's what everyone would like," Sandy agreed earnestly. "Including Grandma. I know you'll do a fine job convincing the community council that this is the right thing."

"Me? What about you? You're the persuasive one!"

"That's not true! You're much more convincing than I am. Not only that, you're available."

When he stared at her in confusion, Sandy went on. "You can't really expect me to leave Christmas Town next weekend? Not with Christmas coming and a family to think of?"

Nick had nearly forgotten Sandy had two newborns under foot and a stepdaughter and a husband to care for. A wave of shame washed over him for not being more sensitive to Sandy's plight. "Naturally, you're right. You can't go. You have to stay here."

"We can't trust the others," Sandy confided carefully. "Both Kris and SJ are itching to take the job, but—truthfully? I'm not sure either one is up to it."

"Why not?"

"Kris is too much of a randy bachelor," she whispered hoarsely. "Until he settles down, we can't have someone like him bringing a rotating bevvy of beauties to the…" She glanced around as if fearful someone was listening. "To…you know where!"

"And SJ?"

Sandy thoughtfully scrunched up her lips. "I suppose he'd do a satisfactory job. But 'satisfactory' is not stellar, Nick. Only someone like you—"

"*No-ho-ho!*" Nick burst in emphatically. "You can leave me out of it. Our parents promised us both regular lives. Remember? At least, as regular as we can manage." And, now that Nick had found a woman he could imagine spending forever with, he not only wanted a regular life, he *craved* one. Nick pined for a wife, home, and family, and a life in a regular town, like this one. Okay, so maybe Christmas Town wasn't completely regular, but—from the perspective of Nick's family—its needle definitely titled toward normal.

"You've got to be reasonable about this, Nick. Your abilities have always been stronger than mine. I'm betting that—now that they are getting even more powerful—they're surely stronger than Kris's and SJ's, too."

"Sandy…"

"And, if Olivia has started experiencing signs—"

"She hasn't, all right?" Nick's voice cracked harshly on the lie. "I'll agree you have a point about Kris. But SJ can grow into the job. Either of them probably could in time."

"But Nick—"

"There are no *buts* about it. I said I'd go help, but don't expect me to go volunteering—for anything beyond that."

"I didn't mean for *right now*, gosh."

"Not now, and not down the road, either," Nick said sternly. "I mean it, Sandy. That case is closed."

Olivia got to Santa's Sandwich Shop early and busied herself studying the menu, even though it never changed.

"What looks good today?" Jade asked, sliding into the booth beside her. "Lobster tails and champagne?"

"Lobster?" Olivia was taken aback. Had someone actually gone through their trash before Nick had been able to discard it at the Grand Hotel? The only person Olivia could think of who was that nosy was—

"Lou found the carry-out cartons," Jade explained in low tones. "From the Peppermint Bark! Totally posh."

Olivia hoped they hadn't smelled too badly.

"Lou said she followed her nose to the kitchen."

Uh-oh.

"You know how it is with fish?" Jade shrugged. "It can get its stink on if left out unrefrigerated."

"But the building was so cold!" Olivia protested.

"I'm sure it was…at night," Jade said slyly.

"I meant the next morn—" Olivia bit her tongue and Jade's eyebrows arched sharply.

"What would you know about the hotel the next morning? Unless…" She gasped and cupped a hand to her mouth.

"Hello!" Sandy shrugged out of her coat, sitting across from them. "What's happening?"

Hannah joined her next. They must have entered the restaurant at nearly the same time. "Happening?" Hannah asked, with a happy smile. "Does someone have news?" She gazed expectantly at Olivia, and Olivia sank down in her seat.

"Olivia was just reporting on the temperatures at the Grand Hotel...*on Saturday morning*," Jade added with undue emphasis.

"Morning?" Sandy asked, surprised.

"Yeah," Hannah said in a sing-songy tone. "Morning!" Her dark eyes shone and Olivia got the very distinct impression that Carter had told her everything.

"*Nooooo...*" Sandy shot a sidelong glance at Hannah and covered her eyes. Then she peeked between her fingers to stare at Olivia. "Really? You *did it* upstairs?"

Olivia's skin was so hot she felt like she'd bathed in five-alarm chili. "I...er..." Then suddenly, she wondered how Sandy had known that? "Wait a minute!" she said, flummoxed. "Did Hannah say...?"

"Nuh-huh," Sandy and Hannah parroted in unison. "Not a word."

Olivia narrowed her eyes at the pair, and Jade leaned forward with interest.

"I just sometimes, um..." Sandy bit into her bottom lip, trying to explain. "Get a glimpse into what Hannah's thinking."

"Really?" Jade asked, enthralled. "Then stay away from my brain, baby," she said to Sandy. "It's a dark and scary place in there! You don't want to *know* about me and Wendell when—"

Sandy's hands shot to her temples. "No! Right! I don't!" She smiled tightly at her friend. "Sorry, Jade. I love you, but I'll...take a pass."

"O-*kay*," Hannah said, appearing extremely intrigued by the entire conversation. She turned her bright eyes on Olivia. "So, tell us... Details! How did you wind up upstairs?"

Olivia goggled at them in disbelief then dropped her voice into a whisper. "I mean, seriously, guys... That's private."

"So, it's true?" Hannah asked with a stunned gasp. "I thought Carter had made the whole thing up!"

"Carter?" Jade asked.

"That's right." Sandy thoughtfully tapped her chin. "He was in the building investigating."

"He didn't tell any of us that he'd found something, though," Jade commented breezily.

"Maybe he kept it secret because it was an *undercover* operation," Hannah teased with a giggle.

"Ha-ha," Olivia said, flush with embarrassment. "You all are too funny!"

They started peppering her with questions at once.

"Weren't you cold?" Hannah questioned.

"Did you at least have a sleeping bag?" Jade wanted to know.

"Did he sweep you off your feet and carry you upstairs?" Sandy asked dreamily.

"Guys!" Olivia hissed, hushing them. "*Puh-leeze*."

"Oh, right. Right." They all seemed to collect themselves. They also appeared to be earnestly waiting on her answers. They couldn't be serious!

"I just knew you and my brother would make a good match," Sandy said knowingly. "I just knew it!"

"Do you think he'll move here?" Jade asked eagerly.

"I...don't know." Olivia's cheeks burned hot. "We haven't discussed things...that far."

"Well, I, for one, think that would be an excellent decision," Hannah said. "For the record, Carter does, too."

"Carter?" Sandy asked with obvious surprise.

"He said, he didn't know how Nick had done it, but he'd seemed to have won Olivia over 'fair and square.'" Hannah lifted a shoulder. "Whatever that means."

"I think it has something to do with Virginia Cookies," Sandy said solemnly. "Or the lack thereof."

Olivia decided not to mention that she and Nick had shared a Commitment Cookie only yesterday. Her friends were already into her business enough.

"Well, whatever charms he's employing," Jade said, referring to Nick, "they seem to be working."

Thankfully, their server finally appeared. Olivia had noticed that service was a little slow since Liz had left her job as a waitress here. Then again, Liz had enjoyed years of practice in the same slot, and the new person, Pam, was still learning. Pam had straight black hair, which she wore in a ponytail, and blue eyes. She'd been good friends with Lou's granddaughter, Noelle, in high school. When the twins went away to college, Pam had stayed home to work here and train as an apprentice at South Pole Pottery.

Pam took their orders, then the others agreed to leave Olivia alone for the rest of the meal. It helped that she'd threatened to disown them as friends if they didn't stop razzing her. She wouldn't have—really—of course. But there was only so much badgering a lovesick woman could endure.

They eagerly finished their lunches with Jade sharing stories about Alexander's latest antics at school, and reporting on Josiah's recent milestones progress.

He was starting to talk now! And, sit up on his own! Soon, he would be crawling…then Jade said she'd really be in trouble, with two kids to run after. Hannah and Sandy laughed easily, swapping stories about their babies, too.

Olivia felt a contented glow spread across her face. Not long ago, she'd felt so separate and apart from the rest of them. Now, nothing could feel further from the truth. Because, in her heart of hearts, Olivia was starting to imagine herself in the same way, as the mother of a baby boy or girl. And, in her mind's eye, that tiny tot had beautiful bright blue eyes—just like Nick.

Chapter Twenty-Six

The following Wednesday evening, Nick and Olivia entered the county courthouse building and headed upstairs. They were presenting their ideas concerning the restoration of the Grand Hotel to the Town Council, and Olivia was inexplicably a jumble of nerves. Nick sweetly took her hand before they entered the courtroom and gave it a squeeze.

"Everything will go just great," he whispered. "Think positive."

She nodded and pushed open the big oak door. The courtroom was jam-packed with all of its benches full, and people crowded in at the back and along the side walls. "Wow," she said quietly to Nick. "Full house."

He winked reassuringly. "Let's take that as a good sign."

It was actually hard to hear him above the roar of conversation in the room. Some folks were talking loudly, and others in thinly veiled whispers, which weren't technically so hushed.

"I hear they had a very romantic dinner at the hotel," one voice confided.

"Word is they're going out," someone else chirped.

"Ooh, I hope they'll marry!" *Hang on! That voice is Jade's!* Olivia whipped her head around trying to spot her. There she was! Sitting with Hannah, who started to agree, before spying Olivia and Nick.

"Me, t…oh! Look! There they are! Hi, guys!" Hannah's whole face brightened, but Jade's natural color darkened a shade. They waved meekly to Olivia and Nick, who stood near the back of the center aisle.

"This meeting will now come to order!" That was Ben sitting at the bench. He smacked his gavel twice and a hush fell over the courtroom, as the various conversations petered out.

"We could use someone like him here," Stan Martin commented to his sister, Liz.

"Absolutely," Liz agreed.

"Lots of old buildings in need of help," Buddy rumbled from beside them.

"Order!" Ben smiled genially and then added, "If you please." He continued by saying how delighted he was that Nick and Olivia had prepared a formal proposal, before asking Tilly if the AV equipment was ready. Tilly gave a cheery thumbs-up, and motioned Nick her way so he could connect his laptop for the big-screen presentation. While that was going on, Lou Christmas took the floor, welcoming everyone as the town mayor.

Olivia had only expected the Town Council members here, but apparently the public had also been invited to attend. "So as not to waste much time," Lou merrily went on, "we're prepared to cast a vote this very evening on Nick's architectural plan and his proposed budget. This will give Nick and Olivia time to set certain things in place for the actual work to begin just after the start of the year." She caught Olivia's eye, indicating an empty spot had been saved for her in the front row on the AV equipment side.

Olivia slid in beside Kurt Christmas, who said in hushed tones, "How's it going, Olivia?" His knowing wink said it all. "I hear really well."

She elbowed him hard, as Lou Christmas cleared her throat, shaking her head at them both. Walt was on Kurt's other side. He was attempting not to look at Olivia, but even from her vantage point, she could tell he was grinning. Either Ray or Meredith was probably here somewhere, with the other one staying home with Kyle, just as Sandy was at home with her kids.

Lou introduced Nick, who smiled at the round of applause. Olivia clapped loudly, too. She couldn't help but be extra enthusiastic. She was so proud of him and the fabulous plans he'd created. She just knew the Town Council would be wowed. Hopefully, the rest of the Christmas Town citizens in attendance here would approve, too. Ninety-nine percent of the effort that had gone into this proposal had been Nick's. She'd only helped with a bit of brainstorming. Olivia's real contributions would come in later with the finer details, in regard to interior decorating. She might help select furnishings, artwork, and light fixtures, for example. Though she would also have a say in choosing wallpaper, paint colors, and other rudimentary finishing touches first.

After Tilly dimmed the lights, Olivia glanced around the darkened room as Nick gave his talk. She detected interested smiles on several faces, and witnessed various people commenting positively to those seated beside them. More than once, appreciative sighs were heard when Nick flipped to a new slide, projecting the possibilities for the Grand Hotel. By the time he had finished, the entire courtroom of people was nodding and grinning happily.

"Well, I think that was just fabulous!" Lou said, stepping forward and encouraging a new round of applause. "Thank you, Nick! And a very big thank you to Olivia, too, for her excellent ideas," she added, citing the ones that Nick had mentioned. Lou then opened the floor to questions, inviting Olivia to step forward and join Nick in delivering the answers. She stood proudly beside him, beaming his way.

"Great job," she said quietly, but everybody heard her. Nick's face colored brightly, as Ben smacked his gavel and Lou instructed everyone to calm back down.

"Now!" Lou said cheerily, glancing around the room. "Who would like to ask a question first?"

"When are you two getting married?" Frank Cho shouted from the back. Chuckles rippled throughout the courtroom, and both Nick and Olivia blushed even brighter than before.

Lou held up her hand, silencing the group. "Serious questions, now!" But when she gazed at Olivia and Nick, Olivia could tell Lou wanted the answer to that question, too.

"I believe he *was* serious." Lou stared in shock at Carter, who'd apparently slipped in the back. "Why, Sheriff Livingston! I'm surprised at you!" Lou said in joyful tones.

Olivia was a little stunned, too. She hadn't been convinced that Carter was in her and Nick's corner. He'd obviously come around. Olivia secretly wondered if this had to do with what Carter had said to Hannah about winning Olivia's affections "fair and square"—whatever that meant, or whether Hannah had simply been working on Carter—on Sandy's behalf.

Ben smacked his gavel again. "Okay, folks. Let's leave their personal business to Olivia and Nick, and get things back on track."

Olivia heaved a sigh of relief, but Nick still looked slightly petrified. "You doing okay?" she asked him in a very low whisper.

"Sure," he whispered back. "*No-ho-ho* worries."

One hour later, and with the wholehearted support of its citizens, the Town Council unanimously approved Nick's architectural plan and budget, agreeing that work should go forward in the way that he and Olivia had proposed after the start of the New Year. The first three phases of the project would begin right away, and would concern restoring the exterior and interior of the building, from the basement through the third floor, while making it fully handicap-accessible. The final phase would begin around this time next year, with a consultant brought in to oversee the aspect of the fourth floor's conversion to a theatrical space.

Meanwhile, the Town Council would discuss the types of artisans they'd like to see included in the studio areas, and design an application process for renters. They'd also develop parameters for the type of restaurant they'd like to see in place and create a bid procedure, so any prospective restaurateurs could submit their specific ideas. Ben volunteered to provide his legal oversight in all these areas.

As people clapped and cheered, Nick grabbed his briefcase, then took Olivia's hand.

"Let's get out of here," he suggested happily. Nick was clearly relieved this was over, and he probably yearned for a bit of peace and quiet. After the noisy ruckus in the courtroom, Olivia completely understood.

As they departed, townsfolk congenially slapped Nick on the shoulder, saying their thank-yous. Many waved and smiled at Olivia as well, telling her they appreciated her input in the project. She and Nick bustled through the crowd, making their way out of the overheated room and quickly down the stairs to the first floor, before anyone else could catch up with them.

Olivia giggled as they burst out the front door facing the roundabout. "Oh, my!"

"You can say that again!" Nick grinned. "I think we can consider *that* a success."

"You were fabulous," she said, holding his hand as they scurried down the steps.

"So were you," he told her. "You didn't lose your composure for a minute. Not even…" He shook his head with a grin. "In the face of great odds."

"Before Frank and Carter, you mean?" she asked incredulously. "I'm going to get those guys! Seriously!"

Nick chuckled in return. "I'm starting to get the hang of this place."

"Yeah?"

"Yeah."

They paused when they reached the sidewalk. Night had moved in, and it was snowing lightly again with new mounds of flakes coating the town sign. Most of its message was still visible, though.

"You know, I'm starting to believe that," he said in a deep rumble.

Olivia's pulse pounded.

"Believe that great things really *do* happen here."

She stared up at him, her breath catching. "Great things have certainly happened for me…since you've been around."

With his free arm, he tugged her up against him. "You know what I think?" he asked, gazing down at her. "I think that we should celebrate!"

"Our victory tonight?"

His blue eyes danced. "Your place or mine?"

Olivia laughed with delight. "My place is closer."

"Plus, you've got a bigger stash of cookies," he added with a wink.

"We're going to need to rectify that," she said lightly. "You're going to have to take some of them home."

"All right," he said, kissing her soundly.

A gaggle of townsfolk streamed out the courthouse doors, and somebody pointed their way. "Look! There they are. Let's go ask them!"

"You think it's a business inquiry?" Nick asked Olivia quickly.

"Doubt it!" she said with a grin.

"Then let's get going," he said, giving her hand a happy tug. Then, together, they took off dashing down the snowy sidewalk…laughing all the way.

A little while later, Nick and Olivia snuggled together on her futon, having cocoa and eating cookies. "I believe these are the best you've made so far," he said with a jolly chuckle. "You'll need to stop doing this. You're spoiling me."

"I like spoiling you," she said, contentedly smiling up at him, and he cheerfully thumbed her nose.

"And, I like spoiling you back."

"I'm really happy about the Town Council meeting," she said. "Everybody loved your ideas."

"Everybody loved *our* ideas, Olivia. I never would have come up with such a great plan without you."

"I guess we make a great team."

"Yeah." He bent down and gently kissed her lips. "It's great spending time with you," he said. "I'm always happy when we're together."

"I know. Me, too."

"I hope we can still go skiing?"

"Of course."

"When I get back."

"Get back?" She sat up suddenly, pulling out of his embrace. "Where are you going?"

"I haven't wanted to tell you, because I hate the thought myself." He pulled a regretful face. "But that family business Sandy mentioned?"

"Yes?"

"It's a little more serious than I thought."

She viewed him with concern. "Is there some way I can help?"

"That's so like you." He smiled warmly. "Always thinking of others first."

"I mean it, though. If there's something I can do…?"

He set down their mugs and pulled her into a hug. "Just keep the home fires burning here."

"When will you leave?" she asked, her heart thumping against him.

Nick gently stroked her hair. "Tomorrow, I'm afraid."

"Tomorrow?" A tear burned in the corner of her eye. "Oh."

"I know it's a little sudden, and I'm sorry. So sorry about that." He kissed the top of her head. "I didn't have much warning myself."

She gazed up at him and his eyes were glistening, too. "What happened?"

"My grandpa, he's... He's going to need some help." Nick face was awash with sadness, and Olivia's heart ached for him. "Hopefully, I won't be gone too long. Just a few days."

Olivia reached up and stroked his cheek. "Isn't there anything I can do?"

Nick swallowed hard. "Say that you'll be waiting when I return."

"You know I will," she told him surely.

"Olivia?" Surprisingly, his voice was hoarse. "I so wish..."

She reached up and traced his lips with her fingers. "What do you wish, Nick?"

"I wish..." He seemed to muster his courage. "I wish that things were different. That I could give you the kind of life you want."

His admission both stunned and saddened her. "How do you know what I kind of life I want?"

He eyed her lovingly. "I can imagine."

"Then, what's so wrong with me imagining, too?" she asked softly.

"I imagine we both dream of the same things." His gaze washed over her. "A warm home...family...."

"A partner to rely on," she filled in boldly. "Nick," she challenged. "If this is about your job in Bangor and me living here, then there are ways—"

"I'm afraid the distance that threatens to divide us is far vaster than that."

Olivia's brow wrinkled in confusion. "I don't understand."

He hugged her tightly up against him and whispered against her hair, "I know you don't."

Nick held her a long while without speaking, but the tension in the air was thick.

"Nick," she said tenderly. "Please tell me what's wrong?"

His heartbeat pounded between them as he held on tighter.

"I'll come back for you, all right?" His voice cracked apart. "I'll find a way."

"Of course you will." She pulled back and cradled his face in her palms. "I love you, Nick. And you love me." She searched his bleary eyes. "Whatever the trouble is, we'll work it out together."

Later that night, Nick packed his bags with a heavy heart. He'd thought a lot about his conversation with Sandy since Monday, and he understood she was right about SJ and Kris. And yet, how could Nick even ask such a thing of Olivia? To change her way of thinking, and completely upend her life? None of his girlfriends from the past had been able to endure even the mildest hint of his powers. Olivia had brought them out in him ten-fold, and yet—the more powerful he became, the more Nick seemed to please her.

Nick was frightened by what this meant and extremely worried about Olivia. She said she loved him now, but would she really want him once she learned the truth? Perhaps she wouldn't even believe him, and would cast him aside as insane. Nick raked a hand through his hair, thinking he wouldn't blame her. If he hadn't grown up how he had, he'd have a hard time believing, too. And still...Nick held onto the tiniest glimmer of hope. While Sandy didn't have all the abilities Nick did, she had some pretty special powers of her own. Those notwithstanding, she'd found her perfect partner in Ben. Ben loved Sandy and accepted her—with his whole heart—just as she was. Could Nick be lucky enough to have Olivia feel the same way about him?

He might have a chance if his situation wasn't so different. For Sandy, things had been less complicated because she'd been able to commit to spending her life here. By contrast, Nick's future was totally uncertain. Was it really fair to ask a wife to shoulder that sort of uncertainty with him? Nick knew he needed to get some shut-eye before his long trip tomorrow, but he doubted very seriously he could sleep. He was tied up in knots over Olivia and afraid of certain decisions that might be made, which were beyond his control.

Nick's day-to-day existence might not change this year, or next...or even the year after that. But, sooner or later, his destiny was bound to catch up with him. Certain abilities in the Claus family skipped generations, and those particular genes were only inherited by males. If Nick denied his future, he'd be letting the world down, perhaps at a time when its people needed to believe in the magic of Christmas the most. Could Nick really be so selfish as to put his own desires above the happiness of countless others? But what about Olivia's happiness? Shouldn't that count for something, too?

Nick sat weightily on his bed and hung his head in his hands. He'd searched everywhere for answers, and had scanned endlessly through *Santa's Little Helper*. But at the end of the day, there was no better place to find the truth—than deep within his heart.

Chapter Twenty-Seven

Olivia woke up with a jolt. Someone was ringing her bell and it was… She squinted at her clock… Three in the morning? She groggily stumbled out of bed, grabbing her robe. *This must be some kind of emergency. Who in the world would call at this hour?* Olivia flipped on the overhead light and headed down the stairs, gripping the railing as she went. Her heart pounded harder as she approached the door, as she feared for the worst.

Against the darkened backdrop of the street, a familiar figure appeared framed by her front door's windows. "Nick!" she cried, yanking the door open in shock. His hair and field coat were buried in snow as winds howled around him. She latched onto his arm and pulled him inside, frantically surveying his features. "What's wrong?" His expression was haggard, and a frown tugged at his lips.

"I'm sorry to come by so late, but I… I had to see you." His eyes were like the ocean roiling in a storm. "We need to talk."

Olivia nodded, sensing something was very, very wrong. "Of course. Why don't you come upstairs?"

Nick followed her in a zombie-like trance, and Olivia's pulse raced. Whatever what happening, it was serious. She felt it like an icy river snaking through her veins.

When he sat on her futon, Olivia offered to make him some coffee to warm him up.

Nick said okay, but there was an eerie distance about him, a demeanor she hadn't witnessed before. After starting the coffee, Olivia returned to the living area and sat by his side. He still hadn't removed his coat.

"I couldn't sleep," he said hoarsely. "I just couldn't go…" He turned to stare at her and there was a harrowed look in his eyes. "Without telling you the truth."

"Take off your coat," she instructed kindly. "It's all wet. You'll catch your death."

Nick dropped his chin. "Maybe that would be a blessing."

"Nick Claus!" she said sharply, righting his chin in her hand. "I don't ever want to hear those words from you again."

His eyes bored into hers but she steadily held his gaze. "I mean it," she said fiercely. "If I have any say in this, you're going to be around for a long, long time."

"And just how will you ensure that?"

Her demeanor softened. "By feeding you lots of cookies."

This elicited a laugh, but it still sounded like a sad one.

Olivia let go of his chin and patted his cheek. "Don't give up on yourself—or me. Whatever it is, we'll fix it." She pointedly eyed his coat until he begrudgingly removed it. As she hung it on a hook, she turned to him. "This has something to do with your trip tomorrow, doesn't it?"

Nick's shoulders sagged with his admission. "I'm afraid so."

"Are you worried about your grandpa?

"Yes. But…it's more than that."

The coffeemaker beeped in the kitchen. "Hold that thought," she told him. "I'll be right back."

When Olivia returned with their mugs of coffee, Nick was still stewing over his problem. She'd never seen him so preoccupied before, and it worried her. Almost as soon as she passed him his coffee, Nick set it down.

"I love you so much." His voice was rough with emotion. "I can't bear to think…"

Olivia firmly took his hand. "Nick, please, babe. Tell me what's going on?"

"If I did, you probably wouldn't believe me," he said with a mournful look.

"Have you ever heard the expression 'try me'?" Olivia sported her brightest, most encouraging grin. "Come on! I'm ready."

Nick drew in a deep breath, then spoke quickly and without preamble.

"I'm Santa Claus's grandson and someday I might have to take over the family business. No, not *might have to*… The thing is, it's really pretty likely." He exhaled sharply. "Eventually!"

Olivia's eyes widened like saucers as she stared at him. She was still stuck on the first part. "Santa Claus's grandson?" she asked with incredulity.

"I know how that sounds…"

Yeah. Wacky! Whoa… Olivia sat back against the futon, her head spinning. How was she going to tell poor Sandy that her brother had become unhinged?

"Er…how long have you felt this way?" she asked, treading lightly, wondering all the while if she should call Kurt. He wasn't a psychiatrist, but maybe he had a sedative. Or…or would know what to do.

"For as long as I can remember," Nick said sincerely.

This was worse than Olivia suspected. A long-term delusion! How had Nick kept it hidden from her so well until now?

"When I was about five years old, I accidentally made a reindeer fly."

"A reindeer?" Olivia asked, swallowing hard. "As in one of Santa's…?"

Nick nodded blankly. "That's right."

"Was it…er…" She tried to think of reindeer names but only came up with one. "Rudolph?"

"Rudolph's not real." Nick smiled indulgently. "There are only eight official reindeer. Everyone knows that."

"Oh, right. Right!" Olivia laughed, playing along, hoping her laugh didn't sound manic.

"Dasher, Dancer, Prancer, and Vixen," Nick began, as if reciting. "Comet…Cupid…"

"Donner and Blitzen!" Olivia added cheerily, the names coming back to her from her children's book.

"Exactly!" Nick's expression brightened. "You know them?"

"Well, um…no. Not personally."

Nick frowned in concentration. "It's no use, is it? You think I'm nuts."

"No! I mean, not *totally*… You've got a really rational side!"

"A rational side?

"That architect thing!"

"It's not a *thing*, Olivia." He sounded significantly dismayed. "It's my career."

"But, it won't be your career forever, will it?" she asked fretfully. "You're eventually aspiring to be—"

"It's not an aspiration," he corrected. "It's a calling."

"A calling. I see."

"I'm afraid you don't."

"Maybe, that's because I can't?"

They both frowned sadly, staring at their coffee mugs.

This entire relationship had taken a really strange turn. Just last night Olivia was ready to marry Nick. But…that was before she learned he thought he was a Jolly Old Elf.

He slowly turned to look at her, and raised one eyebrow. "In all our time together, you have to have suspected…*something*?"

"Well, sure. I knew you were…extra special…" *And wonderful, and charming and kind*, Olivia couldn't help thinking. *Wait.* What was wrong with her? She couldn't go remembering all the good things! She needed to think clearly here…and put some emotional space between them.

"Olivia…" His blue gaze penetrated hers. "I think you knew more than that. Maybe not consciously, but somewhere deep inside."

She wasn't going to let him do this! Snare her into his delusion somehow. "I'd like to know where you're going with this?" she asked reasonably.

Nick hung his head in defeat. "Nowhere, I suppose. I just wanted you to know the truth. I thought I owed it to you." He stood to grab his coat, and Olivia gaped at him in disbelief.

"And now you're leaving? Just like that?"

"You clearly don't believe me," he said in pained tones. "So there's not much point in my asking."

As he walked to the door of her apartment, she queried weakly, "Asking what?"

Nick turned slowly on his heel. "I'd hoped that you would be my wife, Olivia." Agony was written in his eyes. "My forever partner, in good times and in bad…through thick and thin. For better or for worse," he said hoarsely. "No matter who my family was, or where I came from. I guess I was expecting too much."

Then he left her standing there stunned as his footfalls landed heavily on the stairs.

When Olivia heard her shop door slam shut, she burst into tears. Nick was absolutely right. He probably *had been* hoping for too much.

The wretched thing was, Olivia had been hoping for it, too.

Chapter Twenty-Eight

The next afternoon, Olivia was surprised to get a call from Sandy.

"Olivia, hi!" she began cheerily. "I'm calling you about Christmas Eve!"

"Christmas Eve?" Olivia tried to keep her chin from wobbling. "What about it?"

"With Nick being away, Ben and I were hoping you could join us for Christmas church?"

"Well, I don't know…"

"Come on," Sandy insisted. "The family service is so much fun. There will be candlelight, carols and everything."

"I know, I've been to it before."

Sandy must have detected the note of sadness in her voice. "Olivia? Is everything all right?"

Olivia wasn't sure how to answer that, because her world couldn't have seemed more wrong. The joy had gone out of her day, and she couldn't seem to put things right. She'd gone to Nutcracker Sweets on her lunch hour and had purchased an enormous box of dark-chocolate-cherry truffles. But, when she'd gotten the delicious treats home, Olivia hadn't been able to eat even one. She'd had absolutely no appetite. In fact, she couldn't remember eating this morning. Or later today—at all.

"I'm just a little under the weather," she lied. "I might have caught a touch of something." *Yeah,* Olivia thought gloomily to herself, *a touch of something over six feet tall with stunning blue eyes.* She sighed heavily, resisting the urge to weep again. She'd already cried through all her paper products once, and had to dash across the street to the Merry Market for more. And that had been before she'd opened her shop at ten o'clock!

"Oh, dear! I'm sorry to hear that," Sandy said sympathetically. "I hope you'll feel better by Christmas. Remember, we're doing the dinner at my place."

Olivia recalled that Jade's annual Christmas dinner with their friends had been shifted to Sandy and Ben's house this year, due to their increasing numbers. Jade and Wendell's small town house was no longer large enough to accommodate the growing group, with all the new spouses and babies. Olivia thought about how foolish she'd been to believe she was finally fitting in with a serious boyfriend of her own, and she almost burst into tears again.

"Thanks, Sandy," she answered shakily. "I'll try to make it."

"Try?" There was silence down the line and Sandy appeared to be stewing about something. "Did Nick get off okay?" she finally asked.

"I wouldn't know," Olivia said with a sniff. Those blasted tears were leaking from her eyes again and there wasn't a tissue box in sight! Olivia nabbed one of her old receipts from the stack by the register and dabbed her cheeks.

"Oh, dear…" Sandy softened her tone. "You two had a fight, didn't you?

"I wouldn't exactly call it a fight," Olivia said, sniffling again. "More like a misunderstanding."

"Do you want to talk about it?"

Olivia worried that might be awkward, with Sandy being Nick's sister. Then again, Sandy was also Olivia's good friend. And maybe Sandy needed to be made aware that her brother was having…mental trouble. "Maybe." Olivia's voice trembled. "Maybe that would be good."

"Do you want to meet somewhere?"

Olivia wasn't sure she could trust herself to keep it together in public. "How is the gallery right now? Busy?"

"Nope. Not a soul here." Since it was ten minutes till closing, most of the shopping traffic at the local stores had thinned out.

"Then, maybe I'll stop by."

"Great," Sandy said. "I'll have some cider ready."

Sandy rushed to take Olivia in her arms the moment she walked through the door. "Sweetheart," Sandy cried with dismay. "You look a mess!"

"Thanks." Olivia shared a half-hearted smile. "I'm hoping my customers didn't notice."

"Did you have a lot of them today?"

"Yes, quite a few."

"That was probably a good thing, eh?" Sandy said intuitively. "Kept your mind occupied."

Olivia nodded gratefully and slipped off her coat, as Sandy poured them each a hot cider. She locked the door and put out her closed sign, inviting Olivia to sit on a stool by the entryway table holding her gallery brochures and the cider set-up.

Sandy sat to join her, taking a sip from her mug. "We had a lot of shoppers come through here earlier, too."

"We?" Olivia asked with interest.

"Joy Christmas is back in town," Sandy informed her sunnily, and Olivia recalled that Joy was interning for Sandy during school breaks.

"How great! What hours does she work?"

"Just twelve until four. That's long enough for her to get a taste of things, but not so long as to overwork her. Plus, now..." Sandy smiled happily. "I can keep the gallery open during lunch."

"I'm sure that's a help."

"Yeah, and Noelle is back working for Hannah, too."

"I hope the girls had a good first semester at school," Olivia continued, making casual conversation.

"They did," Sandy responded pleasantly, before angling toward her with concern. "Now, tell me about you?"

Olivia suddenly felt stupid for coming here. What was she going to say? *Your brother and I had a falling out because Nick thinks he can make reindeer fly?* "I...I'm not sure where to begin," she said haltingly.

"How about at the beginning?"

Olivia tried to think back...all the way to Tilly's dog, and its strange behavior toward Nick on the street. No, that was way too much history. "The beginning's not important," Olivia said, deciding that it wasn't. "What matters is what happened in the end."

"Go on," Sandy said kindly.

"Well…you know Nick had to go? Had to go out of town?"

"To Canada, yes." Sandy shook her head. "He and I talked about it. I hope you don't… Oh, dear!" She worriedly viewed her friend. "I hope you don't think that Nick wanted to go and leave you in the lurch at Christmas. More than anything, he really wanted to be here."

"Oh…I…I see."

"I would have gone if I could have." Sandy's sincere blue eyes met hers. "But I've got the kids now; it's not so easy."

"I don't imagine it would be." Olivia sipped from her cider, gathering her nerve. As hard as it was, she should really tell Sandy the truth. In the end, it would be better for Nick. In spite of his nervous condition, Olivia still loved Nick dearly. She couldn't help it! Try as she might, she hadn't been able to talk her heart out of it. He was such a good guy—and he'd been so great to her. Nick deserved Olivia's compassion, more than anything. And her help. There *had to be* a way to get him help. Olivia would move heaven and earth to find the proper resources, and she was prepared to do that confidentially. It would be beneficial to have an ally in Nick's sister. Sandy would naturally want what was best for Nick, as well.

"So, tell me," Sandy said, sweetly patting her hand. "What's my blockhead of a brother done?"

"He…well…." Olivia struggled to find the good parts. "Mentioned something about marriage."

Sandy's whole face lit up. "Marriage! That's wonderful!" Then she read Olivia's expression and frowned. "Or, not. What did he do?" she asked with concern. "Totally muck up the proposal?"

"It wasn't a proposal—exactly." Olivia wrinkled up her nose in thought. "It was more like he said, he'd been *thinking about* asking me to marry him?"

"Hoo-boy." Sandy nearly choked on her cider. "I'm so sorry, Olivia. Nick's a really wonderful guy, but sometimes I wonder if he got animal crackers for brains in the romance department."

"It's not just in the romance department," Olivia ventured lightly.

Sandy's brow rose. "What do you mean?"

"I'm not sure how to put this…"

"Then, just state it plainly!"

Olivia bit into her bottom lip, and rushed ahead. "Nick thinks he can make reindeer fly."

"Is that all?" Sandy laughed and flamboyantly waved her hand. Then, she quickly got herself under control. "What I mean is…oh! Oh, yes. I see!" Her eyebrows knitted together, but somehow her expression looked fake. "I can see where that would pose a worry."

Olivia eyed her friend astutely before continuing. "He also thinks he's Santa Claus."

"Santa himself? Nick said that?" Sandy appeared taken aback. At last, she was reacting rationally.

"Well, not *Santa* Santa…" Olivia replied, correcting herself. "More like his relative, or something."

Sandy exhaled with relief. "Well, that's something."

"Something *what*?" Olivia pressed, flummoxed.

"A very important technical point!"

Okay, now Sandy was losing her. Olivia honestly didn't see what difference it made whether Nick thought he was Old Saint Nick or the guy's uncle or nephew! The whole thing was ludicrous anyway. "I can hardly see how that makes a difference?" Olivia blinked in alarm, thinking Sandy must not have heard her clearly.

"Nick's last name is Claus, isn't it?"

"Yes, but—"

"Same as my maiden name."

"Of course. Because you are brother and sister."

"So, if Nick says he's related to *someone*," she paused for emphasis. "Then, that means I must be, too!"

Good heavens above, the lunacy was spreading. "Sandy, er… I'm not sure what you're saying?"

"Don't tell anyone else, but it's true." She leaned forward in a confidential whisper. "Nick's and my granddaddy is known to the world as—"

Olivia shrieked as Buddy Christmas appeared from out of nowhere.

"*Ho-ho-ho!* How's it going?"

"Buddy?" Olivia said, blinking hard. "I thought Sandy locked the door?"

"Did you?" He turned and looked over his shoulder at the door that was locked up tight. "Oops! Sorry! I sometimes forget I can do that."

Olivia felt the color drain from her face.

"It's a Claus thing," Sandy whispered to her. "You thought maybe it was about going down chimneys? Nope! Not everybody has one."

"But…your name's Buddy Christmas?"

"The Christmas and the Claus families go way back," Buddy boomed. "My grandpa and Sandy's great-grandmother were brother and sister!"

Olivia was too stunned for words. Buddy viewed her carefully then said to Sandy, "Odd, that I could do that with Olivia sitting here? Does she have special powers?"

Sandy shrugged. "Don't know!" She and Buddy turned their watchful gazes on Olivia and she wanted to melt into the floor. *Special powers? Me?*

"I'm sure I don't know what you're talking about," Olivia stammered.

"Have you noticed anything different about yourself since meeting Nick?" Buddy asked hopefully.

"Developed any particular urges?" Sandy queried.

"Urges?" Olivia's face flashed hot. She was still trying to wrap her head around the fact that Buddy had seemingly walked through that solid door. "Like...er...what?"

"A compulsion to do something," Buddy explained. "Over and over again."

"Beyond reasonable expectations," Sandy put in.

"You mean, like...uh...baking cookies?"

"You've been baking cookies?" Sandy asked gleefully.

Olivia nodded frantically. "Loads and loads of them."

Buddy held up one chubby finger. "I knew you were *the one*."

Olivia's pulse raced. "One for what?"

"Buddy," Sandy said to him seriously. "I think I'd like a moment alone with Olivia."

"Of course! I just stopped by to see if Joy was still here." He straightened his overcoat and glanced around. "She and Noelle are expected at our house for dinner."

"You might try Jolly Bean Java," Sandy said with a wink. "Devon's working there this afternoon," she said, referring to Joy's high school boyfriend.

"Will do!" Buddy turned toward the door and gave a deep *ho-ho-ho*. "No worries!" His blue eyes twinkled merrily. "I'll use the doorknob this time."

Olivia sat up on the stool stock-still in fright. It wasn't just Nick, the whole town had gone mad. And they were dragging her down with them!

Sandy read her frozen look. "Olivia," she said kindly. "There's nothing to be afraid of. There's nothing in Christmas Town but goodness and love."

"And your family?" Olivia's voice squeaked. "And Buddy's? What's the deal there?"

"Our ancestry goes way back," Sandy explained. "We share very special DNA. None of us can help it; it's just who we are. Just like your eyes are green and your hair is red."

"Yes, but I don't go…walking through doors, or—"

"Knowing things about others?" Sandy asked pryingly. "Like when they are drawing near?"

"Well, I…" Olivia's cheeks burned hotly. "I hardly see how a little intuition—?"

"That's it, exactly! Intuition! It's what all of us have, to varying degrees. Nick claims he experiences his more as *impressions*. But, whatever…" Sandy shrugged mildly. "It's all a question of semantics."

Olivia couldn't believe she was following Sandy's logic, like it was almost making sense. She vehemently shook her head, thinking no, it couldn't. That would mean believing in magic, and all sorts of other things that couldn't be rationally explained.

"It's not a question of believing—or not, Olivia," Sandy continued further. "It's more about opening your mind—and your heart."

"To what?" Olivia asked, flabbergasted by this entire conversation.

"To everything that's beautiful—and possible— within you, and within me. Within all of us."

"Did you…tell all this stuff to Ben?"

Sandy nodded warmly. "In the beginning, it was hard for him to understand, too."

"I'll bet!" Olivia suspiciously eyed her friend, wondering what else Sandy and the rest of the town had been keeping from her. "Who else knows about this Claus thing?"

"Only a very limited few," Sandy assured her.

"Jade?"

"No."

"Hannah?"

"She suspects, but doesn't know for sure. Then again…" Sandy grinned. "Hannah makes some pretty special magic of her own with those Virginia Cookies."

"Yes, that's what I've heard." Olivia turned her eyes on her friend. "But, magic doesn't work on magic, does it?"

Sandy answered craftily. "That kind of depends…"

"On what?"

"On how strong someone's powers are," Sandy explained. "If a person already possesses extraordinary abilities, it would be unusual for simple magic to influence them. They'd be immune…"

"Like Nick," Olivia said with a gasp.

"Have you and Nick…" Sandy appraised her knowingly. "Made some kind of magic of your own?"

Tears burned in Olivia's eyes. She *had* experienced magic with Nick, she had! While dancing…and kissing…and certainly when making love. And, even in the forest…for a fraction of a second, she'd actually thought that their horses had levitated right off the ground.

"The best kind," Olivia answered with a sigh. "Oh Sandy, I love him! I do! I just can't… Don't know what to think about any of this."

"You don't have to make peace with it immediately," Sandy said gently. "You can take your time."

"Do you know when Nick's coming back?"

Sandy sadly shook her head. "I'm afraid that depends on a lot of things."

"And, Nick's magic…is…very powerful, you say?" Olivia asked this carefully, wanting to get it right.

"As powerful as they come!" Sandy's grin broadened. "Buddy reports Nick's abilities are stronger than any that have been seen in the family for generations."

"For generations? Really?" Olivia experienced an unexpected prickle of pride. "Wow."

"That's why the NPC Council…" Sandy quickly cupped her mouth. "Oops! Sorry! I'm not supposed to tell you. Not until you're officially in the family, anyway," she said with a wink.

"This has something to do with Nick's calling, doesn't it?" Olivia asked sagely.

Sandy's eyebrows rose. "Maybe Nick's shared more with you than I believed."

"He didn't tell me everything," Olivia confided. "Just enough."

"You mean, he mentioned the North Pole?"

"He said something about Canada."

"The Maritime Provinces, sure. That's where the *actual* pole is…" Sandy grimaced, stopping herself again. "Sorry! I'm not supposed to tell you!"

Olivia eyed her appraisingly. "In any case, yeah. Nick said some…interesting stuff."

"And, how did you respond?" Sandy asked cautiously.

Olivia sadly shook her head. "Pretty much as you'd guess."

"It's okay," Sandy said. "Give yourself time to come around."

Olivia lightly touched her arm. "It's not just about Nick, though," she told Sandy seriously. "It's about everything. About what that might mean for someday."

"I know, honey. I know," Sandy said warmly. "That's why nobody will fault you for whatever decision you make. Believe it or not, not even Nick."

When Olivia stared at her in surprise, Sandy added, "My brother loves you, I'm certain he does. And if I know my brother, then I'm sure of one thing. He wants you to be happy."

Chapter Twenty-Nine

Nick returned to his room, feeling down. By all accounts he should be happy about the way things had gone. The North Pole Community Council had been able to work things out, so his granddad could continue in his job for a few more years. Several, if he was lucky. Yet, the future remained uncertain, like a clouded-over crystal ball. Nick so wished he could see what was to come. More than anything, he wanted Olivia to be a part of his life, but this was looking less and less likely every day. She hadn't exactly been receptive to his story, when he'd told her about his family, and Nick clearly couldn't blame her. Even if she did believe him, what kind of woman would want to take his kind of baggage on?

"Knock-knock? Can I come in?" His dear grandma entered slowly, gingerly balancing a tray. She wore a festive holiday frock, lace-up leather boots, and a red velvet cape with a high fur collar. Her long, silver hair was tied up in a bun. She had once been a beauty, and that was evident still. The contours of her face were subtle in their elegance, with small laugh lines surrounding her mouth and eyes.

"I brought you some cookies and milk," she said, setting her tray on the dresser. Nick was in the same room in the cabin he used to occupy as a boy. His parents, who customarily stayed there during vacations with Nick and Sandy, now lived in the main house with the senior Clauses.

The room with split-log walls and a low rough-hewn ceiling was rustic and warm. Animal fur coverings draped over chairs and were piled high on the single bed. Ambient heat from the woodstove in the main room drifted in the door, as a real candle flickered on the bedside table. There was no electricity in the cabin, or running water. Both things had made it seem terribly exciting to Nick as a child.

"You shouldn't have gone out in the cold," he admonished her fondly. "It's far too chilly tonight."

"Nonsense!" she said cheerily. "I'm used to it, you know."

His grandmother unwrapped her snow-speckled cape and draped it across a chair.

"Nicholas?" she said, sitting beside him on the bed. "What's wrong?"

He studied the gorgeous older woman with a heart of gold. He'd never known his Grandma Claus to be anything but patient and kind. "I don't know what you mean," he answered.

"Ah," she replied stoically, "but I think that you do." Candlelight flickered against the cabin walls, as she continued. "Your heart is hurting, isn't it? You're at a crossroads?"

Nick's mouth dropped open as he gazed into her deep-set eyes.

"It's one of my talents," she explained quietly. "*Feelings.* I can sense them. And right now…" Her dark eyes glistened. "That well of emotion within you is about to make me cry."

"Grandma, no," he said hoarsely. "I'm sorry."

"*Never* be sorry for what you feel," she told him sternly. "Not when it's powerful and good."

"But how can it be good when I feel like I'm being cleaved in two?"

"That's part of the process," she said gently. "You're working through it."

"What process?"

She observed him tellingly.

"Becoming your own man. Reconciling with who you are."

"I don't know if I want to be that person—without Olivia."

His grandma reached out and took his hand. "Then go to her, son, and tell her. Tell her that you can't see a way forward without her. Because it's true." She smiled softly. "Isn't it?"

Nick smiled in understanding.

"How did you get to be so wise?"

Her musical laughter filled the room.

"Through *years* and *years* of living with your grandfather!"

She studied Nick in the shadows, then spoke more seriously. "If you think for a minute that he and I were sure in the beginning…that we knew we could make it—with this kind of life…then you're wrong. You have to take a leap of faith, Nicholas, and go where your heart leads you. If it leads you to Olivia, then I'll be happy. If it ultimately leads the two of you back here, then I'll be happier still. But, mostly, my child." She squarely met his eyes. "I want you to listen to that small still voice inside you. It's your conscience, and it will never steer you wrong. Do you want to know why?"

When Nick nodded, she said, "Because you're a Claus, Nicholas, and you will find your way. The right way—to the life you're meant to lead." Her dark eyes twinkled. "Just as your grandfather found his way to me."

She gave him a kiss on the forehead and stood, before turning away.

As she tugged on her cape, Nick said, "Grandma…"

"Yes, dear?"

He'd always thought the world of her, but now he adored her even more. "I don't think I've ever appreciated this as deeply until now… But Grandpa…" Nick swallowed past the lump in his throat. "…is a very lucky guy."

"I know he is," his grandma returned with a wink. "But I've never forgotten that I'm pretty lucky, too."

Olivia awoke early on Christmas Eve morning, after a very restless night. She'd had that dream again about flying in Santa's sleigh, and now she knew why. Could it be that Nick was right? Had she been subconsciously detecting something about the truth all along? Olivia tossed aside the covers and climbed from her bed, padding to the closet. After slipping on her robe, she reached for the children's book she'd stashed high on a shelf. *The Night Before Christmas* by Clement C. Moore. Olivia carried it in a daze to her futon and sat to leaf through its colorful pages. The artist's rendering of the "Jolly Old Elf" certainly didn't look like Nick. Though there was that familiar twinkle in his eyes and they *were* bright blue.

Now she was being ridiculous! Of course the artist's rendering looked nothing like the real thing. Because the real thing didn't exist! Olivia paused in doubt… Did it? Her head whirled in confusion, when Olivia realized Nick wasn't the real deal anyway. He was just some sort of unusual understudy. *Or, is he more like an heir? An heir to a magical kingdom?* If that were the case, then that would make Nick something akin to royalty. Olivia gasped in understanding. And, he'd asked her to be his queen! She ran and grabbed her computer off the coffee table, her mind snagging on an important detail. It was somewhere in Nick's PowerPoint presentation. Since she'd downloaded the file to her desktop, she was able to find it quickly. Olivia rapidly flipped through the slides one after the other until—*there*.

This was the one she'd been seeking. It was a color sketch of the mural painting Nick had planned for the ballroom featuring Mr. and Mrs. Claus dancing against a Christmassy backdrop. The older middle-aged couple was charmingly classical, and yet…*wait!* Olivia could spot the resemblances now. Mrs. Claus was clearly a redhead with deep green eyes, and Mr. Claus… *Oh my goodness*. Olivia's heart pitter-pattered. It was hard to deny it. He was a future glimpse at Nick! Olivia goggled at the screen, her mouth hanging open. It was like one of those talented police sketch artists had fast-forwarded time to show Nick and Olivia in another thirty years. *Well, gosh*, Olivia thought, eyeing Nick's projected girth, *we're going to have to really cut back on those cookies!*

She flipped shut her laptop and sat back on the futon in wonder. What else could this mean? Olivia had definitely been experiencing *urges* to bake lots of cookies, and she did seem to detect when Nick was around...What's more, Nick was very special, more special than any other guy she'd met—in the most extraordinary ways. Her rational side didn't want to believe, but her more emotional heart yearned to hang on to the fantasy. Olivia thought back to some of the historical love stories she'd read, and those tales of besotted women following the adventuresome men they loved to the far ends of the globe. Did she have it within herself to be equally daring? Was love truly enough to conquer all? And, what would this mean for their children, assuming she and Nick had them someday?

Olivia folded her face in her hands, her head and her heart pounding. She felt utterly overwhelmed. This was almost too much to process. Too much to comprehend. No regular person could be strong enough, she thought surely...except Ben.

Later that morning, Olivia took it upon herself to do the unthinkable. She went to see Ben in his chambers to ask what it was like being married to the granddaughter of Santa Claus. Since Christmas Eve fell on a weekday, all the businesses closed early. She'd called ahead to make sure Ben was still at work before heading over to see him. When she arrived, he was just closing up shop.

"Olivia," he said pleasantly, snapping shut his briefcase. "Good to see you! Merry Christmas."

"Uh...merry Christmas, Ben!" Olivia suddenly felt really, really stupid for being here. Maybe she was the one who'd gone nuts. Perhaps nothing from this past week had really happened. *Maybe Nick Claus doesn't even exist?* Olivia shuddered in fright, wondering if she'd concocted an imaginary boyfriend. She'd heard of weird things like that happening to seriously deranged people!

"Won't you have a seat?" He viewed her curiously, obviously wondering what she was doing here. He sat behind his polished mahogany desk and Olivia took a chair facing him and the window positioned behind him. It was snowing harder than ever today, with vehicles circling slowly through the roundabout, their wiper blades swishing furiously.

"Is this about your store?" Ben queried professionally. "All Things Christmas?"

Naturally, he had to believe her visit had to do with a work concern. A business license snafu or a city licensing problem. Why else would she be here? *Why, indeed? Ha-ha.*

Olivia's face grew hot. "No, actually, it's..." She suddenly lost her nerve and leapt to her feet. "I'm really sorry to have troubled you. It was silly of me! Uncalled for! I'll just run along and—"

"Olivia," he said calmly. "Please, sit back down."

There was an odd sort of understanding in his dark brown eyes. Understanding and compassion, too. "You've made it a point to come here, so I wish you'd tell me what the trouble is?"

Olivia swallowed hard. "Trouble?"

"I've been in this post less than a year, but, believe me, already I've heard plenty." Ben smiled kindly. "There's probably nothing you could say to shock me."

Olivia wished she could be sure about that. She fiddled with the end of her braid that was slung forward over one shoulder. "I'm…er…having a bit of a personal issue, that's all."

"Personal?" Ben's neck seemed to redden. "Oh! Well…" He uncomfortably cleared his throat. "In that case, perhaps I'm *not* the best one to—"

"It concerns Sandy," she put in and this stopped him in his tracks. Ben seriously met her gaze.

"What about her?"

"I…oh… Gosh, Ben! I'm not really sure how to ask it."

"Ask what?" he replied, flummoxed.

"Is Sandy really Santa Claus's granddaughter?" she asked with a squeak.

Ben's complexion paled. "Who told you that?" he asked slowly.

"Well, um…nobody directly. It was just kind of implied." Olivia stared meekly at Ben. "By Nick…"

Ben leaned back in his leather chair, appearing to take this in. He lifted a pen from his desk and thumped the end of it against his desk blotter. Again, and *again* and *again*. Olivia was just about to snatch it out of his hand when he dropped it suddenly. Ben leaned forward and spoke in a hushed whisper.

"How involved are you and Nick?"

"Pretty involved, I'd say." Heat flashed at her temples. "He's asked me to marry him… Sort of," she added, not wanting to mislead in any way. It really hadn't been a formal proposal. More like a preempted proposal withdrawal. In any case, Nick clearly had been thinking about the long-term for the two of them.

Ben nodded solemnly. "I see." He studied Olivia carefully before asking, "You're worried there might be some sort of family issue, aren't you? That the Clauses aren't quite…" He tapped his skull with his finger. "…right?"

"Uh, no! Not Sandy! She's a jewel!"

"Granted."

"Nick is, too! It's just that…" Olivia realized that she was in pretty deep now, so she might as well forge ahead. "This Santa Claus thing?" Her eyebrows rose as she waited for Ben to agree that the notion was ridiculous. Instead, he shot her an unexpected wink.

"Pretty spectacular, isn't it?" he said in hushed tones.

Olivia blinked hard, not once—but twice. "You mean, you…believe?"

"It was hard at first, I'll concede that. But, over time?" He considered her carefully. "Yes, I've certainly come to believe."

"But it's so fantastic! The whole story!"

Ben's dark eyes sparkled. "What's more fantastic than love? And hope? And joy?"

"I…I'm not sure."

"The Clauses are a special clan, Olivia. Their magic isn't suited for everyone, but if Nick's convinced that it's suited to you, then you might want to think about trusting him."

Olivia's heart sank. "I'm not sure if Nick's convinced…any longer."

"Why?" Ben asked gently. "Because you rejected him?"

Well, she hadn't exactly done that. Olivia hadn't precisely *accepted him*, either.

"It's not even Christmas," Ben went on. "And, you'll be working with Nick a little longer. There's still time."

"Time?" she asked feebly.

"To sort things out. Decide what you want to do."

"How did you decide?"

Ben smiled warmly. "I looked into my heart, and you know what it told me?"

She waited for him to continue.

"It said that I'd be a fool to let a woman like Sandy go. Someone so genuine and kind and wonderful, just because of her birthright...because of things completely beyond her control."

Olivia finally got what he was telling her, and that understanding warmed her soul.

"Thanks, Ben. That...that was very helpful."

"Merry Christmas, Olivia," he said when she stood to go. "I hope it's your best one ever."

Chapter Thirty

When Olivia exited the old stone church, snow was drifting lightly, dusting the cars in the parking lot and cloaking the lampposts lining North Main Street. Pastor Wilson warmly took her hand as he stood in the doorway. "Merry Christmas, Olivia." Then he added with a wink, "I hope Santa's good to you!"

Olivia yanked back her hand with a jolt. "Santa?" Her whole face steamed. "Right!" But the kindly minister was already engaged in conversation with Sandy and Ben behind her. He said something to Lily, and she wished him a merry Christmas, asking the clergyman whether he'd been naughty or nice.

Pastor Wilson chortled in reply. "We'll leave that to the Man Upstairs to decide," he said good-naturedly.

As they headed out into the cold, Sandy caught up with Olivia. "Thanks for joining us tonight. We're really glad you did."

Olivia was glad, too. Seeing Sandy and Ben's relationship in action only made Olivia realize how precious love was. The couple shared a deep affection for each other, and they were excellent parents. They'd left the twins at home this evening with Joy Christmas to babysit. Joy had a special way with the babies, and had been happy to help out since she'd planned to attend the eleven o'clock service with Devon later.

Ben was extra kind in not mentioning Olivia's earlier visit to the courthouse. While Olivia suspected Ben had told Sandy about it, the two of them obviously had decided that this was now a private matter for Olivia to wrestle with on her own. One way or another, they were there for her as friends, and wouldn't judge her, regardless of the choice she made. Good friends stood together, and Sandy and Ben were no exception.

Since they lived on Church Street, their home was only a few short steps away. "Can I grab my SUV and drive you home?" Ben offered gallantly. Olivia thanked him, but declined, saying she enjoyed walking in the snow, and that it wasn't more than a few blocks anyway. The sidewalks were bustling besides. Olivia parted from her friends, wishing them all a happy Christmas and saying she'd see them tomorrow. Because she was unsure of Nick's plans, Olivia had decided to go ahead with her previous arrangements.

Olivia strolled down the festive avenue, her spirit feeling light. Everywhere she looked, she saw loads of friendly faces… People she knew very well and others she was acquainted with just barely. Yet, all of them were glowing with good cheer and exchanging Christmas tidings. Christmas Town was in its element, with the sound of Christmas carolers filling the air. Olivia stared up at Buddy and Lou's front porch, spying a band of merry carolers holding flickering candles high in the darkness. The joy of the season was spreading through Christmas Town, and all of its residents were swept up in the jubilation.

It was hard for Olivia to imagine leaving this place.
She loved the town and its people dearly. There was
only one thing Olivia loved more. He stood over six
feet tall, had rich dark hair and stellar blue eyes. When
he grinned, his left cheek creased in a dimple. Olivia's
heart fluttered just at the thought of him. On a very
basic level, she understood that things were finally
falling into place. Olivia didn't need to know her plans
for next week or even next year. She only needed the
certainty that Nick would be with her.

She passed the Grand Hotel, recalling the amazing
evening she spent there with Nick. He'd gone out of his
way to woo her, and in doing so he'd won her heart.
Olivia could never feel that way about another, or make
that special kind of magic with any other man. *Nick* was
the only man she wanted, now and forever going
forward. It didn't matter about his family, or the future
that might confront him. All that mattered was the love
between them. And, Olivia realized with a certainty,
she loved Nick with all her heart.

Olivia thought of Savannah, and how poorly the
conversation had ended between them, the last time
they spoke. Naturally, Savannah had been concerned by
some of the things Olivia said. When Olivia stepped
back and viewed them from Savannah's perspective,
she could understand why. Still, Olivia missed her sister
and didn't want to stay at odds with her. While Olivia
obviously couldn't be expected to tell Savannah
everything, Savannah was sure to come around after
Olivia explained more fully about what a wonderful
person Nick was. Olivia was further betting that
Savannah would approve of Nick, once she'd met him

in person. Olivia wanted to have Savannah visit
Christmas Town at the first opportunity.

She also hoped to get Savannah interested in the
Grand Hotel project. The fourth floor's conversion to a
dramatic space presented the perfect chance for
Savannah to become involved. Since Savannah worked
at a school, perhaps she could be brought in as a
consultant over her winter break? That would mean
extra money for Savannah, and the project would be the
ideal outlet for her creative energies. If things went
really, really well, Savannah might even stay in
Christmas Town to manage the theater! Olivia found
herself growing more and more excited about the
possibilities, until she recalled one minor problem:
James.

Oh well, even having Savannah in Christmas Town
for a short while would be a joy. Carter would love
having their sister here, too. Olivia reached All Things
Christmas, contentedly deciding on two things. One,
she would call Savannah on Christmas Day to wish her
a happy holiday and make amends. And two, she
couldn't wait to see and make things up with Nick
Claus. Her pulse pounded as she imagined Nick taking
her in his arms. She'd grown lonely for him since he'd
been away, and Olivia couldn't wait for his return.

Nick unlocked the door to his rental unit at Sisters'
Row at five minutes past midnight. He'd returned to
Christmas Town as quickly as he could. Unfortunately,
it had been a long journey. His grandpa had set out very
early this morning with his assisted care team for the far
side of the world, where hopeful children lay sleeping.
Not all little ones were lucky enough to have parents

who could buy them presents. Some were in need of very basic necessities, like food, clothing, medical care, and shelter. If Santa could plant the proper seeds of compassion within the right hearts, more good could be done for a greater number of children throughout the earth.

While naysayers bemoaned the commercialism of Christmas, some failed to see the forest for the trees. There was joy in the season and love, and Santa was merely the messenger of these very important beliefs. Those who kept Christmas in their hearts were certain to love their neighbors, and deliver charity to communities they engaged with near and far. For, the world was definitely becoming a smaller place, and all people were bound to love each other, just as they themselves were loved.

Because of his upbringing, Nick inherently understood these truths. Now, he yearned for Olivia to understand them, too. He wanted her as more than a wife. Nick longed to have Olivia as a helpmate and friend, someone who could assist him in his ultimate mission of spreading the holiday spirit and forever protecting the season's joy. Nick removed his coat and hung it on the hook by the door, understanding what he had to do next. He had to talk to Olivia, and see if she'd be willing to give their relationship a chance. For now, Nick was content with being a restoration architect, and he believed he could develop a business for himself in Christmas Town. He'd move from Bangor without a second thought, and would be happy to stay here as long the fates allowed. There was only one important condition.

Chapter Thirty-One

Olivia woke up before daybreak in giddy anticipation. Nick was *coming home*, she could feel it! She didn't know when she'd see him next, but sometime today for certain. Olivia had stayed up half the night baking extra cookies, yet she wasn't the least bit tired. On the contrary, she was energized. Plus, she had a sneaky little plan for the man of her dreams. After a couple of hours of Internet searching, she'd amassed a number of healthy, low-fat, low-sugar cookie recipes! *Yay!* Nick could indulge to his heart's desire and never develop that family tummy. Not that she wouldn't love him, anyway. If it came to that, Olivia knew she'd merely believe there was more of Nick to love! Ooh, she couldn't wait to get her hands around that hunk of a man, and tell him that she'd thought things through.

Everything was *okay*. Nick's family history was okay, his potential future occupation was okay, the whole notion of North Pole magic was a little crazy—but, *okay*, Olivia had accepted it. If a rational man like Ben could believe in Santa, then why couldn't she? Ben had a law degree, for heaven's sakes, and was used to examining all the angles. And, his closing arguments had certainly made sense.

The one thing Olivia wanted to know now was....*is there a tiara involved?* Not that it really, really mattered. And a tiara would probably be impractical anyway, especially if it contained real gemstones. But it should be all right for special occasions! Olivia paused briefly, wondering what those might entail. She didn't suspect the Maritime Provinces Clauses got out much, but one never knew! And if they didn't, then... Well, Olivia could help her and Nick make couple friends! Sure! She'd take the neighbors plates of...um...cookies. Olivia gulped hard, staring around her cluttered apartment. What had she done?

Cookie tins were stacked high everywhere, even crowding the futon. She'd need to move a few of those if someone wanted to sit down. Olivia stared down at what she'd slept in, which was basically Nick's sweater, deciding she'd better get dressed for the day. At any moment, the love of her life could appear, and she wanted to be ready! Olivia raced toward the bathroom, doing a little cheer with her fists pumping skyward. Goodness, she felt great today. *So, alive! And happy! And freeeeee...* Olivia looked down with fright, seeing her feet had left the ground.

She knitted her eyebrows together and commanded fiercely: "*Down!*" When nothing happened, she added sweetly: "*Please?*" Despite the shrill squeak in her voice, that seemed to work. Her slippers descended gently onto the bathmat, making an excellent landing. Olivia's knees wobbled. *Gracious!* She took a mental note. Who knew that magic required manners?

Olivia cautiously glanced around, waiting to see if anything else was going to happen, but her equilibrium seemed steady now. She slid back the shower curtain with a trembling hand and turned on the water. This was really charged stuff! Just the thought of Nick sent her soaring! Her insteps started tingling again and Olivia decided she'd better focus on something else. Like another cookie recipe, or something. She wondered about brownies, and if they'd qualify?

She'd have to ask Nick, when—*Oops! Noooo!* Olivia fiercely gripped the towel bar as her feet swung out sideways, levitating over the toilet. Hopefully, *he'd* have some tips on how to deal with this, she thought frantically, taking great care not to even *think* his name again.

Her legs were straight out to the side as if lifted by a big gust of wind, but they didn't hurt or anything. They felt lighter than air! *Maybe because they are? Gosh!* Olivia's knees were still shaking though, and that wobble went all the way down to her ankles and feet. One slipper worked its way off, and—*kerplunk! Ew!*— dropped straight into the open toilet bowl.

Olivia sucked in a breath and shut her eyes, gripping the towel bar tightly with one hand, while trying to force her legs toward the floor with the other. But every time she batted her legs down, they popped back up again like helium balloons! Olivia focused hard, remembering to ask nicely. *"Pretty please with a cherry on top! Land, feet! Land!"*

Her legs dropped suddenly like a ton of bricks. *Oomph!* She righted herself just in time, landing in a crouched position. Olivia stared down at the soaked slipper in the toilet, thinking she was definitely going to have to work on this. Then she had a stellar idea.

Although he sensed that Olivia was awake, Nick decided to wait until sunup to visit her. He'd sat all night on the sofa without sleeping a wink. Then again, that wasn't unusual for Nick on Christmas Eve. He'd always had insomnia on that particular night, and last night was no different. Of course, this time, he hadn't been able to sleep from hopeful anticipation. Would Olivia say yes? Could Nick convince her that his heart was true, and that his emotions were sincere? Together, they could work through anything. Nick was sure of it. If only she'd be his.

Nick finished his morning coffee, setting his mug down on the coffee table. He had two wrapped packages there, and both were for Olivia. The larger gift had been provided by Nick's grandmother. She'd handed it to him joyfully before he'd departed Canada, giving him a warm hug and wishing him the best of luck. The smaller present was something Nick had purchased on his own with exceptional care.

Nick was cautiously optimistic, yet nervously skittish, as he slid on his coat and headed out the door, his Christmas packages in hand. Nick had always been more about giving than receiving, but—this year, and this year alone—he desperately wanted something for himself. He wanted the beautiful redhead who lived down the street to say she'd be his wife.

He stepped onto the porch, his spirit feeling light. More heavy snow had fallen last night, completely covering the street and sidewalk. Nick had to be the first one out in it, as it glistened pristinely, unmarred by footprints anywhere. As he made his way along, his boots crunching crisply beneath him, odd animals began to appear. Deer scampered out of the forest, prancing up Santa Claus lane, squirrels skittered down branches, and morning birds landed behind him, hopping right along with the band of bunnies, raccoons, and skunks that had joined them.

Nick joyfully greeted them all, sensing deep in his heart that things would be all right.

"*Ho-ho-ho!* Merry Christmas!"

More birds flitted out of the tree tops and a faraway hoot owl called, answering the distant trill of a whippoorwill and the soft coos of two mourning doves perched on an overhead lamppost. Nick cheerfully glanced behind him, eyeing his feathered and furry friends and the multitude of new tracks they'd left in the snow. He passed the Grand Hotel, imagining it in centuries past, and envisioning its glorious new future. When the town held the opening reception there next winter, Nick wanted Olivia on his arm.

The way they'd worked together on that project was a telling precursor to how they might collaborate in the future. Nick would always seek Olivia's input, and her guidance, as a partner. But, more than anything, he longed to pamper her and make her happy, day after day. No other woman wore a smile as bright as Olivia's, and no other person could so completely capture Nick's heart. He reached All Things Christmas, noting the lights were on in Olivia's apartment upstairs. Nick rang the bell, his pulse pounding, as he hoped for the best.

Chapter Thirty-Two

Even before he rang the bell, Olivia knew Nick was there. She'd raced to the window the second she'd sensed him approaching. And there he'd been! With a whole host of animals trailing behind him. Plus, he was holding something in his hands. They looked like... *Oh, no!* Olivia blanched, realizing Nick was bringing Christmas gifts for her, and she hadn't thought to get anything for him! How could she have been so *stupid*? Okay, all right. So, she'd been a little preoccupied with baking cookies. Still, those hardly seemed enough.

Think, Olivia! Think! She had a huge supply of Christmas stuff right in her shop. Surely, she could dash down and quickly pick up something? Olivia rushed downstairs in clunky movements. She glanced at her legs, remembering the ankle weights. She'd applied them shortly after her shower. Once she'd gotten dressed in her jeans and pretty red Christmas sweater, that was. The flexible ten-pound weights looked a little weird strapped around her knee-high brown leather boots at her ankles, but they did seem to be doing the trick.

Olivia waddled through her darkened shop, frantically searching the shadows. *What? No, not that! Definitely not a Christmas barrette. Tree ornaments? Lame! A homemade stocking? Nice! That will work!* It had a handstitched design and it was Christmassy. Olivia yanked it off its hook and scuttled behind the counter, whipping out a gift bag and popping it open with a swift jerk of her wrist. The bell rang again.

"Coming!" she called, her heart racing.

Perspiration dotted her hairline as she shoved the stocking into the bag and nabbed some giftwrap tissue off a mounted roller. *Eeek!* She'd pulled out too much. *No matter. Push, punch, shove!* She tamped it all down in the bag. *There!* Her eyes darted toward the door, where Nick was cupping a hand to the glass, attempting to peer inside. Olivia grabbed her gift bag off the counter and awkwardly toddled over, her legs bowed out sideways like an old Western movie cowboy's.

She unlocked and opened the door with a joyful smile. "You're back!"

But instead of smiling in return, Nick worriedly surveyed her legs. "Are you all right?" he asked with concern. "You seemed to be having trouble mov—?"

"Oh, that!" She dismissively waved a hand like she dealt with this all the time. "It's nothing. Just levitational issues." She lowered her voice conspiratorially. "*You* know."

Nick blinked hard and she grabbed his arm, dragging him out of the snow. "Come in! You must be freezing."

As she shut the door behind him, Nick chortled a *ho-ho-ho.* "Not anymore!" His blue eyes danced. "It's so great to see you, Olivia."

She beamed up at him, about to explode from happiness. "Yeah, you too."

"I wanted to stop by and say…" His voice grew rough. "Merry Christmas."

"That's perfect!" Olivia grinned. "I want to say merry Christmas, too."

They stood there staring at each other like dopey teenagers, until Nick finally said, "Should we go upstairs?"

"Upstairs," Olivia answered eagerly. "Sure!"

Nick studied her ankle weights. "Don't you want to take those off first? It might be a little hard climbing the—"

"Nope," she said decidedly. "Don't think I'd better." She shot him a sunny grin. "Not just yet."

Nick followed behind her as she clambered up the stairs…one—*arghhh*—leg at a time. If Olivia did this all the time, she'd have thighs of steel! When they reached her apartment, she gasped in horror. She'd completely forgotten about all those cookie tins.

"Wow," Nick said with a pleased grin. His gaze poured over her and Olivia's heart stilled. "Been baking again?"

She brought her thumb to her forefinger in a pinching motion. "Just a…tiny bit."

Nick's laughter rumbled. "Well, thank you if it's all been for me."

"It has been! Most definitely!" she answered, dropping her bag on the coffee table and starting to clear room on the futon. Nick set down his packages to help her.

He slowly looked around, observing the jam-packed countertops. There were even cookie-tin towers on the stove! "I'm not sure where I..."

"Oh, anywhere!" Olivia's gaze swept her living area, searching out some free space. "There!" She pointed to a spot beside a director's chair. The seat of the chair itself was naturally loaded. "Let's put them on the floor by that chair."

Nick obliged, helping her relocate the tins, so they had a place to sit on the futon. Then he removed his coat and Olivia hung it up for him. He considered her ankle weights again, apparently fretting over them. "Don't you want to—?"

"In a moment," she answered sunnily. "I'm still feeling a little...er...light."

Nick's lips creased in a frown. "Olivia, I'm sorry if—"

"Don't be silly," she told him in frothy tones. "Every girl I *know* would *love* the feeling of losing twenty pounds...uh...thirty...probably more!"

Nick smiled warmly and shook his head. "You're really special. You know that?"

She flushed happily in return. "Coffee?"

"Sure."

Olivia motioned for him to sit then ambled into the kitchen with jerky movements to pour their coffee. She returned huffing and puffing, finally feeling the burn from her morning workout.

"How was your trip to the North...er...Maritime Provinces?"

Nick accepted a mug, as she sat beside him. "Very productive. You'll be happy to know my grandpa is doing better."

"Oh, Nick! That's wonderful news."

"The care team we've put in place is top-notch."

"So…he'll be able to continue on then?" Olivia asked tentatively. "With his job?"

Nick eyed her curiously. "I thought you had questions about his job."

"No…not questions. Doubts." Olivia thoughtfully raised her coffee mug to her lips. "Doubts were more like it." She took a soothing swallow of coffee, thinking this was going well. *Nick is back! Yay! And we're having coffee!*

"Olivia?" He leaned closer and viewed her worriedly. "Are you all right?"

"Yes!" she answered joyfully. "Why?"

"Because…I don't know… You seem a little…" He appeared to be struggling with the word. "Enthusiastic?"

"I'm just glad to have you home," she said with a grin. "Did you know that I could sense you?"

A delighted expression crossed his face. "Really? Since when?"

"Since early this morning." Olivia thought hard, rolling her eyes toward the ceiling. "I'd say, it started just after midnight."

Nick grinned in surprise. "That's just when I got back! Returned to Christmas Town."

"I know." Olivia giggled contentedly. "I had a feeling."

The dimple in Nick's cheek deepened. "That's a very good sign."

"I've been experiencing a lot of them," Olivia confided.

"Yeah?"

"Such as," she dropped her voice into a whisper. "Urges." Her eyes swept the room, roving over the mountains of cookie tins. "You know what I mean?"

Nick followed her gaze with understanding. "Yes. Yes, I think that I do… Anything else?" He viewed her questioningly, and Olivia pointed to her ankle weights. "Oh, right. Right! I get that one sometimes, too."

"Like when we were on the horses?" she asked cagily.

Nick's blue eyes sparkled. "I thought you didn't notice?"

"Oh, I knew something was going on, all right. It just took me some time to put it together." She studied him a beat. "What else can you do?"

"More and more each day, it seems." He brought a hand to her cheek and said huskily, "I attribute a lot of it to you."

"Me?"

There was warmth in his eyes. Warmth and tenderness, too. "You're my perfect match, Olivia. That's what all these signs mean. That you were meant for me, and I for you."

"I was confused about that before, but I believe it now." Olivia fell into his gaze and her breath hitched. "I believe in *us*, and the idea that we're somehow meant to be together."

He searched her eyes. "What changed your mind?"

"Christmas Town," she answered on a sigh. "You. Me. Everything."

"I brought you something," he said, picking up the larger of the two gifts. "Something for Christmas. I hope you'll like it."

Olivia eagerly dug into the package, unsure of what to expect. The medium-size box was gorgeously wrapped in shimmering wrapping paper showcasing intricate snowflakes against a glittery background. It was tied up with a satiny silver ribbon. She cast aside the wrapping then gently lifted the lid off the box, exposing a swath of red velvet. "What's this?"

Nick set down his coffee then helped her by gently unfolding the fabric.

Glimmering gemstones shone up at her and Olivia caught her breath.

"It's a tiara, fit for a queen." Nick reached into the box and lifted the crown, carefully placing it in Olivia's outstretched hands. "But for now?" He grinned warmly. "You'll have to settle for being a princess."

Tears formed in Olivia's eyes. She'd never seen anything so beautiful in her life. Its design was delicate and elegant. Despite its vivid display of rubies, emeralds, and diamonds, the piece was surprisingly lightweight. "It's incredible."

"It's been in my family for generations," he explained. "I'm afraid you won't have much occasion to wear it in public." A sly grin warmed his face. "But you can wear it around the house any time you want… Let's try it on, shall we?"

He gently lifted it out of her grasp and settled in on her head, as Olivia's long red hair spilled past her shoulders. "You look absolutely stunning, my love. Regal."

For a moment, Olivia's head felt light, but then gradually she adjusted. It was like acclimating herself to a slightly different altitude. Higher than the Great Smoky Mountains.

"Want to take a look?" he asked sweetly.

Olivia nodded and got unsteadily to her feet.

"Let's take these off now," Nick said, indicating her ankle weights. "You won't need them. I'm with you." Olivia wasn't so sure about that. Because, at the moment, she felt lighter than the wisp of an eyelash. Nick removed the weights, then tenderly took her by the elbow and queried gently, "Mirror?"

"It's…in the bathroom," she uttered in stunned disbelief. Was this really happening to *her*? It seemed so surreal and yet so totally wonderful! Olivia met her reflection with a blush.

"I'm glowing!"

Nick happily hugged her from behind. "It's called the royal glow," he quipped admiringly. Nick leaned forward and warmly kissed her cheek. "It looks great on you."

Unexpectedly, his gaze snagged on something near his knees. "Is that your…slipper in the toilet?"

Olivia was consumed in a lava-wave of heat. "Er…" She pivoted toward him, steadying her crown. "Collateral damage, I'm afraid!"

"Collateral?" His brow rose.

"I experienced a little blip in here earlier." She shrugged sheepishly, then fluttered her arms out beside her like wings.

"My poor darling!" Nick pulled her into an embrace, and her tiara tilted sideways. "No wonder you were wearing those weights." He hugged her tightly up against him and Olivia spied their sideways profiles in the mirror. *Cool… That tiara actually looks kind of good on me.* But Nick looked even better, as he stood there with his strong arms wrapped around her shoulders. Olivia's heart *boom-boom*ed, and she pushed back to stare at him. "Did you hear that?"

"Yeah," he grinned sexily. "I felt it, too."

"What?"

"Darling, I've been feeling it ever since we first met."

"Well. Uh…" Olivia self-consciously adjusted her crown. "Maybe we should get out of the bathroom?"

Nick laughed joyfully and released her, taking her hand. "Most definitely!" he said. "You've got one more present to open!"

"I've got one for you, too…" Olivia said temptingly.

He paused halfway to the futon. "Olivia," he said ultra-kindly. "You've already baked me all these cookies." His hand swept grandly around the room.

"That wasn't enough," she told him resolutely. "I wanted to share my own merry Christmas."

They sat on the futon and she excitedly passed him her gift bag. It took him quite a bit of time to paw through the tissue, but once he'd gotten it all out of the way, Nick exclaimed, "A stocking! How great! And it's so Christmassy…" He held it by its hanging hook, allowing it to unfurl all the way. "It's personalized, too?"

To Olivia's horror, she saw the name read: *Jack.*

"Jack?" Nick shot her a confounded look. "Who's Jack?"

Olivia stared in dismay. Rather than select a plain stocking, she'd mistakenly grabbed one of the customized ones! She sold several sporting common names, and others could be made to order. "Oh, that.

Ha-ha!" She tried biding for time, thinking quickly. "Can't you guess?"

Nick slowly shook his head. "No, no. Not off the top of my head…" He cocked his chin to the side. "Is 'Jack' some kind of nickname?"

"*Yes!*" Olivia replied emphatically. "Spot on, *Jack*." She winked in collusion, but her cheeks burned. "Jack, as in jack-of-all-trades. Just like your grandpa! Isn't that what you said he was?" Olivia's face kept getting hotter. At this rate, she'd soon burst into flames.

"Actually, I think you're the one who said that."

"Oh, *yeah*! I knew it was…" Olivia swallowed hard. "One of us."

A smile warmed Nick's handsome face. "You were so sweet to think of me, Olivia. I'll hang it every year— with pride. We can use it to decorate our house."

"Our house?" she asked, her voice quaking. While Nick had certainly skirted around the issue with the tiara and everything, he hadn't officially popped the important question.

"Sure," he replied evenly, as if they'd previously discussed it. "I thought we'd buy one of those fixer-uppers on Church Street, and, well…" He beamed at her. "Fix 'er up!"

"Together?"

"Isn't that what you want?"

"What about the future?"

"Can we take that one step at a time…?" He took the smaller box from the table, handing it to her. "Starting with this?"

She accepted his gift and Nick took her hand. "Sandy told me I did a terrible job the first time, so now I'm going to try to get it right."

Olivia's pulse fluttered. This was it, their big moment!

"Olivia Livingston," he said, meeting her eyes. "I knew from the moment I saw you that you were special, but I only had an inkling of how very dear to me you would become. They say perfection only exists in fairytales; in that case my fairytale has come true. I've fallen in love with a gorgeous woman with enchanting green eyes and a beautiful heart."

"Oh, Nick," she whispered, her lips trembling. "I love you, too."

Nick slid off the futon and dropped down on one knee, still holding her hand.

"I've thought about this long and hard," he told her. "Considered the burdens I might be placing upon you. I'm sorry for any of those that may pose challenges for us ahead, but there's one thing I won't apologize for—it's what I feel in my heart." His blue eyes glistened. "I love you so much, Olivia, and though my future is uncertain, I want you by my side. Because the truth is…" He paused as his Adam's apple rose and fell. "I can't see a way forward without you."

He nodded toward the package and she unwrapped it with shaking fingers, revealing a small velvet box. Olivia pried it open and the most glorious diamond she'd ever seen glimmered in the lamplight. Nick plucked the solitaire from its pillow and held it above Olivia's left ring finger.

"Olivia Livingston," he said, "will you be my lifelong partner and the queen of my domain? Will you allow me to love and cherish you forever? Stand by your side and our family's—"

"Family's?" she cut in with a happy gasp.

Nick's eyebrow arched. "You do want babies?"

Olivia nodded eagerly as tears streamed down her face. "Loads and loads of them! Please!"

"I'd be happy to oblige." He shared a warm grin. "If you'll only say, *I do*. Say that you'll marry me, Olivia. Make me the happiest man alive by telling me you'll be my wife?"

"Nick Claus," she said, smiling broadly. "Don't you know I'd go to the ends of the earth for you?"

"Unfortunately, that might be part of the package."

"That doesn't sound so unfortunate to me." She shared a jaunty look. "I'm game!"

Nick viewed her admiringly. "I imagine you're capable of handling just about anything."

"I...er...except for reindeer," she said a tad uncertainly. "I might need your help with those..."

Nick burst into a happy *ho-ho-ho*, before tightening his hold on her hand.

"I'll help you with everything. Nothing would give me greater joy."

He gazed at her hopefully, and Olivia's heart soared.

"*Yes!* I do! I will! To all of it, Nick. Nothing would make me happier than spending the rest of my life with you. It doesn't matter if we're here—or there. As long as we're together."

Nick slid the ring on her finger and Olivia leapt into his arms as he stood to catch her. The sudden motion dislodged the tiara from her head, and it dropped backwards onto the futon. "Oh, no!" Thank goodness she hadn't broken it. That could have been an inauspicious beginning, damaging the family jewels...

"It will just take some getting used to," Nick said with a sexy grin. "Soon, you'll be wearing it with no difficulty at all." He kissed her for a luscious moment, and Olivia sighed in his arms, sagging up against him.

"About those babies...?" Olivia queried lightly, thinking it really didn't matter. She was determined to have them, anyway. Still, it would be helpful to know. "Will they...uh...have special abilities, too?"

"They might." He beheld her adoringly. "But their powers will never be as great as ours."

"No?"

"Certain things skip generations," he told her with a twinkle.

Nick gently kissed her again, then lovingly stroked her cheek.

"You're all I wanted for Christmas, Olivia."

She gazed at him dreamily. "You're what I wanted, too."

"It can only be you," he said surely. "From this day forward. Only you."

"Only me at Christmas?" she asked with a saucy edge.

Nick's lips brushed over hers and Olivia's skin tingled. "Then, and the whole year through."

Then he swept her off her feet and carried her into the bedroom, where the real magic between them began.

Epilogue

You are cordially invited to attend
The first annual
Christmas Town Ball

Celebrating the reopening of
The Grand Hotel
209 South Main Street
Christmas Town, Tennessee

Christmas Eve
Next winter
Eight o'clock in the evening

Champagne reception and
Hot hors d'oeuvres
Dancing to follow
Formal attire requested

Donations to the Lena Winchester
Good Works Memorial Fund
May be made at the door

The End

A Note from the Author

Thanks for reading *Only You at Christmas.* I hope you enjoyed it. If you did, please help other people find this book.

1. This book is lendable, so send it to a friend who you think might like it so that she (or he) can discover me, too.

2. Write a review at the site where you purchased this book and at Goodreads.

3. Sign up for my newsletter so that you can learn about the next book as soon as it's available. Write to GinnyBairdRomance@gmail.com with "newsletter" in the subject heading.

4. Come like my Facebook page: https://www.facebook.com/GinnyBairdRomance.

5. Follow me on Twitter: @GinnyBaird.

6. Visit my website for details on other books available at multiple outlets now: http://www.ginnybairdromance.com.

Next Christmas, won't you come home to Christmas Town? Watch for Kurt and Savannah's story in Book 4!

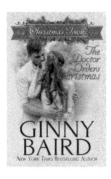

THE DOCTOR ORDERS CHRISTMAS
Christmas Town Book 4

Christmas Town doctor Kurt Christmas has loved high school guidance counselor Savannah Livingston his entire life. While he's had plenty of opportunity to meet beautiful and accomplished women, playboy bachelor Kurt hasn't become seriously interested in any of them. He still pines for the stunning redheaded rebel with emerald-green eyes, who took his breath away at sixteen. When Kurt and Savannah reconnect in Tennessee at Savannah's sister's wedding, that old flame reignites and Kurt finds himself hoping for a brand new start. Yet Savannah's current circumstances in Miami threaten to hold her at bay. If Kurt could write a prescription for anything, it would be to win Savannah's heart. But will love be enough to conquer the secrets that stand between them?

CPSIA information can be obtained
at www.ICGtesting.com
Printed in the USA
LVHW041553311018
595486LV00003B/537

9 781942 058236